nine wives

nine wives

dan elish

 St. Martin's Griffin ❧ New York

www.stmartins.com

Design by Phil Mazzone

Library of Congress Cataloging-in-Publication Data

Elish, Dan.
    Nine wives / Dan Elish.—1st St. Martin's Griffin ed.
        p. cm.
    ISBN 0-312-33943-7
    EAN 978-0-312-33943-2
    1. Bachelors—Fiction. 2. Commitment (Psychology)—Fiction. I. Title.

PS3555.L435N56 2005
813'.54—dc22

                                                                2005043200

First Edition: August 2005

10 9 8 7 6 5 4 3 2 1

For Andrea and Cassie

acknowledgements

I would like to extend special thanks to the many people who helped me bring *Nine Wives* to life.

First and foremost, to Leslie Pietrzyk and John Canaday for encouraging me to give this book a shot and then putting their money where their mouth was by reading multiple drafts. Also, big thanks to two other first readers: Margo Rabb, whose laughter kept me going, and Matthew Gartner, who remains "the man." Other family members and friends read early drafts and gave me helpful comments. Thanks to: Skip Weinstock, Jonathan Rabb, Billy Aronson, Lisa Vogel, Beth Hassrick, Harry and Nora Elish, Helen Ellis, Leah Stewart, Matthew Benson, Dave Hill, Michael Harvey, Alexandra Shelley, Mark Sullivan, and Jonathan Levine. I am very fortunate to have a great agent, Matt Bialer, whose insightful comments were instrumental in getting the book into publishable form and whose persistence got it into print. Also, great thanks to Matt's then-assistant, Lynn Ward, for her support and insights into the manuscript. I've also been lucky to have a wonderful editor, Ben

Sevier, a great guy whose suggestions for the final rewrite brought the book up another major notch.

Finally, I'd like to thank my wife, Andrea, for her love, support, and encouragement in all things, and Cassie, our daughter, whom I love dearly and who I sincerely hope will never read this book.

Gatsby believed in the green light, the orgiastic future that year by year recedes before us.

—F. Scott Fitzgerald

nine wives

1

tamar

henry Mann forced himself up the final steps to his fifth-floor walk-up with the heavy gait of a man who has had two marriage proposals rejected in the same evening. After fumbling with his keys, he finally managed to gain access to his small apartment, where he tossed his tie onto the beat-up console piano and flopped backward, spread eagle, onto the couch. The effects of the four whiskey sours were finally wearing off. Also, the three glasses of champagne and the two—or was it three?—tequila shots. But this was one night when Henry would have been perfectly happy to remain permanently plowed.

Had he really done it? Proposed to two women? At the same lousy wedding? Sadly, the answer appeared to be yes. That the mother of the bride was actually pretty damned good-looking didn't soften the blow, or that Charlotte, the cousin of the groom, had seemed flattered. Facts were facts: It was inappropriate to pledge one's eternal love to a total stranger, especially while attempting to keep the beat to an anemic rendition of "Brown Sugar." Further, it was wrong to grab the bride's mom by the waist directly after she had delivered an emotional rhymed toast. It was even worse to pay homage with one's own short poem:

> *In your arms, the bride you carried.*
> *You're old! So what? Let's get married!*

That both of Henry's intendeds could tell that he was drunk and joking was beside the point. He had turned himself into the guy at the reception that everyone was talking about. Not because he was cute, smart, witty, tall, clefted, buff, talented, rich, or in any way desirable, but because he was, well, pathetic. That nice but sort of sad young man who better get a girlfriend—or better yet a therapist—fast, before his head caves in.

When a full five minutes of staring at a small crack in the ceiling did nothing to lift his flagging spirits, Henry finally rolled off the couch and found his way to the bathroom. There he threw his coat over the shower curtain and doused his face with cold water. After that came a long, appraising look in the mirror. True, this had been what one friend had called "the year of weddings." Eight of them to be exact. And yes, it had been difficult to devote so many weekends to other people's happiness. The most confirmed playboy would have felt left out. But left out was one thing. Desperate was another. Was Henry really so lonely that his drunken alter ego had felt it had no other choice but to embark on a covert take-no-prisoners bridal mission?

Before he had time to ruminate on the issue in greater and possibly more humiliating detail, Henry was saved by the phone. Given the lateness of the hour, he knew exactly who it was. Even so, at the first ring, Henry decided to screen. In his current state of mind he couldn't bear to talk to anyone, not even Glenn. But by ring number two a vain hope took root in his mind. After all, Henry wasn't usually a big drinker. What if all that booze had clouded his memory? What if he hadn't proposed to two total strangers at all? "No, dude," Glenn would reassure him. "The cousin followed you around all night like a homeless beagle, and Mrs. Miller grabbed your ass on the receiving line. They proposed to you!"

Henry answered on the fourth ring. A millisecond after he pressed TALK his fate was sealed. Before the receiver reached his ear he could hear Glenn's laugh registering loud and clear.

"Man oh man, Henry!"

Henry slumped on the piano bench as though he had taken a hard kick to the stomach.

"I know. I know."

"You are a case, my friend! A fucking case!"

Of course, Henry knew it was true. On the other hand, where was the sympathy? Hadn't he been sympathetic when Glenn's wife, a thirty-seven-year-old knockout named Diana, had recently decided to take some time off in Colorado? Had he laughed? Made jokes? Of course not. Then again, Henry knew that a potential divorce was not joking material. But two drunken marriage proposals in a single night? Open season.

"Alright, alright," Henry said, a bit gruffly. "I know it was bad, OK?"

Glenn was undeterred.

"Did any of them say yes?"

The perfect opening. Perhaps there was a way to save a little face.

"Actually, the cousin took my hand on the dance floor," Henry said. "I think she liked me." Then he paused. "If only she didn't live in Zaire."

"Focus on Mrs. Miller, then," Glenn said. "I don't care if she is pushing fifty-five, she is hot."

Henry had to agree.

"Then again," Glenn went on, "I don't suppose Mr. Miller would appreciate his wife taking a second husband."

"Guess not," Henry said. "It'd be pretty weird to be Jane's stepfather anyway."

Henry knew it wasn't that funny a line, but the sound of Glenn's laughter worked wonders. For a brief moment, the cloud of mortification lifted and Henry saw himself in an entirely new light. True, he didn't rake in a ton of cash. On the other hand, he was only thirty-two, an excellent musician, a good writer, a perfectly acceptable athlete, disease free, and straight. The city was his to conquer. Who gave a damn about a couple of drunken proposals? No one.

Henry almost believed it. He even started to stretch out on his couch, ready to get Glenn laughing at some of the other wedding guests. Then Glenn lowered the boom.

"So," he said, "I guess that leaves the rabbi."

Henry was back on his feet as though he had been branded.

"The . . . *rabbi?*"

"You mean you don't remember?" Glenn asked. "The sexiest since the age of Moses. You're probably too assimilated for her, though. Better start rereading the Torah or call off the engagement."

Henry sat back on the couch and gasped. Apparently those drinks had taken their toll. Now, with Glenn's reminder, the last installment of the evening's horrors came rushing back.

It had been near the end of the festivities when Henry had spotted the comely Rabbi Anna Weinstein chatting with the groom and assorted relatives across the room. After downing his fourth whiskey sour, he had marched across the dance floor and gotten down on one knee. There he had performed an impassioned, if slurred, rendition of "I've Got a Little Dreidel," then segued into "Oh, Promise Me." But that wasn't all. Indeed, the singing portion of the program had been followed by a short speech. Though Henry didn't remember much of it, he was chagrined to recall one short phrase in its entirety, "You part my waters, baby." Only when his rambling proposal was complete did Henry notice that the band had stopped playing and that he had drawn an audience. That would have been bad enough, but the mother of the bride and the cousin of the groom had felt it their duty to inform the guests that Henry had spent the night collecting prospective wives like party favors.

The rest of the evening had been death by mortification—a never-ending series of backslaps, handshakes, and mock congratulations, all peppered with such witty comments as "Where are you registered?" and "How many kids are you having with each?" Worst of all was the moment when the sexiest rabbi since the dawn of man had given Henry her card. For a second Henry had allowed himself to believe it was for a date.

"I know it can be hard out there," she had said with a sympathetic nod. "My specialty in grad school was premarital counseling. Feel free to drop by the shul anytime if you want to chat."

Now Henry sank back into his couch, wishing that it had the magical powers to transport him to a parallel universe where weddings didn't exist and it was other people who were drunken idiots. Aware that it would take more than the next few seconds to figure out a way to defy the laws of time and space, Henry focused on his more immediate problem: how to save face with Glenn. As he saw it, there was only one way out—pretend it had all been a dare. "That's right," he could say. "I got ten bucks for every proposal and an extra five for women who were into God or old enough to be my mom." It was a fine plan, except for one thing: Glenn wasn't a moron. No, the only thing left was to come clean and throw himself on the mercy of the court.

"I know it's pathetic," Henry said, voice quivering with self-pity. "It's just that I'm on such a frigging losing streak."

"Aw, no you aren't."

"Oh, yes I am. Ever since—"

"God, Henry. Don't say it."

Henry said it.

"Ever since Sheila!"

Indeed, Henry, the man who craved marriage, had actually once come close to joining the institution. Sheila was the willowy blonde he had dated for a year and a half at college, then hooked up with again at their fifth reunion. The WASP goddess of Henry's high school fantasies, she was smart, forthright, and seemed, at least for a while, to genuinely love him. After a ten-month stint of living to-gether in a small studio in Brooklyn Heights, Henry was more than ready to ask her to take the plunge.

Just as he had been gearing up for the big proposal, Sheila had unceremoniously dumped him, citing "lifestyle differences," a phrase that Henry, no fool, immediately understood to mean "Get a real job." In the end, Sheila, a Top-Sider-wearing prep from Darien, was not cut out to be the wife of an aspiring artist. The last Henry heard of her—and this through the classnotes—she had moved to Seattle and married a top executive at Microsoft. Though Henry didn't consider himself particularly vindictive by nature, on more than one occasion over the past few years he had hoped that Sheila's husband had lost his job along with his stock options and was now overseeing the fried dough machine at a local A&W.

Once the initial shock of desertion had worn off, Henry had moved from Brooklyn into his small walk-up on Washington Place in Greenwich Village. Settled into his bachelor pad, Henry had put to work his master plan: to exact revenge upon the evil Sheila by screwing whomever he could get his hands on. Sadly, he couldn't get his hands on anybody. At least not with the regularity necessary to make single life worth it. Yes, there was the occasional conquest, even several affairs that lasted long enough almost to be consid-ered relationships, but the last of these had ended a full year ear-lier. Since that time, the other side of Henry's bed had been occupied by a warm body only three times: once by a visiting cousin and twice by a friend's dog.

Then came the year of weddings. And each time Henry returned home in his limp, sweat-drenched suit, he wondered whether he should have fought harder to get Sheila back. Had he missed his one big chance? Much to his dismay, questions such as "When's my turn?" or "When do I find love?"—queries he had considered the sole dominion of a certain breed of relationship-obsessed female—had begun to haunt him. Even worse was the answer that most fre-quently came to mind: "Never, loser."

Glenn knew better than anyone how hard it had been. He was the first to give Henry a hard time, but he was also the first to help.

"OK, Romeo," he said. "Time to forget Sheila once and for all. Your losing streak is officially over."

"Oh, yeah?" Henry said. "What's that supposed to mean?"

"The reason I'm calling. I met someone."

"Already?" Henry asked. "Diana just moved out."

Glenn sighed. "Not for me, idiot. *You!* We met at a party a few weeks ago, but I just ran into her coming out of the subway on the way home. It's fate, dude. She's a good-looking lady, too."

Henry wouldn't be budged.

"Why don't you want to date her, then?"

"Will you shut up. Her name is Tamar. Like I said, she's cute."

"Cute, huh?"

"More than cute. Very cute. Pretty."

"OK. How pretty?"

"Very pretty."

"As in *pretty?* Or pretty pretty?"

"Shut up."

The quality of her looks thus established, Henry sat on the edge of his one nice piece of furniture, an oak desk that had once belonged to his grandfather. He picked at a New York Knicks sticker he had placed four years earlier on the side of his computer monitor.

"Henry?" Glenn said. "You there?"

Henry sighed.

"Yeah, I'm here."

"I'm telling you, this could be the one."

What did he have to lose? Henry picked up a pen.

"Just give me her number."

Two weeks later, Henry paced the subway platform, anxiously waiting for the uptown local, the train that would carry him to the girl he intended to marry. Unfortunately, Tamar herself had not yet been made aware of this fact. Nor had Henry yet informed his friends and family, for despite his confidence that he had finally truly found the woman of his dreams, he knew that his beloved might well need time for her feelings to catch up. At any rate, a first date would be in order. After all, Henry realized that before he proposed it might be useful to know what his wife looked like.

Though it had taken Henry a full week to recover from the embarrassment of his three drunken proposals—not to mention the resulting hangover—and work up the nerve to place the call, to his surprise it had been a meeting of the minds from the very first moment. For starters, he and Tamar were both Jewish (nonpracticing), both grew up in New York (he in Manhattan, she in Queens), and both went to summer camp (he: Camp Waconda, "the Camp With the Pioneer Spirit"; she: Camp Willimonka, "the Camp With the Song in Its Heart"). And though Henry was three years older, they surmised that they might even have met approximately seventeen years earlier when he, a high school sophomore, chaperoned a junior high dance at her girls' school.

Tamar had passed other tests with flying colors as well. Most important, even though she worked in marketing for a major corporation and undoubtedly pulled down a substantial salary, she seemed genuinely delighted to hear that Henry was an aspiring writer. "You're a starving artist?" she had said with a giggle. "Most of the guys I meet are lawyers and bankers. Are they dull or what?" Needless to say, that comment elicited no argument whatsoever on Henry's part. In fact, Henry had seized this opening and skillfully maneuvered the conversation to his ability to play jazz piano by ear. This gambit had reaped even greater benefits than he had expected. Not only did Tamar sing alto in her college a capella group, but her favorite band was the Beatles. Trembling with the momentousness of the news, Henry had taken a daring risk and informed his future bride that he and his friends had a New Year's Eve party every year—a party at which, after ample intake of alcohol, they

threw caution to the wind, set up an electric piano, bass, and guitar, and played, sometimes even sang, the greatest hits of the past
fifty years. The event culminated with a tongue-in-cheek boogie-
woogie rendition of "We Are the World" at the stroke of midnight.

"Last year I was Bruce Springsteen," Henry had said.

"Bruce Springsteen!" Tamar had hooted. "Well, next year I'm
Michael Jackson."

By the time the phone call was over (a life-changing thirty minutes) Henry was in a state of near paralytic happiness. Here was
the woman who would miraculously lift him out of his downward
spiral—the first woman in what seemed like ages with whom he
had felt such a strong connection, a connection so powerful it had
"soul mate" written all over it. True, they had only spoken for thirty
minutes, but in the past year he had fantasized just as much based
on far less, and that half hour had given Henry something he desperately needed: hope. Eight weddings in a year? Give him a couple of months and he'd raise it to nine.

Now, as the headlight of the number 1 train floated toward him
down the dark tunnel, Henry let the name of his betrothed roll de-
liciously off his tongue.

"Tamar," he said.

Then he paused, thought a moment, and took the liberty of at-
taching his own last name to the end. "Tamar Mann."

No, better yet. "*Mrs*. Tamar Mann."

Yeah, that had a nice ring to it.

After a short train ride uptown, Henry found himself standing in
the dark entryway of Tamar's Upper West Side brownstone. Despite his eagerness to get the evening under way, he was suddenly
frozen by a surprisingly daunting sight: a small brown button. The
cause of this particular button's fearsomeness could only be attributed to its direct proximity to a frayed piece of masking tape directly to its right. On it, in faded black ballpoint, was an exciting

yet terrifying arrangement of letters—letters that spelled the maiden name of the future Mrs. Mann: BROOKMAN.

"Relax, goddammit," Henry told himself.

The sad truth was that Henry couldn't relax. With each stop of the subway he had grown more and more nervous, as though he were on his way to meet not a woman but a lynch mob. Try as he might, he hadn't been able to stop thinking about the coming evening. Wild fantasies, wonderful and horrific, danced through his mind. One minute he and Tamar were rushing off to get blood tests before eloping to Fiji; the next he was accidentally spitting a wad of chicken Marsala into her hair. The combined effect of these various scenarios had turned Henry into a quivering wreck.

Luckily, he was wise enough to know that what he needed was a few moments to collect himself. After all, a cliff diver doesn't jump until the tide is in and the moment is right. Likewise, years of experience had taught Henry that to press that brown button, thereby setting the evening irrevocably in motion before he was good and ready, would be tantamount to tossing himself off a precipice onto a shoal of jagged coral.

He glanced at his watch. Five minutes early, he had just enough time to perform the predate ritual he called upon in times such as these. Three rotations of the block usually did the trick. Four when the need was particularly dire.

So Henry got walking. With the very first step he began to repeat a series of soothing words, a mantra that he hoped would help him face that brown button like a man. "You're good-looking. You're smart. Women love you," he told himself. "You're good-looking. You're smart. Women love you. You're good-looking. You're . . ."

It is perhaps a testament to Henry's agitated state that it took a record seven trips around the block before he found the inner strength to face that foreboding doorway at 83rd Street and Columbus Avenue. Even then, a final, desperate flurry of "You de man! You de man! You de man! You de man!" was required before he could muster the courage to jab that evil brown button with his thumb.

"Hello, Henry?" a voice sang.

Her voice!

"Yeah, it's me," he replied. (Shit! Did his voice actually crack!?) He cleared his throat. "Should I come up?"

"No, that's OK. I'll be right down."

Stage one complete, Henry leaned against a parked car, drew in a lungful of air, and willed himself to relax. But he was soon pacing anew, the age-old plaint of the single man drumming through his head: "Please God, don't let her be ugly! Please God, don't let her be ugly!" Despite Glenn's repeated assurances as to the quality of Tamar's looks, Henry knew that there was no accounting for personal taste, and like most men, he was a full-fledged, dues-paying member of the chronically looks-obsessed. As much as he hated to admit it, no personality, no matter how wonderful, could push a so-so-looking woman across that invisible cutoff line into the realm of the attractive. Was he shallow? Maybe. In Henry's view, he was a victim of biology, perhaps even of social forces beyond his control. Genetics and a lifetime of alluring magazine covers had wired him for babedom.

This brought Henry to the subject of his own appearance. He caught his reflection in a nearby apartment window. Dressed in standard dating garb—blue khakis, checked Gap shirt, black workboots—he liked what he saw: a reasonably well built guy with dark hair, green eyes, and a nice smile. Though he would rather die than admit it, Henry sometimes dared think himself very handsome. Dashing even. Of course, this view was tempered by the times he felt hideous, those moments when a glance in the mirror revealed love handles no amount of crunches could flatten, a chin that was a shade on the weak side, and a nose half a size too small for his face. The truth was that Henry was perfectly decent looking. He'd had girlfriends who thought he was cute. Once upon a time, Sheila had even called him a piece of ass. And a week and a half earlier, a few days after the fateful three-proposal wedding, Glenn's soon-to-be ex-wife, Diana, had called from Colorado and left a message on Henry's answering machine informing him of her desire to "fuck him on her dining room table." On the other hand, Henry was sadly aware that there were plenty of women in the world who had no desire to fuck him anywhere. Certainly not on a dining room table. Not even in a bed.

"Hi . . . Henry?"

Henry had been so involved in ruminations over personal appearance and dining room tables that Tamar's sudden presence took him by surprise. It took him a full second to focus on the actual woman who had so occupied his thoughts for the past week. It seemed almost odd that she was an ordinary human being. Having imagined her so intensely, he had half expected Venus herself to glide onto 83rd Street and whisk him away to a heavenly cloud.

When he was finally able to see reality for what it was, Henry found himself exhaling an enormous sigh of relief. No, Tamar wasn't gorgeous, but Glenn had been right. She was cute. Alright—she was very cute. Curly dark hair, ski-jump nose, smooth white skin, pale blue eyes. Jewish but not too Jewish, she could pass for a Protestant in a pinch. Although there were initial concerns as to the size of her butt, the largeness of which, Henry feared, was masked behind a loose skirt, closer inspection revealed Tamar's rear end to be perfectly satisfactory. Enough to grab, not enough to be crushed by.

"Hi," he stammered, awkwardly extending his hand for her to shake. "How you doing?"

She took his hand and kissed him on the cheek.

"Fine," she replied. "Wanna get a drink?"

At 4:00 A.M., Henry glided into his apartment wearing the sort of shit-eating grin that appears on a man's face only a few times in life, the sort of smile reserved for lottery winners, Olympic medalists, and the recently converted. A mere eight hours earlier, Henry had been on the outside looking in, his face pressed against the window of the proverbial candy store of life. Now he was inside that store, grabbing great gobs of chocolate with both fists and cramming them down his throat. What an evening it had been! Reality had not only equaled expectations but had blown them clear out of the water. As Henry collapsed on his couch and kicked off his shoes, he allowed himself a brief retrospective of the evening's greatest hits, a grab bag of images he would keep in his private mental scrapbook forever.

Stop one, a pub on Amsterdam Avenue. A grizzled Irish barkeep serves them cheap beer. With the first Bud, Henry's nervousness disappears. With the second—miracle! Henry becomes downright charming. He soon has his intended in stitches.

"Seriously. The man was a pedophile."

"Your junior high basketball coach?" Tamar says, laughing hard despite the unusual subject matter. "A pedophile?"

"Right. He used to try to corner us in the showers."

Henry then describes various ploys (including hiding in his locker) used in order to shower and change without Coach Bryant sneaking a peak.

Stop two, a cozy Italian restaurant. Over a bottle of house red, Henry takes Tamar through the entire plot of his jazz musical: *The Green Light!* based on F. Scott Fitzgerald's *The Great Gatsby*. At her insistence he describes these numbers in painstaking detail:

Nick's opening solo, "Younger and Vulnerable Years."

First-act modern ballet—"Those Eckleberg Eyes."

Grand finale—a choral number, "Boats Against the Current" (which Henry has imagined again and again setting off a torrent of cathartic tears from the audience).

To Henry's delight, Tamar is not only intimately acquainted with the novel but pipes in with a suggestion for a new song, "My Pink Suit," a second-act soft-shoe for Gatsby and Nick.

Stop three, a piano bar (Tamar's suggestion). A few beers and two shots of tequila later, he and Tamar are making out in a corner booth while a quartet of gay waiters sings "Doe, a Deer."

At 1:00 A.M., Henry turns to his new girl and croons (to the tune of "Maria" from *West Side Story*), "Tamar! I just met a girl named Tamar."

At 2:00 A.M., Henry is lost in a consideration of what font to use on their wedding invitation.

At 3:00 A.M., he and Tamar are the proud parents of six—two boys, four girls—and the owners of a Riverside Drive brownstone and a ramshackle Vermont farmhouse, complete with a handful of sheep, a horse or two, and the requisite friendly dog.

Stop four, Tamar's front door. Henry showers her with kisses. "I have to see you again," he whispers.

Another date is made. Just like that, four years of bad luck is wiped away.

Take that, Sheila.

Every one of life's truly great moments needs a final touch, that certain something to nudge the merely excellent across the line into the realm of the inspired. Now, still lying on his couch, luxuriating in the evening's success while watching the 4:00 A.M. repeat of *SportsCenter*, Henry got such an idea. More than an idea, really. A brainstorm. A grand romantic gesture, the type of charming maneuver that would ensure Tamar's enduring love.

Before he lost his nerve, Henry hightailed it across the room, logged on to AOL (his screenname, HEMAN), selected "Compose Mail," and typed in this address: TJBROOKMAN. He paused a moment to consider the subject heading, then wrote, "Fantastic Date." With that, he turned to the letter itself.

Dearest Camp With the Song in Its Heart,

Your song is in my heart. Thanks for the great evening.
xxoo, Gatsby

It was perfect—short, to the point, and filled with two of what he was sure would be a lifetime's worth of inside jokes. Henry reread his masterpiece and wagged his head at the genius of the gesture. He could just picture the look on Tamar's face when she logged on the following morning, could see her giggling with delight, then reaching for the phone to read the note to her friends. "Is he a keeper or what?" she'd gush. "I've hit fucking pay dirt!"

He pressed SEND, then leaned back in his swivel chair and allowed himself the luxury of one final prebedtime fantasy. Of course, Henry knew full well the ramifications of what he was about to attempt. A typical man's man was conditioned from birth to shun anything remotely connubial, but that didn't take into account the protracted ignominy of those eight miserable weddings. Besides, the last time he checked, his male buddies weren't mind readers. In the privacy of his daydreams he could think whatever he wanted, then go happily about his business without anyone being the wiser. That being the case, what was keeping him from pulling out all the stops? Nothing. With that thought, Henry leaned back even farther in his chair, closed his eyes, and got busy.

The time: his wedding day (of course). The setting: Vermont. The place: certainly *not* some gaudy hotel ballroom off an indistinguishable New Jersey exit. No, he and Tamar would be more creative than that, asking friends and family to gather in the pasture of his summer camp on a stunning autumn day when the leaves were blazing with color. His wife would put even that gorgeous scenery to shame. After their vows—vows that would leave the judge glad he had remembered his handkerchief—the guests would retire to a local inn for dinner. Friends and family would raise their glasses in a series of toasts, each more flattering than the one before, culminating with Glenn, his best man, who would inform the gathered crowd that Henry was "the best damned friend a guy could have." Then Henry would sit down at a tinny upright and belt out the song he had written especially for the occasion, "When I Look in Tamar's Blue Eyes, I See a Window to My Soul." By the time Tamar and her mother had dried their eyes, it would be time for the usual array of wedding rituals: the bouquet, the garter, the cake, and, finally, the first dance, where Henry would stun the guests with an exuberant imitation of John Travolta.

"It's so unfair," Tamar's aunt would tell him later on, grabbing his cheeks with both hands. "Is there anything you can't do?"

Henry would shrug and grin as if to say, "Probably not."

Later that evening, Henry would carry his beloved across the threshold of their honeymoon suite and set her gently down in front of a stone fireplace. There he would look her in her pale blue eyes and tell her he loved her. As they kissed, he would expertly undo the buttons of her wedding gown and watch it tumble to the floor, a cascade of white, leaving his wife dressed, to his delighted surprise, in a pair of black, see-through undies. "Happy wedding, hon," she would murmur, and Henry would thank God and sweep his wife into his arms, lift her again and carry her to the bed and . . .

"You've Got Mail."

The voice was so unexpected that Henry's rear end rose two inches in the air. He had been so lost in his fantasy that he was somewhat irritated that he and Tamar actually had to date for a period of time before it could become a reality. He glanced at the digital clock on the upper right-hand corner of his computer: 4:25 A.M. Who could possibly be writing him at this hour?

It is perhaps important to note that it never crossed Henry's mind that it was Tamar herself who was the mysterious author. In fact, Henry, suddenly exhausted (the sheer magnitude of his triumphant wedding day had left him with no energy), decided to read his mail in the morning, reached for the mouse, and scrolled to the word "Quit." But just as he was about to release his finger, curiosity got the better of him and he moved to the "New Mail" icon. Seconds later, these letters appeared before him.

GETDOWN, from best friend Glenn. Subject heading: Yo, brother!

MELLY, Melissa, Henry's sister, writing to remind him about her housewarming party the following day. Subject heading: See you there!

TJBROOKMAN, his future bride. Subject heading: Hey there.

Henry skimmed the list so quickly he had to do a double take before the third name fully registered. Once it did, he couldn't believe his good fortune. It was a turn of events beyond even Henry's capacity to imagine. Not only had Tamar read his note, but she was already writing back! No matter what the actual text of her letter, the very fact of her immediate reply made its subtext unmistakable: She was as excited as he was. His feelings were returned! She might as well have picked up the phone and asked if she could move in.

Trembling now, Henry clicked her name and watched the wonderful letter—the letter that would unambiguously seal the deal—bloom gloriously before him.

Hey there,

I just got your note and it was sweet. That makes what I'm about to write even harder.

I'm sorry to do this over e-mail but I'm too wimpy to call and I don't believe in drawing these things out. I don't know how else to say this but to say it: I'm involved with a woman. I suppose I should have told you before the evening began that I've been experimenting with my sexuality. But these things are complicated, you know? I thought I was interested in men when we talked on the phone a week ago. Since then, my relationship with Abby has deepened. Since you and I had already made a date I didn't want to cancel. Anyway, seeing that we've only just met, I can't imagine that this news will upset you.

I write you this because I had a really good time—much better than I expected. I guess I let myself get carried away.

Say hi to Glenn for me and good luck with your musical. A jazz version of Gatsby could be a winner. Don't forget "My Pink Suit"—it could be a showstopper.

Tamar

Henry slumped back in his chair, eyes glazed. It was a full half hour before he was able to harness the energy required to wash and get to bed.

When the phone rang the next morning, a vain hope took root in Henry's mind: It was Tamar calling to tell him that she'd made the mistake of her life. Wracked to the core by the ludicrousness of a decision that led her to reject the man of her dreams, she had tossed and turned until dawn, roused herself from bed, thrown on a pair of Keds, a T-shirt, and sweats, marched to Abby's apartment, and announced, "I'm in love with a man, dammit! A man!"

Like most vain hopes, this one blew quietly away. Instead, when Henry finally managed to fight his way to semiconsciousness and prop his portable phone by his ear, he was greeted by the proverbial booby prize.

"Am I calling too early?"

His mother. About as far a cry from an ex-future wife as one could get.

"No, no," Henry lied. He yawned and glanced at the clock: Sunday morning, 9:00 A.M. "I'm just getting up."

"Good. How are you, Henny, honey?"

Henry had come to view conversations with his mother as little battles. He was the Union soldier running through the fields at Bull Run without a gun while musket fire—in the form of motherly suggestions and "helpful" criticisms—crackled around him. If he was lucky and ducked for cover at the appropriate times, he could escape with a flesh wound or two. Those instances were rare, however. Usually Henry hung up the phone in desperate need of the type of medical treatment that had been woefully unavailable during the Civil War. At the very least a MASH unit was required, if not the entire cast and crew of *ER*.

With the seemingly simple words "Henny, honey," his mother had already drawn first blood. In Henry's view, this endearment had become unacceptable the moment he had outgrown jungle gyms. Unfortunately, this belief was not shared by his mom. Despite repeated requests that she stick to the basic "Henry" or, for those dire moments when she simply couldn't help herself, "Hen," she had yet to prove herself up to the challenge. It often struck Henry as odd that a woman who had raised two children, written a series of successful self-help books (notably *The Inner You*, a best seller), and was now happily remarried to Henry's high school history professor—in other words, an intelligent and sensitive person—was seemingly unable to execute such a simple request. But that was the way of mothers. In her mind he was still "Henny, honey," the adorable eight-year-old. She didn't seem to care that he was trying to be "Henry," a real live adult.

In any event, the first round had been fired. Two seconds into the conversation and Henry was already limping. Little did he know that in another few seconds he'd be begging for mercy.

"I'm fine, Mom. How're you?"

"Good, good. Just getting ready for your sister's housewarming this afternoon. Are you bringing a date?"

Henry closed his eyes and lay back on his pillow. Yes, the one-woman Confederate brigade had come out with rifles blazing. In one sentence Mrs. Mann—for she still used the last name of husband number one—had successfully, even brilliantly, Henry thought, not only referred to his sister's lavish new Fifth Avenue apartment (actually, two apartments that had been converted into one) but also touched upon the most taboo subject of them all: Henry's love life. A double whammy. In his own way, Henry had to admire her skill. Ten seconds into the conversation and she had already (a) made him feel like a six-year-old, (b) obliquely made reference to his low income (though Henry knew it wasn't his fault that his brother-in-law was an investment banker), and (c) not so subtly inquired whether he finally had a girlfriend or, short of that, any available female suitable for display at a family gathering. General Lee would have been proud.

"No, no date," Henry muttered. He was sprawled on the battle-field, looking vainly for a medic.

"No date?"

A sigh.

A pause.

"You know, the Pinafore Players have a set of auditions Tuesday night."

Aha! Her first tactical error in an otherwise brilliant opening set of maneuvers. Though he was mere seconds from last rites, this comment gave Henry the will to drag himself to his knees and face the enemy.

"Listen, Ma," he said, sitting up in bed. "You know I hate Gilbert and Sullivan. I don't want to prance around the stage in a community theater production of *H.M.S. Pinafore* dressed up in a sailor suit just to meet girls!"

There. That showed her. Maybe he didn't need that medic after all. Sure, Henry was well aware that his passing interest in musicals was not exactly the hippest thing in the world. He even felt somewhat embarrassed by it. But singing Gilbert and Sullivan? Every man had his limits.

"Suit yourself," his mother replied. "But FYI—Sally Harris thought you were cute."

Henry sat up with a start. Sally Harris? Thought he was . . . *cute?* He was suddenly more excited than he cared to admit. It didn't particularly matter that he had no idea who Sally Harris was. Age, looks, weight, race, and temperament were secondary.

The mere fact that a female currently alive on the planet was attracted to him was enough to raise his spirits.

This left Henry in a sticky situation. How could he ask for more details about this mystery woman when the very act of asking would imply a definite willingness on Henry's part to join the very theater group he had just ripped to shreds? If only his mother had mentioned Sally Harris *before* she had mentioned the auditions, then Henry, with all the facts at his disposal, would've been able to adjust his initial response accordingly.

"Gilbert and Sullivan operettas certainly are treasures of the musical theater," he could have said. "Brimming with delicious wit and robust yet surprisingly plaintive music. I'd love to join you."

Or, "Funny you should bring that up, Mom, because I've had a hankering lately to give something back to the community. Since the Players donate money to charity each year, I think it would be the perfect forum in which to express myself artistically while simultaneously helping my less fortunate brethren."

Or, if he didn't want to meet Sally (yeah, *sure*), "Listen up and listen up good, Mother dear. I'm not as hard up as you might think. In fact, there's a thirty-seven-year-old woman in Colorado who wants me to hump her brains out on a dining room table. Hear me? Hear me?!"

The trouble was that Henry *was* hard up. Given the previous night's fiasco, he was in no position whatsoever to push away a potential date. It also occurred to him that there was a chance, maybe even a good chance, that Sally was one of those cute female pirates who had caught his eye when he had attended the players' production of *The Pirates of Penzance* a few weeks back. Clearly it was time to raise the white flag, admit total defeat with as much dignity as he could muster, and get more info.

"Sally Harris?" he said. "Which one's she again?"

"Hmmmm." Henry's mother clicked her tongue. "Let's see if I

can describe her. She's twenty-four, dark hair. Very pretty. She was in the show."

Henry sat up a bit straighter.

"Was she the girl who played . . . ?"

"That's right! One of those cute pirates!"

Yes!!! Henry catapulted to his feet and paced the room in his boxers. He suddenly loved Gilbert and Sullivan. Gilbert and Sullivan were his friends. There was nothing embarrassing about dressing in a sailor suit. It didn't even imply that he was gay. Even if it did, Henry was much too secure in his sexuality to be bothered. Community theater was a wonderful thing. A sterling American tradition. He wanted to be a part of it.

Like Mozart envisioning a symphony in a single instant, Henry now allowed his entire romance with Sally to come to life before his eyes. He'd play his hand with the cool precision of a Vegas card shark. The first few rehearsals he'd lie low, act as if he had no idea Sally was even interested. Then he'd strike, wooing her with his self-effacing wit, his stunning piano technique, his "I have enough going for me to be conceited if I wanted, but I choose not to be" charm. By the time the show went into dress rehearsal they would be an item. By opening night, well . . . Henry smiled. While the rest of the male chorus was onstage belting out "Oh, we sail the ocean blue," he'd be behind the set sticking his hand (if not his head) up Sally's petticoat. While everyone else was onstage during the first-act finale, they'd be naked on the dressing room floor, painting each other's bodies with stage makeup.

"She's a sweetheart, Henry," he heard his mother continue. "She works in publishing. You have things in common. Lots of marriages come out of the Players, you know."

Oh, yes, Henry knew.

"She comes from a nice family, too. Grew up in Katonah, I think. I like girls from Westchester. They aren't jappy up there, you know?"

Again, Henry knew.

"And she loves music, of course, and sings like a little bird and . . . Wait a second. Oh, darn it!"

Henry stopped short. Something in his mother's tone worried him.

"What's wrong?"

"Oh, Henny, honey. I'm such a fool. Sally just got engaged to a stockbroker."

Henry crumpled to his bed. A mere second earlier, he was a proud soldier on the move. Now he was taking a cannonball to the solar plexus. How could his mother do this to him? Didn't she know about his plans? The petticoat? The dressing room floor?

"Engaged?" he squeaked.

"Well, never you mind about her," his mother stated. "She's too stupid for you anyway. A real airhead. Sort of slutty, too, if you ask me. There's lots of others in the troupe anyway. There's one named Kathy Monroe, a bit chunky, but cute as a button and . . ."

A bit chunky? Henry was suddenly in no mood to hear about the other prospects. How could he be when in the last twelve hours two of his future wives had been so cruelly snatched away? By a woman and a stockbroker. He didn't know which was worse.

After another five minutes of idle chat, which Henry spent with the phone a good six inches from his ear, he reached for a pen and scrawled the address of his sister's new apartment on the back of a book cover. Then he said good-bye and hung up.

Though Henry often played basketball in Riverside Park on Sunday mornings, his mother's call left him more exhausted than a full-court three-on-three. Lying back down for what he thought would be a few seconds, he soon fell back asleep. In fact, it was eleven by the time Henry managed to rouse himself from a fitful dream (in which he was making love to Tamar on a sandy beach only to discover that she was an enormous sea lion) and stumble into his living room. Still in his boxers, he plopped himself down at his desk. Realizing that a show of restraint was a virtual impossibility, Henry immediately booted up his computer and logged back on to AOL. True, the odds were long, but there was a chance, albeit slim, that Tamar had woken that morning, seen the error of her ways, and had sent along a retraction. After all, hadn't the '69 Mets been a hundred-to-one shot? All things being equal, Henry figured his chances had to be at least as good as his favorite team's—a team that won the World Series after coming in next to last in the National League the year before.

Of course, the '69 Mets had Tom Seaver, a man who could throw a ball ninety-five miles per hour, along with a team of skilled role players and a superb manager. Indeed, the Mets had a whole squad of finely tuned athletes to call upon in their quest to defy the odds, whereas Henry was just a simple guy in a fifth-floor walk-up whose only notable features were the antique oak desk and the beat-up piano, as well as a scratched oak coffee table, a TV (27 inches, Columbus Day sale), two IKEA bookshelves, and a fireplace whose chimney actually carried smoke up and out of the apartment approximately once a year when the draft was just right.

So when his list of new mail flashed on the screen, Henry wasn't really very surprised to be greeted by the same three letters that had been there at 4:00 A.M.: Glenn's "Yo, brother," his sister's "See you there," and finally that laser to his heart, Tamar's "Hey there." To make his torture complete, Henry reread her short note not once but three times. Then, with a sigh that could only be categorized as mournful, he laid his head down on his desk and shut his eyes. He was half tempted to compose a stinging reply—a rebuke so astute, so laced with vicious wit, that Tamar would be reduced to tears while simultaneously realizing that she had missed the catch of a lifetime. But such notes are easier to imagine than to write. Since Henry knew that "Have fun with the lesbo" (all he could come up with after a good ten minutes' thought) wasn't exactly what he would call incisive or, for that matter, politically correct, he wisely decided to hold back and soon lurched to his small kitchen, where he made a pot of coffee, then stumbled back to his living room and flopped down on the sofa.

It was there that Henry's level of despair reached an entirely new low, a level that could only be termed profound. To this point the evening's outcome had saddened him greatly, but it now embarrassed him as well. To his dismay, new recollections flashed through his mind. Though he closed his eyes in a vain effort to ward them off, the images danced across his eyelids one after another, coming as fast as curves in a roller coaster.

At dinner (while taking her hand, looking deeply into her eyes): "You're everything Glenn said you'd be," he had said. "Only even more beautiful."

Henry grimaced. Had he really uttered a line so sappy that it would have been cut from a bad episode of *The OC?*

Yes, he had.

Over dessert (with a casual wave of his hand): "That's right," he had remarked. "I won the photography prize in junior high."

Another grimace. Had he really bragged about a photograph of a fire hydrant, an award he had won at age thirteen? In a field he was no longer even interested in?

Again, yes.

Even worse were the depths to which Henry had stooped while on their way to the sing-along bar. Here he had done everything in his power to portray himself as a tragic figure, tortured by a cruel and wicked fate. Not only had Henry informed Tamar that his parents had gotten divorced on the first day of tenth grade, but he had topped it off by mentioning that this sad event had been followed a week later by the death of his dog. That this happened to be true didn't especially matter. What Henry despised was the tone he had used to communicate this information, a tone calculated to bludgeon Tamar into seeing that he was a deep and sensitive soul— a man who had known pain and could therefore empathize with hers. Why did he feel the need to be a walking résumé of achievement and grief, spewing out information calculated to impress her with every breath? Couldn't the photography award and the dead Yorkshire terrier have waited? At least until date two?

Henry closed his eyes and tried to clear his head. He had hoped to devote the entire afternoon to spreading the good news to his friends—the joyous "Guess what? I got a little!" postdate phone call. Now any communication would be of an entirely different nature. Though Henry had plenty of friends who would have gladly spent the afternoon inventing a never-ending series of imaginative epithets to describe Tamar, somehow that seemed even more depressing. Besides, he was far too emotionally involved to stand aside and listen to his buddies call the love of his life names.

Sometimes a man must reach the very end of his rope before he can hope to find redemption. It was at this low moment that Henry happened to glance at his phone machine, where the number 1 was lit up on the console. That number was the branch that Henry now grabbed hold of, the branch that saved him from careening all the way down the icy glacier of self-loathing into the pit of abject humiliation. After all, desperate times cried out for desperate measures. With no further hesitation, he pressed PLAY, leaned back in the sofa, and listened as the voice of Diana, that gorgeous thirty-seven-year-old, filled the room. It was her fourth message in ten days.

"Henry, baby. Just got my dining room table sanded. Ha, ha! It's official. It's over between Glenn and me, and you've simply got to visit. Get your cute butt out here. Call me."

Henry was half tempted to play the message into Tamar's answering machine.

"See?" he would shout. "This could have been you!"

Instead, he lay back on the sofa and allowed himself to remember Diana's long body, her dirty blonde hair, those puffy lips, that tight little butt. She was one of the most sexual women he'd ever met. On top of that, she was more experienced as well and, by her own admission (stated during a phone call earlier that week), "one horny bitch."

Was a friendship with a soon-to-be-ex-husband enough to pass up a woman like that? Even if that soon-to-be-ex happened to be Henry's best friend? After last night's debacle, he wasn't so sure anymore. Sure, Glenn was a great guy, someone Henry depended upon in times of need, a man who trusted him unconditionally, but . . .

His wife was one horny bitch!

Henry reached for his address book and phone. He got her machine on the second ring.

"Hi, this is Diana. I'm out, so leave a message."

More excited than he would have cared to admit, Henry cleared his throat. He hadn't thought of exactly what to say. After all, how does one respond to a request to get on a plane to have sex on a piece of furniture usually reserved for dining? ("Polish the silverware, babe. I'm coming down!") The next thing he knew, there was that beep and he had to speak.

"Hi, Diana. Yeah, it's me. Henry. Anyway, not much going on here. Listen, listen . . . I've been thinking about what you've said and . . . *(moral and spiritual crisis of epic proportions)* . . . well, I still feel funny about it. Maybe it's a bad idea. I don't know, I just, well . . . you know, the Glenn thing still bothers me. I know it's lame. Speak to you. Bye."

Henry hung up the phone, his spirits deflating faster than a birthday balloon with a three-inch gash. He didn't know if it was fear of Diana, his friendship with Glenn, or worry that he'd get caught that had made him say no, but even though it hadn't been the exciting thing to do or the satisfying thing to do, deep down he knew it was the right thing to do.

There would be no trip to Colorado. No sex with the added enticement of finding a fork up his ass.

"I'm too damned honorable," he muttered.

With another mournful sigh, a sigh that bemoaned the loss of everything—Tamar, Sally Harris, and the now mythic dining room table—Henry took a sip of coffee, forced himself to his feet, and headed to the shower. He would have preferred to stay put, order in, and watch the Knicks, but the housewarming party was an unqualified command performance—and he figured that he might as well be clean.

2

amanda

later that afternoon, Henry found himself standing on the park side of Fifth Avenue across the street from a red prewar building, home of his sister's new apartment. A freshly washed green awning flapped back and forth in a cool April breeze as a doorman, a dapper elderly man in a gray suit, flagged a cab for a couple in a tuxedo and gown. Henry shook his head, unable to fully believe that his sister, Melissa, had actually moved into an apartment building where people had so much money that they dressed up just to go to lunch. Then again, Henry reminded himself, when Melissa had chosen a husband, she had struck gold. Not only was Adam loaded, but he was also a sensitive soul who read good books, could talk openly about his feelings, and even volunteered occasionally in a soup kitchen. It often seemed unfair to Henry that such a person could exist. In his view, someone with his brother-in-law's kind of money should at least have the decency to be an asshole.

In any case, the "dream apartment" had been in the works for a solid year now. Once a serious painter, Melissa had placed her easel and brushes into storage and turned the full force of her creative powers on the renovation. It was a job she took seriously. In that time she had gone through two architects, three interior designers, six carpenters, two therapists, and a masseuse. Interestingly enough, Henry had yet to so much as glance into the lobby. Though he had been invited over at various phases of the process, he had always declined, saying, "I want to wait until it's finished." In truth, Henry was afraid that the minute he stepped inside he'd throw a jealous fit of *Exorcist*-like proportions.

In more lucid moments, however, Henry reminded himself that even if he had been lucky enough to have Adam's kind of money, he wouldn't have wanted to live on the Upper East Side anyway. Rather, Henry saw himself in a hipper part of town. Certainly, his *60 Minutes* interview would play better in a café outside his SoHo loft than in a stodgy Fifth Avenue apartment. There, over a cappuccino and baguette, he could more easily assume the role of the bohemian artist and wax poetic on the state of the modern musical, impressing Steve Kroft and viewers at home alike with his brilliant wit, astonishing talent, and telltale humility. Now, after taking a final moment to imagine that interview in greater detail (Steve Kroft: "Tell us, Mr. Mann. Are you a genius?"), Henry crossed the street and presented himself to the doorman.

"Adam and Melissa Richardson," he said.

"Very good, sir. And your name?"

"Henry Mann."

As the doorman referred to the guest list, Henry allowed himself a first peek into the lobby. Certainly, he had expected it to be big. On the other hand, he hadn't expected it to rival the main entryway of Versailles. Indeed, the lobby was cavernous, decorated with eight chandeliers, a string of Persian carpets, assorted sculptures, elegant potted plants, and a wall full of art that looked like it had been lifted straight from the Metropolitan Museum.

"Go on up, sir," the doorman said. "Eighth floor."

With a nod of thanks Henry headed down the long lobby to where another man in another gray uniform followed him into the elevator. As Henry reached for the number 8 the man raised his hand. "Allow me," he said, and spared Henry the inconvenience of having to lift his finger and press the button himself.

Moments later, Henry stood before his sister's front door. Given the massive size of the lobby, Henry wouldn't have been particularly surprised at this point to find Melissa and family ensconced in an apartment as large as the Meadowlands. Before he even had the chance to ring the bell, the door flung open.

"Henry!"

Standing before him was a dark-haired seven-year-old girl wearing a blue and orange Knicks jersey. It was his niece, Jill.

"Hey, sweetie!" Henry said, and kissed her on the top of her head.

"Watch the game with me later?"

Like Henry, Jill was a die-hard hoops fan.

"You got it," Henry said. "Knicks all the way."

With that, he tried to enter the apartment, but Jill proceeded to wrap her arms securely around his right leg, forcing Henry to carry her along with him. As he did, he couldn't help wishing that Tamar had been there to bear witness to this unabashed display of affection. How would she have been able to turn down a man with such a natural affinity for kids? Someone who would make such a wonderful father? It seemed a crime to let such an opportunity go to waste.

"Henny, honey!"

His mother appeared in the entryway. An elegant woman with closely cut blonde hair, at fifty-eight, she was still attractive. As usual, she was well dressed, wearing a lavender blouse, blue silk pants, and an Armani scarf. With Jill still attached to his legs, Henry positioned his cheek for the requisite kiss.

"Have any trouble finding the place?"

Henry was half tempted to remind his mom that he had been fully capable of getting around the city since age ten. In an effort to get the festivities off on the right foot, he opted for the polite response.

"No. Not at all."

"You'll never believe this apartment, Henry," she said. "Or apartments, I should say. I mentioned that they broke down a wall and joined two together, didn't I?"

Henry decided not to remind his mother that he had known for a solid year that two apartments would, in fact, be joined at the hip. She took him by the arm.

"I hope you circulate here, dear," she continued. Then she whispered, as though conveying top secret information, "Adam hangs with a very well-connected crowd."

Henry knew what that meant. Through the years, he had found it deeply ironic that his mother, who had made a career out of writing books designed to help people better realize their deepest dreams, didn't want her own son to realize his. Yes, she appreciated his talent, but she could never quite manage to turn off a pestering voice of doom that whispered in her ear that Henry would spend his golden years playing electric organ in a bar mitzvah band.

"Adam's college roommate John is at Davis, Polk," she said now. "Entertainment law."

Before Henry could come up with a suitable reply (such as "fuck off"), a meaty paw entered his field of vision: Adam's.

"Hey there."

Henry finally detached Jill's arms from his leg and took his brother-in-law's hand. Along with his other sins, Adam had one of those extrafirm handshakes that made Henry feel like the type of guy who had gotten cut from his junior high football team (which he had quit, opting for the less violent soccer and hoops).

"It's great to see you," Adam said. "How's the musical going?"

"Pretty well, thanks," Henry said.

"Remind me again. It's based on *The Sun Also Rises*, right?

The Great Gatsby."

"That's right," Adam replied. "Good idea. If you want to play any of it later, there's the piano."

He waved toward the enormous living room. In the corner sat a brand-new baby grand. Henry shuddered. It was a beautiful instrument, glistening in the afternoon sunlight. It would have taken up half of his own living room.

"Is Henry going to play?"

His sister, expecting in four months, waddled his way. Still, she looked good, having what Henry had heard described as "that glow." Though he had been somewhat surprised that his older sis had bagged a man of Adam's quality, petty sibling jealousies aside, he had to admit that Melissa wasn't half bad. Of course, as kids they had had their moments, but to Henry's surprise, that petulant, vain child had grown into a nice, supportive adult. In fact, she seemed to take a certain pleasure in showing Henry off. Requests to play piano were de rigueur for any social gathering. Given his current state of mind, though, Henry preferred to remain anonymous.

"I don't think so," Henry said. "Not in front of all these people."

"OK," Melissa said. "But I'd love to hear it sometime."

"Well, I might have a reading when it's all done," Henry said.

"Make sure to invite us," Adam said. "And if you need money to help organize it, don't hesitate."

This wasn't the first time his brother-in-law had offered financial assistance. As always, Henry was touched. He liked to think that if the tables had been turned he would be as generous. Secretly, however, Henry feared that he would've taken his cue from Silas Marner and shamelessly spent every last cent on himself.

"Thanks," Henry told Adam now, "but readings don't cost much to put together. Actors usually work for free."

"Whatever you say," Adam replied. "But lemme know." Then he tossed a muscular arm around Henry's shoulder. "Now let me show you around."

Half an hour later, Henry stood in the corner of the living room, sipping a mimosa, watching Sunday afternoon joggers huff and puff around the Central Park Reservoir. The dreaded tour was over. After so much buildup, the actual event hadn't gone nearly as badly as he had feared. Though enormous by any standard, the apartment hadn't lived up to Henry's inflated expectations; at seven rooms, plus a kitchen, dining room, and living room, it was no Meadowlands. As Henry had followed Adam, Melissa, and Jill, who soon tagged along, from room to room, he had miraculously managed to temporarily expunge all traces of envy from his mind and allow himself to share in his sister's joy. In fact, his main problem became an inability to find increasingly expressive ways to convey his admiration for her remodeling job. "This is so beautiful!" and "Wow!" only took him so far. By room number three Henry found himself wishing that he had brought along a thesaurus so he could have had a never-ending supply of choice descriptive words at his fingertips. Left to his own brainpower, Henry soon found himself settling on less elegant alternatives such as "Goddamn!" or the always descriptive "Yes!" And by the time they reached the last stop, the kitchen, all Henry could manage was a double-thumbed-up "Fuckin' A!"

With the tour behind him, Henry's goal for the remainder of the afternoon was simple: to avoid as many conversations as possible. He would defy his mother's wishes and be aggressively antisocial. Not that it was an unfriendly group. The living room was packed with Adam and Melissa's friends, several of whom Henry had known for years. The trouble was that most of these people had "real jobs" and spent inordinate time talking about their work—work that Henry had nothing against but didn't pretend to understand. His ignorance had led to trouble in the past. At his sister's wedding, Adam's best man had gone on a roll describing to Henry some "hot deal" that looked like a "slam dunk" but then "went hostile" until a "white knight" appeared and "closed the fucker." When the conversation had ended, Henry had felt exhausted, having said "uh-huh" and nodded in the appropriate places for a full half hour while having no idea whatsoever what the guy was talking about.

So when Henry felt a hand on his shoulder, he immediately tensed.

"Hey there."

Henry turned to find himself face-to-face with his stepfather/ex-high-school-American-history-teacher. An angular man who wore a beard with no mustache, Rye (whom Henry still sometimes called Dr. Bertolini out of habit) bore a somewhat striking resemblance to Abraham Lincoln. Just as the South had unfairly blamed Lincoln for starting the Civil War, Henry had blamed Rye for his parents' divorce, spending much of his high school years shooting barbs and sneers his way with only the slightest provocation. In the end, it took Henry until college to realize that his parents had simply grown apart and that Rye had had nothing to do with their divorce or, for that matter, the untimely death of his dog. Now the two got along extremely well and the only thing Henry held against his stepdad was the B-minus he had given him in Urban Politics.

"How's the writing going, Henry?"

Henry quickly opted for a vague, noncommittal answer that he hoped would lead to a quick changing of subjects.

"Pretty good, Rye. How's school? Teaching any good classes this year?"

Rye scratched his beard and, like any good teacher, refused to let Henry throw him off track. "Still working on your novels? Or is it poetry now?"

Henry knew he was lost. Once Rye wanted to talk about a subject, that was the subject that got talked about.

"I've actually put them aside for the time being. I'm concentrating on the musical."

"Oh, yes. Now it's the musical."

Henry sighed. He knew that his mother, and Rye by extension, thought his writing career had suffered from a certain aimlessness. What's worse, they had a point.

"Your mother told me about it," Rye continued now. "Based on *Dubliners*, is it?"

"No, *Gatsby.*"

Rye beamed. "*Gatsby,* eh? Now there's a fine work of literature, Henry! Written in the Roaring Twenties. Hmmmm." His hand returned to his beard. "You know, Henry, that musical of yours could be a gold mine. Fitzgerald was a true symbol of his era. The twenties were much like the eighties, come to think of it. A time in our history when greed ruled the day. A decade defined by a certain recklessness, if you will. Of course, the stock market crash changed all that, as you know."

Henry knew he was at a critical point. Like many historians, Rye loved to talk. Henry was too busy feeling sorry for himself to get mired in a discussion about the leading causes of the Great Depression. Perhaps he could read a book to Jill in her room? Or maybe he could try out the piano? Or maybe . . . ?

Just then, Henry glanced across the room. What he saw caused his jaw, literally, to drop. Smiling at him from the bar was a stunning creature—twenty-five tops, auburn hair, and a body worthy of Jennifer Aniston (*Friends* reruns were one of Henry's most loathsome yet unbreakable habits). Henry shivered. Under most circumstances, such a woman would be quickly tossed into the "out of my league" file, but something in that smile—a certain welcoming quality— made Henry leave her index card out of the drawer for a moment. Maybe this one could slip into the rarely used "gorgeous yet attainable" folder. Not only was she smiling directly at him (still), but she appeared to be alone. Further, Henry had home court advantage. Perhaps he'd be getting over Tamar more quickly than he thought?

"Sorry, Rye," Henry said.

"What?" the professor said.

Henry nodded across the room. Rye glanced over his shoulder. When he turned back to Henry he was all smiles.

"We'll talk about Herbert Hoover some other time."

"You think she's single?" Henry asked.

Rye shrugged. "She sure seems to be standing alone. Go! Go! Before somebody beats you to it!"

Henry didn't need to be told twice. He chugged the rest of his mimosa, laid the glass on the windowsill, and surveyed the terrain. His challenge now was to find the quickest possible route across the crowded living room while simultaneously avoiding all conversations. Directly before him and facing his way was his first obstacle: his mother. Not only that, but she was talking to John, the famed entertainment lawyer.

"Society constantly tells us that a woman over sixty is worthless," she was saying. "My new book is going to lay out twenty simple steps today's modern ladies can take to stay active and psychologically on top of their game."

"Oh, really?" John asked politely.

Without having to be asked, Rye winked at Henry, then joined the conversation, positioning himself in such a way that his lanky body partially blocked his wife's field of vision to her left.

"Why, yes," she continued as Henry slipped by. "I believe that women should be giving birth into their fifties. Menopause is a thing of the past. It's extraordinary what medical science can do these days, and I see no reason for women to . . ."

Now in the epicenter of the party, in a swirl of chatter, Henry accidentally met eyes with Adam's best man. Henry didn't have a spare hour to hear about another incomprehensible deal, so when the best man made a motion his way, Henry threw civility to the wind, made a quick cut left, and edged past his sister.

"You've got to get Pampers," she was telling another pregnant friend. "Disposable. The ads are right. They really do hold in all that poop."

When he thought of marriage, Henry imagined nonstop sex and nonstop companionship. Excrement was low on his list. Temporarily ecstatic to still be single, he hurried by but soon found himself in a particularly knotted part of the crowd, sandwiched between three separate conversational groups bunched in a tangled muddle near the bar. Henry edged right, then back to his left, but found himself firmly wedged into an assortment of elbows. Just as he was considering continuing the journey on his stomach, some-thing miraculous occurred. Suddenly, the crowd shifted—and lo and behold, a direct path to the woman opened up! And she was still smiling right at him! Like Moses crossing the Red Sea, Henry rushed toward the Promised Land.

But Henry didn't see what was lurking to his right. A mere three steps from his prime objective, a large, globlike mass lurched di-rectly into his path. Horrified, Henry found himself staring down upon the heavily made-up features of Joan Fitz, a childhood friend of his mother's.

"Your mother tells me you're going to join the Pinafore Play-ers!" she cooed, holding up a plate of whitefish and bagels.

Henry feinted right, then left, but Joan Fitz, a rotund creature, blocked his way without even having to move.

"We're doing *H.M.S. Pinafore* next year," she continued. "You'd be such a cute sailor!"

Out of his peripheral vision, Henry noticed a beefy stockbroker named Pete approaching the girl from his left flank! Disaster!

"Well?" Mrs. Fitz asked. "Will we see you at auditions?" She pushed her face an inch away from his. Henry could count at least three layers of lipstick. "There's lots of pretty young ladies who would love a good-looking boy like you. Your mother tells me you've been having trouble meeting girls."

At this point Henry realized he had three options.

1. Deck one of his mother's best friends.
2. Dash back across the room and deck his mother.
3. Get the hell away however he could and deal with the fallout later.

With Pete closing fast, Henry simply reacted. In a dazzling dis-play of party-maneuvering pyrotechnics, he cut wide around Joan Fitz, slipped in between two of Adam's college roommates, and butt-checked Pete out of the way.

"Henry Mann," he said.

"Amanda Sullivan."

She took his hand.

At this juncture, Henry let out a nearly audible gasp. Amanda was even more beautiful up close than she had been across the room. Her eyes were pale blue with the slightest hint of sea green— a few stray flecks, really—near the irises. Her auburn hair spilled onto her shoulders like little waterfalls. Her skin was pale pink, unblemished but for three (or was it four) freckles that adorned a nose that was charmingly pugged. Then there was her smile! Indeed, Amanda was in possession of a set of teeth to put toothpaste models to shame. She was the absolute personification of "wholesome," Henry thought. An Iowa farm girl, reared on porch swings, church suppers, and buckets of cold goat's milk. Though they had exchanged only two words, Henry was already half in love.

Now the rest was simple: The introductions complete, all Henry had to do was upshift to genuine conversation. A natural talker, he usually had no trouble getting the ball rolling, but today was different. Amanda's radiant beauty was making it nearly impossible for him to get his tongue around any sort of statement or question that seemed at all appropriate or even comprehensible. To make matters worse, he couldn't take his eyes from her breasts—breasts that displayed an astonishing, even Anistonian, roundness. In fact, Henry was so overcome by the sight of that chest that the only words that came to him at this point were "nice tits." Wisely realizing that Amanda might not take that comment in the right spirit, Henry panicked and blurted out the most clichéd line in the book.

"So . . . come here often?" he asked.

Amanda laughed, possibly thinking Henry was kidding.

"No. It's my first time."

"Uh . . . well, I . . . mine, too."

Suddenly, Henry was struggling in Arctic waters going down fast. From out of nowhere, a life preserver bobbed to his side.

"Your sister tells me you write music," Amanda said.

"She did?" Henry replied, surprised. "I mean, I do. That's right."

"That's funny, because I'm a music teacher."

It took all Henry's powers of concentration not to jump in the air and click his heels. There was a God! Undoubtedly this woman had been sent to this party by some divine power as reparation for the ignominious treatment he had received the previous evening at the hands of . . . uh, whatshername?

"That's incredible," Henry said. "Do you play an instrument?"

"Piano."

"Me, too."

"Cool."

"What grade do you teach?"

"High school mostly. You know, I introduce the kids to the classical composers."

Despite a music minor, Henry had never been much of a classical fan. His true loves were jazz and rock. Still, he knew enough music history to keep the conversation rolling.

"Oh, really? Who's your favorite?"

"That's hard to say, really, because I like so many. Brahms, Bach. Copland, too."

"Oh, I love Copland," Henry said. "*Appalachian Spring* is one of my favorites."

"I adore that piece," Amanda said. "I try to listen to it every Sunday morning when I get up. It's so, I don't know, serene."

"So tranquil," Henry offered.

"So uniquely . . ." Amanda paused, searching for the right word.

"American?" Henry asked.

"That's it," Amanda said. "It's American. About the American experience."

At this point, Amanda launched into a somewhat detailed description of a dance recital to *Appalachian Spring* that she had seen the previous year. Though Henry could see that she was continuing to talk, he was vaguely aware at best of the actual words coming out of her mouth. Truth be told, he was busy replaying the previous evening's wedding fantasy, this time X-ing out Tamar and replacing her with his new love, a woman who was clearly much better suited for him. A fellow music lover, no less! If Henry wasn't sure exactly what else they had in common just yet, he felt certain that their range of mutual interests would be vast.

"What's your favorite?"

"What?"

Henry willed himself to focus. He had been told that a prerequisite for any meaningful relationship was an ability to listen and respond on cue.

"The Beethoven symphonies," Amanda said. "I like number six the best."

"Yeah, the Pastoral," Henry said, rallying. A pause. "In F major."

Amanda smiled, impressed. "F major. Very good, sir. The second movement is gorgeous, don't you think?"

"Oh, yeah, I love it," Henry said, though he couldn't for the life of him remember how it went. "Very plaintive."

At this point, Amanda seemed to nod, as though she were considering what Henry had just said. Then she glanced toward the kitchen.

"You know," she said, "I really want to grab some food before it's all gone."

Henry was stunned. With that simple statement, he was rudely tossed back into Arctic waters, this time surrounded by a school of man-eating sharks: Indeed, he had taken the single man's equivalent of an uppercut to the jaw. Amanda's meaning couldn't have been clearer. In not so subtle party code she was informing him that he had not measured up in some critical area and that, as a result, she had decided to move on in search of a man of higher quality—someone better-looking, funnier, richer, better in bed, possibly even more well endowed. Maybe Pete the stockbroker (that slimy asshole) or another of Adam's single friends.

But then . . . what was that?

Was Amanda touching his hand?

"Don't go anywhere, OK?" she said, leaning toward him, close enough for Henry to get a knee-weakening whiff of hair. "I'll be right back. Promise."

Just like that, Henry was standing, broad-shouldered, chest out, in the captain's cabin of the USS *Stud*. Giddy now, he leaned back against the wall and watched his love disappear into the kitchen. He loved the way her long legs carried her confidently through the crowd. He loved her slim hips and her hard, muscular calves. Oh, yes! Henry could love a woman with hips like that. And those calves? They could carry him through a lifetime.

As the party swirled around him, Henry closed his eyes and allowed himself to mosey back to that Iowa farm he and Amanda would soon call home. Henry had always fancied himself a gentleman farmer. Though raised in the city, he could see himself as the type of guy who'd wake with the rooster to milk the cows. While he tended to the herd, Amanda would be inside getting the kids breakfast. Then, when the school bus had carried their brood off for a day of learning, Amanda would head off to the local university to teach music history while Henry retired to his study to create stunning works of art.

Sometimes, schedule permitting, Amanda would come home early and surprise him. Diligent at his desk, Henry wouldn't hear her until she was at his side. Then, without saying a word, she'd take his hand and lead him to the hay barn. There, on the spot where they had conceived all six of their children, they would make love with a fervor that only got stronger with each passing year. When they were through, they would lie peacefully in each other's arms, luxuriating in the sounds of nature—the playful coos of the robins, the gentle buzz of crickets. Maybe Amanda would walk, still nude, to a beat-up old piano they kept by the lawn mower and play some Mozart or Liszt. Henry would prop himself up on his elbow, listening to the lovely strains fill the barn, watching the arch of his wife's back as she leaned over the keys. The concert finished, she'd return to his arms and they'd doze, drifting in and out of a tender sleep for the better part of an hour. Only when they heard the distant rumble of the school bus would husband and wife scramble back into their clothes. Henry would be safely back in his office, tying the laces on his boots, by the time his youngest daughter would rush in, all smiles, waving a spelling test with a big *A* printed on top.

"Hi there, Henry."

Henry blinked. He had been so involved in his new life in Iowa that for a second or two he was genuinely surprised to find himself back in New York. Further, it wasn't Amanda's voice that had carried him back from the farm. She was still in the kitchen, loading up her plate with bagels and muffins. Rather, it was Henry's father, Gregory Mann, who now stood before him, a distinguished businessman in a blue blazer. With bright green eyes (which Henry inherited, one of his best features) and a strong chin (which Henry did not inherit, one of his worst), he looked a good deal younger than his sixty years.

Though the first years of Henry's folks' divorce had been acrimonious, Mr. and Mrs. Mann were now able to inhabit the same room without feeling compelled to scowl, bicker, or broadcast embarrassing information about the other (e.g., "Tell us, Gregory. What was the name of that preschooler you met on our honeymoon?"). With time, venom had melted into polite cordiality. Though Henry hadn't been sure if his father had been invited to the party, he was happy to see him. He would certainly take great pleasure in introducing him to Amanda.

Right on schedule, she glided out of the kitchen, plate of food in hand, and flashed him another vintage smile. Henry felt a slight stiffening below his waist.

"Dad," he said proudly, as his love approached. "I'd like you to meet Amanda."

Henry expected his father to hold out his hand and introduce himself. Instead, Amanda gave the elder Mr. Mann a playful punch in the arm.

"Hey there," she said. "What took you so long?"

"Sorry. I had to drop by the office."

A sickly feeling welled in Henry's gut. Did they know each other? Become friendly at some other family function? Before Henry had a chance to parse it any further, his carefully constructed future life crumbled to dust. Mr. Mann took Amanda by the shoulders and pulled her close. Then, to Henry's horror, they kissed—and it was no peck; tongues were involved. By the time it ended (a good fifteen seconds later), Henry's heart had disintegrated into the consistency of gruel.

"Hey there," his dad said to his son when he finally came up for air. "I see you've met my new honey."

Met and married, Henry might have said. Instead, he muttered an anemic "yeah" and left it at that. Back in the Arctic waters without a lifeboat in sight, he began to seethe. This was the latest and most egregious example of a phenomenon that had been a thorn in his side for years: His dad had a better track record with women than he did. Not only that, these women—and there had been a string of them—had some significant attributes in common.

Average age, 25.
Average measurements, 36-24-36.
Average intelligence, extremely high.
Average skill in bed, Henry didn't want to think about it.

What made matters worse was the way these "relationships" ended. Henry's dad was always the dumper. Not once had one of these women given *him* his walking papers. It was an uncanny record that, in Henry's little universe, left Barry Bonds in the dust. A record that made Henry proud, jealous, and embarrassed all at once. Now it made him furious and desperate for a quick escape.

"I need a refill," he said.

"Going so soon?" his dad said.

"I'll be back," Henry lied.

As he cut through the crowd, Henry thought that he would've liked to see his father with an elderly widow—someone along the lines of Miss Havisham.

"It was real nice meeting you," Amanda called.

"Yeah. You, too."

As Henry cut across the foyer, he knew what he needed. It was time for a total retreat to Jill's room. There he could wallow in misery with the one woman on earth who truly understood him. That this "woman" was only seven was inconsequential. This wasn't the first time that Henry had stooped to letting his spirits be lifted by the unconditional love of his niece. After the last twenty-four hours, he needed that sort of boost more than ever. They would watch the Knicks, play gin rummy, use her bed as a trampoline. Perhaps Henry would comfort himself by snuggling with her giant stuffed polar bear.

"Henry!" he heard a voice call. It was Adam, waving from across the room.

Busted! Henry stopped in the foyer.

"Yeah?"

"Do you have a minute? I want to talk to you."

"Can it wait?" Henry asked. "I'm going to check in on Jill."

Without waiting for an answer, he turned for the hall and bumped right into his mother.

"Oh, Henry. Have you had a chance to chat with John?"

"Not yet," Henry said.

"Just do it, Henry. It can't hurt. It's always good to have a fall-back."

If Henry had had the energy, he would have taken great pleasure in pointing out that chapter nine of his mother's book *The Inner You* was entitled "The Evils of Fallbacks! Pursue Your Dream!"

"I've got to go," he said, continuing down the hall.

"Where?"

"To see Jill."

"You're going to play piano for us later, right? You're so wonderful."

"Sure, Mom. Sure."

Alone at last, Henry glanced over his shoulder again. Across the living room, his father and Amanda were looking out over Central Park, holding hands. Henry was suddenly worried that he might christen his sister's new apartment by barfing all over the back hallway. Minutes earlier, he and Amanda had been making love in their hay barn. Now she was fucking his dad.

With a final painful glance back toward the party, Henry hurried down the hall. Yes, he needed Jill and that giant stuffed polar bear now more than ever.

3

patricia

SIX that evening found Henry sitting in a conference room in the largest corporate law firm in New York. Though he resented the fact that his limited earning power required him to work as a part-time proofreader, Henry had come to view this monstrosity of a law firm, Albright, Pierce & Dean (twenty-two floors and four hundred attorneys in the New York office alone), as his home away from home. His sanctuary within that home was this room—number 34 North—where he hung out with his two best friends, Glenn Roth and Doug Buchanan.

Glenn was a tall man with a receding hairline and horn-rim glasses. When he wasn't advising Henry on the varied facets of his love life, he was a playwright whose most ambitious work, *The Broccoli Indictment*, had run a year earlier off-off-Broadway. Though the *Village Voice* had called Glenn's work "unusually adventurous," Henry had to admit that his own feelings were more in line with the reviewer from *Time Out* who had observed, "Ten minutes of *The Broccoli Indictment* made me crave a plate of steak tartare." Not that Henry didn't think Glenn was talented. He simply found his friend's artistic vision, which included human beings taking on the roles of talking pieces of food, furniture, or animals, a bit odd. At any rate, it was certainly not the type of work that was likely to earn Glenn a cent anytime soon. In fact, an almost complete lack of concern regarding future income (along with a predilection for a certain young actress) had played a part in leading Diana, lover of dining room tables, to move to Colorado. Already thirty-five, Glenn showed no signs of changing his writing to suit commercial tastes. His next play, *Hoo, Hoo! Haw, Haw!* took place in a monkey cage and told the story of a zookeeper's relationship with three talking chimps. According to Glenn, the piece was a metaphor for man's inability to connect with his fellow man. Henry, who had edited one of the early drafts, had his doubts.

Then there was Doug, the poet. A slightly built man with short, sandy hair, in many ways Doug had had the most success of the trio, having recently won a nationwide poetry competition. Unfortunately, the list of people who had made a good living writing poems in the history of mankind was very short. That Doug had recently married Ellen (feelings regarding dining room tables unknown), who was devoting her career to pinhole photography, didn't increase his odds for economic security anytime in the near future.

Now the three friends sat around an oval conference table, catching up on the weekend's news. Though each man had a pile of proofreading before him, work was pushed aside for a few moments in order to let the room fulfill its other more important function. After five in the afternoon, four nights a week, 34 North became a makeshift psychiatrist's office. Not that there was anything inherently therapeutic about the space itself. Aside from the oval table there were half a dozen swivel chairs, some legal pads, a tray of sharpened number two pencils, and a phone. A picture window afforded a view of 44th Street just east of Times Square. The room's most prominent feature was a formal portrait of Wynn Hamilton Albright, the founding partner of the firm, now deceased.

Albright was a gray-haired man, somewhat pudgy, with reddish skin and jowls like a St. Bernard. Even though he had had an international reputation in the field of corporate law, it made Henry feel somehow better to know that if he had dressed this man in a white apron, he'd look a lot like the guy who sold sausages at the corner deli.

The first topic of conversation this evening had been Glenn's rewrites of *Hoo, Hoo! Haw, Haw!* Soon the discussion turned to Henry. Working backward, he touched upon the housewarming fiasco, then quickly launched into a full-blown description of the main event: his date with Tamar.

"You're kidding." Glenn said once Henry laid out the basic facts of the case. "By e-mail?"

Henry nodded. "Right. Now I guess there are fifty-one ways to leave your lover, huh?"

"How'd you meet her again?" Doug asked Glenn.

"At a party. I thought of Henry the minute we got talking."

"Yeah," Henry said, "and she was probably thinking of Abby."

"E-mail!" Glenn repeated. "That's such a bitchy thing to do." He turned to Doug. "Is she a bitch or what?"

Prone to great bursts of moral outrage, Glenn often turned to Doug, the slow, steady sage, to confirm his pronouncements. In the small universe of 34 North, Doug's opinions were the equivalent of binding UN resolutions. Now he seconded Glenn's opinion.

"She's a bitch alright."

"Damn straight," Glenn said.

Henry smiled. His friends were responding on cue.

"I guess it was pretty crappy," Henry said. "She could've called."

"Exactly my point," Glenn said. "She owed you a phone call." Once more to Doug, "Didn't she owe him a phone call?"

Again Doug ruled in the affirmative. "She should've called."

"What he said," Glenn said.

A silence filled the room as the three friends pondered the pointlessness of a universe that included women who could dismiss a man of Henry's obvious qualities. After this contemplative moment, Glenn reached for a pencil and held it loosely between the thumb and index finger of his right hand. Henry knew what was coming next—a game Glenn used to pass the time virtually every shift. The goal was to flick a pencil toward the ceiling with enough force that the point stuck. On a good night, twenty or more pencils would hang down from the ceiling like a rare collection of tropical plant life. Henry often grew annoyed at Glenn's devotion to a pastime most eight-year-olds would have abandoned after a couple of weeks. Then again, Henry knew that at heart Glenn was really no more than an overgrown kid with a severe case of the fidgets.

"You know," Glenn said as he glanced toward the ceiling, taking aim, "there is a good side to all this. I mean, at least you made out a little, right? When the pain fades, you'll always have that memory."

Henry forced a smile. Unfortunately, he'd also have the memory of singing, "Tamar! I just met a girl named Tamar!" along with the heartwrenching description of his dog's untimely death. Just then, Glenn snapped his wrist and the evening's first missile was launched. Unfortunately, it slapped lengthwise against the ceiling and dropped to the carpet.

"Fuck!" he said.

Henry and Doug remained silent for a moment out of respect for the misfired pencil, then carried on with the conversation.

"Something still bothers me, though," Doug said. "Do you really think she's gay?"

Henry sighed. With customary insight, Doug had zeroed in on the one aspect of Tamar's letter that hadn't rung true. As much as he hated to admit it, Henry knew that Tamar's professed bisexuality was likely an elaborate lie, calculated to let him down easy.

"I don't know," Henry replied. "She sure didn't seem it last night."

"Oh, she's gay, alright," Glenn said, taking another pencil from the tray. "Why else would she turn you down? I mean, come on! You're a stud!"

With that, he flicked his wrist. Henry saw a yellow blur rocket toward the ceiling. This one stuck with a satisfying *thwap*.

"Me? A stud?" Henry said. "My mother and sister sure the hell don't think so."

"What do you mean by that?" Doug asked.

Henry paused. Indeed, there had been a final humiliation in the weekend from hell. After watching the Knicks with Jill for half an hour, he had been badgered by his mother into playing piano for a sing-along—an event highlighted by a stirring falsetto rendition of "I Cain't Say No!" by Adam's boss. When Henry had finally been able to pry himself from the piano and fight his way toward the front door, Adam had corralled him in the kitchen by the new eight-burner stove.

"I feel awful about this," he had begun. Henry hadn't remembered ever seeing him look so uncomfortable. "But your mother and sister wanted me to talk to you about something."

Henry had known instantly that "something" had to refer to either his career or his personal life—either a job Henry was completely unqualified for or a woman with whom he would have nothing in common. In this case, it was even worse than expected. With great embarrassment, Adam informed Henry that it was the belief of the female members of his family (minus Jill, who didn't offer an opinion) that since Sheila his social life had been floundering. Though it seemed drastic, they felt that a personal ad was in order.

"What?" Glenn said now. He began to clean his glasses on his shirt. "No way do you need to place an ad. Right, Doug?"

Henry fully expected Doug to give his assent, thereby dismissing the topic. To his surprise, his friend seemed to think the idea worthy of some discussion.

"Well, of course, Henry doesn't *need* to take out an ad," Doug said.

"What does that mean?" Glenn asked, returning his glasses to their rightful place.

"Yeah," Henry said, eyes narrowed. "What does that mean?"

"Nothing bad. Just that it's something worth considering. There're lots of good dating Web sites."

"Oh, come on," Henry said. "You've got to be kidding."

Doug shrugged. "Whatever. But it could work."

Before Henry could engineer an appropriately dismissive response, Doug's wife, Ellen, pushed the door open and bubbled her way into the room.

"What could work?" she cooed. Without waiting for an answer, she immediately turned to her husband. "Hey, cutie!" Then, to Glenn and Henry, "Isn't he cute?" Then back to Doug. "You're so cute!" After which she zeroed in for a big, wet kiss.

Henry often wondered how his friend stood sharing his life with this member of the pathologically perky. Perhaps the quiet poet in him fed off of her liveliness. Whatever the reason, Henry knew that he himself wouldn't have been able to stand it. It wasn't as though Ellen compensated for her overbearing (though admittedly affectionate) nature with great looks, either. Sure, in isolated instances, from very specific angles she could be considered attractive, but her Brillo-pad hair and pale complexion, matched with a wardrobe that leaned heavily upon L. L. Bean and J. Crew, gave her a sterile, boyish look that left Henry completely cold. Of course, there was the possibility that Doug, being the most mature member of the group, had considered more than just her appearance when he had proposed. Henry was aware, after all, that some men actually did that. He was also aware that Ellen, despite her annoying perkiness, was in possession of many fine qualities. She was loyal, loving, sometimes amusing, and, if one cared about such things (which Henry didn't), an expert on the intricacies of pinhole photography.

"We're talking about a personal ad," Glenn said, as Ellen finally unwrapped herself from Doug and took a seat.

"For you?" Ellen replied.

"No way, José," Glenn said. "I'm not ready to date yet."

Henry suddenly imagined the conference room table covered with a tablecloth and six place settings with Diana as the centerpiece, fully naked, legs spread, an apple in her mouth. He looked to the floor and shut his eyes.

"Gosh, I'm sorry," Ellen said, patting Glenn's hand. "Still no word?"

"None," Glenn said. "She's still ski-bumming out west, I guess." Glenn marked that comment by flicking another pencil toward the ceiling (this one also lodging there successfully).

"The ad is for me," Henry cut in, changing the subject.

"For you?" Ellen said. "Well, there's nothing wrong with it. My brother met his wife through a personal."

Yeah, Henry wanted to reply, *but he's a loser.*

Instead, he kept his mouth shut and let a silence fill the room. Henry knew, of course, that Ellen was right. There was nothing inherently wrong with taking out a personal. People met that way every day of the week—some of them even worthy of being seen in public without bags over their heads. Henry just couldn't picture doing it himself. The way he was feeling now, he could only picture the sort of ad he'd place:

> Single man, 32. One sad case. Totally broke. Dumped over e-mail. Mother pushing him to sing G&S with losers. Father gets more ass. Brother-in-law (rich stud, but taken, sorry) forced him to take out ad. Principal skills: whining, piano, beating off. Wanna fuck?

"I know someone you can ask out."

Henry looked up to see Ellen twirling her hair, smiling his way.

"Oh, really?" he said skeptically. Ellen had set him up once before, and it turned out that her definition of "pretty" weighed over two hundred pounds and sported a "Save the Whales" nose ring.

"Who?"

"Christine."

Henry knew her well—a fourth-grade teacher who worked at Albright once a week to make extra spending money.

"There's a choice!" Glenn said. "Cute girl."

"Yeah, she's cute," Henry said. "But . . ."

"But what?" Doug asked.

Though Henry had never mentioned it to his friends, he had come close to asking Christine to a movie a short month earlier, but when he had approached her, something had caught his eye—something that, though essentially insignificant, he knew would bother him down the line. Christine's eyebrows didn't stop at the inner edge of her eye but rather continued, albeit with less hair (really only a thin layer of fuzz but, since her hair was jet black, noticeable fuzz), across the bridge of her nose. The result was a unibrow. Perhaps not as obvious a unibrow as the one made famous by Bert the Muppet, but enough to be distracting. Even worse, the second after Henry noticed the upsetting joined brow, he was confronted by a largish pimple that had taken up residence on her slightly crooked nose. Any of these imperfections (brow, pimple, nose) by itself could have been easily overlooked, but in tandem they stopped Henry dead in his tracks. Instead of asking Christine to dinner and a movie, he asked her to double-check a table in a document. As he had walked back to the conference room moments later, Henry had felt irredeemably shallow. Even so, he had felt confident that he had done the right thing. The pimple would heal, of course, but Henry knew that he would never be able to stop staring at that eyebrow or have the guts to tell her to shave it. And the nose? Short of surgery, she'd take her slightly lopsided shnoz to the grave. He could just picture their wedding day. Their vows complete, he'd lift the veil to kiss his bride. Instead of gazing into the eyes of the woman he loved, he'd be compelled to gaze at her forehead.

Now Henry was faced with a difficult dilemma: The three people in the room were among his closest friends in the world, but were they close enough to embrace the full depths of his superficiality? Could he tell them that the reason he hadn't asked out a perfectly attractive woman—in fact, a very attractive woman—had to do with an unruly eyebrow, an off-kilter proboscis, and a zit?

"Out with it," Ellen said. "What's wrong with her?"

"I'm not sure," Henry said haltingly. "I considered her once . . . Is she funny enough?"

"Sure, she's funny," Ellen said. "She's hilarious. You've got to give her a chance to warm up, that's all. She thinks you're cute."

"Wait a second here!" Glenn said. "Wait a second! Isn't she the one who xeroxed her butt?"

"That's her," Ellen said.

"Well, that's a funny thing to do, right?" Glenn said. "I mean, fuck! What kind of girl puts her bare ass on a color xerox machine, then hangs the copy in the supervisor's office?"

Henry had to admit that he had admired that picture enormously. Maybe there was hope after all? He could overlook the eyebrows and focus on the rear.

Now Ellen smiled even more broadly.

"What?" Henry said. "What?"

She giggled. "You're going to kill me."

"Why?"

"Well," Ellen said, "I may have just read her your poem."

"My poem?"

"Yeah. The one you wrote for your niece. About the otter."

Henry couldn't believe the betrayal.

"That was just for Jill. How'd you find it?"

"It was in your bookbag," Ellen said.

"You looked through my bookbag?"

"It was on top."

"Oh, Jesus," Henry said.

"You act like it was obscene or something," Doug said. "It's just a poem about an otter."

"You mean you read it, too?"

"Blame me," Ellen said. "I showed it to him. Anyway, Christine teaches elementary school. She's the perfect judge. And she loved it."

"So did I, by the way," Doug said. "A lot."

At this point, events spun out of Henry's control. Before he knew it, Ellen produced a piece of paper and Glenn snatched it from her.

"How come I've never heard this?" Glenn said.

"Gimme that!"

Henry lunged across the table. Glenn stood up and held it over his head.

"Read it!" Ellen called.

Henry knew Glenn too well. He could either chase him around the room like an idiot or resign himself to his fate. So he slumped back in the chair and listened as Glenn cleared his throat dramatically and began to read:

> There once was an otter
> Named Benjamin Potter
> Who had quite a crush on the zookeeper's daughter.
>
> The zookeeper's daughter
> Walked by the water
> Each morning at ten with a millionaire yachter.
>
> The millionaire yachter,
> John Witherspoon Kotter,
> Spotted the otter admiring the daughter.
>
> Then Witherspoon Kotter
> Got hotter and hotter
> And aimed a small rock at the dewy-eyed otter.
>
> The zookeeper's daughter
> Cried out, "You rotter!
> How dare you assault Mr. Benjamin Potter!"

And that's when the otter
(That quick-thinking plotter)
Cried to the daughter: "Wed me, you oughter!"

The zookeeper's daughter
Spied the otter that sought her
And thought to herself: Why not tie the knotter?

"Good-bye, Mr. Kotter!
I'll become Mrs. Potter!"
And later that day they wed underwater.

So ends the tale of how
Benjamin Potter,
A lovable otter,
Defeated a yachter
In pursuit of a daughter . . .

And finally got her.

Glenn lowered the paper from his eyes and looked directly at Henry.

"Man!" he said. "That's fucking great."

Henry knew the praise was sincere. In Glenn's lexicon, the word "fuck" was reserved for only the most heartfelt raves.

"What he said," Doug agreed. "You should write more."

Henry shrugged. "Yeah, maybe. After I finish the musical."

"You should," Glenn said. "You're onto something."

With that, he folded the poem into a paper airplane and sent it gliding back Henry's way.

In time, the four friends hunkered down and actually did a little work. It was Henry's theory that legalese was a language developed years ago by a group of cunning lawyers as a way to confuse potential clients and enable attorneys to bill ten times more than necessary. Still, despite thick verbiage, most proofreading jobs were fairly mindless. All that was required was to check the most recent copy of a document against the previous draft to make sure that the changes indicated by the attorney had been made by the word processing department. It was a job that called for a limited knowledge of grammar and spelling, along with a highly developed ability to decipher a never ending variety of semi-incoherent attorney scrawl. After five years at the firm, Henry and his friends had become old pros and could chat, listen to music, and otherwise coast while they worked. Of course, there were those times when Henry really had to concentrate—those indentures, proxy statements, and briefs with sentences so long that he had to look halfway back up the page to find the subject. Sometimes, when a document was truly impossible to get through, Henry was tempted to add in his own inappropriate clauses:

> In view of said litigation, URCO (the "Company") will have the right to sue the defendant if and only if said Company fulfills the aforestated conditions *[i.e., the supplying of CEO with lifetime supply of urological creams ("Pleasure Balms") and sexual devices ("Happy-Toys")]*, provided, however, that said Company does not engage in any . . .

Though Henry was desperate to pencil in such language, he knew that to be caught would mean immediate dismissal. Still, he, Glenn, and Doug often amused themselves by reading documents out loud, inserting obscene words or phrases *(i.e., provided, however, the defendant's vagina is of suitable shape . . .)*. True, it was infantile, but Henry speculated that seven hours of reading legal documents four nights a week would turn even Jerry Falwell and Ralph Reed into perverts.

In fact, Henry was just about to ask Glenn if he was up for such a game when the phone rang. Doug answered.

"Hello?" Seconds later, he held out the phone to Henry. "For you."

"Who is it?"

"Steve."

The call could not have come at a worse time. If his mood wasn't yet cheery, these few hours with his friends had at least rescued Henry from the ranks of the presuicidal. A summons from Steve, their supervisor, could only mean bad news—news that in Henry's delicate condition might send him hurtling back down into the abyss. And the news *was* bad. Not wasting any time, Steve quickly informed Henry that he would have to put down what he was working on, go up to the forty-seventh floor, and "help out an attorney for a couple of hours."

Like all proofreaders, Henry positively detested being "sent out." Even when faced with an illegible document with microscopic print, a proofer had the comfort of working in privacy. Out "on the floors," anything could happen, one became "a legal assistant." One might be forced to stand for hours in front of a xerox machine clearing jams, or check piles of documents for missing pages, or be screamed at by a rabid associate for not making a deadline there was never a prayer of making in the first place.

"Who's the lawyer?" Henry asked Steve.

The deathly pause on the other end of the line told Henry that things were going to be even worse than he thought. Something was very wrong indeed.

"It's Patricia Gergen."

Henry's face went white.

"Hello, Henry? You there?"

"Yeah, I'm here."

"Sorry, buddy."

"That's OK, Steve. Not your fault."

He hung up the phone.

"Who is it?" Glenn asked.

Henry smiled ruefully. "Patricia."

Henry didn't think the degree of shock displayed by his friends would have been any more pronounced had he informed them that his grandfather was Hitler. Even Ellen found herself unable to give this unwelcome bit of information an upbeat spin. All she could manage was a short inward breath, followed by a sympathetic "Oh, dear," after which Glenn muttered, "Ouch!" and Doug shook his head. "It's not your day, my man. Not your day."

Indeed, Patricia Gergen was the least liked attorney in the firm. One of the world's leading authorities in the elusive art of making anyone, regardless of IQ, feel like an idiot, her life goal seemed to be to humiliate everyone with whom she came in contact. Her unique talent for screaming, coupled with what seemed to be a positive passion for cruelty, had earned her the nickname "the barking hyena" from the night staff.

Henry had had the misfortune of working for her a year earlier. The assignment had seemed easy enough: to send three documents to an important client in Paris, Texas. Unfortunately, Henry, who had been too busy imagining his acceptance speech for the Best Jazz Album of the Year Award at the Grammys to listen carefully, had only heard the word "Paris" and sent the documents to Europe. (Though it did briefly occur to him as he addressed the envelope that "1010 Appletree Way" didn't sound particularly French, he had decided not to double-check.) Upon discovering the mix-up the next day, Patricia picked up the phone and, with characteristic restraint, informed Henry's senior supervisor that "the fucking moron who fucked up my job better be fired ASA-fucking-P!" Luckily, Henry's good reputation within the department had saved him. With a letter of apology the matter was quietly dropped, but though he had escaped with his job, Henry's senior supervisor had made the terms of his future tenure at Albright very clear: If he screwed the hyena again, he was history.

Then something strange happened—so strange Henry hadn't even told Glenn. A week after the smoke had cleared from his mail misadventure, Henry had found himself alone in an elevator with a young associate, Sarah Wald, one of his favorites due to her practice of ordering in large dinners on the client and including Henry in the feast. One particularly lavish Indian meal had come to $320, tip included. When Henry had nervously handed Sarah the receipt, she hadn't even blinked, just rubbed her belly and said, "That tikka masala was to die for, didn't you think?" No doubt about it, Sarah was Henry's kind of lawyer—a woman who realized the value of a well-fed support staff.

In any case, though Sarah and Henry came from different social strata of Albright, their mutual love of fine dining had led them to enjoy a casual work-friendship. Typical conversation, however, usually focused on movies or Sarah's desire to go back to grad school in marine biology. So Henry had been surprised when Sarah had pressed the button for her floor, then turned to him and said, "Word around the xerox machines is that you made quite an impression on a certain partner."

Henry had been surprised. As a general rule, nighttime proofreaders didn't make impressions on much of anyone.

"That's weird," he said. "Who?"

Sarah grinned.

"Patricia."

"Patricia?"

"Yeah, as in Gergen."

"Oh, right," Henry said, slightly embarrassed. "Must've been the package I accidentally sent to France."

Sarah bit her lip, suppressing a laugh. For some reason she was positively giddy. "Nope. Wasn't that."

"What then?"

"Turns out she thought you were cute."

Henry was stunned. The idea of Patricia Gergen finding anyone or anything attractive seemed impossible.

"Cute?" Henry said. "You're kidding."

"No, her secretary told me," Sarah said. Then another smile. "Hey, go for it. I hear she's single."

With that, the elevator doors had opened. With a quick "This is me!" Sarah was gone, leaving Henry alone and more than a little bit agitated. Normally, he would have been thrilled to hear of a member of the opposite sex who had thought he was good-looking. But Patricia Gergen? Said he was ... *cute!?* It was almost an insult—one that actually made him feel temporarily less attractive, not more—but despite his deep disgust, or perhaps because of it, Henry had found it hard to get Patricia out of his mind. Late that night he had imagined the worst: sex with the hyena—Patricia ripping off her clothes down to a pair of black garters and shouting, "Don't just stand there, you asshole. Do me!"

Now, standing within the safe confines of 34 North, that same terrifying image came roaring back, this time with Patricia wielding a giant staple remover. Henry cringed.

"Well," Ellen said. "See you in the next life."

"Yeah," Henry said, shaking the black-gartered Patricia away. "The next life."

He took a moment to resign himself to his fate and walked to the door.

"Wait a sec," Doug said as Henry reached for the doorknob. "I'll do it for you, if you want."

Henry looked at his friend. It was an offer perhaps even more generous than Adam's earlier that afternoon to pay for a reading of his musical. Given his fragile emotional state, Henry was half tempted to take him up on it, but even as he was dying to say yes, he knew he couldn't ask someone as nice as Doug to do something so onerous. Staffing was a game of Russian roulette. Tonight, the bullet happened to be in his chamber. Henry knew that he had to take it like a man and pull the trigger.

"Thanks," he said. "But I've got it."

"Hey," Glenn said as Henry reached for the doorknob again. "Make sure to check out her new office."

One of the perks of partnership at Albright was the opportunity for an attorney to put a personal stamp on a spacious new corner office. Interior decorators were consulted, rugs bought, furniture selected, art hung.

"What's so special about it?" Henry asked.

"You mean you haven't seen it?" Ellen said. She seemed genuinely surprised.

"No."

Henry saw his three friends share a smile.

"Come on. What is it?"

"Should we?" Glenn asked.

Clearly, Glenn was desperate to tell, but this time Doug ruled in the negative.

"Let him see for himself."

"Right," Glenn said, smiling broadly now. "We wouldn't want to ruin it. Have fun, Henry."

Some sights in life are so surprising that it seems to take hours for what the eye sees to fully register in the brain. Perhaps if Patricia Gergen had been a man, Henry wouldn't have been so shocked. Perhaps if Albright, Pierce & Dean hadn't been in New York City he would have taken the view in stride. But given the set of conditions and assumptions under which Henry was working (that he was, after all, in New York City and that Patricia Gergen was, in fact, a woman—or some approximation thereof), when he took his first peek inside the hyena's lair, he quite simply couldn't believe his eyes.

Henry found himself gazing into a room that looked more like the den of a big game hunter than a business office. Not only that, an extremely successful big game hunter. Indeed, in rapid succession, Henry was assaulted by four extremely distinctive sights:

1) An enormous stuffed lion, teeth bared, mane flapping in an imaginary breeze, standing smack in the middle of the room.
2) A zebra head, suspended next to a shelf of law books and black binders.
3) The head of an elk or llama, Henry couldn't tell, hanging over the desk, engaged in an eternal staring contest with . . .
4) A defiant white rhino head, hanging on the opposite wall.

Taken as a whole, it was a truly awful sight—four animals, once the pride of Africa, now sacrificed to the altar of interior decoration. But Henry's tour through the wonderful world of taxidermy wasn't over yet. At just that moment he felt his foot knock against something hard. Looking down, he saw that there was a final trophy in the Hall of Patricia. Henry found himself standing on the matted fur of what appeared to be a dead grizzly bear. To make matters worse, the object Henry's foot had knocked against was the great animal's head. The vacant eyes stared up at him lifelessly. Henry cringed. Then he was tempted to apologize to the bear. It seemed an awful shame that such a majestic animal, one of nature's greatest creations, should end up in the atrium of one of the biggest bitches in Manhattan. It would have been preferable, in Henry's view, for Patricia herself to be laid out on the floor while the bear, lion, rhino, elk, and zebra used her office for a screening of *Free Willy*.

The sad truth, however, was that the killer was alive and clawing. In fact, the barking hyena was now leaning back in her desk chair, legs up, wearing blue jeans a size or two too tight, which served to highlight the alarming stubbiness of her legs. Across the room was a man in a polo shirt, an associate whom Henry recognized and immediately pitied. Getting hooked up with the barking hyena was on par with discovering that one's dorm head was Stalin. Things weren't going well for the young lawyer, either.

Though Henry had missed it, he had clearly just made a suggestion that Gergen found absurd.

"What kind of asshole are you?" she shouted in a voice loud enough to put most drill sergeants to shame. "Come on! Think!"

A deadly silence filled the room. Henry half wished that the lion would spring to life and devour her, but the young associate (Henry thought his name was Jim, maybe John) seemed to believe that this question warranted a response.

"Gee, Pat," he said, "doesn't the third party have some rights here?"

"No! No! No! Jesus! What kind of asshole are you?"

This time Jim/John wisely took the query as rhetorical and kept his mouth shut. To Henry the answer was crystal clear: He was the kind of asshole stupid enough to accept a job at Albright, Pierce & Dean. With this momentary breakdown of communication, Henry thought the time ripe to announce his presence by clearing his throat. He could only hope that she wouldn't recognize him as the cute guy who had sent her documents on vacation to Europe.

"Yeah?" Patricia said, glancing up.

"I'm your legal assistant," Henry said.

"My legal assistant?" she growled suspiciously, as though Henry had just informed her that he was her undertaker.

"That's right," Henry said, willing himself not to be intimidated. "I hear you need help?"

At this point, Patricia scrunched her brow and began to munch a pencil. As she narrowed her eyes, Henry feared the worst: that she (a) was remembering the unfortunate mailing escapade and was about to send a stapler or some other blunt object flying in his general direction or (b) was rediscovering her appreciation of Henry's good looks and plotting how to get him naked on her bearskin rug. Neither option was appealing.

To Henry's surprise, something completely different occurred. In short, the hyena suddenly smiled, exposing a row of surprisingly white teeth, perhaps the only attractive feature on a face that could at best be described as "charmingly rodential."

"You know what?" she said, abruptly swinging her legs off the desk. "You sort of look like my husband, Alan. Only taller and thinner with more hair."

Henry gasped. Apparently, Sarah Ward had been right. Patricia really had thought he was cute. After all, assuming that she was attracted to her husband, didn't it make sense that she'd be attracted to the better-looking version as well?

"Oh, really?" Henry stammered.

"Yeah," Patricia said. "We just got married."

"I had no idea," the associate said. "Congratulations, Pat. Where'd you go on your honeymoon?"

To that, Patricia smiled playfully and waved her hand, gesturing to the animals.

"On safari," she said. "My sixth, his first." Her smile grew into a full-fledged self-satisfied grin. "I bagged another elk."

Henry was now faced with another problem. Were congratulations in order for the murder of another in a series of innocent and possibly endangered wild animals? He wasn't sure. Luckily, fate intervened. As he was scrambling for something to say, Henry was saved by the phone. What followed then was a series of grunts that grew louder and louder as Patricia grew increasingly dissatisfied with whatever the caller was telling her. As those grunts escalated into growls and shouts, something in what she had just said hit Henry in a new way. Though it seemed difficult to believe, Patricia *actually had a husband.* To the extent that he had thought about it at all (which was virtually never) Henry had assumed that the barking hyena was single, but now he noticed the gold band around the chubby ring finger of her left hand. He also noticed a picture on the mantle, under the rhino, of Patricia in a bridal gown, standing with what Henry assumed was her idea of a short, fat, bald version of himself, the man who had pledged to live his life with her, Mr. Barking Hyena.

Though Henry often had trouble controlling the ramblings of his overly fertile imagination, his mind had almost never betrayed him the way it did now. As he gazed at that wedding picture, Henry began to wonder what it would be like if *he* were Alan—if he were married to the hideous Patricia. After all, the attraction was there, on her part, anyway. Henry sucked in a deep breath. It was an alarming concept, one he had to expunge from his mind as soon as possible. To that end, he glanced at the stuffed lion and tried to steer his thoughts toward a recollection of Bert Lahr singing "If I Only Had the Nerve." That only made things worse. Henry's mind did not travel to the Land of Oz. Rather, the office suddenly transformed into the African grasslands.

Just like that he was Mr. Henry Gergen, on a safari honeymoon. His bride walked before him, her puffy frame stuffed into a suit of khaki, a giant rifle slung across her shoulder as she surveyed the veldt for game. Now she was stopping to consult a map, then sinking to her knees to investigate a pile of droppings. "Excellent," she hissed. "We're getting warmer!"

Moments later, the stillness was broken by the sound of pounding hooves. A string of gazelles bounded into view. While Henry admired their stunning beauty, their effortless grace, the hyena's eyes narrowed. She dropped to her stomach, rifle at the ready. "Come to mamma," she said, taking aim. "Come to mamma."

The gun's report sent a flock of birds flying. One of the gazelles appeared to freeze in midair and hang there suspended, but then he faltered, stumbled, tottered back and forth, and collapsed, legs akimbo, on the African green. Patricia jumped to her feet, fists clenched, and kissed Henry passionately on the lips, forcing her thick tongue into his mouth. Then, with an ecstatic howl, she bounded across the plain. In minutes, the unlucky animal was skinned. Still not satisfied, Patricia pulled Henry close, ripped off his clothes, and forced him to make love to her directly on the kill. Henry imagined a cataclysmic orgasm in which Patricia's mighty legs clenched, squeezing him to death. Suddenly, Henry could see the mourners at his own funeral, his family and friends walking by his casket (which given the condition of his body would be closed) and shaking their heads.

Now Henry looked at Patricia's wall and imagined his own head hanging there next to the elk, his green eyes staring blankly across the room. With a horrified shudder, he turned his attention back to Patricia. Yelling at the unfortunate soul on the other end of the line, a fleck or two of spit on the mouthpiece, she appeared more hideous than the Wicked Witch herself. Indeed, if ever there was a walking advertisement for remaining single it was she, and as Henry watched the hyena continue to transact business, he initiated an immediate reappraisal of recent idealized thoughts of marriage. In short, was the grass really greener on the "Do you take this woman to be your lawfully wedded wife" side of the street? Had he been too focused on the minuses of single life to see the benefits? As things were, there were millions of things he could do each and every day that marriage would make impossible. He could go out every night, sleep until noon, go to the bathroom with the door open, crank Pink Floyd on the stereo, eat fettuccine with his bare hands, feel the sweet anticipation of a date, watch *Law and Order* three times a day—even beat off into a dirty sweatsock. Not that Henry had done all these things or even wanted to, but the point was that he could.

As Henry mulled it over, an old song from the sixties began to knock through his head, a tune that hadn't occurred to him in years but had never seemed more appropriate. As he remained in the hyena's doorway, a full orchestra joined in. Brass took the melody, underscored by strings and winds, punctuated by the *boom-boom* of timpani. In fact, the melody soon grew into something so stirring, so majestic, that Henry half expected the Three Tenors to leap out of the hyena's closet for the grand finale: "Born free! And life is worth living! But only worth living if you're . . . born . . . free!"

"Sorry," Patricia said, slamming down the phone. "Now where were we?"

Just like that, the music stopped. The Three Tenors retreated to the closet. The musicians packed their instruments and caught a bus to their next gig. But their work had been done. Henry shook himself and looked the hyena square in the eye, feeling as light as a hiker who has taken off a sixty-pound pack after a day on the trail.

"Just awaiting my orders," he said, his tone airy, almost jaunty.

After all, nothing the mighty Gergen could do could upset him now. No matter how cruel she was, Henry held the ace. Somewhere in the city was a poor schmuck named Alan. And that poor schmuck wasn't him.

"Orders, huh?" Gergen said. She tossed a velobound book at him. Henry assumed it was something he'd have to xerox, then mail to a client. Instead, he saw that it was a compilation of menus from restaurants in the neighborhood.

"Since you weren't able to handle a simple mailing last time," the hyena continued with a wry smile, "why don't we see if you can manage to order some dinner?"

At 2:00 A.M., Henry and Glenn stood at the corner of 44th Street and Seventh Avenue, both waiting for the car service supplied by the firm to take them home. Despite the late hour, Times Square was still lit up, a nonstop tribute to neon and one of America's greatest contributions to modern culture: advertising. Everything from shows to shoes still burned bright.

"All you did was order dinner?" Glenn asked.

"That's it," Henry said. "Once she ate, she was actually pretty nice."

"So that's the key to the hyena, hmmm?" Glenn said. "Like any wild beast, she becomes docile after the feed."

"Right," Henry replied. "Maybe marriage has mellowed her."

"It's possible," Glenn said, nodding. "When sexually satisfied, most animals are forgiving. We should get *Wild Kingdom* to do a feature."

"Not a bad idea."

With that, Glenn lit a cigarette and inhaled deeply. Though it was a habit Henry had avoided, he sometimes couldn't help feeling that he was denying himself a prop that would enable him to get in touch with his hipper self. Bottom line: Despite years of surgeon general's warnings, Henry still thought cigarettes looked cool. Of course, small matters such as cancer and heart disease, not to mention the latest and possibly, depending on one's point of view, most dire smoking-related health hazard, impotence, made it a nonstarter. As a result, Henry was duly resigned to living a healthier if somewhat geekier life.

"Well, at least something went right for you this weekend, right?" Glenn went on. He tossed the match into the gutter.

Henry smiled. *Yes, thank God for small favors,* he thought as a Lincoln Town Car pulled to the edge of the curb. The driver placed a sign in his passenger window: BIG APPLE NO. 345.

"Yours?" Glenn asked.

Henry glanced at his car voucher. He was waiting for number 211.

"Nope," he said. "You?"

Before Glenn could answer, an attorney walked by them and got in.

"By the way," Glenn went on, "we were having us a little chatski in the conference room after you left. About you."

"Yeah? What about?"

"It's unanimous. Call Christine."

Henry thought of her xeroxed butt. "Maybe so."

"Just do it," Glenn said. "Then write me a postcard with all the details."

Henry glanced sideways at his friend. He knew it had been hard on Glenn since his wife moved west. For a second, he was tempted to confess all, drop to his knees, and beg Glenn for forgiveness. What did he really have to feel sorry for, though? Yes, he had been shocked, then excited, when Diana had started to call. But was it his fault his best friend's wife suddenly found him irresistible?

"You miss Diana?" he asked.

"Yeah." Glenn gazed into the lights of Times Square wistfully. "And I'm horny as hell."

Henry was well acquainted with the feeling. It wasn't pleasant. "Oh, yeah?"

Then Henry saw a smile that bordered on a leer spread across Glenn's face. "Sex is a wonderful thing, Henry."

Though Glenn had stated the obvious, both friends thought the comment worthy of a moment of silent appreciation.

"Diana was funny, though," Glenn went on.

"Oh? How so?"

Glenn drew a deep breath. "Well, she always wanted to do it in the weirdest places. The floor, the tub." He glanced at Henry. "Once even on the dining room table."

For obvious reasons, Henry found this bit of information riveting. From the start, he had wondered whether Diana's request had been particular to him or an ongoing fetish of some sort. A pretty fair college actor, Henry was able to assume an appropriately detached yet bemused air.

"And did you?" he asked.

"Don't try it," Glenn said. "It's not too comfortable."

Somehow, this answer pleased Henry immensely. Though he had known he had done "the right thing," he couldn't help feeling that he had denied himself some sort of uniquely perverse experience. With his suspicions regarding the comfort level of sex-on-a-table confirmed, his faith in the wisdom of his decision grew. Flying all the way to Colorado to perform an act so physically challenging—even with a woman of Diana's obvious appeal—simply didn't seem worth it. (On the other hand, Henry was aware that there were some women in the world so beautiful that it would be worth having sex with them anywhere. Gwyneth Paltrow on a bed of nails? Henry would gladly take the bottom.)

"Do you think she's going to come back?" Henry asked.

Glenn shrugged. "Don't know. I think she just needs to get

some stuff out of her system. After what I did, I guess I can't blame her."

The "did" referred to Missy Grant, an actress in *The Broccoli Indictment* with whom Glenn had had a two-month affair.

"She'll forgive you," Henry said. "You'll see."

"I hope so," Glenn said. "Last time we spoke I offered to do the couples therapy thing."

"And?"

Glenn took a final drag of his cigarette, then stamped it out on the pavement. "Let's just say she didn't go for it."

"Still pissed?"

"Oh, yeah. That's an understatement."

Of course, it had occurred to Henry on more than one occasion that that was why Diana wanted him: payback.

"She'll come around," he said.

"You think so?"

It was clear that Glenn was bobbing for a yes. Though Henry had no crystal ball, he quickly decided that this was one of those times when his role was to tell his friend what he wanted to hear.

"I'm sure of it," he said.

That seemed good enough for Glenn.

"Thanks, man," he said.

Just then, an old Lincoln pulled up in front, the number 92 decaled onto the window.

"This is mine," Glenn said. He turned to Henry. "Getting back to the issue at hand, remember what I said about Christine, OK? I could see you guys together. Much, much better for you than Tamar."

"Wait a second," Henry said, somewhat taken aback. "You were the one who set me up with her in the first place."

Glenn nodded. "True. But now that I think of it, Christine is someone you can get to know slowly, be friends with first. Listen, I know what you've been going through lately. It's rough."

"Yeah, yeah."

Glenn smiled.

"What?" Henry asked.

"Ah, forget it."

"No, what?"

Glenn draped an arm around Henry's shoulder. "Tell me if I'm wrong, but this time last night, you were dancing at your wedding."

At that moment, Henry wished more than ever that it was within human capability to cut off a blush in the formative stages. Glenn had an uncanny ability to know what was on his mind— usually something embarrassing.

Glenn patted his back. "Ah, don't sweat it. I'm just giving you shit."

"No," Henry said. "You're right. It's pathetic. This afternoon I had myself married to my dad's girlfriend."

"Oh, really? Kids?"

He sighed. "Six." Henry walked to the curb and looked out over Times Square. Even at this late hour people milled about, rushing who knew where. Suddenly, he felt the need to explain himself. "It's just that I've been on such a losing streak," he said, turning back around. "I feel like I'm the only single guy left in the city."

"Yeah, I know how it is," Glenn said. "Or I think I know. But look at me. Marriage is no miracle cure. Besides, taking things too fast isn't going to help you get what you want anyway. Relationships have to develop. Try to put that active imagination of yours in a headlock for a while."

Henry nodded and leaned back against a parked car. He knew Glenn was right, but like so many things in life, it was easier said than done.

"You know what's really crazy?" Henry said.

"What?"

Glenn had his hand on the door of his Lincoln, ready to go home. Henry paused. He knew full well that he was about to sound irredeemably stupid. Then again, hadn't he just mentioned his six children?

"My college reunion is coming up."

"What's that got to do with anything?" Glenn asked, taking his hand away.

Henry paused while an older couple approached, arms linked. "Well," he said with a grim smile, "if you really want to know, I sort of worry that . . ." He shook his head.

"What?"

"Well, that everyone is going to think I'm gay."

It was a piece of information that left even Glenn temporarily flustered.

"Gay?" he said, finally. "You mean, as in . . . ?"

"I mean, look at me!" Henry said. He began to pace. "A single guy living in New York. Writing show tunes. Not to mention an occasional children's poem. Who hasn't had a serious girlfriend in four years. Christ! I live a block from Christopher Street. I might as well write the word 'homosexual' on my forehead in red lipstick!"

All Glenn could do was laugh.

"I know, I know," Henry said. "Like I said. Crazy, right?"

He felt like throwing himself in front of the next conveniently fast-moving bus and getting it all over with.

"I love it!" Glenn said. "The first gay man in the history of the world who spends every waking minute thinking about being with a woman. Don't worry, Henry. You've got pathetic heterosexual written all over you."

"Gee, thanks. That's real helpful."

"Anytime."

Just then, Glenn's driver leaned on his horn. "Alright, already," Glenn called. He turned back to Henry. "Listen, Sheila's going to be at this reunion, right?"

"Don't remind me."

Indeed, Henry couldn't bear the thought of seeing the woman who had destroyed his life on the arm of her rich husband. They'd probably be wearing clothes made from carefully sewn thousand-dollar bills.

"Well," Glenn continued, "if anyone thinks you're queer, you can get her to set them straight."

Henry forced a sad little smile. He could just see it. Sheila and Mr. Microsoft, chatting with the beautiful set at the Hamden College alumni cocktail party. "Uh, Sheila," he would say, sidling pathetically to her side. "Sorry to interrupt, but could you have a few words with Phil? There seems to be a small misunderstanding regarding my sexuality . . ."

"I was kidding," Glenn said.

Henry shook himself. "Yeah, I know. I know."

For the first time, Glenn looked concerned. "Christ. You're worse off than I thought. You've got to relax. No one is going to think you're gay, Henry. The truth is that half the married guys are going to be jealous you're still single."

Henry nodded. "I suppose."

"Now I better roll."

"OK. Catch you later."

"Life ain't so bad, you know."

"Yeah, I know."

"Good," Glenn said. "Do me a favor and keep reminding yourself."

Henry watched his friend jog to the car. Just as Glenn was reaching for the door, he stopped short and rooted through his knapsack. The next thing Henry knew, a video sailed into his arms.

"What's this?"

"You know what it is."

Henry glanced at the side to make sure.

"Don't you still want it?"

"I made my own copy. It's yours. It'll help you relax."

With that, Glenn flashed Henry a quick smile and shut the door. As his car pulled out, Henry leaned back against the building and tried to clear his mind, to look at the bright side. Corny as it sounded, there was some truth to what Glenn had said. At least he wasn't married to the hideous Patricia Gergen. And thank God he wasn't a lawyer. One look at the hyena's associate was enough to convince him that the hardships of the starving artist were greatly preferable to the humiliating climb up the corporate ladder. No, Henry was still a free agent—life was wide open, full of as many possibilities as there were lights in Times Square. Henry now took a look at a billboard that advertised the musical *Mamma Mia!* Then he imagined his billboard: THE GREEN LIGHT! NOW AND FOR-EVER!

Moments later, as he leaned back into the plush interior of his own Lincoln, Henry imagined it was a private limo, come to whisk him off to the opening-night cast party.

4

tori

though Henry realized early on in college that he wanted to be a writer, figuring out where his true talents lay had proven difficult. As a result, he had spent much of his twenties jumping from project to project, producing this slap-dash array of work:

- *Music 101*. A novel. The searing portrait of a music history professor in love with an undergraduate botany major (one chapter complete at 90 pages).
- *Greener Pastures*. Another novel. The epic tale of a Vermont dairy farmer's struggles for survival after discovering irregularities in his herd's milk (two chapters, 186 pages).
- *Young Paul Bunyan*. A children's musical about the famed lumberjack in his youth struggling to fit in as a "big kid" (complete, performed at Abracadabra!, a children's theater on the West Side).

- Brief tenure as artistic director of Abracadabra! Left to pursue own "creative work."
- *Willow Trees and Strip Malls.* The beginning of a collection of self-conscious poetry (23 pages).
- *Cannibal Stew and Other Poems.* Four children's poems written for Jill (4 pages).
- One side of a cassette's worth of jazz songs, featuring a range of influences from Armstrong to Coltrane.
- *Tribeca Rhythms.* Five minutes of a Gershwin-influenced symphonic tone poem.
- Played the role of Onion in six staged readings of *The Broccoli Indictment,* by Glenn Roth.
- *You, Jane!* The first seventeen and a half minutes of a twentieth-century grand opera based on the life and times of Tarzan. Some sample lyrics:

JANE: You swing from trees?
TARZAN: In rain or shine.
JANE: Swing with great ease?
TARZAN: Yes, using vines!

- *The Green Light!* A musical based on *The Great Gatsby* (in progress).

In his more confident moments, Henry liked to think of himself as a Renaissance genius—a man who wasn't just *good* at lots of things but rather had the capability to be *great* at a lot of things. One day he might be convinced that his destiny lay in being the next Gershwin, a composer for the Broadway stage who also dazzled the musical community with his classical works. The next morning, Henry might wake to imagine himself on the cover of the *New York Times Sunday Magazine,* heralded as a novelist with Fitzgerald's beautiful, florid prose style coupled with the macho realism of Hemingway. Other times, Henry might aspire to be a jazz pianist—the Art Tatum of his generation—playing to sold-out houses around the world, or a one-man Lennon and McCartney, a pop star of genuine talent whom women routinely chased down the street.

These were just the goals that had at least some sort of grounding in reality. Henry also spent some time each week fantasizing about various careers in professional sports, most typically as a center fielder for the Mets, a point guard for the Knicks, or an Olympic medalist in any number of events from downhill to the decathlon. He was also prone to daydreams that involved the winning of Academy Awards in writing, directing, and acting. And though, as has been noted, he had no interest in business, Henry had been known to imagine himself as the next Bill Gates, an entrepreneur worth billions (he never got as far as what he would actually invent or sell).

Of course, Henry did have some perspective. He knew he'd never play for the Mets or star in a movie. He realized that he was no Beethoven or Shakespeare. Maybe not even a Gershwin or Hemingway. His principal talents (piano and comic writing, in particular) were most definitely not in the touched-by-God category. On the other hand, Henry still felt that he had something to contribute, and he'd spent years looking for an idea that would let all his talents merge into one, so he could finally emerge as a mature writer.

It had been six months since Henry had reached up to his bookshelf for a bent copy of *The Great Gatsby*, one of his favorite novels from high school. By the time he had hit page twenty, he knew that he had finally found his subject. Yes, he was aware that an operatic version had been performed recently at the Met, but the history of theater was filled with reworkings of the same story. Weren't there multiple operatic versions of *Romeo and Juliet* in existence before Bernstein wrote *West Side Story*? Henry felt that Fitzgerald's novel was better suited to the musical form anyway. Set in the roaring 1920s, it was a work that called for a lighter touch. In *The*

Green Light! Henry could exhibit his superior talent for writing moody jazz tunes and intelligent, witty lyrics. At the same time, the story of Jay Gatsby's pursuit of the American dream would give it depth. Indeed, Henry would be able to have his cake and eat it, too. He would be recognized as a writer with the popular appeal of Irving Berlin coupled with the dark, haunting power of Stephen Sondheim.

Now Henry sat at his grandfather's oak desk, contemplating the blank screen on his word processor. Though he hoped to fill the space before him with a dazzling array of words (the lyrics to the new number suggested by Tamar, "My Pink Suit"), the morning had been a complete bust. The brief sense of perspective afforded him by his encounter with Patricia Gergen had disappeared overnight. With the horror of the weekend pounding at his temples, he felt like a discarded sponge, wrung dry of every conceivable ounce of optimism. As a result, instead of writing, he used the time to brood over his current lot in life.

Of course, despite those eight pernicious weddings, Henry knew that on paper he had it pretty good. With no biological time clock, the ball was in his court. Indeed, he was the living personification of that classic American mythic figure, the freewheeling stud, self-reliant King of the Road. The trouble was that, in Henry's view, that sort of man only found happiness in movies. In real life, Henry was beginning to realize that the man who professed to be more content alone was usually lying. And fear of commitment? More and more it seemed like a euphemism for not having met the right girl. Though Henry assumed that it was only a matter of time before he hooked up with his special someone, it didn't stop him from feeling that something was missing now, and following a weekend of near misses, the ache was more pronounced than usual. To fill the void, his mind began to roam. Soon it was bouncing like a Super Ball from one woman to the next. First to Tamar, then Amanda, then back to Tamar, then to—what was her name? The woman in the Pinafore Players? Sally!—then back to Tamar, then to Amanda. Though each thought was brief—ten to fifteen seconds at most—a general theme emerged: sexual gratification, each including ample amounts of nudity, cries of passion, and protestations of undying love.

Soon enough these sexual thoughts culminated in a final fantasy that included all three women. Surprisingly, this one wasn't sexual in nature. Rather, Henry used it to channel his feelings of frustration and anger. With an innate feel for dramatic structure, he conceived a little revenge play in three tidy scenes. What follows is a rough synopsis.

Scene One. Time: The morning after *The Green Light!* has opened to raves on Broadway. Place: Outside the Richard Rodgers Theater. Cast of characters: Tamar, Sally, Amanda, and a chorus of eager theatergoers. As the curtain rises, Tamar, Sally, and Amanda enter from Seventh Avenue. Brief dialogue establishes the fact that their love lives are in a state of complete disarray. Abby has just left Tamar for a man, Sally has discovered that her fiancé is a Scientologist, and Amanda is bemoaning Henry's father's Viagra addiction. It is in this state of profound dissatisfaction that the three heroines come across a long line that stretches all the way down the block and around the corner. At first, they have no idea what it is that they have stumbled upon. Finally, Amanda asks a ticket buyer, who points to a marquee that reads, in bright block letters, THE GREEN LIGHT! The three ladies exchange glances of heart-wrenching dismay as they realize, simultaneously, that they have missed the chance of a lifetime. In short, they've traded the chance to be the better half of a genius for lesbianism, Scientology, and Viagra. As Henry walks by, surrounded by a coterie of hangers-on, Tamar drops to her knees sobbing while Amanda hits her temples with her fists. As the scene ends, Sally calmly decides that her life has been rendered meaningless and throws herself in front of a speeding cab.

Scene Two. Time: The night of the Tony Awards. Place: A split set showing two dingy studio apartments—the homes of Tamar and Amanda. The two ladies, both obese due to months of non-stop bingeing, sit in front of their respective TVs, eating pints of Ben & Jerry's with their hands. As they watch Henry accept the award for Best Musical, both women dissolve into tears. Tamar curls into a ball, then pounds her sofa pillow until her entire living room is covered in down feathers. Amanda stumbles to her CD player, cranks the finale of *The Green Light!* to ten, then commits hara-kiri in the middle of her living room with a corroded ice cream scoop.

Scene Three. Time: Two months later. Place: Broadway. Now homeless, Tamar wanders the streets, dressed in rags, living on scraps. Dressed in a new overcoat and Armani suit, Henry struts down Broadway, arm in arm with his new twenty-two-year-old girlfriend, Lulu, a brain surgeon, novelist, and *Sports Illustrated* swimsuit model. When Tamar sees them coming, she reaches for Henry's coat to beg for forgiveness, but as she lurches his way, she trips and falls into the trash compactor of a nearby garbage truck. As Henry and Lulu stroll down the street on the way to his new penthouse, where they will spend the remainder of the afternoon in bed, Tamar is reduced to the size of a can of Alpo.

Curtain.

Henry knew he should be somewhat embarrassed by this violent train of thought, but the little playlet proved so effective at diffusing his frustration that he rewound it to the beginning and thought it through again from start to finish, this time adding Scene Four (cast of characters: Henry and Lulu; setting: Henry's bed), which Henry envisioned with an eye for detail that would have made Fellini proud.

By the time he finally looked back to his computer screen, Henry knew that any further attempts at writing would be pointless. Having squandered his morning's ration of creativity on his fantasy life, he knew from experience what he needed to do: go outside, clear his head, and try again later. Then he remembered something. There was at least one thing he could accomplish before lunch. At the housewarming he had promised his niece a complete collection of his four children's poems. Henry clicked open a folder labeled DR. SEUSS LOOK OUT and scanned down the list of titles: "The Tale of the Otter," "The Enterprising Camel," "The Bald Gorilla," and "Cannibal Stew." After printing them one by one, he dropped them into an envelope addressed to Jill Richardson and headed out the door.

It was already 1:30 in the afternoon. Most Americans had been hard at work for four and a half hours. In that time, Henry had slept, killed off three women, had sex with a swimsuit model, and printed out four poems.

All in all, an extremely productive morning.

After mailing the letter to Jill and picking up his lunch—two burritos and a Coke—Henry strolled up Sixth Avenue toward home. With his mind on the opening of his musical, it was perhaps the first time in forty-eight hours that he wasn't thinking about Tamar. Ironically, that was when she walked right by him.

Unfortunately, Henry was so lost in his thoughts that by the time he had fully registered her presence, she was gone. But it *had* been her. That much he was sure of. The two days since their date had not clouded the memory of her face. Quite the opposite; he remembered it perfectly, feature for feature. With only one minor difference. Two days earlier she had been happy. Now it seemed as though she had been crying. Indeed, in that split second between noting her presence and her disappearance out of his line of vision, Henry could have sworn he saw two tears rolling down her right cheek. This brought him to a consideration of a final question. What on earth was she doing in his neighborhood, possibly crying, no less, on a weekday? Though Henry briefly entertained the idea that she had been stalking him, he quickly dismissed it for what it was: the vain hope of a desperate man.

With the entire incident shrouded in mystery, Henry returned to his apartment. On his couch, his burritos and Coke spread on the coffee table, he turned from a general overview of the facts of the case to a more detailed consideration of the subject herself. Though his glimpse had been just that, a mere glimpse, it was of long enough duration to imprint an extremely pleasing image in his mind. Tamar had looked even better than he had remembered. On their date she had been dressed casually. Now a tight gray business suit highlighted the curves of her body and showed off the slightest dash of cleavage. Her eyes appeared to be an even deeper, icier blue. When he had glanced over his shoulder for a rear view, the arch of Tamar's back down to her rear end had appeared even more enticing than on the night he had first fallen in love. No, Henry didn't need a color xerox to see that her ass was distinctive. Round, pert, and firm—he now viewed it as one of Mother Nature's most stunning achievements.

As Henry lay back on his couch, ruminating on the sundry glories of Tamar's physique, he happened to glance across the room. There his eye fell upon an object of great interest. Sitting atop his TV was a certain video that a certain best friend had tossed to him the evening before. It was a film with a varied history of ownership. Henry had originally borrowed it years earlier from Ricky Feldenzer, a buddy from college. After enjoying it for a while, he had given it back with his heartfelt thanks. Then, a month or so later, Henry had found that occasional viewings had become a matter of habit and asked Ricky if his personal library would be willing to extend another loan. This time he had held on to it for a month or two, after which he had loaned it to Glenn, who had then kept it for the better part of a year until its unexpected return the night before. Though Henry had been tempted to watch it the minute he got home, a combination of guilt and exhaustion had stopped him. Now, with Tamar's body on his mind, it suddenly beckoned him, calling across the room with the low, incessant undertones of tribal drums, "Watch me! Watch me! Watch me!" Though he had planned to give the video its inaugural re-viewing later that night, Henry realized that there was no need to stand on ceremony. How did that old tune go? "Skyrockets in flight. Afternoon delight!" Even though that song had been about a couple, Henry surmised that there was nothing in the lyric to suggest that the author wouldn't have approved of a solo act.

Moreover, it was a worthy film—beautifully photographed, expertly acted by a cast who exhibited a startling command of their chosen profession. Indeed, unlike most movies, it seemed to improve with repeated viewings. It was a film to study, to learn from. In short, a work of art.

With those thoughts in mind, Henry roused himself from the couch and approached the TV. There he held the video in his hands with the sort of reverence usually reserved for the rarest of jewels. The title was written on its side on masking tape in careful print: *The Doctor's Wife*. Henry unfastened his belt buckle and slipped the tape into the VCR.

Seconds later, he was leaning back on his sofa watching not just a film but a cinematic event. After the opening credits, the plot quickly unfolded. Apparently, there had been trouble at the Virginia State Hospital. Dr. Reginald Montgomery had been experimenting with a new cure for premature baldness. Unfortunately, his wife, played by Tori West, an actress of startling range, had spilled the concoction on herself. The result: Instead of developing a baldness cure, Dr. Montgomery had accidentally developed an aphrodisiac of unparalleled potency. With the setup established, *The Doctor's Wife* got down to business. Scene One was set in a back room of the hospital where a handsome intern was reviewing a set of lab results. Enter the Doctor's Wife.

WIFE: (leaning over intern's shoulder) Hey? What're you working on?

H. INTERN: (uninterested in the Doctor's Wife) The evolution of amino crystals.

WIFE: (kissing his neck) Oh, really?

H. INTERN: Really, Mrs. Montgomery . . . Please. You know the rules. I'm trying to concentrate . . .

The Doctor's Wife begins to unzip his pants.

H. INTERN: Mrs. Montgomery! Please! I'm married! Mrs.— (long pause) Don't stop . . .

Seconds later, Henry was witnessing something extraordinary. Shining out of his 27-inch TV, the Doctor's Wife was giving the intern the type of blow job that he understood, in theory, could conceivably occur but that he had yet to have the good fortune to experience. Indeed, no part of the lucky intern's anatomy was left unexplored. Even so, for the first few moments Henry sat still, somewhat stunned, his pants now splayed out on the floor. Though he had thought about the film with great fondness time and again over the past year, he had forgotten just how graphic it was. In fact, Henry was so dazzled by the virtuosic display of technique that he didn't even find it immediately arousing. It was as though he were observing a biological experiment on the sexual predilections of the human species. As Henry watched Tori West's stunning approach, he couldn't help but be mystified by the actor's response. Lying back on a cot, eyes closed, his expression denoted at best casual interest in the remarkable technical display being brought to bear below his waist. Who was this guy anyway? Some sort of superhero? *Pornman?* Henry longed for the day when he had so much sexual experience that he could afford to be cavalier about something like that! Especially with the Doctor's Wife giving an Academy Award performance. As a friend of Glenn's who knew about these things had once informed him, Tori West was the indisputable Meryl Streep of her trade. The intern, however, was responding as though he were watching a rerun of *The Brady Bunch*.

Not being a member of the pornographic acting community, Henry was much more aroused. Keeping his eyes on the set, he soon grabbed hold of his hardening penis. *Wouldn't it be incredible to be married to someone like that?* he thought, as he began to stroke. Someone with that kind of energy and enthusiasm, not to mention raw technical know-how? Wouldn't it be even better if there were some way to tell which women were in possession of such skills just by looking at them? Perhaps the government could start some sort of licensing process, like the Department of Motor Vehicles, where all women over age eighteen would be required to pass a basic test or else be relegated to remedial coursework. More than once, Henry had wished a school existed that he could refer his girlfriends whose kissing wasn't up to par to. He had even considered asking a recent lady friend (who could kiss well enough but was otherwise orally deficient) to watch this very scene with him as a sort of tutorial. Given that she had dumped him a week later, Henry had been grateful that he had decided against it.

In any case, he was fully erect now. While Tori West continued to further exhibit her startling mastery of her craft, Henry allowed himself to imagine that, instead of making living expenses proofreading dry legal documents, he supported his writing habit in a much more interesting, not to mention satisfying, profession. More than once, he and Glenn had joked about *The Doctor's Wife* and the various benefits of a life in porn. Perhaps the adult film industry really was on the lookout for new stars? Maybe even one who broke the mold—a wry, artsy intellectual who could still deliver the goods: *Henry the Man!* Truth be told, Henry even thought his penis was almost large enough. When he had been eighteen, a girlfriend at summer camp had measured him at six and a quarter inches. With proper lighting and trick photography, Henry surmised that they could probably get that number up to at least ten. Then again, given that he hadn't even felt comfortable making out in front of other couples in high school, Henry knew that the likelihood that he would enjoy having sex under lights in front of a camera was slim. As much as he longed to experience the total majesty that was Tori West, he was sadly aware that it wasn't likely to happen in this lifetime. Glenn had once suggested that he look her up through the Screen Actors Guild and ask her out, but something told Henry that a woman who had cut her teeth, so to speak, on a never-ending stream of one-footers wouldn't be interested in a six-and-a-quarter man.

Despite Henry's size-related insecurities, it wasn't long before he began to imagine that he was the Handsome Intern. As the Doctor's Wife lay back on a conveniently placed bed and took the intern inside her, Henry grew more and more turned on, wondering what it would really be like to screw a gorgeous porn star. Like anyone, Henry had occasionally felt bedroom anxiety of the "What the hell do I do next?" variety. Maybe he would feel less pressured with a team of film technicians there to cheer him on? And there was no underestimating the value of a good director.

"Good, Henry! A little bit deeper! Now lick her neck. No, her neck, Henry! That's it! Excellent, baby! Keep driving. Deeper! Good! Now give me a little groan! Kiss her left breast! Now her right! Good! Good! Who loves ya, baby? Who loves ya?"

Whatever the inspiration, the Handsome Intern (aka Henry the Man!) had to be doing something right. The Doctor's Wife's moans were now filling his apartment.

"Yes!" she cried. "Don't stop!"

(*Brilliant dialogue*, Henry thought as he stroked a bit harder and imagined himself going in a bit deeper.)

"Do it! Do it!"

(*Coarse, yet effective.*)

At this point, the Doctor's Wife began to moan so loudly that Henry grew concerned that the neighbors might hear and magically know that he was watching a porn video as opposed to actually having sex himself. In fact, he was even considering whether or not to turn down the volume a notch or two when an unwelcome sound filled the room. As often happens, the phone rang at the least opportune time. All morning, when Henry had been daydreaming—when he would have killed for a distraction—it had remained silent, choosing instead the very moment Henry was getting reacquainted with the Doctor's Wife to crash the party.

Which brought Henry to his first major decision of the day: to answer or not to answer? Ideally, he would have liked to finish what he was doing before engaging anyone in a conversation. On the other hand, he wasn't so far gone that if the call was from someone with whom he wanted to speak (Tamar, for instance) he couldn't regulate his breathing and pretend that he was slightly winded due to running in after taking out the trash. So Henry decided to continue at his task, albeit with a bit less fervor, and to find out who was calling. Seconds later, he heard the beep, followed by Glenn's voice.

"Hey, bud, Just calling to say hi . . . Where the hell are you? Watching a certain wife of a certain doctor? Henry? . . . Henry? You there? Come on. Pick up!"

Henry almost allowed himself to be swayed until a glance at his groin made it obvious which instrument he'd rather be holding.

"Anyway, listen," Glenn went on. "I've been thinking. You seemed so down last night, man. But don't sweat it, because I have the solution. Her name is Christine. Since she's teaching full-time now and is hardly ever at the firm anymore, I took the liberty of looking up her number: 545-6783. Also, don't forget my play reading next weekend. I guess that's it. But call me. Later."

Glenn's intuition had always amazed Henry. This wasn't the first time Henry had screened his friend's call to hear Glenn wonder whether he was watching *The Doctor's Wife* when, in fact, he had been watching it. As for Christine, in his current aroused state, she sounded great. If she were half as talented as Tori West, he'd overlook her unibrow in a New York minute.

With the message heard and digested, Henry gave his full attention back to the movie. Unfortunately, as he slipped back into his role as the intern, there was a new person on the set. Yes, he and Glenn had joked about moving to L.A. to launch their careers in adult films, but Henry never figured that they would be starring in the same movie! Clearly, the sound of Glenn's voice on the answering machine had interrupted the single-minded focus that Henry usually brought to bear on his fantasy life. While Henry continued to imagine himself making love to Tori West, Glenn was suddenly on the next bed—with two women! Worse, one of them was coating his chest with hot fudge sauce while the other was nibbling on his kneecaps, inching her way farther north.

Henry gasped. Yes, he loved Glenn, but did that mean he had to take time from his own precious fantasy sex life to imagine him receiving a chocolate-dipped ménage à trois? Absolutely not, especially when he felt positive that Glenn was fully capable of creating his own vividly detailed fantasies. That was one department no guy needed help with.

Luckily, the action on Henry's TV screen soon helped him put all thoughts of Glenn's porn career aside. Just then, the happy couple rolled out of the missionary position. Tori West took the top, arched her back, and began moving up and down. It was a highly appealing visual, one that Henry had called up from his vault of appealing visuals many times over the past year. Indeed, Henry thought that this sequence represented one of those rare moments when all those involved in a project had worked in brilliant unison; the cinematographer, director, lighting designer, and sound man had blended their various talents into a perfect artistic whole. Also the actors. Once again, Henry imagined lying on his back, gazing up at the beautiful Tori West, cupping her perfect breasts.

Unfortunately, what followed was the one flawed segment (or so Henry felt) in an otherwise perfect piece of cinematic art: The camera moved to an extreme close-up. Directly on the heels of the stunning midrange shot, Henry found this view deeply disappointing, too clinical to be arousing. Watching a penis go in and out of a vagina from point-blank range reminded him of a filmstrip he had seen in junior high on the mating habits of the praying mantis. No, Henry greatly preferred the wider angles—shots that enabled him to see the whole act in some context, to enjoy the entirety of the woman's body, the arch of the back, the curve of the hips. He was extremely pleased when the camera finally panned back out. As the heroine began to moan anew, Henry applied a bit more pressure, allowing himself to fully enjoy the filmmaker's resurgent artistry.

It was at this juncture, however—just as Henry was getting back to the job at hand with renewed vigor—that the phone, in another impeccable show of timing, rang for a second time. Though there have probably never been formal scientific studies on the subject, phone calls often come in flurries. Under normal circumstances, Henry would have welcomed a second call so close on the heels of a first, but these circumstances were far from normal. Obviously, the answering issue was moot. Even if it was Tamar calling to propose, this one would have to be screened. Henry heard the beep. Then he heard a voice.

Diana!

"Hey there, gorgeous. OK, I got your message. And I guess I have to admire your friendship to that rotten husband of mine. But, oh Henry. There's so much to do here, and I don't have anyone to do it with. Remember—the invitation's open. Call me . . . just to say hi. Or to book a flight to paradise. I miss you."

With the click, Henry immediately began to imagine that the Doctor's Wife was Diana. It was perfect! Still inhabiting the role of the intern, Henry could imagine that he was screwing his best friend's wife with no guilt! OK, so maybe they were on a bed as opposed to a table, but to Henry that was a net plus. As the intern rolled back on top and Tori West wrapped her legs around his back, Henry brought years of practice and hard work, not to mention raw talent, to bear on his task. He knew from past viewings that the Doctor's Wife and the Handsome Intern would climax any second. If he stroked with expert precision, Henry could time his own orgasm so it would coincide exactly with the two fine actors'. And the intern was actually responding now. The Doctor's Wife had finally managed to break through the wall of his nonchalance.

"Oh, yeah," the intern murmured.

(Henry had always appreciated the Mamet-like succinctness of the dialogue.)

With an instinctual grasp of high drama, West and her partner gave themselves even more fully to their jobs, demonstrating an assiduousness of purpose that workers everywhere, regardless of profession, could study and admire.

"A little more," the intern gasped.

(At this juncture, Henry gasped as well, his knee knocking against the coffee table, sending the burritos flying to the floor.)

"That's it, baby! Oh . . . Yes!!!"

(Going for his own Academy Award, the intern was letting loose.)

Seconds, later, Henry's legs stiffened. Soon it would be all over . . .

"Ah!" the intern cried.

"Oh!" Henry moaned.

"Ohhhh!" (The intern.)

"You like it?" (The wife.)

"Yes!" (The intern.)

"Henny, honey!" (What?!)

"I was just calling to say hello, dear, and to . . ."

His mother! Henry had been so intent on the task at hand that he hadn't even heard the phone ring or the answering machine beep! Since the sound of his mom's voice most definitely did not fall into the aphrodisiac category, Henry knew he had to shut her up fast, especially after she briefly—for a mere instant, but still horribly—took Diana's place in Henry's mind! With his strong hand (his right) occupied, Henry was forced to assign his weaker left the task of locating the volume control on the answering machine. Finding it difficult to stroke with one hand and search with the other (especially while also trying to concentrate on the film and simultaneously block out the sound of his mother's voice), Henry quickly grew frustrated and simply swept the machine and phone onto the floor, where they landed upside down next to the burritos. Which only made matters worse. Yes, the machine stopped recording, but the phone had come to rest two feet from the TV.

Off the hook! That meant his mother could hear the movie—just as intern and wife were nearing the moment of truth.

"Hallelujah!" the intern shouted.

"Praise be to God!" the wife cried.

Then, together, "ARRRRRGGGGGHHHHH!"

As the Handsome Intern and the Doctor's Wife enjoyed orgasms of earth-shattering intensity, Henry scrambled for the phone (nearly slipping on a burrito), hung it up, then dove back for the couch, where he continued to stroke like a madman. Unfortunately, his mother's call had left him so frazzled that by the time the actors were finished, spent and satisfied, all Henry could do was watch his own penis grow smaller and smaller. Though he tried valiantly to jump-start his engines, he soon recognized it for what it was: a lost cause. Rather than the anticipated pleasure of release, Henry knew that all he would have to show for his efforts was a severe case of blue balls.

In fact, ten full minutes passed before he felt well enough to hobble across the room and gingerly pull up his pants. Then he collapsed at his desk, head in hands. At times, it seemed to him as though he had been put on the earth as a sort of test case—a subject to be studied by a team of specialists researching the effects of unrelenting humiliation. And that humiliation wasn't quite over, for at just that moment, the phone rang again, and Henry knew exactly who it would be: his mother calling back.

What to do this time? The way Henry saw it, there were two options: (a) screen or (b) pick up and play dumb. Given that he was too agitated to carry on a normal conversation, especially with his mom, he opted for the former. Had she been able to hear the video? Henry wasn't sure. Duly resigned, he prepared for the worst.

"Henny, dear," his mother said into the machine. "Are you there?"

Yes, Henry thought. *With my balls in a sling.*

"The oddest thing just happened, dear. I was leaving you a message, and suddenly the line switched over to . . . I don't know, it

sounded like some sort of loud sporting event. Or a religious re-
vival meeting. It was hard to tell. You really ought to get your line
checked. Anyway, I wanted to know what you thought about what
Adam discussed with you at the housewarming. Don't be angry,
dear. It's just a suggestion, OK? And I have John's number for you.
So give me a call sometime, honey. Don't be a stranger!"

With that, she hung up.

Henry sighed. His first good news all day. He had dodged the
bullet. Still, he was depressed. After a positively hideous weekend,
filled with inflated hopes and crushing rejection, his one solace
had been stripped away. What was the world coming to? Couldn't a
red-blooded American man jerk off in peace anymore?

Luckily, Henry had enough perspective to realize that he couldn't
let his entire day be ruined due to a single poorly timed masturba-
tion attempt. He had to move beyond it. Focus on the positive. After
a moment or two straining to find anything in his life that even
remotely fell into that category, he remembered Glenn's message.
Maybe there was a step he could take to get things back on track.
After all, why waste his day thinking about women who were uninterested (Tamar), inappropriate (Diana), or wholly out of his league
(Tori West) when he could pursue someone who was available and,
by all accounts, liked him?

Henry retrieved the answering machine, replayed Glenn's message, and jotted down Christine's number. Then he paced around
his living room twice, repeating the same mantra that had served
him so well in the past ("You're good-looking. You're smart.
Women love you."), before finally turning to the phone and dialing
the number of the cutest woman in New York City . . . with one
eyebrow.

5

christine

NO matter how he tried, Henry couldn't take his eyes off it. It was there when he picked her up at her apartment, there as they stepped through the turnstile to the subway, there as they entered the restaurant. Though, as predicted, the pimple had healed weeks earlier, it was small consolation in light of the fact that Christine's two eyebrows appeared to be linked even more substantially than Henry had remembered. Perhaps more mature, well-adjusted souls wouldn't have noticed. Not Henry. All he could see was the thin tuft of fuzz over the bridge of her lopsided nose, sprouting like an overfertilized lawn through cracks in a sidewalk.

What made it so upsetting was that by the time they were settled in for dinner at a local Master Wok, Henry realized that Christine was everything Glenn, Doug, and Ellen had promised: funny, sexy, easy to talk to. Indeed, the conversation meandered easily from subject to subject—first to movies (Christine's favorite: *Talk to Her*; Henry: *Lord of the Rings*, with *The Doctor's Wife* an unspoken second), then their upbringings (Christine's: Ohio, relatively happy; Henry's: New York, significantly tortured), eventually wending its way to careers, politics, and then sports. Upon discovering that they shared a mutual love of basketball—her father was her high school coach—the couple devoted a good portion of the main course to a vigorous discussion of the best point guards in the NBA. Henry knew that Jill would have been pleased to hear that his date's all-time favorite was Walt Frazier, the star of the Knicks championship teams of the early seventies.

By the time he paid the bill, something that Henry never would have thought possible had taken place, an occurrence that seemed to fly in the face of his very genetic makeup: For the first time in his life, the sheer force of a woman's personality had actually altered his perception of her looks. Be it the charming idiosyncrasies of Christine's character, a newfound maturity, or simply a case of good lighting, the unibrow and the crooked nose were no longer deal-breakers. In the course of a single meal, Christine's face had morphed from a lukewarm interesting into an emphatic cute. As a result, Henry's predate expectations—a quick dinner, then home in time for reruns—had been blown out of the water. This date would continue. Further, Christine seemed like the kind of woman who would appreciate a visit to one of Henry's favorite spots in New York: the Lookout.

On the fiftieth floor of the Shearing Plaza Hotel, this restaurant was known for a slowly rotating outer floor that allowed patrons to spin in a slow circle, taking in the view of the city as they ate dinner and sipped drinks. Set in the heart of Times Square, the Lookout catered to the bridge-and-tunnel crowd and had therefore been designed with the type of cheesy charm usually associated with Holiday Inns. Henry loved it for just that reason. At the Lookout he could enjoy the best suburbia had to offer right in the heart of the city—the décor that leaned heavily on glitter and mirrors, the all-you-can-eat buffet, and, most of all, the band. Though the actual group had been different the half dozen or so times Henry had visited, they shared a unique sound that could only be termed bar-mitzvahesque. Tonight, the musical entertainment was being provided by the Tritones, three women in matching red uniforms who performed the greatest hits of the seventies on two synthesizers and a drum set.

As the maître d' showed them to their table, Henry was pleased that Christine found the restaurant as delightfully tacky as he did. Working on their first beer, they devoted several minutes to arch comments at the expense of the interior decoration and clientele (notably the man in a leisure suit at a nearby table), then turned their attention to the stunning view of Manhattan. After they picked out a few landmarks, the conversation got around to Christine's work as a fourth-grade teacher. Here, she found the opportunity she had been waiting for all night—to discuss Henry's poem, "The Tale of the Otter." Not only had she loved it, but she had read it to her class!

Henry was stunned.

"I hope that was OK?" Christine said.

"You're joking," Henry said.

"Nope. No joke. You aren't mad?"

Henry wasn't quite sure how he felt. That poem was meant for Jill and Jill only. Suddenly, it seemed that the entire world was hearing it. On the other hand, his curiosity was piqued. He couldn't resist finding out the reaction of his target audience.

"Did they like it?"

"They loved it."

"No kidding?"

"No kidding. And fourth graders don't lie, Henry. In fact, they want you to come in and read some more if you have any others."

"No!"

"Yes. Will you?"

Henry hesitated. Though he was having a good time with Christine, he was unsure whether he wanted to commit himself to another meeting quite so soon, even if it was to be chaperoned by a room full of nine-year-olds.

"Come on," Christine said. "They really want to meet you. I'll even throw in a free juice."

"A free juice?" Henry said.

"And an unlimited supply of graham crackers."

Henry smiled. "Well, since you put it that way, sure."

By that time, the outer floor had nearly completed one full rotation of the restaurant, bringing Henry and Christine back in sight of the Tritones. On the dance floor, four couples were trying, with little success, to feel the beat to "Nights on Broadway." Henry and Christine watched them struggle gamely along, eight people with the collective soul of Mr. Rogers.

"God," Christine said. "We can do better than that. Wanna join them?"

Though Henry would have been more than content to stay put, it somehow seemed wrong to come to the Lookout and not dance at least once. Even more, despite the success of dinner, he felt a need to further establish his I'm-a-fun-guy credentials.

"Why not?" he said.

"Let's go, then," she replied, standing up.

On the way to the dance floor, Henry's spirits were high. After a week of nonstop work on his musical, coupled with vain attempts to forget the horror of the preceding weekend, this date had turned out to be just what he needed. Each time he made Christine laugh, he felt his self-esteem rise that much closer to pre-Tamar levels. Further, he was playing the evening flawlessly. Some guys would have suggested an after-dinner movie. Others would have tried everything in their power to rush Christine back to their apartment. Henry had chosen the Lookout, a place so devoid of taste it was hip—a place designed to charm his date into a stupor. So far it seemed to be working.

Halfway to the dance floor, though, Henry's self-congratulatory good cheer took a sudden nosedive, for it was at that precise moment that he realized that agreeing to a dance was a mistake of monumental proportions. What had happened was this: The minute he and Christine had stood up, the Tritones had segued to a new song, "More Than a Woman." At that point, the other four couples, perhaps realizing just how terrible they looked, had sat down en masse. Though Christine seemed perfectly fine with the idea that she and Henry had, in effect, been ceded the dance floor, Henry was terrified. Despite years of piano lessons and several college courses in composition, Henry had never been able to translate his musical abilities into a talent for rhythmic movement. True, he knew the difference between a quarter and a dotted eighth, but something in his nerve endings wouldn't allow that information to be transmitted to his arms and legs in sync with an actual beat.

Ironically, Henry had been told more than once that he was a good dancer. Though he viewed his technique, if it could be called that, as nothing more than an erratic splaying of arms and legs coupled with sundry random, spastic body shakes, these disjunct movements apparently meshed together more fluidly than he thought to make up a dancing style that was more aesthetically pleasing than he realized. Still, in Henry's view, dancing was only enjoyable, and then only moderately so, when certain conditions were in effect: a dimly lit room, a crowded dance floor, and unlimited access to alcohol. Faced with a bright room, an empty floor, and an intoxication level that was close to nonexistent (one lousy beer!), Henry began to panic. Especially since Christine was already clapping her hands and marching around him like the leader of a high school pep squad.

"You sure you want to do this?" Henry called.

"Sure I do," Christine replied. "Come on!"

Technically, Henry knew, he was a free agent, at liberty to turn on his heel and head back to his seat. On the other hand, he was also aware that an action that drastic would make him look socially awkward at best and like an asshole at worst. So as Christine marched backward to the center of the floor, beckoning with her hands, Henry forced himself to take a few tentative steps forward.

"What're you waiting for?" she called.

"Another song," Henry said desperately.

"Why? This one's great."

"I never dance to the Bee Gees."

"Never dance to the Bee Gees?" Christine replied. Henry thought that her tone wouldn't have been any different had her question been *You mean, you believe in slavery?*

"That's stupid," she said. "Get your butt out here."

Then she got right to it, shaking her body every which way, wildly even, eyes closed, lost in her own world. For a second Henry thought he might be able to get away with simply standing still, watching until the song ended, but he was not to be that lucky. Soon enough Christine opened her eyes and shot him a look that communicated a sense of disappointment so deep it bordered on contempt. Like the terrified skydiver who knows that there's no turning back, Henry knew that it was time to throw caution to the wind and jump out of the plane. True, there were great risks involved. His parachute might not open. He might crash to a painful death on a rocky ravine. At least he wouldn't die a coward.

The history of the Broadway stage is filled with many wonderful performances, but none of the theater's greatest luminaries from Barrymore to Hayes ever pulled off a transformation as startling as the one executed by Henry Mann that night. Henry realized in short order that the only way he would be able to overcome his insecurities would be to reach for a metamorphosis worthy of Jekyll turning into Hyde. When the song reached the second chorus, that's exactly what he did. With the raw, searing power of a young Brando crying, "Stella! Stella!" he revved his engine from zero to a hundred and began to move furiously with the music. In seconds, the insecure nondancer had been supplanted by Henry, wild man extraordinaire—a shaking, shimmying, twisting, turning, rocking, rolling tornado. If Christine thought his style a bit too energetic, she didn't let on.

"God!" she said. "You're good!"

Thus encouraged, Henry ponied all the way across the floor and shuffled back. Then he pretended he was holding a mike and sang along with the Tritones in his best falsetto: "More than a woman! More than a woman to me!" Christine laughed and took his hands. Just like that, Henry had to change character again—this time into a finger-pointing, hip-shaking John Travolta clone. Luckily, he remembered a few disco moves from his junior high days. As a result, he was able to bluster his way through the final verse and chorus calling upon a mixture of spins, twirls, and strategically planted goofy expressions. At the coda, Henry tangoed Christine down the length of the floor. When the final chord of the song played, he dipped her so low she almost fell to the ground.

"That was great!" she said, and threw her arms around him.

"Yeah," Henry said. "Had enough?"

"No way! We've got to see what the next song is."

In truth, Henry had enjoyed the dance more than he ever would have thought possible. Though slightly winded, he was actually loose enough to try again. That all changed the moment the leading Tritone turned to her microphone and uttered a series of fateful words—words that had struck fear in his heart since the seventh grade.

"OK, folks," she said. "We're going to slow things down a bit."

Henry shuddered. Seconds later, the opening chords of "Desperado" filled the room. Once again, the pressure was on. Henry glanced at Christine. Was a first-date slow dance taking things too fast? Though it was difficult to read her expression, he guessed that she was allowing him his male prerogative, leaving the decision entirely in his hands. The fact was that Henry would have loved to hold her. His eyebrow/nose fixation had never, even from the beginning, stopped him from appreciating Christine's body. She was tall and slender with small but firm breasts. Her interest in professional sports had apparently carried over to her personal habits, giving her the hard, lean look of a woman who had logged serious gym time. No wonder she had wanted to display her backside for the entire night staff of Albright, Pierce & Dean.

Unfortunately, slow dancing caused Henry even more anguish than fast. With a slow dance there was no place to hide. In fact, the way slow dancing was practiced in Henry's youth didn't seem like dancing at all—more like authorized groping, featuring hugging couples moving their feet only as much as absolutely necessary to keep up the charade that they were paying any sort of attention to the song at all. In high school, Henry had sometimes thought it would be better if they turned off the music every half hour to let the couples who wanted to slow-dance have a three-minute group hug.

"You want to?" Christine asked. "Or should we bag it?"

The opening was there. Henry could gracefully decline and be back at his seat in seconds, but a final evaluation of Christine's body made that option untenable. In the end, the needs of his libido ruled the day, and without a word Henry took her hand and led her to the center of the floor.

There, they hesitated. Like two dogs getting each other's scent, they approached each other slowly, nervously. Finally, Henry took her in his arms, and Christine tucked her head in the crevice between his chin and right shoulder. Finding that uncomfortable, she switched to his left. Still dissatisfied, she switched back. Settled in at last, Henry felt her pull him close. Swaying mechanically from foot to foot, he closed his eyes and willed himself to feel the beat along with Christine. *This is fun*, he told himself. *This is fun. This is fun. This is fun* . . . As the leading Tritone belted the first chorus— "Don't you draw the queen of diamonds, boy. She'll hurt you if she's able"—Henry felt Christine tighten her grip even more, felt her hips gyrate into his, her breasts push against her chest. Then he felt a soft breath blow into his ear, followed by a throaty whisper.

"You feel so nice."

"So do you," he said. Reassured, he shut his eyes and rubbed her back, letting his body mesh into hers. The "This is fun" mantra, at first an admonition, faded from his mind and slowly became a reality. This *was* fun. Lots of it.

That was when something wholly unexpected—even astonishing—happened. Something that hadn't happened to him in years. Something that, if he had ever taken the time to consider the subject, Henry wouldn't have thought would ever happen to him again, certainly not in a manner so conspicuous. In short, Henry suddenly found himself in possession of an enormous erection. Not half or two-thirds hard but rock solid, all six and a quarter inches, sandwiched against his abdomen and underwear as though a tube of steel casing had been surgically implanted in his jeans. Obviously, something about Christine—her scent, the way she was grinding her hips, her warm personality—was turning him on. Despite the very best evidence—evidence that was close to bursting out of his pants—it was still hard to believe. Yes, Henry found Christine sexy. On the other hand, he would never have thought her capable of inducing a reaction of such magnitude.

Henry was so hard his pants felt two sizes too small. So hard it hurt. So hard that he couldn't quite remember the last time he had been so hard. Though getting it up had never been a serious problem, he couldn't count the times when, naked in bed with a woman (where erections were appropriate and, in most cases, the bigger the better), he would've given a year of his life for what he was packing now. As fate would have it, it seemed to Henry that his best hard-ons seemed to occur when he couldn't use them—on buses, at ball games, while picking up pastrami at the deli. With a certain sadness, he realized that he would likely remain stiff for twenty minutes or so and then this miraculous boner would disappear forever, completely undocumented.

Or would it? After all, Christine would have had to be wearing a suit of armor not to have noticed. As Henry ruminated on the various strategies he could use to defuse the situation, he remembered with startling clarity the last time this had happened. High school, sophomore year, the fall mixer. The young lady had been a big-boned blonde with slightly horsey features who had introduced herself as Libby and asked him to dance. Flattered, Henry had said yes before he realized that the song was slow. It is a testament to the sex drive of the average fifteen-year-old that despite a decided lack of enthusiasm regarding his dancing partner's looks, Henry had become erect in less than ten seconds. Even worse, in that case his penis had angled downward as it had hardened, causing it to press painfully against his right leg. Unable to tactfully maneuver his swollen member into a more comfortable position (pointing upward toward his belt), Henry had soldiered through the duration of the song in agony, mumbled thanks, and waddled to his father's apartment, whereupon he set out to block the humiliating incident from his mind through the consumption of inhuman quantities of beer. As a result, he had spent a good portion of that evening's wee hours hunkered over a toilet bowl.

Henry almost wished his old man were there to help him now. Given his sterling track record with younger members of the fairer sex, Henry figured that this sort of thing must happen to him on a near weekly basis. If anyone would be versed in the proper etiquette for such an occurrence—a sort of Emily Post for the unexpectedly aroused—it would be the elder Mr. Mann. Perhaps an apology was in order? Or a written note? "Handle with care. It's loaded." Or was the best strategy to simply admit it? Put on his best soul-singer voice and whisper, "Don't fear, my dear. This is for you."

But Henry was well aware that he was no Barry White. Suavely using this erection to his advantage was well beyond his capabilities. No, the only course of action was clear: close his eyes, finish the dance, and pray that Christine either didn't notice or was simply too polite to say anything.

So Henry settled in for a siege. Unfortunately, never before had a musical group taken such artistic liberties with "Desperado." By the same token, never had a hard-on showed such staying power. As the Tritones moved to the second chorus, Henry tried to shift his weight onto the balls of his feet in a vain effort to make more room in his jeans. The area was simply too tightly packed to allow for even a millimeter of wiggle room. So tightly packed, in fact, that Henry became briefly concerned over the durability of his zipper—and that didn't even take into consideration the possibility of further growth! It was a thought that brought Henry to the uneasy borders of an out-and-out anxiety attack. But as Tritone number two flipped on the electric guitar sound on her synthesizer and took an instrumental, Henry rallied, reminding himself that he was no Handsome Intern. *I'm six and a quarter,* he told himself. *Everything's fine. Just six and a quarter.* In this way, he made it to the top of the third verse, and knowing that all things—even overwrought seventies ballads—must eventually come to an end, he gritted his teeth and hung on for the home stretch. Though the singer milked the final chorus within an inch of its life, throwing in enough glissandos, repetitions, and dramatic pauses to make even the most die-hard Barbra Streisand fan cringe, the band finally took it home for the big finish. "Before it's too"—long pause—"late!" Then the playoff, followed by the last merciful chord. Finally over. Christine gave Henry an extra squeeze, then lifted her head.

"Thanks," she said simply.

"No," Henry replied, as gallantly as he could given the circumstances. "Thank you."

He tried to read her face. Did she know? If so, she was certainly playing it coy. Now she took his hands and stepped back.

"Wanna keep dancing?"

A simple question, but unfortunately one beyond Henry's current ability to answer. Though he didn't dare look down, he still felt virtually naked, as though his swollen state were obvious to everyone not only in the entire restaurant but in the entire city. He half expected the mayor to rush in and declare him the Big Apple's latest tourist attraction. ("Step right up, ladies and gentlemen. See what put the grin back on Lady Liberty's face!")

"Henry?" Christine repeated.

"Oh," Henry said. "No. I don't think so."

"OK," she said. "Let's grab a seat, then. Come on."

She took a step toward their table.

"Wait."

She stopped.

"Changed your mind?"

Henry brushed a hand through his hair. "No. But come to think of it . . . Listen, I think I'll use the bathroom, if that's OK?"

Christine smiled. "I know I'm a schoolteacher, but you don't have to ask permission."

"Right," Henry said awkwardly. "That's true . . . Listen, I'm going to go ahead, then. I'll meet you back at the seats. Sound like a plan?"

With that, Henry turned on his heel and cut across the dance floor. As soon as he was out of Christine's line of vision, he began to move at the pace of an above-average Olympic speed walker. The crowd was thick, though, and a near collision with a waiter caused him to temporarily lose his bearings and make a wrong turn. It wasn't until Henry was halfway around the strange rotating restaurant that he realized his mistake and doubled back, now at a gentleman's jog.

When he reached his destination, Henry finally caught a break. Amazingly enough, the men's room was empty! Indeed, Henry had six glistening urinals and four stalls all to himself. That didn't even take into account a row of marble sinks stocked with aftershave, combs, tissues, and mints, but now wasn't the time to take advantage of the free Brut. In seconds, Henry was at the closest urinal, jeans unbuckled. Freed from its tight quarters, his penis burst out of his pants as if on a spring. Henry never would have imagined that he could be so angry at a body part. "Christ," he whispered. "Will you go down already?" Though his member was incapable of speech, the answer was clearly an unqualified 'no'. Like a pigheaded two-year-old, it was going to do whatever the hell it pleased.

To make matters worse—perhaps due to a strong power of suggestion—Henry felt a slight pressure in his bladder. He had to pee. On the one hand, he couldn't have been standing in a more appropriate place. On the other, Henry knew that in his current state the act of urination was fraught with risk. The main issue was one of control. Indeed, there was the distinct possibility that the stream of urine (assuming he was even able to force one out) might well hit him in the face or shoot sideways, perhaps even onto his leg. Henry shuddered. The last thing he needed was to return from a trip to the bathroom with a dark, wet mark on his jeans. No woman, no matter how down-to-earth, could be expected to pursue a relationship with a guy who wasn't fully toilet trained.

"Shit!" he muttered. He looked down. "Why—the—hell—don't—you—*go down!*"

Frustrated, Henry pounded a fist against the marble wall. At this point, he was close to certain that he'd be hard for life, a freak of nature featured in medical journals and on *Dr. Phil*. Then he was struck by a thought—a thought so painfully obvious he couldn't believe it hadn't occurred to him the very second he had entered the room. After all, a urinal was a versatile receptacle. What if he forgot about his bladder for a moment and revisited his more pressing problem? Glenn had once spoken of being so horny that he had beat off in a urinal, an experience he had referred to as "kind of a rush." But that was Glenn, a man in possession of a slightly more daring nature. Henry being Henry couldn't stop himself from flashing on a variety of worst-case scenarios. What if a woman barged in at the moment of truth? Ask her to help? Or a group of teenagers? Henry didn't know if he was up for a circle jerk.

Sweating now, Henry glanced toward the door. He then turned his attention to his open palm as if trying to reassure himself that, should he decide to go ahead, there wouldn't be any equipment failures. Everything appeared to be in order. Then he looked to the door again, this time feeling somewhat scandalous. It would certainly make a good story. The truth was that the entire exercise wouldn't last long enough for anything to go wrong anyway—a quick thirty seconds, forty-five tops. A final look to the door. The coast was still clear. Only one question remained. Did he have the guts?

As it turned out, Henry never had a chance to find out. Just then, a crashing sound—the mighty flush of a toilet—filled the room and resounded off the marble walls. The door to the last stall down at the end flew open, and a doughy middle-aged man in a black tuxedo appeared, zipping up his fly. Henry responded as if struck by a cattle prod. In a flash, his underwear was up, his pants buckled. As the man walked by him, Henry remained stone still, heart thumping. Soon the intruder was at the sink, washing his hands, humming lightly. Henry studied him with his peripheral vision. If the man had seen anything, he certainly appeared unfazed. Just as Henry was considering his next move, the man smiled his way.

"Lovely evening, eh?" he said.

Henry was shocked. Typical public restroom decorum did not generally call for sink-to-urinal discourse. Further, the man spoke in a bright English accent. Perhaps lavatory protocol was different in the mother country? Not wanting to be a boorish American, Henry answered in kind.

"Sure," he stammered. "Terrific."

"I simply love your city!" the man intoned as he reached for a paper towel. "Absolutely fabulous place!"

Indeed, this gentleman was downright chummy. Henry couldn't suppress a smile. Had he exited the stall ten seconds later, he probably would have slapped Henry's back and cried, "Bully for you, old chap! I spank several times a day. Jolly good fun!"

"Yes, it is nice," Henry said.

"Saw a fantastic show tonight," the man went on as he patted down his hair with his hands. "*Mamma Mia!*"

Under normal circumstances, Henry would have found it impossible to resist the urge to lecture the man on the sundry evils of European degrading of the musical form (bad lyrics, schlocky music, melodrama, amplification, etc.). Given his present condition, Henry simply smiled and choked out, "It has some catchy tunes, alright."

"Extremely catchy! Abba is genius!"

Henry was briefly concerned that he would have to use the urinal as a vomitorium, but before he could think up an appropriately neutral response, the man, who didn't seem to require a confirmation of his musical tastes, shot Henry a quick nod.

"Well, cheers!" With that, he was gone.

Alone again, Henry began to tremble, terrified by the narrowness of his escape. But perhaps that terror had worked to his benefit? He quickly unbuckled his pants and took a peek, hoping against hope that the wood had been scared out of him. No—still going strong. Henry sighed, knowing that his options were becoming increasingly limited. With a date on hold, he didn't have time to wait this problem out. The time had come for manly action. Further, he knew where to do what he had to do. The privacy of the back stall. In a flash, Henry was inside. Before he could change his mind, he locked the door and got down to business. A minute and a half later he emerged, a new man. Never in his life would he have thought he'd be so happy to be going limp. At the sink, he washed his hands, embarrassed by what he had just done but also somewhat bemused by the absurdity of the situation and the ridiculousness of his past week. He splashed cold water on his face, then toweled himself off. There. Finally, he was ready to face the world. A close call, yes, but miraculously, disaster had been averted.

Or had it? For when Henry returned to the restaurant, he was confronted by a surprising sight: Christine wasn't at their table! After a quick glance to make sure he wasn't in the wrong part of the restaurant, the full force of what seemed to have happened hit him like a medicine ball to the stomach. Obviously, Christine, offended by his slow-dance shenanigans, had gathered her things and vacated the premises! What else could possibly explain such an abrupt desertion? Lost, Henry slumped in his chair, head in hands. Was there no end to his anguish? Had he committed some heinous act in a previous life for which retribution was only now being exacted?

"Can I get you another drink?"

The waitress, college age, pathologically cheerful, was beaming down upon him. Perhaps that was the answer: alcohol and lots of it. But Henry had been down that route before. He had no desire to degrade the night any further through intense physical illness.

"No, no thanks," he said. As the waitress turned away, though, he couldn't resist. "You haven't seen my date, by any chance, have you?"

Though the waitress began to stammer out some semblance of an answer, at just that moment, the moving floor brought the dance floor back into view. To Henry's surprise, Christine was in the room, after all—chatting with the Tritones' big-haired singer!

"Aha!" Henry said. "Found her."

He hustled past the waitress across the room.

"Hey there," Christine called over. "I'm just getting some advice."

"Advice?" Henry said.

"Yeah," the singer said. Her accent was pure Brooklyn. Or was it Bronx? Henry never could get the boroughs straight. "Your girlfriend wants to be in a band. I invited her to sing a song, but she's shy."

Henry felt relieved and surprised at the same time.

He turned to Christine. "You sing?"

"And writes songs," the singer said.

Henry looked at his date with renewed appreciation.

"No kidding?"

"Oh, I just dabble," Christine said. "Folksy stuff, mostly. You'd think it was incredibly corny."

"No, not at all," Henry said, even though he often did find folk music just that and sometimes even worse. Though he had liked Peter, Paul, and Mary as a kid, he'd rather die than admit it now. "I'd love to hear it sometime."

Christine looked pleased, but she didn't exactly jump at the chance. "We'll see about that." Then she turned to the singer. "Nice chatting with you."

"Anytime. Enjoy!" She turned back to the band. "What next, girls? 'My Sharona'?"

"Sorry I wasn't at the table," Christine said as the band started up. "I hope you didn't think I had deserted you or something."

Henry laughed. "Deserted me? Not at all. I'm sorry I ran off so fast."

"No problem."

"So . . . you wanna grab another drink?"

Though he had expected a quick assent, Christine seemed to take the question quite seriously. Then, much to Henry's surprise, she shook her head.

"Let's take a walk instead."

"What?"

"This hotel is so big and goofy. Let's explore."

"Is that alright?"

"If we get arrested I'll take the fall. Come on."

Though most explorers would have given the Shearing Plaza Hotel a pass, Henry and Christine found a lot to discover. Their initial wanderings led them to a smoky piano bar. At first glance, dim lights and soft music seemed to make for an ideal romantic setting, but on their way to their seats, Henry heard the pianist play the opening few chords of "Maria." He steered Christine toward the door.

"Sorry," he said, thinking of his embarrassing serenade to Tamar. "I have a bad association with that tune."

Stop two was the gift shop. After a careful investigation of the wares—postcards, key chains, posters—they each settled upon a New York Knicks mug.

"For my dad," Christine said.

"For Jill," Henry replied. "She's a Knicks maniac. We shoot hoops in the park sometimes."

"Oh, yeah?" Christine said. "I played in high school, you know."

"Yeah, that's right."

"Maybe I can join you sometime?"

It was certainly a bold move—especially considering she had already asked him to speak to her fourth-grade class—and Henry didn't usually like sharing his time with Jill. But something told him that adding Christine to the mix for an afternoon would be fun.

"Sure," he said. "We'll set it up."

The tour continued. Soon Henry faced a most unusual test. On the top floor of the hotel, he and Christine passed the honeymoon suites. Showing uncharacteristic resolve, Henry did not allow himself even a snippet of a fantasy. He was determined to follow Glenn's advice. Christine was a girl he could get to know slowly. There was no need to marry her—at least not yet.

The couple wandered back to the glass elevators. Christine pressed UPPER LEVEL LOBBY. It was there that the evening took its final turn. It was well past midnight by now. Directly to their left was a conference room.

"Hmmm," Christine said. "How about that?"

Upon closer investigation, they discovered it was empty. By this point they were holding hands. It wasn't something that Henry had planned but rather something that simply happened in the elevator, a by-product of how well they were getting along.

"Where do you wanna sit?" Christine asked.

Henry surveyed the choices. Down the center of the room was a long, narrow table. In the corner, as though it had been planted there just for them, was a blue loveseat. At the opposite end of the room was a circle of easy chairs, where they could chat at a safe distance. Again, Christine was offering him the male prerogative.

"The couch," he decided.

As they walked across the room, Henry could not help but bask in the knowledge that, at long last, his dry spell was officially over. Last weekend, Tamar. Now Christine. Two for two! In fact, Henry was so certain that making out would commence the second their rear ends hit the cushions that he felt almost cheated to find that Christine had something else in mind.

"So," she said, wrapping her hand around his. "Tell me about yourself?"

Henry laughed uneasily. "What do you want to know?" Was she subtly inquiring to see if he had any notable STDs?

Christine snuggled closer. "You decide."

Up to this point in the evening, Henry had exhibited admirable restraint in regard to communicating the painful details of his parents' divorce, not to mention his terrier's demise, but now that he had been given a permission slip, it didn't take much to get him going. Once he dispensed with his family situation, Henry was surprised at how easily the conversation meandered to past relationships. In fact, Henry soon found himself talking of Sheila. Perhaps it was taking things too fast, but then again, Henry realized, it was probably a symptom of how well he and Christine were getting along. There was even an unusual point of intersection. As it turned out, Christine's high school sweetheart, the main love of her life, had been the captain of her high school lacrosse team. Ironically, at the end of junior year, a few months into their relationship, Sheila had dumped Henry for the captain of the Hamden College team.

"His name was Hans, if you can believe it," Henry said.

"Hans?" Christine said. "Sounds terrifyingly blond."

"And muscular, too," Henry said. "They were one of those really disgusting couples, you know? All over each other, everywhere, every minute."

"Yucky," Christine said. "Was there a happy ending?"

"Sort of," Henry said.

"Ah, pray tell."

Though he couldn't quite believe that he was having such a nice time with a woman who had actually used the word "yucky," Henry eagerly recounted his revenge.

"It was junior spring, I think. I had a Shakespeare seminar with them. Now, let's just say that Hans wasn't the brightest guy in the world. One day early in the semester, he raises his hand."

"And what's he say?" Christine asked.

Henry paused for dramatic effect. "Well, he told the class that, in his opinion, Shakespeare named one of the evil sisters Goneril because she represented King Lear's inner turmoil, or 'gonorrhea.'"

Christine was dumbstruck. "Gonorrhea?"

"You heard me."

"You're kidding."

"No," Henry said. "Dead serious."

"But that's so dumb!"

"I know. That's the point."

"What happened after that?"

"Well, in a certain way of looking at it, not much, but in another way, it was wonderful. The second after Hans said it, I met Sheila's eye. She turned red. I swear to God, I almost thought she was going to run from the room."

"Hmmm. Sounds extremely satisfying."

"It was." Henry smiled. "Extremely."

Indeed, it had been a glorious moment, but the tale had a tragic second act. Immediately following that fateful class, Henry had gone to lunch. While carrying a tray of chicken cutlets, he had passed a table of Hans's frat buddies. Rising above the hum of ceiling fans and buzz of student conversation, Henry had overheard this brief yet wrenching dialogue between Gus Stampalopolis, an acne-necked football player, and Marty Wright, Hamden's star quarterback.

MARTY: So are they doing it?

GUS: More than doing it. The lucky bastard's fucking her brains out.

MARTY: Fucking, eh?

GUS: Yeah. With a capital F-U-C-K.

Though the proper nouns hadn't been exactly specified, something in the leer Gus shot Henry as he strolled past made it clear that the "lucky bastard" in the sentence referred to Hans and the "her" to Sheila. Needless to say, Henry did not dig into his chicken cutlets with his usual gusto that afternoon. Obviously, he had known that Sheila and Hans were having sex, but the fucking out of brains was something he hadn't bargained for. Now, eleven years later, Henry remembered how unsure he had felt of his own sexual prowess in those days; he would lie in bed, ruminating on his own lovemaking sessions with Sheila, wondering whether they had reached brain fuck-out levels. Indeed, Henry had had some reason to feel insecure. Sheila had been only his second lover and the first he had ever slept with in a bed. (He had lost his virginity the summer before college at camp on the darkroom floor.) Could he have helped it if his skills were not yet fully developed? Sheila, who had lost her virginity at age fifteen, had told him repeatedly that he was a good lover, a natural. That was little solace when virtually every waking minute for the remainder of that school year was attended by thoughts of Sheila and Hans in a never-ending series of compromising positions.

"I take it they broke up eventually?"

Henry blinked.

"Huh?"

"Sheila and Hans?" Christine repeated. "They broke up, right?"

"Right," Henry said, focusing back on the here and now. "Over the summer. But then we started dating again senior year."

"How long did that last?"

"We pretty much decided to go our separate ways at graduation. It was mutual."

Again, Henry had left out a key detail. When Sheila had suddenly decided to accept a job in France, the couple "mutually" decided that the relationship couldn't continue.

"But then we hooked up again at the fifth reunion," Henry went on. "She was moving to New York to work for a bank. That stint lasted about a year."

"What happened then?"

Here Henry paused, faced with a classic decision. Should he let Christine know that he had been devastated? What the hell. He had gone this far.

"She dumped me," he said. "Just as I was getting ready to propose."

"Geez . . . Sorry."

"Nah, it's OK," Henry said. "It's for the best. We were a lousy couple. From two different worlds."

"Oh, yeah? How do you mean?"

"Well, lemme put it this way," Henry said. "The first time I laid eyes on her she was wearing Top-Siders and a monogrammed green sweater."

"Say no more," Christine said. "Extreme displays of preppiness should be punishable by death."

Henry nodded. "Tell me about it."

They paused. Henry wanted to tell Christine more. How after Sheila had dumped him he had been so depressed that he had taught photography at his old summer camp, this at twenty-eight, making him six years older than the counselor closest to him in age. How he had had to fight daily urges to mix darkroom chemicals with his morning orange juice.

Then he had a better idea. Thinking back to the embarrassing incident on the dance floor, something funny occurred to him. Perhaps his penis, acting with a mind of its own, had been a compass, pointing him after all these years toward what he really wanted. Certainly, Christine was not a woman whose ticket to happiness lay in the comforts of a big house and barrels of money. Why was he wasting time talking about Sheila? Let her remain in Seattle with her materially full life but barren soul. He would stay east with a woman who appreciated him for who he was.

With that thought, Henry slowly lifted Christine's head and looked into her eyes. They were deep brown, warm, the eyes of a person he could trust. Then he studied the rest of her face.

Imperfect, but beautiful. Who cared about the unibrow and slightly lopsided nose anyway? He moved closer and slipped his arm around her shoulder.

He'd concentrate on the full, perfectly aligned lips.

jennifer

FADE IN:

EXT. BEVERLY HILLS POOL PARTY—DAY

A smattering of L.A. types mingle, sip drinks, dip in the pool. FOCUS ON: Henry Mann, a dashing thirty-two-year-old writer. He's a tan, fit, confident stud. One sexy fucker. Right now he's chatting with JENNIFER ANISTON, the voluptuous star of FRIENDS. She wears a tightly fitting bikini that leaves nothing to the imagination.

> JENNIFER
> (giving Henry a playful shove)
> Get over yourself! You won a Grammy?

> HENRY
> (modestly)
> Well, I . . .

TWO GORGEOUS STARLETS happen by.

> GORGEOUS STARLET ONE
> (to Jennifer)
> Did you know that his latest novel just got
> nominated for the National Book Award,
> too?

> GORGEOUS STARLET TWO
> (to Henry)
> And aren't you signed up to write the new
> Spielberg flick?

Henry meets eyes with Jennifer. He shrugs, the
very definition of humility. She's duly impressed.

LATER—IN THE POOL

Jennifer and Henry lie side by side on inflatable
rafts.

> JENNIFER
> Yeah, I know the show was a huge hit. But
> it got hard sometimes to balance my phenom-
> enal TV career with film offers.

> HENRY
> Yeah, some people don't realize how tough
> it can be to be wildly successful.

> JENNIFER
> Tell me about it. And then there's the
> whole L.A. dating scene. Ever since I
> dumped Brad . . . well, it's a huge time
> drain.

                    HENRY
     Oh? A woman as beautiful as yourself must
     be seeing someone?

                   JENNIFER
                  (coy grin)
     Actually, I'm currently unoccupado.

With that, she dives off her raft and knocks
Henry into the water. A lively splashing fight
ensues.

EXT. DESERTED BEACH—THAT NIGHT

A dark, starry night. Jennifer and Henry lie
side by side in the sand.

                    HENRY
     It really all began in third grade. My
     mother took me to see *A Chorus Line*. By the
     end of the first number I knew that I had to
     devote my life to writing.

                   JENNIFER
     That's incredible. *Chorus Line* is the show
     that made me want to act!

They pause, look deeply into each other's eyes.

               JENNIFER (cont'd)
     I can't believe how much we have in com-
     mon . . .

He reaches for her. They kiss, roll in the sand.
DISSOLVE TO:

INT. HER BEDROOM—NIGHT

A lavish boudoir, overlooking the beach. In bathing suits, the couple kisses on a loveseat by the bed.

                    HENRY
          You're so beautiful.

Despite her great celebrity, Jennifer is shy, unsure of her sex appeal.

                    JENNIFER
          Do you really think so?

Henry kisses her again and removes her bra, exposing the breasts that men across America have admired for years. He kisses her neck.

                    JENNIFER
          Oh, Henry! You're such a man . . . Take
          me, Henry! Take me!

Henry lifts her in his arms and carries her to the bed. As the choral theme from Beethoven's Ninth plays, they make love with a passion to make *The Doctor's Wife* seem like Disney.

DISSOLVE TO:

THE BEDROOM—LATER THAT NIGHT

Henry and Jennifer lie in each other's arms.

                    JENNIFER
          That was unbelievable . . . My life is
          forever changed.

Henry kisses her anew as we DISSOLVE TO:

MONTAGE.

As Barbra Streisand sings, "People. People who need people":

Jennifer and Henry walk into a crowded restaurant. The other patrons stop and stare. Several applaud.

Henry and Jennifer chat with Nicole and her man of the moment at the Golden Globes. Nicole laughs uproariously at one of Henry's telltale witticisms.

Henry and Jennifer stroll down the Champs d'Elyssées in Paris with Demi and Ashton. Henry impresses all, asking for directions in perfect French.

Henry and Jennifer ski at Vail with Rosie and Madonna. Henry executes a stunning freestyle jump.

On the set of a *Friends* Reunion Special, Henry wows the cast with a dead-on imitation of Jimmy Durante.

END MONTAGE

INT. TV STUDIO—DAY

Jennifer is being interviewed by BARBARA WALTERS.

> BARBARA
> Now let's get to your love life. Word has it that you're involved with a handsome genius.

                    JENNIFER
                (gently weeping)
Oh, yes, Barbara. Henry is everything a man
should be. Sensitive yet strong. Forceful
yet kind. He's my friend, my soul mate, my
lover.

                    BARBARA
Sounds serious. Do I hear wedding bells?

                    JENNIFER
Oh, Barbara, I don't know if a man that
independent could ever be tied down. (giggling)
But here's to hoping!

EXT. CHAPEL—DAY

Henry and Jennifer run out of a chapel. Papa-
razzi snap pictures. Guests cheer wildly, throw
confetti.

EXT. THE RECEPTION—DAY

A cast of thousands looks on admiringly. As the
bandleader sings a rubato version of the theme
from FRIENDS, Henry leads his new wife to the
dance floor. Her eyes are glistening.

                    JENNIFER
        Mrs. Jennifer Mann!

                    HENRY
        Mr. Henry Aniston!

                    JENNIFER
        Oh, Henry. I'm so happy!

HENRY

So am I!

(quietly singing)
So no one told you life was gonna be this way.

"You're singing, Henry."
"Your job's a joke, you're broke . . ."
"Stop it!"
"Your love life's . . . Ouch!"
Henry shook himself. To his surprise, he was suddenly no longer dancing at his wedding but sitting in a small theater in the East Village. Disoriented, it took him a few moments to realize that he was sitting between Doug and his wife, Ellen, who had just pinched his thigh—*hard.*
"What did you do that for?"
"You were singing to yourself," she hissed.
"I was?"
"Yes. Shhhh!"
With that, Ellen nodded back to the stage. The fantasy had been so powerful that Henry was almost surprised to find himself back at the reading of Glenn's play, *Hoo, Hoo! Haw, Haw!* Right now, two actors playing chimpanzees, one a male, wearing a Walkman, the other a female, holding a tattered copy of *War and Peace,* were engaged in a pedantic debate over humankind's corrupting influence on twentieth-century civilization. Monkey suit aside, something in the female chimp's smile had reminded Henry of Jennifer Aniston. That, coupled with the fact that he found the play largely indecipherable, had caused Henry's mind to wander far, far afield.

Though this was hardly the first time that Henry had daydreamed his way through a boring play or movie, he was more than a bit troubled that Jennifer Aniston had been the subject. Not that he had anything against her. *Friends* reruns were one of his favorite guilty pleasures, and Jennifer was his favorite of the six pals. No, he had thought about the comely Ms. Aniston many, many times. It was the timing of his thoughts that concerned him. After all, hadn't he just had a killer date with a woman named Christine the very night before? Shouldn't he have been thinking about her? Here his new relationship wasn't even twenty-four hours old and he was already cheating with a movie star. It didn't bode well.

At least the play was almost over. Onstage, the two talking chimps had been joined by a third, another male, along with a burly zookeeper. After being captured in the African jungle in Act One, taught how to speak English by the zookeeper in Act Two, and thrust upon the world stage as international celebrities in the beginning of Act Three, the three monkeys were in the process of rejecting the human influences they had initially welcomed. In fact, the very moment Henry turned his full attention back to the footlights, Chimp One ripped off his Walkman and began to stomp it to bits. Seconds later, Chimp Two spit on her copy of *War and Peace*. As for Chimp Three, he shook the bars of their cage, screaming, "Hoo, hoo! Haw, haw!" The zookeeper, sensing that something was very wrong indeed, began to back slowly toward the door. Seconds later, in an act that bespoke their deep, burning desire to be free, the chimps burst through the bars of the cage and, after a series of celebratory yelps, approached the zookeeper, who, terrified now, brandished a pistol. This dialogue ensued:

ZOOKEEPER: You can't go! Back in the cage!

CHIMP ONE: Never! We want to be free!

ZOOKEEPER: But why? I've given you the power of human speech! I've opened up new, glorious worlds to you!

CHIMP TWO: Yes! The world of lies! Disease! Hate! Hypocrisy! True, you have the power to communicate. You are rich in material goods! But give me a bushel of bananas and a few good trees over the corrupt world of men any day! You, my friend, and your kind are rapists!

ZOOKEEPER: (tearfully) No! Noooo!

CHIMP TWO: Rapists of the land!

CHIMPS ONE AND THREE: (chanting now) Hoo, hoo! Haw, haw! Hoo, hoo! Haw, haw!

CHIMP TWO: Rapists of morality!

ZOOKEEPER: (holding his ears in mortal pain) Stop! I beg of you!

CHIMP TWO: Rapists of our divine animal soul!

At this point, the zookeeper tossed his gun aside and crumpled to his knees, weeping, while all three chimps danced around him in a circle, gesticulating wildly, shouting, *"Hoo, hoo! Haw! Haw!"* as the lights faded to black.

Though Henry always tried to look for the good in his friends' work, Glenn's play left him at a loss. In fact, he was so confused by it (or at least the parts he had actually heard) that he spent a good portion of this final scene desperately trying to come up with some sort of consoling words to lift Glenn's spirits when it was through. After some thought, he narrowed it down to two choices: either "Who gives a damn what other people think. They aren't deep enough to get it," or the old standby, "Well, *I* loved it." To Henry's surprise, however, these comments turned out to be unnecessary. The moment the lights went back up, the applause wasn't just appreciative but thunderous. During the first curtain call, several of the most enthusiastic patrons even rose to their feet. With the second, everyone else followed suit, Ellen and Doug included, which put Henry in the unhappy position of either getting up as well or remaining conspicuously seated.

He stood.

"Wasn't that great?" Ellen said.

She was applauding so hard, Henry grew concerned about the health of her palms' capillaries.

"Yeah," Henry said. "Great."

He was mystified. Never before had his feelings about a piece been so out of line with the general consensus. Was he envious that Glenn was getting his work read in public and he wasn't? Possibly, but even though Henry was as prone to fits of jealousy as the next guy, he liked to think that he wasn't so maladjusted that he would hate something out of pure spite. No, the most likely explanation was that he just didn't understand Glenn's writing, plain and simple. Of course, there was also the possibility that the rest of the audience didn't understand it either but was simply being polite. After all, Henry figured that, this being a reading for invited friends, at least half the crowd knew Glenn personally. In a gathering that partisan, it was hard not to take a standing ovation with a healthy grain of salt. As they headed up the aisle moments later, Henry decided to test his theory on Doug.

"What did you think?" he whispered. "Did you really like it?"

"Oh, yes," Doug replied. "His stuff is so original."

"Yeah," Henry admitted. "But you didn't think it was sort of, I don't know . . . heavy-handed?"

Doug considered the question. "Maybe a little at the end. But all in all, I was moved."

"Come on," Ellen said. "Let's say hi to the playwright."

Soon Henry found himself with Doug and Ellen near the head of a makeshift receiving line in the back of the lobby as Glenn— bride, groom, parents, and best man all rolled into one—greeted each well-wisher in turn.

"Great job!" Doug said, after what seemed to Henry an interminable five-minute wait.

"Thanks, man," Glenn said.

"So moving," Ellen said. "I cried!"

As if to prove her point, she took this opportunity to wipe her eyes with a Kleenex. Now it was Henry's turn. Still unsure of precisely what he wanted to say, he took Glenn by the shoulders and looked him deep in the eyes.

"Well?" Glenn said.

"Loved it, man," Henry said.

"You mean it?"

Had Henry been a member of the pathologically truthful, he might have suggested that several hits of acid might have contributed to his comprehension of the play. Instead, he nodded as sincerely as he could.

"What can I say?" he said. "Your stuff is so fucking original!"

Soon Henry and a coterie of well-wishers were stationed at DBG, a hip new bar on First Avenue. It was here that an astonishing coincidence took place. At least, it seemed to be a coincidence, for of all the bars in all the different neighborhoods in New York, the odds that Tamar would choose to visit this particular bar in this particular neighborhood on the very same night as Henry were slim indeed. The truth of the matter was that Tamar's presence in DBG was no fluke. Rather, she had sought Henry out. To that end, she had entered the bar a couple of minutes after he had arrived, then positioned herself out of sight across the room. After giving her prey a moment to order a beer, she had cut purposefully through the crowd to say hello.

Henry was ostensibly participating in an in-depth analysis of Glenn's play with Doug and Ellen. The reality, however, was somewhat different. Henry had just caught a glimpse of the chimp-actress who resembled Jennifer Aniston in the bar mirror, a sighting that caused him to immediately revisit his life as husband to the big-breasted sitcom star. In fact, at the precise moment of Tamar's approach, Henry and Jennifer were about to conceive their first child, an event he was looking forward to rendering in some detail. So when he felt Tamar tap him on the shoulder, Henry's first emotion was annoyance. What kind of person would have the nerve to bother him at such a time? Didn't he know that Henry was about to fuck Jennifer Aniston?

"Hey there," Tamar said.

Henry wheeled around.

"Yeah?" he said gruffly.

As it had on the street, it took Henry a long moment to register just who was standing before him.

"Oh, my God," he said quietly. Then, louder, "Hey! How are you?"

"Pretty good. Pretty good."

"What are you doing here?"

Tamar smiled. "I was at the reading."

"What?"

"I'm a friend of a friend of Glenn's, remember?"

"Yeah, yeah. That's right. So you were at the play, huh?"

"Yeah. In the back." She looked both ways. "I thought it sucked."

Perhaps it was Tamar's mischievous glance to make sure no one would overhear. Perhaps it was her blunt choice of the word "sucked." Then again, perhaps it was nothing more complex than a renewed appreciation of her body. Whatever the reason, Henry was once again a card-carrying member of the critically smitten. His mantra of the past week, "I don't care about Tamar," had been officially exposed as a sham.

"We're in the minority," Henry said. "Everyone here thinks it's a work of genius or something."

"Genius?" Tamar said. *"Please."*

"I'm just not sure if I get his writing," Henry said. "I mean, it could be us. It took Sondheim a while to catch on."

"True," Tamar replied, "but at least Sondheim had the good sense to avoid singing monkeys. He never musicalized *Planet of the Apes*, did he?"

Henry laughed and took a sip of beer, suddenly completely at ease, ready to enjoy what he hoped would be a long, luxurious conversation. But Tamar hadn't schlepped over to the East Village for idle chitchat. By the time Henry brought his glass down from his lips, she had leaned in close.

"It's pretty crowded in here," she said. "Can we go someplace and talk?"

"Now?" Henry said.

"Yeah."

"What about?"

Her smile was inscrutable. "Come with me and you'll find out."

"Glenn just got here. I really should stay for a while and help him celebrate."

Tamar and Henry glanced down the bar. To his surprise, Glenn had an arm draped around none other than Chimp Two!

"He seems well taken care of," Tamar said. "Come on."

Henry hesitated. It was a devil's dilemma: either stay and celebrate the reading of a play he hadn't liked or desert his best friend for a woman. The shiver he felt when Tamar took his hand made the answer obvious.

"Pretty please?" she said.

Henry smiled. "Just give me a second to say good-bye."

Tamar looked back down the bar. "You may be too late."

She had a point. Glenn was leaning forward, lightly kissing the chimp on the mouth. Henry shook his head. Another young actress—Glenn's specialty. Somewhat jealous (after all, that monkey was his!), Henry wondered what Diana would think if she knew that Glenn was cheating—again. Would it make her push Henry even more to visit? He hoped not. With his hands full in New York, he wasn't looking forward to fielding any more phone calls from the Mountain time zone. Then again, perhaps Diana had already gotten the message. Since the afternoon of the fateful *Doctor's Wife* episode, she hadn't called.

"Should we roll?" Tamar asked.

The chimp was now in Glenn's lap.

"Yeah," Henry said. "He seems a bit preoccupied."

With a quick good-bye to Doug and Ellen, he led Tamar outside.

By the time they were seated at a nearby diner sharing a piece of chocolate cake, Henry's curiosity had had a good ten minutes to build. Unfortunately, he had little in the way of hard facts to help it build toward anything approximating a reasonable guess at what Tamar might say. His hope was that she would grab him by the lapels and cry, "You must forgive me! Take me back, you fool!

Take me back!" Well aware that that could never happen (he wasn't even wearing lapels), Henry's mind was soon brimming with other scenarios, each more outrageous than the last. For a moment or two he had become convinced that Tamar was going to tell him that she was terminally ill. After that, he was sure that all she wanted was for him to write a love song for her wedding to Abby. Of course, deep down Henry knew that the news Tamar wanted to impart probably wasn't anything nearly that dramatic, but given the way his mind was reeling, by the time Tamar finally came clean the truth savored of anticlimax.

"For the past two years," she said, stirring milk into her coffee, "I've been involved with a married man."

Henry took a bite of cake, processing the news. Then, before he could figure out exactly what to say or even precisely what he should be feeling (though he was leaning toward furious), Tamar went on.

"I suppose," she said, "that you want to know why I agreed to go out with you?"

The question helped Henry focus his thoughts and find his voice. "Along with why you told me you were a lesbian, yeah."

Tamar forced a smile. "Fair enough."

For the first time since Henry had met her, Tamar looked suddenly uncomfortable. Though he knew that it was within his power to make a joke or say something to help her relax, he decided to remain quiet and allow himself the pleasure of watching Tamar suffer as she attempted to explain herself. Given the way she had lied, it seemed only fair.

"Well," she finally said. "I said I'd go out with you because I was mad at Robert."

"The married man?" Henry said.

Tamar nodded.

"And the lesbian thing?" Henry asked.

He saw a young couple walk into the restaurant, arm in arm, laughing, obviously happy. Henry hated them.

"I don't know what to say," Tamar said haltingly. "I guess I wasn't thinking clearly. It was late at night."

Henry smiled. "Well, I'm usually pretty sure of my sexual orientation no matter what the hour."

Tamar let the comment pass. "I know there's no explanation for what I did," she said, "except to say that I was confused. I freaked out. I know it sounds funny, but to my way of thinking telling you that I had an affair seemed more embarrassing than telling you I'm gay."

Against his will, Henry was somewhat intrigued. "Why?"

"We live in New York," Tamar said. "Everyone's gay, it seems. But having a two-year affair that has absolutely no hope of going anywhere . . . well, that's pathetic."

Henry nodded. "I see what you mean."

"Your e-mail was so sweet it sort of blew me away," Tamar went on. "I panicked. I wanted to say something that would get rid of you, no questions asked."

"So why are you telling me all of this?" Henry asked.

Tamar drew in a deep breath. "Well," she said, "I'm telling you because . . . Listen, remember passing me on the street on Monday?"

"Sure."

"I was crying, remember?"

"I thought you were."

"Well, I was coming from my shrink."

"Really?"

"Yeah. I had just decided to dump Robert once and for all. And that night I did it. I'm a free lady now."

Henry paused. No, she wasn't grabbing him by the lapels, begging for forgiveness. On the other hand, the conversation was taking a welcome turn.

"Going out with you made me realize that I had to get rid of Robert," Tamar continued.

Two tables over, the couple laughed again. This time, Henry hated them a bit less. Much less, in fact. He looked at Tamar. After a week of his feeling he'd do anything to be near her, the tables had turned. She was the one on the defensive.

"So are you interested?" Tamar was wearing a new look: vulnerability. "Give me another chance?"

Henry faced a crisis of epic proportions. Though tempted to jump up on the table and shout, "Hallelujah!" he knew he couldn't drop everything and take up with Tamar without giving full due to the woman with whom he had spent the previous evening. The time with Christine had been wonderful. They had made out in the conference room for a solid hour, only stopping when interrupted by a night janitor. In the elevator, they had agreed that Henry would read to her class the coming Monday afternoon. Then there was the possibility of that basketball date with Jill. Walking to the subway after seeing her to a cab, Henry had felt downright jaunty. A lifelong malady, *appearancata obsessionetta severite,* seemed to be a thing of the past.

Unfortunately, by the time he had boarded the uptown express, Henry had experienced the first signs of a relapse. Much to his dismay, he had spent the entire train ride home picturing how much better Christine would look sans unibrow. Later on, his condition worsened. That night as he had drifted off to sleep, he imagined asking Christine to have the brow clipped, even offering to do it for her or to pay for a professional. In the morning, he had awoken with the vague memory of a dream in which Christine had gotten a nose job. Despite such thoughts, Henry had roused himself, determined not to give in to his weaker self. After all, no one recovered from an affliction so serious in a single night. He could beat it. He wanted to beat it—desperately. All it would take was time and hard work.

Why do all that work if he didn't have to, though? No, Christine wasn't bad-looking. In fact, she was extremely attractive. But was it a crime to think Tamar was even more attractive? Henry considered her face—the dark, curly hair, the blue eyes, the wry smile— not a hair (or nose, for that matter) out of place. Though Henry hated to admit that it mattered—despised himself for it, even—he couldn't help it. With Tamar there would be no nagging doubts, no convincing himself that a flaw was a charming idiosyncrasy. Simply put, she was extremely pretty.

Besides, it wasn't all about looks. Tamar was a true kindred spirit. A fellow New Yorker, she was a woman who managed to be stylish and ironic without being snobby or bitter, who combined down-to-earth values and city smarts in one shining package. On the other hand, Christine had flaws that transcended mere physical appearance. In fact, as Henry worked it out, he found it surprisingly easy to convince himself that there were several liabilities in regard to Christine's personality that would make a long-term relationship infeasible. Their backgrounds were too dissimilar. At heart, Christine was an earnest girl from the Midwest—a woman who peppered her conversations with "yucky" and "geez." Who taught fourth grade. Who liked—no, *wrote*—folk music. Could a New York neurotic really find happiness with someone so, well, corny? Yes, Henry realized that such homespun qualities might be considered charming, but he now chose, perhaps unconsciously, to give them a negative spin. In one bold stroke, Christine, an otherwise wonderful woman, was reduced to a prissy schoolmarm from Ohio. A square. Sure, Henry wanted someone with girl-next-door qualities, but did he really want Donna Reed?

"So?" Tamar asked. "What do you say?"

Henry took her hand. Perhaps if Christine had been there in person she would have had a fighting chance, but at this moment—the crucial moment of decision—she was most probably home in sweats correcting spelling tests. Tamar was sitting directly across the table, where Henry could look into her eyes, admire her hair, get swept away by her laugh, lose himself in her smell. Yes, she was the woman he had put on a pedestal. How could a day-old memory, no matter how pleasant, ever hope to compete with a dream come true?

"Hello? Earth to Henry?"

He smiled. All systems were go. Still, before he said yes, there was one final talking point. Unfortunately, Tamar wasn't off to a sterling start in the truth-telling department. True, she had had the class to look him in the eye and apologize—but he still needed a final word of reassurance.

"So," he said, withdrawing his hand. "It's really over, huh?"

"What?"

"Your relationship with Robert."

"Oh . . . that."

Tamar stirred her coffee. Then she leaned forward and smiled archly. "Don't you know I'm using you to make him jealous? The minute he comes crawling back, you're history."

Sadly, Henry was so terrified at the prospect of just such a scenario that for a split second he almost thought Tamar was serious. Worse, he was completely unable to keep his anxiety from reading on his face.

"Boy," Tamar said with a laugh, "are you ever gullible." She squeezed his right cheek. "I'm kidding, you big idiot."

Henry felt just that way—like a big idiot.

"Oh," he said sheepishly. "Right."

Seeing she had been too flip, Tamar took Henry's hands in hers and continued more seriously.

"I've moved on," she said. "Robert isn't right for me."

"Oh?"

"He's too rich, for starters."

Henry wasn't quite sure he had heard correctly. If he had known that being poor was an attractive quality, he would have taken care to exploit it on past dates by pleading poverty and not paying.

"And that's bad?"

"No, not exactly. But he doesn't work, really. He just sits in his big house in Fairfield and invests all day. His only hobby is sailing. He's obsessed with it. It's a totally barren existence. Not that it matters really, but he has two teenage kids. He's old. But you're . . . I don't know, different. You live in the East Village."

"West Village," Henry reminded her.

"Whatever," Tamar said. "The point is that you're doing something with your life, you know? You have a passion. That's what I want."

Henry looked her in the eyes. Could he trust her?

"Really?" he asked.

By way of an answer, Tamar kissed him on the mouth.

"Really," she said.

Henry smiled, finally allowing himself to appreciate his good fortune.

"Then let's pay the check and get the hell out of here."

It was while making out passionately with Tamar in the backseat of a cab, halfway to his apartment, that Henry remembered something: At the party where he had met her, Glenn had heard through a friend that Tamar was supposed to be great in bed. Though this memory excited Henry enormously, it also got him thinking about the infamous Millhauser incident. The story went something like this: Back in college, Glenn had taken a woman named Daisy Millhauser to dinner. After Herculean efforts (not to mention expense—she had ordered lobster), he had managed to get her back to his room, where they soon started to make out. Eventually (again, through more Herculean efforts), she had let Glenn remove her shirt and kiss her breasts. Then, instead of the expected sigh or moan, Glenn had heard sounds of a more alarming sort—a sharp snort, followed by these words: "Jesus! Haven't you ever read a sex manual?" As Glenn told it, he was dressed and out the door in ten seconds flat. Even though Henry himself had never been served "a Millhauser" (as he and Glenn came to refer to any cutting rebuke delivered by a female in a compromising situation), he was convinced it was only a matter of time. That his girlfriends had always told him he was good in bed didn't matter. The way Henry figured it, he was bound to run into someone who thought he wasn't sooner or later. As a result, whenever he was lucky enough to find himself with a new woman, Henry couldn't help keeping one ear cocked for a critique.

This brought Henry back to a consideration of the woman he was now bringing back to his apartment. Would Tamar be the first woman to stick him with the dreaded Millhauser? Viewed in light of her alleged skills, it was a definite possibility, for if Tamar was as good as advertised, her own standards for a partner would undoubtedly be high. Assuming that was the case, Henry knew there was a strong likelihood that she might find something in his technique— and it could be nearly anything—to criticize. She could find fault with the way he put on the rubber, with his penis size, with how he kissed, how he touched, how long it took him to get hard for a second time (assuming he could the first), even how his gut hung ever so slightly below his belt line. After all, in any given lovemaking attempt there were generally hundreds of things that could go wrong. From that vantage point, Henry could only assume that there would be several disasters before the evening was through.

What Henry hadn't counted on, however, was how turned on Tamar would make him in the course of the ride home. Indeed, it is a testament to Henry's state of arousal that by the time they made it to the West Village his worries had all gone the way of the mastodon. In fact, it was all Henry could do to pay off the driver and maneuver Tamar to his front door without ripping off her clothes. Apparently, she felt the same way. Once inside his apartment, they were naked in the hallway in a matter of seconds. Though in the past Henry had fantasized about floor sex—a close kin of the dining room table—he soon discovered that the reality (he didn't have so much as a throw rug) was more than a bit uncomfortable. That left him with three choices: (a) to continue where they were, risking anything from floor burn to splinters, (b) to suggest they walk to the bedroom, or (c) to carry her to the bedroom. Though Henry had never successfully carried a woman anywhere, let alone to a bed, (c) was clearly the most romantic choice. Would it be tempting fate to try a move so audacious? What if he wrenched his back and dropped her? Could he risk that? Under normal circumstances, the answer would have been an unqualified no, but in his current aroused state, Henry suddenly felt as powerful as the Incredible Hulk. Before Tamar knew what hit her she was in his arms.

"Oh, Henry," she said, then wrapped her legs around his waist.

So far, so good. Then, just as Henry was about to knock his bedroom door open with his butt, he remembered that his bed was covered with laundry. Take a moment to sweep the clothes onto the floor or choose a new venue? Given the time-sensitive nature of the act he and Tamar were about to attempt, Henry opted for Plan B, pulled a 180, and made a beeline for the living room.

"You're strong," Tamar said as he laid her on the couch.

"Ah, it's nothing," he said.

In fact, even Henry was impressed with the studliness of the maneuver, and he silently thanked his father for helping him pay for that gym membership, but now was not the time to bask in the glow of a single lift and carry, no matter how successful. More pressing concerns were at hand. To that end, Henry dimmed the lights, lit a candle, and turned back to Tamar, now lying back fully naked on his sofa. Her body was as beautiful as he had envisioned. Thin hips, slim muscular legs, flat belly. Though her breasts were by no means Anistonian, they were firm and perfect handfuls.

There had been many times in Henry's life when he had been so concerned about how things would go in bed that he found himself measuring each detail of the act as it was happening, as though he were participating and observing simultaneously. This time was different. Maybe it was because he was so turned on. Maybe it was because Tamar possessed a certain indefinable quality that helped him relax. Whatever the reason, Henry was able to fully lose himself in the moment. Perhaps he wasn't the world's greatest lover, but when he kissed her neck, her ears, her breasts, Tamar responded in all the right ways. And although she was no Doctor's Wife, Tamar soon lived up to her advance billing. Yes, Glenn's friend hadn't lied. She was good in bed. Very.

Later, still naked on the sofa, Tamar lit a cigarette.

"My one vice," she said with a grin.

In Tamar the habit seemed somehow endearing. In fact, Henry found everything about her endearing. As she looked for a place to toss her match, she noticed the fireplace.

"Does that work?" she asked.

"Not really," Henry said, "but I suppose we can try. Just get ready to douse the fire and open the windows in a hurry."

"Let's risk it," Tamar said.

"You sure?" Henry said. "It is April, you know. And pretty warm out."

Tamar grinned. "Crank the AC."

A little crazy, yes, but at this point Henry would have flooded his entire apartment with motor oil if Tamar had asked. After turning the air conditioner to high, Henry, pleased to show off his outdoorsman credentials, had a nice blaze going in a matter of minutes, and he took it as an extremely good omen when most of the smoke actually found its way up the chimney. Then he turned his attention to the CD player. He knew exactly what to pick. Sinatra or Ella was too obvious. No, he'd impress Tamar with his sophisticated tastes. Soon the mellow tones of Johnny Hartman, a bluesy singer from the forties and fifties, filled the room. As Tamar snuggled close, Henry thought about the beginning of the evening and his brief tenure as Mr. Henry Aniston. From where he was sitting now, the person who had had that fantasy seemed like a needier, more pathetic twin. The new Henry didn't need fame, pool parties, *People* magazine. Maybe he didn't even need a Grammy. What he needed—no, what he had—was lying next to him, enjoying the warmth of the fire.

It was while sitting at his desk the following afternoon that Henry first told Tamar that he loved her. The fact that she wasn't currently in his apartment didn't stop him.

"I love you," he said.

"I love you, too," his computer screen replied.

"No, I love you!"

"No, no! I love *you*!"

It was when Henry found himself leaning forward to plant a big, wet kiss on his monitor that he pulled himself up short. What the hell was he doing? Professing love to a piece of machinery? Apparently. Eyes closed, Henry leaned back in his chair and shook his head. Even when measured against his own permissive standards he had reached a new low. Unfortunately, he couldn't help himself. The previous evening had been just that wonderful. Sex and music had been followed by more music and even more sex. Then the requisite back rubs and foot massages. In fact, the mood had been so idyllic that Henry had sacrificed an old bookshelf in order to keep the fire going until it was time for bed. And the morning? Not a trace of awkwardness. At a local diner, the new couple had chatted easily for a bit, then devoted the remainder of the meal to constructing a sculpture out of three forks, two knives, a coffee cup, ten packages of Sweet'N Low, three pats of butter, and a ballpoint pen. When the work was complete, Tamar had christened it "Love in the Post-Vietnam Era."

While the title had seemed enigmatic at the time, it now seemed apt, for despite the ardent protestations he had directed at his Macintosh, Henry couldn't be sure whether the jumble of emotions he was currently experiencing truly qualified as love. Was it even possible to consider such a thing after only two dates? His intellect said no; his heart shouted yes.

In any case, one thing was certain. He was far too distracted to work. Instead, Henry found himself approaching his bookshelf and reaching for a high school textbook, a collection of the greatest poems ever written from the Elizabethans to the moderns. Perhaps Shakespeare, Keats, or Byron would have something enlightening to say on the subject? With that thought in mind, Henry took the book to his couch, ready to devote an entire afternoon, if necessary, to discovering the real answer to life's most elemental question. He began with a sonnet.

> *My mistress' eyes are nothing like the sun.*
> *Coral is far more red than her lips' red.*
> *If snow be white, why then her breasts are dun;*
> *If hairs be wires, black wires grow on her head.*

Henry shut the book with a disappointed sigh. A single quatrain was enough for him to realize that poetry was too imprecise an art to suit his current purposes. What he craved was facts—hard data against which to measure his feelings. He closed his eyes briefly, then, wondering what to do next, happened to glance back toward his desk. Leaning against his word processor was a tattered Webster's dictionary—the one his father had bought him in seventh grade. Maybe he'd find some answers there? Seconds later, Henry was at his desk flipping to the letter *L*. This is what he discovered.

> Love: 1) strong affection for another arising out of kinship or personal ties; 2) attraction based on sexual desire; 3) affection based on admiration, benevolence, or common interests; 4) unselfish loyal and benevolent concern for the good of another; 5) the sexual embrace; 6) a score of zero in tennis.

When he had read it through twice, Henry leaned back in his chair and mulled it over. On first glance his feelings seemed to measure up to the standards outlined in the definitions (excluding, of course, number six—Henry knew full well that Tamar was no tennis score). Already he felt a strong affection for Tamar based on "kinship or personal ties." They had much in common—summer camp, music, religion (not to mention a penchant for making provocative pieces of twenty-first-century art in diners). As for definitions two and five, Henry's strong attraction to and interest in the sexual

embrace were obvious. He quickly flipped to "lust," which was defined as "an intense sexual desire." He was pleased to discover that
he felt that as well. Definition three? Why, Henry admired Tamar
enormously. He admired her intelligence, her wit, her high-paying
job, even the courage she had displayed in searching him out after
Glenn's reading. (For the record: He also admired her long, smooth
legs, the arch of her back, how she purred—(yes, purred!)—when he
kissed her neck. The list was endless.)

As for number four, Henry was sure that his feelings toward
Tamar encompassed "benevolent concern," but were his motiva-
tions "unselfish"? Not purely. On the other hand, he didn't think
the word entirely appropriate. Obviously, he wanted Tamar to be
happy, but did he want her to be happy in the bed of another man?
Of course not. He wanted her to experience her happiness with
him and him only. If that was selfish, then so be it.

His analysis complete, Henry shut the book. So far, so good. According to the dictionary, he was already there, but there were two
more people he needed to consult prior to reaching his final decision: Glenn and Doug, the resident experts of 34 North.

Upon arriving at the firm that evening, Henry didn't beat
around the bush.

"I think," said he, "that I might be in love."

Glenn peered up from his work. Two pencils already hung down
from the ceiling over his head. Doug sat across the oval table, a fat,
heavily marked document laid out before him. Spread out on the
opposite side was a knapsack, a Discman and a package of fig
cookies—a sure sign that Ellen was loose somewhere in the building, probably sent out to work for an attorney.

"I take it things went well with Tamar last night?" Doug said.

Little effort was made on Henry's part to suppress the enormous
shit-eating grin that suddenly bloomed upon his face. At moments
such as these, he wished he were back in high school at that period
in life when it was socially acceptable to cap off a sexual encounter
by telling his friends every last detail. As much as he would have

liked to launch into a lurid description of his night with Tamar, his hands were tied. The best the parameters of mature adulthood (something Henry aspired to) allowed him to do was to flash a coy grin and remark somewhat smugly, "You might say that," as he took his seat between his two buddies.

"So you think you love her?" Glenn asked. "I thought she was a lesbian?"

"Not anymore she isn't."

"What?" Glenn asked. "You converted her?"

Henry took this opportunity to bring his friends up to date on the preceding evening's developments. When he was through, Doug frowned.

"So she lied about it?" he said.

"About what?" Henry asked.

"The lesbian thing."

"Oh, that," Henry said. "Like I said, she explained it. It's all settled now." He could tell Doug was skeptical. "I know it's weird, but trust me, she seemed sincere."

Doug shrugged. "If you say so. The whole thing seems strange, if you don't mind my saying. What about Christine? I thought you guys hit it off."

"We did," Henry said. "But I don't know—she just doesn't do it for me the way Tamar does. I can't explain it."

"Yeah, but—an affair with a married man? For two years? That's bad news."

"And she'd be the first to admit it," Henry said. "We all make mistakes."

"I know that I sure the hell have," Glenn said. He leaned forward and smirked. "So, Henry, how was it?"

"How was what?" Henry asked. "You mean the sex?"

There was something about Glenn's smile that told Henry he was in trouble. "No, no—not the sex." He glanced quickly at Doug. "The *wedding*."

Henry smiled grimly. Once again, Glenn had demonstrated his

irritating knack for going for the jugular. This was one time that Henry was more than pleased to be able to give an honest answer. "Cute," he said. "But for your information, I didn't think about marrying Tamar once all evening."

"Really?" Doug said. "That's an improvement."

Glenn wasn't satisfied. "Wait a second here. You mean to tell me that you didn't have a single wedding fantasy all of last night?"

"No."

"Not about anyone?" Glenn said. "Think, now."

Just as Henry was about to blurt a defiant "No!" he hesitated.

"Aha!" Glenn said. "Who?"

"Well . . ."

He felt a blush coming on.

"Come on," Glenn urged.

Henry looked away. "Jennifer Aniston."

"Jennifer Aniston?" Glenn said.

"Yes," Henry shouted. He stood up. "Jennifer Fucking Aniston, OK? She dumped Brad Pitt. Our wedding was on the cover of *Time* magazine! She walked down the aisle naked! Then we did it doggie style on the set of *Friends!* Alright?"

"Impressive," Glenn said.

"Listen," Henry said. "I'm talking about Tamar here, a woman who I actually know and, what's more, actually slept with last evening. So what about it? Am I in love or not? My dictionary says yes."

"You looked up 'love' in the dictionary?" Doug asked.

"I was curious," Henry said. "Also 'lust.'" The diatribe over, he seated himself and smiled. "Apparently, I've got both."

"Both?" Doug asked.

"Why not? Love and lust can coexist, can't they?"

"Abso-fucking-lutely, they can," Glenn said. "I mean . . ." He struggled for the right words to properly convey the strength of his convictions. "When the two go together it's like . . . fuck!"

Henry and Doug grinned. Glenn-speak could be remarkably precise at times.

"Alright," Doug said. "So lust is accounted for. How about infatuation? Did you look that up, too?"

Henry sighed. Doug's unwavering skepticism was steering a discussion that was intended to be a triumphant acclamation of the deep and abiding love he was feeling toward his new girlfriend in a depressing direction. He suddenly wished that Ellen, the eternal optimist, had been there to take his side. But suddenly, Glenn charged in to the rescue.

"Not so fast," he said. "Henry might be more than infatuated. I can think of, oh, at least two couples off the top of my head who knew they were in love after a day or two. There're no rules, you know."

"Are those couples still together?" Doug asked.

"Don't know," Glenn said. He paused to send yet another pencil flying. "One of them was me."

"Sorry."

Glenn waved off the apology. "Don't sweat it," he said. "Right now I'm satisfied with a certain young actress."

"You mean Chimp Two?" Doug asked.

"That's right. But she prefers to go by her given name, Rachel."

"You had sex with her?" Henry asked.

Despite his own conquest, he was still jealous.

"Close," Glenn said.

"What about Diana?" Doug asked.

"What about her? She's still in Colorado. Probably forever."

At this point, Henry hoped so.

"You're OK with that?" Doug continued.

"No," Glenn said, gathering his fallen pencils. "But at the moment it doesn't look like I have much of a choice. Listen, we're straying from the issue at hand." He looked to Doug. "I rule that Henry's in love. The dictionary says it, and he certainly seems to feel it."

Henry looked to Doug for confirmation.

"Well?" he asked hopefully.

Doug thought for a moment, then looked to Henry and shrugged. "What can I say? I don't want you to get hurt. But if it feels right, it feels right."

It was all that Henry needed to hear. After all, the true purpose of his day's labor had been to confirm what he was already sure he felt. Now that it was official, he was eager to pick up the phone and instantly report the results to Tamar herself. He even thought of transmitting the good news by e-mail; given the nature of the beginning of their relationship, it seemed only appropriate. Before he could, Glenn quickly brought him back down to earth.

"Let me give you some advice, lover boy. If you tell her right away it might freak her out."

"You think?"

"Definitely, señor. Keep it to yourself for at least another couple of weeks."

"Or months," Doug said. "Convention dictates it. Be patient."

Of course, Henry knew his friends were right. Yes, Tamar seemed to like him a great deal. There was even a decent chance that she loved him back. But it was simply too soon to risk it. The proper course of action was to play it cool—to keep those three little words in a way station near the tip of his tongue until he was sure they would receive the welcome into the world they so richly deserved.

"Don't worry," Henry said. "I'll be patient. Hey, I'm the King of Patient."

The King of Patient held out for approximately three hours. As hard as he tried to focus on his proofing, the complex legal sentences he was supposed to be checking for spelling and grammar blurred into a variety of lurid fantasies. After an especially vivid montage that featured Henry declaring undying love to Tamar over the Alps in a hot-air balloon, he excused himself and walked down the hall to an empty conference room. Feelings this strong cried out to be expressed. The trouble was that those feelings weren't quite strong enough to override his overwhelming fear of rejection.

After all, a one-week "I love you" was fraught with risk. Tamar might think him desperate or crazy or, worst-case scenario, might not love him back. Before taking such a blind leap into the unknown, he quickly decided that he needed a few moments to gather himself, and the basic "You're good-looking. You're smart. Women love you" wouldn't do the trick. No, a gamble of this magnitude required space to roam, room to think, time to prepare. So it was that Henry took to the halls. In the following ten minutes he circumnavigated the thirty-fourth floor of Albright, Pierce & Dean more than twenty times, preparing himself for perhaps the most important phone call of his life.

What Henry said (an abbreviated list):

"She loves you" (60 times)
"You de stud. You de stud. You de studly stud." (20 times)
"Tell her, goddammit. Tell her!" (between 50 and 100 times)
"Ohhhh, baby! Ohhhh, bay-bee!" (15 times)
"She wants it! She wants it!" (twice)
"Fuck! Fuck! Fuck!" (10 times)

Henry capped off this rigorous regimen with an old standby, "You de man! You de man! You de man!" He repeated this mantra without pause for an entire rotation of the floor up until the precise moment that he reentered the empty conference room, picked up the phone, and dialed Tamar's number. Though he half hoped that he would get her machine, to his horror she answered on the first ring.

"Hello?"

"Hi . . . Tamar?" (requisite heart-pounding, assorted tremors)

"Henry! I was going to call you."

"You were?" (genuine surprise)

"Sure I was."

"I'm glad," (first full breath since decision to place call) "I had a great time last night."

"Well, so did I. Hey, you're really terrific . . ."

Prior to making the call, Henry had assumed that he would have several minutes in which to gather his nerve before spilling the news. Now, with an expectant silence on the other end of the line, he suddenly realized that he had been presented with an opening a mere ten seconds in. Though there were hundreds of things he could have said to keep the conversation going in a more innocuous direction, Henry, hell-bent on making his deepest feelings known as soon as possible, barreled forward. Despite his exceedingly thorough preparations, he was suddenly too anxious to express himself directly. As a result, in lieu of "I love you," Henry heard himself saying, "I'm falling for you," watering it down even further with the qualifier "I think."

Tamar's response caught him off guard.

"You *think* you're falling for me?" she replied flirtatiously. "You mean you aren't sure?"

What Henry had expected was either an awkward pause or a quick "I'm falling for you, too." Instead, he had gotten lip. Though that lip was a good part of what made him love Tamar in the first place, Henry was slightly irritated that she wasn't a bit more serious in the face of a declaration of such import, no matter how awkwardly expressed. Called on the carpet, he now had no choice but to remove all traces of doubt from his statement.

"I mean," he said, "I'm falling for you, OK? Is that good enough for you?"

Tamar paused. "Hmmm. Yeah, I suppose that's good enough."

"So?" Henry said.

"So?" Tamar replied.

Henry suddenly wished he had chosen a woman who was less of a smartass to be the object of his admiration.

"So? Are you falling for me?"

Tamar giggled. Henry was sitting on the edge of his chair, a heartbeat away from a seizure.

Then her answer. "Of course I'm falling for you, you big pigdog."

It was all Henry could do not to catapult himself through the wall. His feelings were returned! Though he came frighteningly close to expressing his joy with an impassioned "Yes!" Henry caught himself and somehow managed to play it cool.

"Me a pigdog?" he said, downshifting to banter. "What's a pigdog?"

"It's what you are, dumbhead."

"Nope," Henry said. "You're the pigdog."

Suddenly, Tamar assumed a thick French accent. "I am no peegdog."

To which Henry replied (in his own bad accent), "Dream on, swinish one. For you—you are zee true peegdog!"

Tamar laughed. "Oh, yeah?" she said. "The deep and sickening nature of your peegdoggishness is blatantly apparent. I weep for you."

By this time, Henry was looking out a picture window onto Times Square, all traces of nervousness gone. After twenty more minutes of similarly lovestruck conversation (too nauseating to be documented), he strolled back to 34 North, took a seat, and tried to refocus on his work. Though proofing a fifty-page document on the subject of subordinated debt (in small print, no less), Henry found himself smiling like an idiot at every line.

"What's with you?" Glenn asked finally.

Henry couldn't stop himself from an indulging in a disgustingly brazen reprise of the shit-eating grin he had worn upon entering the room earlier in the evening.

"She loves me."

"She does?" Doug asked.

Henry nodded. "She says I'm her leetle peegdog!"

Glenn looked across the table at Doug.

"Well, that's just great," he said.

"What?" Doug asked.

Glenn scowled. "They've already got fucking pet names!"

The grin didn't leave Henry's face for the rest of the shift.

7

sheila

henry woke the following morning to find himself hugging his pillow. Before he knew it, he was staring at it longingly, then engaging it in the same conversation he had had the day before with his computer screen.

"I love you," he said.

"And I love you," the pillow replied.

"I love you more!"

"I love *you* more, my leetle peegdog!" the pillow said.

Henry rewarded that response with a long kiss.

It was directly following this unusual man-pillow interaction that Henry thought of something. Under normal circumstances, he attached no special meaning to Monday mornings, but this particular Monday was a different story. Lying in his bed (still wrapped in a torrid embrace with that pillow), he remembered an appointment he had made in what now seemed like a previous life: He had agreed to read his poems to Christine's class that very afternoon.

In seconds, the pillow was on the floor and Henry was sitting up. It was at moments such as these that he wished that at birth he had received a gene that allowed for displays of flagrant assholery. Unfortunately, however, he was trapped within his own essentially good-hearted skin and couldn't, in good conscience, simply cancel the reading (as he desperately wanted to) and then ignore Christine, leaving her to figure out on her own that their prospective relationship had ended before it had begun. Decorum dictated that he look her in the eye and with a few choice but kind words, a quick surgical strike, nip their relationship in the bud. It simply had to be done. Before he could fully throw himself into his life with his new love, he had to rid himself of the old.

The question now was what to say. Henry picked up the pillow and, with no more hugs, put it where it belonged. Then he flopped back on his bed, stared at the ceiling, and considered the question. The options were these: Go with the truth or come up with a convenient lie. Any of the stock breakup lines would do.

"I need time for my writing right now—about ten years."
"I'm on the rebound from an affair with a United States Senator."
"I'm getting back in touch with my religious roots. Do you speak Yiddish?"
"You see, I've got this sexual problem."

The trouble was that any line Henry could think of had grown transparent through overuse. On the other hand, the truth might hurt her feelings. For a moment Henry considered calling Tamar and asking her opinion. What better way to mark the beginning of a relationship than by scheming together about how to best break another woman's heart? Despite its somewhat morbid appeal, Henry thought better of it. First of all, it wasn't actually Tamar's business. (She hadn't asked Henry's advice before breaking up with Robert.) More important, he didn't have her work number.

At that moment, Henry got help from an unexpected source. The phone rang. Happy for a diversion, he answered right away.

"Hello?"

"Henny, hon—"

"Hi, Mom!" Henry sometimes found it less irritating if he cut off the full "Henny, honey!" with a preemptive greeting.

"Henry, darling, is this a good time to talk?"

Henry slumped back on his bed. Though he considered saying no, years of experience had taught him that delaying tactics usually backfired. It was often better to face the firing squad like a man and get such "talks" out of the way immediately.

"What about?" he said.

"Well, dear, I feel a little funny bringing this up."

Henry closed his eyes. This promised to be very, very bad.

"Uh-huh?"

"But I was calling to do a little follow-up work on what Adam discussed with you last week. You know, at the party. About the personal ad. Have you given it any thought, dear?"

Ordinarily, such a comment would have caused Henry to curl into a fetal position and pray for a speedy death, but in the past week his stockpile of ammunition had increased dramatically. Unknown to his mother, he was now armed and dangerous.

"Actually, Mom," he said, "I have."

"That's wonderful!" she cried. "You know, Henny, it's nothing to be embarrassed about. Lots of fine couples have—"

"I've decided against it."

"Oh . . . Do you mind if I ask why?"

Henry was enjoying this for all it was worth. He picked up the phone and began to pace.

"Not at all," he said. "As a matter of fact, I've met someone. Two people, in fact."

His mother was temporarily stunned into silence.

"Two?" she said at last. "My, that's fast work. Tell me about them."

Henry had been in such a hurry to prove to his mother that he was dating, he hadn't thought through the full ramifications of such a disclosure. Now he had no other choice but to give her a cursory outline of the situation, excluding, of course, the more intimate details.

"So when are you going to tell the teacher?" she asked when he was done.

Henry loved the way she had of cutting to the chase.

"This afternoon, I guess," Henry said.

"Do you have a plan of action?"

"A what?"

"A plan of action, Henny!"

Henry had a strong suspicion that he was about to receive one. He shouldn't have been surprised. Somewhere in the back reaches of his mind he remembered that subheading three of chapter ten of *The Inner You* read: "Breaking Up: How Excising Unwanted Leeches From Your Life Can Point You Toward the Road of Self-Discovery." Soon Henry was listening carefully as his mother took him through a step-by-step procedure, guaranteed, as she said, to quickly but gently cut Christine out of his life.

"You're going to have to strike fast, Henny," she began. "Don't keep the poor girl dangling. Find a nice coffee shop near her school and tell her right after the reading. It's perfect timing, actually. How can she get angry after you've given your time to her students? Am I right? Now, once you've got her seated and you've ordered, get right to it. Don't wait! A sweet boy like you is going to be a bit nervous, Henry. And who wouldn't be? You're going to break the poor girl's heart. It's a well-known fact that it's harder to be the dumper as opposed to the dumpee. Many people don't realize this, but it's true. It's in chapter eight of my new book. The dumper has to wade through weeks, sometimes months, of guilt and anxiety, whereas all the person being rejected has to do is sit there and listen. Then cry. Oh, yes, expect tears, Henry. Lots of them. But if you play it right, you may be able to avoid them. Here's how. Now listen. Are you listening? Good. Tell the truth. No lies! I won't abide a son who fibs! But break it to her nicely. You were such a fine actor in high school, Henny, honey! So play the role of the confused suitor, dear. Play your torment. Make her feel your pain. Your turmoil. You're just one lucky guy, mystified and slightly overwhelmed by the powers of fate that have brought you two such wonderful women at once. Make it seem like the decision has kept you up all week. If you do it right, you watch! Christine might just end up feeling sorry for *you!* 'Don't torture yourself over it,' she'll say. 'These things happen. It was only one date.' When she says that, Henny, dear, you're almost home. Take her hand, look her in the eyes, and say, 'Thanks for understanding. You're the greatest.' Then when it's all over, pay the bill—you pay, not her—and get out. No lingering. Trust me, after you break the news there's not going to be a whole hell of a lot to talk about anyway. Just leave. Then call and tell me how it went."

As Henry hung up the phone, he had to admit that it sometimes paid to have a mother in the self-help profession. That afternoon he presented himself to Christine's class, prepared to do what he had to do (read his poems, jettison the girl), but since he hadn't, for obvious reasons, called Christine and asked her to save half an hour after school to be dumped, it turned out she had already made other plans. The first was a party on Henry's behalf, complete with graham crackers, juice, and homemade cupcakes. After that, she had to run to the dentist. Short of breaking up with Christine in front of a group of nine-year-olds (something Henry briefly considered for its novelty, if nothing else), there was nothing to do but head home, mission unaccomplished.

Even so, Henry remained steadfast in his determination to bring the episode to a clean and speedy finish. Christine had told him she was going to hang out at home that night. To that end, he took off work and spent the better part of that evening pacing his apartment, trying to work up the guts to convey the bad news by phone (after all, there was no reason why they needed to be face-to-face for his mother's strategy to work). But each time Henry began to dial, he stopped short. Now that the moment of truth was finally at hand, he suddenly saw the situation in a new light. The truth of the matter was that he and Christine had been out only once. What sort of explanation did a man really owe a woman after a single date, albeit a date that went well and on which a certain amount of physical closeness had occurred? Viewed from this perspective, Henry figured, the conversation could go two ways. He could emerge unscathed with a disappointed Christine thanking him for being considerate enough to tell her directly that he had met someone else, or he might be forced to endure the kiss-off tirade of a spurned woman. Indeed, Christine might well think him a presumptuous jerk for assuming that she was emotionally invested to the point that a phone call was required in the first place. What if, in her fury, she made disparaging references to the infamous slow-dance woody?

In the end, no matter how many times Henry tried to dial, he couldn't get all the way to the last digit. To his great discredit, when he saw Christine at work the following night, he pretended to be busy. Later on that evening, when she stopped him in the hall to say hi, Henry hurried by, waving a newspaper. "Sorry!" he called. "Bathroom!" No fool, she soon got the point. The next time they saw each other at the firm, a full two weeks later, she looked right through him.

When his mother called for a report, Henry couldn't bear to tell her the truth.

"Your plan," he said, "worked like a charm."

It was a statement that Mrs. Mann marked with an especially ecstatic "Oh, Henny, honey!"

Later that day, on the phone to Glenn, Henry was more honest.

"God," he said. "Did I ever fuck that one up."

"Yeah, maybe," Glenn said. "It was a tricky situation, though. Only one date. Technically, you didn't really owe her anything."

Henry could only imagine what Doug would have had to say about that particular line of logic.

"You think?" Henry said.

He heard Glenn take a drag from a cigarette. "On the other hand, you're probably right. You fucked up."

"Gee, thanks."

"Anytime."

Yes, even Glenn felt that he had handled an imminently manageable situation with all the tact and grace of an average seventh grader.

Though furious with himself for botching what should have been, by all accounts, a straightforward parting, the truth was that Henry was simply too lost in his own happiness to let it bring him down. As time went on, he grew more and more certain that Tamar was the woman he had been waiting for, the elusive "right girl," the living embodiment of his most ardent fantasies. No, he and Tamar were not having sex in an Iowa barn or taking hot-air balloon rides over the Alps. They weren't even being photographed for the cover of *People* magazine. But Henry floated through the spring feeling as though he were trapped, happily so, in a schmaltzy movie montage, complete with soft focus and music by Burt Bacharach or Henry Mancini. Indeed, his relationship with Tamar seemed to develop as if scripted. There were long walks in SoHo, deep kisses in Washington Square Park, outdoor jazz concerts, and, naturally, rainy days in bed. Better still, Tamar embraced Henry's bohemian lifestyle with more than open arms. She let Henry help her begin a collection of jazz CDs. Her wardrobe began to favor black. She even joked about selling her apartment and moving to Avenue B. And one afternoon in late May she arrived at Henry's apartment bearing gifts: his-and-hers matching berets.

"To ensure that we'll be the hippest couple in town," Tamar said.

"We aren't hip enough as it is?" Henry answered.

Indeed, Henry never pictured himself as the beret-wearing type (after all, what was so hip about Maurice Chevalier?), but Tamar took it upon herself to convince him. After making him change into a black T-shirt and jeans, she led him by the hand to his bathroom mirror. Hat perched at a jaunty angle, Henry stuffed his hands in his pockets and twisted his face into an attitude of unspeakable cool.

"It works, doesn't it?" Tamar asked.

Henry shot the mirror a vicious scowl. He liked what he saw—a downtown, slightly more corrupt alter ego.

"Oh, yeah," he decided. "Most definitely."

Unfortunately, the life of this particular beret was destined to be short. Recently, Henry had decided that the time was right to start the process of introducing Tamar to his family, and in an effort to keep things low-key, he had made a date for the following morning with his sister and niece to go to the Central Park Zoo. Proudly wearing their glorious berets, the newly hip couple walked into the park at 10:00 A.M. Coincidentally, Jill was sporting a new look as well—a pair of red high-tops, hip-hop shorts, and, for a change of pace, a Mets T-shirt. Only Melissa, who stood at her side in a plain blue maternity dress, wasn't using the outing as an excuse to make a fashion statement. Though Henry could have sworn he heard Jill whisper, "What's that thing on his head?" and her mom reply, "Shh! Be nice!" as he and Tamar approached, he quickly chalked it up to the ignorance of youth. How could a seven-year-old possibly be expected to comprehend the full implications of his exciting new piece of headwear? *She'll learn,* he thought, and seconds later graciously complimented Jill's new sneakers and saw to the introductions. Soon thereafter, the quartet headed into the zoo, ready for fun.

But it didn't take long for trouble to strike. After a successful visit to the otter pond (where Jill recited Henry's poem by heart), the group moved on to the monkey house. So far, so good, but twenty minutes on a slow-moving line through the world of penguins made Jill antsy. The second she was back outside, she grabbed Henry's beret and cut through the crowd, pretending to run for an imaginary goal line. Just as suddenly, she wheeled around and became the quarterback. "Go long," she called to Henry. Henry, who encouraged such athletic outbursts, did as he was told. "Hit me!" he cried. Jill crumpled the hat into a ball and heaved it with all her might. Horrified, Henry watched the prized beret open up in the air, catch the wind, and come to rest smack in the middle of the polar bear cage, where the largest (and seemingly hungriest) bear took the hat in his mouth. After several unsatisfying chews, he deposited the mangled remains on a rock by his swimming hole.

On the way back downtown, Henry and Tamar mourned the fate of his beret.

"It was my fault," Henry said. "I never should have run for that pass."

The couple was standing on a crowded subway platform.

"I suppose," Tamar said. Her own beret was still perched proudly on her head. "But who ever heard of using a hat for a football?"

"You don't know Jill. She's an athletic kid."

"So you said." Tamar paused as an express train going the opposite direction roared by. "But I still say she's jealous."

"You really think she did it half on purpose, huh?"

Tamar nodded. "How old was she when you were with Sheila? Three? She's used to having you all to herself."

Though he knew it was somewhat pathetic, perhaps even deviant, Henry loved the idea of his niece being envious.

"Maybe if I learn more about sports?" Tamar went on. "Watch ESPN or something. You think that'd help us get along?"

"You got along fine." Henry kissed her. "She's going to love you. She already does."

Two days later, Tamar received a carefully printed note from Jill in the mail.

> Dear Tamar,
> It was very nice meeting you. Thanks for taking me to the zoo.
> I'm sorry that I threw Henry's hat to those bears.
> Love, Jill

Though Henry guessed that the apology had been his sister's idea, it worked like a charm, Tamar was touched. To smooth things over some more, Henry bought himself a new beret. As Memorial Day approached, though, the city began to get hot. As if by mutual consent, both Henry and Tamar quietly relegated their prized hats to the back of their respective closets.

Still, despite a notable lack of image-enhancing headwear, Henry and Tamar's relationship continued to blossom. During the month of June the couple passed many important thresholds. When Tamar left a bag of toiletries and a blow-dryer at Henry's, Henry left a ragged toothbush at Tamar's. A few days later, after Tamar admired Henry's summer camp awards, with a special emphasis on the Junior Woodsman badge he had earned at age nine, Henry read Tamar's fourth-grade social studies report entitled "The Tragedy That Was Crazy Horse." Then, toward the middle of the month, Henry spent a beautiful Saturday afternoon at a three-hour French film about the loves of Louis the Fourteenth. In return, Tamar spent the next evening watching the NBA finals. To their infinite credit, both managed to stay awake.

After that came the obligatory parental introductions. One night late in the month, Henry took a long train ride to Queens and enjoyed a pot roast with Tamar's mother and father, two retired public school teachers. Though Henry was initially intimidated to discover that Mr. Brookman had taught *The Great Gatsby* for thirty years, he was touched when the ex-teacher suggested a Beatles-inspired Act Two solo for Nick: "Ah, Look at All the Careless People!" Later that week, Tamar and Henry met both of his parents and Rye for dinner at a downtown French restaurant. To Henry's delight, Tamar had not only read *The Inner You* but had come prepared with questions ("Does rubbing your kneecaps before bed really give you good dreams?"). She also listened politely when Rye went off on a rant about the rise of populism, and she flirted harmlessly with Henry's dad. Though Amanda had been invited, Mr. Mann had told Henry that they were "on a short break." Luckily, the dinner didn't fall apart when his father's new girl, a twenty-something stewardess and part-time Pilates instructor named Maureen, showed up for dessert drunk and sank her elbow into his mother's crème brûlée.

Even more than these undeniably important milestones, it was Tamar's contribution to his work that Henry valued the most. Soon her insights were steering *The Green Light!* in exciting new directions. In an effort to give the piece more depth, Henry replaced some of the more traditional, catchy numbers with darker, more contemplative songs. Though he eventually decided against Mr. Brookman's Beatles-inspired suggestion, Henry was especially proud of the plaintive ballad "They Call Me Owl Eyes, Baby," as well as a duet for Gatsby and his business partner Meyer Wolfsheim, "The Wail of the Lonely Bootlegger." Henry also added an avant-garde twelve-tone instrumental to the middle of the Act One party sequence, then wrote an intricate dance break in 7/8 time for the opening of Act Two. He began to employ moodier, more expressive keys. Of course, Tamar tried to push things too far at times. For instance, Henry refused to take a cue from the hit musical *Rent* and set the piece in the East Village. Likewise, he blanched at making Gatsby bisexual. But all in all, with Tamar's help, he felt that his work was gaining in maturity and poise—that he was creating something of which he would be truly proud.

Henry was pleased to see Tamar flex her own creative muscles as well. Slightly bored with her job in market research, she got a catalog for the New School and picked out a comedy writing workshop for the fall. As preparation, she continued to cultivate a refined sense of the absurd. Aside from a knack for funny accents, Tamar soon made a specialty of composing impromptu nonsensical songs (notable titles, "I Am a Liver Pizza" and "101 Chickens"), usually performed a capella between 2:00 and 3:00 A.M. One morning in late June, she took inanity to new levels, spontaneously renaming Henry's kitchen appliances: the coffeemaker Jesabelle, the refrigerator Mr. Mazzola, the stove Sebastian, and the blender J. J. Elmer McBean. That very night, she incorporated these new names into one of her late-night ditties.

> *J. J. Elmer McBean*
> *You bring a teardrop to my eye.*
> *Please blend for me*
> *A daiquiri*
> *At liquefy.*

At 2:00 A.M., giddy with exhaustion, such songs smacked of genius. Who couldn't love a woman so delightfully inane? So refreshingly silly?

In fact, it seemed that things were going so well that one night just after the July Fourth weekend, Henry took a deep breath and asked Tamar the question that had been brewing in the back of his mind since they had started dating. His tenth reunion was two weeks away now. Would she be willing to drive upstate to Hamden for the weekend? It was a request Henry expected Tamar to want to discuss, maybe even take a few days to think over. When the answer came back an immediate yes, he could barely believe his good fortune.

"Really?" he asked.

"Why not?" Tamar said. "Sounds like fun."

It was all Henry could do not to leap in the air and Charleston till dawn. He knew full well that many of his classmates would have already achieved the material vestiges of success—money, homes, wives, and kids. Now he could show them that he had something better, that he wasn't put on this earth to be yet another suit in yet another office, trapped in a life that was predictable and dull. No, he was put on earth for a higher purpose: to screw gorgeous women and create stunning works of art—works that would resonate down through the ages. Gay? No way! Nerd? *Not!* With Tamar on his arm, his current career pursuits would be legitimized. He'd be the guy whose star was on the rise, the bohemian artist with the bitchin' babe.

That night, Henry was so excited it took him two hours to fall asleep. In the morning, he was still flying high. So high, in fact, that Tamar took the bull by the horns and dared him to really live on the edge, to do something to put his fellow alums back on the ropes. He had worn his hair in the same conservative style for years now—medium length, parted to the side. Wouldn't it better suit his new persona to glide into his reunion with one of those hipper Village cuts? Maybe even with a streak or two of yellow thrown in for an extra dose of kick-ass funk?

Once again, Tamar led him to the mirror.

"Think how sexy you'll look with it clipped short," Tamar said. "Not quite a crew cut, but, well, a George Clooney kind of thing."

"George Clooney, huh?"

"Yeah."

Henry nodded. He could live with that.

"And then the killer—a dash of yellow . . . right there!" Tamar brushed her hand through the left side of his hair. "Your classmates won't know what hit them."

The more Henry studied his reflection, the more he began to feel that Tamar was right. A yellow streak would be the pièce de résistance, the final masterful touch that would make his classmates shake their heads and wish that they were in his shoes—shoes that had shunned the easy path and dared to set out on the road less traveled.

"So?" Tamar said. "What do you say?"

Henry looked to Tamar. Ever since he had moved to the Village, he had secretly envied the cooler set. Now Tamar was showing him how to be one of them. A run-of-the-mill "I like it" wouldn't come close enough to conveying his true feelings. Instead, he picked his love up by the waist, then attempted to carry her to the bedroom in order to express his appreciation more fully. Unfortunately, halfway there he accidentally walked right into the coffee table. Laughing, the couple fell harmlessly to the sofa.

"I take it you're OK with it?" Tamar said.

Henry held her tight. He could only imagine the galvanizing effect his presence would have on the Hamden campus now. Perhaps classmates would ask for autographs? Maybe even Sheila's husband?

"Oh, yeah," he said, kissing her again. "It's terrific."

As excited as he was, however, Henry was still smart enough to realize that to hesitate was to lose his nerve. After Tamar finally left for work, he jumped in the shower, threw on some clothes, and marched straight across town to the Astor Place barbershop, a salon known for its punk dos. Once inside, he was directed to Zoe, a youngish woman clad in purple cutoffs, black hiking boots, and a yellow halter top that exposed a pierced belly button, which was hooked by a thin chain to her pierced lip. As Henry slid into the chair, he noticed a tattoo on her right shoulder, an intricate etching of two skeletons. Underneath were the words MY PARENTS.

"A funky cut and a streak or two," she said. "I gotcha."

It crossed Henry's mind that engaging such a person to perform a task so delicate was tantamount to hiring Genghis Khan to renovate one's bedroom. Suddenly nervous, Henry thought it wise to lay down some ground rules.

"Now, don't go overboard or anything. I—"

"Relax." She smiled. Henry suddenly had a thought worthy of his mom. Why did such a pretty girl have to dye, pierce, and tattoo herself into a state of indisputable ugliness? "I won't send you out of here with an orange Mohawk. Scout's honor."

As it turned out, Zoe was in complete command of her chosen profession. As she let fly with scissors and comb, Henry sat transfixed, happily watching the new him bloom before his eyes, a man—no, a dude—better still, a *stud*—with a closely cropped do and a streak of yellow (he opted for one) down the left side. When it was all done, Henry handed Zoe a five-dollar tip and floated home on the fumes of his stunning hipness, all traces of geekitude in permanent remission.

That night was one of the happiest in Henry's life. Not only did Tamar approve of the new look, but she took him to their favorite bistro to celebrate. For the next two weeks Henry's work suffered. Why work when he could be spending his time sneaking peeks at himself in his bathroom mirror? "You are good-looking," he would whisper. "You are smart. Women do love you!" It was all he could do not to kiss his reflection.

When the big day finally arrived, Henry continued his one-man admiration society on the New York Thruway. Constant reevaluation in the rearview mirror of their economy-size Rent-A-Wreck assured him that the desired effect had most assuredly been achieved: unspeakable coolness—coolness to make his classmates, Sheila in particular, shudder. In fact, she might well see the error of her ways, perhaps even throw herself at his feet and beg Henry to take her back. But would he? Of course not. He had already traded up for Tamar. "Sorry, babe," he'd say. "The USS *Stud* has sailed." Upon hearing this news, she would flop on the floor like a freshly caught trout. As stunned classmates looked on, campus security would be forced to subdue her with a tranquilizer dart, then take her by stretcher to the infirmary for observation. The next Hamden alumni magazine would provide the denouement: Sheila had divorced her husband and moved to Peru to join a convent for wayward preppies. Happily occupied by these and similar thoughts, Henry found that the trip went by in a blink. By the time they reached the outskirts of Hamden, New York, he was practically salivating at the chance to get the ball rolling.

He didn't have to wait long. After a quick tour of the campus, Henry and Tamar changed clothes in their assigned dorm—Henry into a vest and jeans, Tamar into a short, strapless dress (black, of course)—and made their way across campus to the reunion cocktail party. As he began to bump into fellow alums, Henry was delighted to see that the haircut and Tamar, working in tandem, were making the precise impression he had hoped for. Some came right out and said it. "Wild haircut, man. You look good." Others simply adopted an attitude of subdued reverence. Then there were those who openly ogled Tamar. Best of all, though, was the woman from

Henry's freshman hall who stopped him to gush about how much she had admired the cantata for brass, prepared piano, and bassoon (cryptically entitled "Rhapsody for a Melon") he had written sophomore year. Indeed, by the time Henry reached the alumni center, he was walking on air, a slave to his own radiant glory. Let the news be spread unto the four corners of the campus! Henry Mann hath gone forth into the world of the arts—and Lord have mercy, how he hath conquered!

Sadly enough, Henry's carefully constructed sense of cool wasn't equal to the supreme challenge. As fate would have it, Sheila was standing no more than twenty feet from the entrance, sipping a glass of wine, when Henry floated into the reception. The minute he saw her, he was jolted out of his narcissistic reverie, consigned back to the world of mortals. Though Henry knew it was unrealistic to think that his ex would have completely lost her looks, nothing prepared him for what she had become: even more beautiful. Indeed, her hair—so blonde it bordered on white—cascaded all the way down to her lower back. Her skin looked whiter, smoother. The slight hint of baby fat she had carried into her midtwenties had disappeared. Even the hint of crow's feet lent her face a welcome touch of maturity. In short, the girl was gone. In her place stood a woman, poised and elegant. Henry suddenly remembered the first time he had seen her, on a hike during freshman week. Awed by her looks, he had placed her in the "out of my league" file and barely said another word to her until they met again in an American literature seminar the fall of their junior year. How could he have known that almost fifteen years later he would find her more beautiful still?

"Is that her?" Tamar asked.

"Yeah," Henry gulped. "That's her."

"Hmmmm."

"What's that mean?"

"She's pretty, alright, but boy—even preppier than you described."

Indeed, Sheila was wearing a yellow cotton dress that might have cost five hundred dollars. She looked every bit the suburban housewife, sharing cocktails at a lawn party.

"Yeah," Henry agreed. "She always was."

"Totally wrong for you," Tamar said.

Though Henry still felt that attraction—an attraction that dredged up old feelings, feelings that bordered on love—he knew Tamar was right. Then, just like that, Sheila glanced his way and smiled. The next thing he knew she was cutting confidently through the crowd. A nice-looking man in a white tennis shirt was beside her, holding her hand. The husband, no doubt. Henry felt his mouth go dry.

"Hi, Henry."

"Sheila . . . hi . . ."

Henry leaned forward to kiss her cheek, then thought better of it and pulled back. Sheila kissed him anyway, then turned to Mr. Tennis Shirt.

"Henry, I want you to meet Frank."

It was at moments such as these that Henry wished he carried a blackjack. Unarmed, he forced himself to simply extend his hand and smile.

"So nice to meet you," he said. "Oh, and this is Tamar."

Two handshakes later the quartet was poised for conversation, but just as Sheila and Henry were fumbling for a neutral subject to get them started, none other than Hans, the Shakespearean scholar and lacrosse player, stopped by to say hello. Though Henry was more than tempted to inform Frank that this was the gentleman who had fucked out his wife's brains junior year, he managed to hold his tongue. When Hans (who now, to Henry's surprise, taught eighth-grade English) took his leave, the conversation finally gained some momentum.

As it turned out, Henry's information had been largely correct. Sheila had moved to Seattle and met Frank three months later. They had gotten married nine months after that. "I just knew," Sheila said with a giggle (a comment that caused Henry to consider kicking her in the shins at the same time that her giggle reminded him of the one time he had tried to suck her big toe). Now they were the proud parents of Megan, a chipper one-year-old. To Henry's dismay, the conversation then became rooted in Megan's fledging efforts to join the ranks of the ambulatory. As a result, Henry found himself dipping and weaving in and out of the discussion.

He realized that this very room had been the site of the big blowout party senior week—the party where, on a whim, he had gotten down on one knee and drunkenly proposed, an offer Sheila had drunkenly accepted. Now he remembered how their friends had taken them to an all-night diner to celebrate. More painfully, he recalled how the following afternoon, while they were having wine and cheese on a blanket on her dorm-room floor, naked, Sheila had informed Henry that she was accepting a job in France. Further, she would be rooming with Josh, another hulking lacrosse player. Though Sheila claimed they were just friends, Henry had had his doubts. Now Henry glanced around the room. Thank God, that miserable bastard wasn't here. Hans was bad enough.

"So, Henry? How's the music biz?"

Henry blinked. Apparently, while he was revisiting the various ups and downs of senior week, Sheila and Tamar had begun to hit it off. Left alone, Frank had taken a bold step.

"Oh, pretty good," Henry replied. "Pretty good."

Drawn into a one-on-one, Henry was forced to leave his memories behind and focus on the enemy—but Frank turned out to be another Adam, rich and disgustingly likable. Indeed, he seemed so interested in *The Green Light!* that Henry almost thought he was going to whip out his checkbook and invest on the spot. In fact, after years of devoting countless hours to detesting him, Henry began to find himself having a nice time. To his horror, Henry could almost imagine (gasp!) being his friend. No wonder Sheila had fallen for him the minute she moved west. He was everything Henry wasn't, with an emphasis on rich and chiseled.

As the conversation shifted and Frank began to describe a new line of software Microsoft had coming down the pike, Henry found himself remembering the day Sheila had pulled up in front of their Brooklyn apartment in a rented moving van; despite Herculean efforts to hold it together, he had cried when he and Sheila had hugged good-bye. Once again, Henry reminded himself that Sheila wasn't his type, but with a quick glance to his left, where she was talking to Tamar, he couldn't help wondering what things would've been like if they had stayed together. Suddenly, Henry transported himself out of the Hamden gym into a parallel universe where, instead of handing him his walking papers, Sheila had offered him her hand, a universe in which he was the grand prize winner. And Frank? Well, he was back at A&W working that fried dough machine.

Indeed, a struggling composer no longer, Henry was now the world-famous multimillionaire who had gone public with Henricon, a biotech company that had developed an adventurous new procedure used to treat certain brain cancers through gene therapy. As the first scientist to clone a goat, Henry adorned the cover of every leading science journal. "I admit that my choice of cloning subject is a bit unusual," he would comment in *People* magazine when it picked him as one of the fifty sexiest men of the decade. "But the cell structure of the goat's left hoof has fascinating ramifications for the cure of many debilitating spinal conditions."

Henry could see it all. After a long day in the lab discovering exciting new ways to better the world, he would return by train to suburban paradise: Scarsdale. Ambling home, he might stop to pick up a quart of milk or take a quick swing at a local softball game. Soon enough he would round the corner of Henry Way (so named after he had donated six million dollars to the Scarsdale Public Library) to find Sheila, his love, waiting on the doorstep of their modest twelve-room home with three-year-old Jane (for Austen) hugging her knee and baby Art (for Tatum) in her arms. "Daddy!" Jane would cry and break away from Mom and bound across the spacious lawn. As she leapt into Henry's arms, he would transform from scientific genius into Superdad. Over the next two hours he would change diapers, construct elaborate dollhouses out of Lincoln Logs, oversee finger painting, heat up the chicken fingers, run the bath, lay out the pj's, read the story, and then, after the kids were down, roll up his sleeves and prepare a sumptuous six-course dinner.

Yes, it would be a busy life. Sometimes hectic. Occasionally exasperating. But always fulfilling. Because through it all, there would be Sheila. Sheila the beautiful. Sheila the well coiffed. Sheila the loving mom. Sheila the high-powered stock analyst/homemaker. Sheila who would still look hot in panties at sixty. Sheila who would spend all day at a fund-raiser for cystic fibrosis and still have the energy at night to treat Henry to a fervent reenactment of *The Doctor's Wife*.

So what if Henry didn't really want Sheila anymore anyway? Who cared if she had dumped him four years earlier and never looked back? For one brief instant, they were perfect.

"Well, I suppose we should probably mingle."

Henry blinked, and just like that he was back at the Hamden gym. Sheila stood before him with Frank and Tamar on either side.

"Great," Henry said. "I mean, great seeing you, Sheila."

She gave him a funny look—Sheila was as well acquainted as anyone with the unusual ramblings of Henry's imagination. Though Henry had always suspected that she was secretly horrified, she had always claimed to find it endearing.

"OK," she said now. "What are you smiling at?"

Henry shrugged. "Me? Smiling?"

"Same old Henry," Sheila said. "Always dreaming."

"Hey," Henry said. "Keeps me young."

With a single glance at Tamar, he let his suburban dream world and career as a world-famous scientist dissolve. Yes, he had loved Sheila. He even loved the idea of a life in a beautiful suburb. But deep down he knew that it wasn't for him. On the first day of home-ownership he'd most likely break the lawn-mower blade on the curb, then crash the minivan into a stop sign. Henry turned to Frank.

"Hey, really nice chatting with you." To his surprise, he meant it.

"Likewise," Frank said.

They shook hands.

"I'm glad you two hit it off," Sheila said. "But when's my turn?" She looked to Tamar, her new best bud. "Do you mind if I steal him for a bit tomorrow afternoon so we can really catch up?"

If Tamar was surprised or jealous, she didn't show it. "Fine by me."

Frank, in his infinite maturity, agreed as well.

"Sound good?" Sheila said. "Henry? The snack bar, say two o'clock?"

"Why, sure." What else could he say?

After a round of good-byes, Tamar shrugged. "She's actually quite nice."

Later, back in their dorm room, Henry couldn't help wondering why Sheila wanted to see him again. Tamar had her own theories.

"Simple," she said, as they pushed the two flimsy single beds side by side. "She's either going to apologize for how she dumped you or she's going to talk about me."

Henry, who had reverted to his previous fantasy and assumed that Sheila would, in fact, be begging him to take her back, was slightly disappointed.

"Oh, no," he said. "She's not the type to apologize. She seems friendly, but she's hard as nails."

Tamar shrugged. "Then she wants to talk about me."

"No way."

"Yeah, I think so."

"Really?"

"Really."

The next afternoon, while Tamar retired to the shade of a tree with the *New York Times* and Frank hit the Hamden links, Sheila (country-club casual in a pair of white tennis shorts and polo shirt) and Henry (starving-artist casual in cutoffs and a GO NBA T-shirt) grabbed a couple of sodas and wandered out to the college green. The day was clear. So clear, in fact, that Henry could see the top of the Catskill Mountains that surrounded the campus. Closer to home, he noticed a couple, college age, walk by arm in arm.

"There goes us," he said as he and Sheila sprawled out on the grass. "Ten years ago."

"No way!" Sheila laughed. "We were never that young, were we?"

"Well, you were never that young," Henry said. "But me? Back in college I was about nine."

"I had my moments, too," Sheila said. She made a face. "Like Hans, for instance. I mean, what was I thinking?"

"About his biceps, probably."

"Couldn't have been his brains."

Using Hans as a springboard, Henry and Sheila launched into a discussion of old times, with special emphasis on the memories that could be placed in the "good" column. When the conversation veered back to the present, Henry, to his infinite credit, asked several questions in regard to the development of Megan and even admired a picture or two. It seemed that Tamar was wrong—Sheila wanted to simply catch up, to spend a pleasant afternoon, maybe heal a few wounds in the process. But Henry had been lured into a false sense of security. Just as he was beginning to feel it was time to pack for the drive home, Sheila got to her real agenda.

"By the way," she said. "Your girlfriend, Tamar? She's all wrong for you."

The boldness of the attack, especially following an hour of light banter, caught Henry completely off guard.

"What?"

Sheila met Henry's eyes, seemingly relaxed, oblivious to the fact that what she said might be construed as out of line.

"Tamar. She's wrong for you."

She stared across the green with a somewhat annoying serenity. Henry glared at her. Who the hell was she to tell him anything? This was the other side of the sweet, intelligent woman he had chatted with the previous night. The woman who stated her mind whether or not her opinion had been asked for. Unfortunately, Henry knew from experience that she was often right. Though he should have told her to fuck off, he couldn't resist asking what she meant.

"It's just a sense, that's all," Sheila said. "Like when I talked to her about your music."

"You talked about my music?"

"Yeah. She didn't seem to really understand it, you know? Like she was trying to make you into a bohemian Stravinsky or something. I don't know . . . but I feel she doesn't know what she wants. Isn't grounded. Listen, I hope I'm wrong. She's a smart girl. Great wit. Very pretty in an ethnic sort of way . . . and she seems to be crazy about you. But still . . ." Sheila shrugged. "I don't know." Then she said something Henry couldn't quite believe. "You're a special person, Henry."

"Oh, please."

"No, you are. I feel bad about how things ended between us. I mean, about how I ended things."

The apology. Tamar was two for two.

"Which time are you referring to?" Henry asked.

Sheila smiled weakly. "The last time. I was out the door pretty fast. But you've got to admit that it was the right move. I mean, look at my life. I live in a frigging suburb. You'd rather be dead."

Despite his brief, glorious career as Superdad and founder of Henricon, Henry knew she was right.

"Yeah," he said. "I suppose I'm a city kid."

"You know what you need, Henry?" Sheila said. "Someone who really gets you. I mean, deep down."

Henry looked away, suddenly furious. Who was Sheila—a woman

who had dumped him twice, after all—to tell him what he needed? Though tempted to assault her with a diatribe he would undoubtedly regret, Henry forced himself to draw in a deep breath of clean country air and look out over the Hamden green. The Catskills rose above him. As corny as it seemed, he felt that his love for Tamar was as strong as those mountains—and as lasting. Indeed, he realized that he loved her more than he had ever loved anyone else. Including Sheila.

"Tamar's the best thing that's happened to me in ages," he said finally. He couldn't resist a dig. "Maybe ever."

Sheila nodded. "Point taken. I just want you to be happy, that's all."

Again, Henry was tempted by that diatribe. But how could he? As much as it pained him to admit it, he believed Sheila was telling the truth. She wanted him to be happy, to assuage her guilt if nothing else.

"Anyway," she said, standing up. "We've got a plane to catch."

"Yeah," Henry said.

"Bye, Henry."

He rose to his feet and kissed her cheek. It seemed silly not to.

"Bye."

With that, she walked across the green. Then she suddenly wheeled back around.

"One more thing?"

Henry sighed, resigned to more criticism, a dog waiting to be kicked.

"Yeah?"

"Your hair. Lose the yellow streak, OK?"

Henry watched Sheila walk a good hundred feet down the campus, then turn right behind the science building. Once again, she got the last word. It was maddening. Worse, what she said planted a pernicious seed of doubt. Packing the car for home, Henry caught his reflection in the sideview mirror and cringed, suddenly feeling less like a hip George Clooney than like the Bride of Frankenstein.

"Christ," he whispered. "I look like a world-class idiot."

"What?" Tamar said.

"My hair—look at it!"

"I am," Tamar said. "It looks great."

Henry simply glanced in the mirror again and grimaced, suddenly positive that his classmates had spent the weekend humoring him. He was the class joke. A nerd trying to hide behind a ridiculous haircut.

Tamar put her arms around his shoulders.

"Did Sheila say something?"

Henry nodded sheepishly.

"I'm not surprised. She'd do anything to bring you down."

"What do you mean by that?"

Tamar pulled away and leaned back against the hood. "Well, I felt funny saying this last night, but I didn't like her at all. She's an ice queen, Henry. Really closed up. Very manipulative, you know?"

Henry nodded. In a way, these dueling put-downs were flattering. But also confusing. Which one should he believe?

"And your hair looks good."

Henry glanced in the sideview mirror. "You don't think I look too much like a skunk, do you?"

Tamar brushed a hand through his streak and considered the question. "Maybe. But a cute skunk. A punk skunk."

"Oh, yeah?" Henry allowed himself a small smile. "I thought I was your pigdog?"

"You were," Tamar said. "But now you're even better. You're my pig-skunk-dog-punk. How's that?"

That was fine by Henry. Reassured, he finally finished packing the car. After a stop for dinner an hour or so down the road, though, Sheila's words came back to haunt him—so much so that when Tamar leaned her head against the passenger-side window and fell asleep, he forced himself to take a step back and view their relationship as an impartial observer. Was she really as good as she seemed? Certainly, she had her faults. She smoked, tended to run late (sometimes even neglecting to call ahead), and rarely made the bed. But these were minor grievances. Others were more troublesome. Like the fact that she was in touch with several of her ex-boyfriends, including Eddie, a sax player who had blown through town in mid-May. And another (Rick, was it?) who was scheduled to crash on her couch for a long weekend toward the beginning of August. But Henry had been trying to work on what Tamar had called his "jealous side." After all, the ability to maintain solid friendships with ex-lovers was a sign of maturity, wasn't it? Something to admire. Just as Henry admired the hard work Tamar had put in with her therapist. All eight years of it. It took courage to wrestle with one's demons three times a week. Besides, who was he to question someone else's mental state, anyway? Self-absorbed, prone to periodic bouts of whining, and sensitive to a fault, Henry knew he was no bargain. And the good news? He was poor. Moreover, he spent half of his waking hours lost in grandiose fantasies that had virtually no chance of ever coming true.

What was really amazing, though (at least to Henry), was that Tamar didn't think his fantasies at all unrealistic—at least not insofar as they pertained to his career. This was where he had Sheila dead in the water. No, Tamar got his music completely. She was just pushing him to be better, that's all. Where Sheila had humored his artistic ambitions, Tamar championed them. With her help he would make it to the top of the proverbial heap. She believed in him.

"Screw you, Sheila," he said to himself. "You don't know me. Not anymore."

With those words, she was summarily dismissed. At best, she was well intentioned but wrong; at worst, a pernicious bitch who, not wanting Henry for herself, would do anything to sabotage his chance of future happiness with someone else. Soon the George Washington Bridge rose up on the horizon. Tamar stirred and stretched.

"Wow," she said. "Have I been asleep since dinner?"

"Yep."

Tamar rubbed her eyes, then looked up.

"God."

"What?"

The New York City skyline loomed before them, majestic and welcoming.

"I forget how beautiful that is sometimes."

With that, she slid over in the seat and leaned her head on Henry's shoulder. As Henry drove the car up the ramp toward the bridge, he took a good look. Yes, the city was beautiful. It was his to conquer. And he had the right woman by his side to help him do battle.

8

jill

as it turned out, the trip back to Hamden did Henry more good than he ever could have predicted. No, Sheila hadn't crawled across the campus, licked his kneecaps, and pledged her eternal love. To Henry's surprise, something even better had happened. By the end of the weekend, he realized that had she actually done it, he would have been a fool to take her back. Over the past four years Sheila had been like a mosquito buzzing around his ear, a memory he could never quite slap away. Now the buzzing was gone, and in the sweet silence, Henry felt free to take some risks, to flex his creative muscles in a way he never had before. Look out, Broadway! Watch out, Stephen Sondheim! Henry Mann was back and dressed to compose!

So when an old high school friend invited Henry to the country the first week of August, he said no. When his father asked Henry to join him in the Berkshires with Maureen, he declined. Henry even passed up a day trip to Coney Island with Doug and Ellen. Though it was the time of year when most New Yorkers took a break, Henry realized that his muse wasn't in a vacationing sort of mood.

After all, there were new songs to be written. Old ones to be re-
vised. Lyrics to hone. Dialogue to write. Whatever needed to be done
to make *The Green Light!* as good as it could be. Of course, Henry
did do some socializing. To avoid eviction and keep food in the
house, he worked his shifts at Albright. He saw Tamar, obviously.
But in truth, at the beginning of August she was busy entertaining
Rick, ex-boyfriend number two, and it is a testament to the intensity of Henry's creative fire that he didn't even throw a tantrum
when Rick extended his visit to a week. So what if he and Tamar
were sharing a one-bedroom apartment? Rick was in the other
room. Henry had seen the foldout couch with his own eyes. Why
should he be jealous? Not with Tamar continuing to lend a critical
ear, cheering him on, making invaluable suggestions. In fact, as
The Green Light! started to gel, Henry even began to consider her
most radical idea of all, an idea she claimed would set his musical
apart and guarantee it lasting success. Tamar encouraged Henry to
make the main character, Gatsby, black.

Initially, Henry thought the idea ludicrous. A twelve-tone dance
break was one thing (after all, Bernstein had worked a twelve-tone
fugue into *West Side Story*), but changing the race of his main character? It was absurd—the equivalent of making Huck Finn Chinese, or Madame Bovary an American Indian—but this was one
suggestion that Tamar wouldn't let lie. She had accepted Henry's
decision to keep the show set in Long Island without argument.
Likewise his decision to keep Gatsby straight. Skin color was another matter, though, and as she pushed, Henry was surprised to
find himself becoming swayed.

Her main argument was this: Gatsby was the quintessential
American dreamer—a man who grew up poor, became rich by
mysterious means, then used his wealth to attract Daisy, the upper-
class girl he loved. Wouldn't Gatsby's quest to cross class lines be
even more resonant if such a character were African American,
trying to woo the white woman of his dreams? It was a good point.
And as Tamar pressed her advantage, Henry thought of another

compelling reason to make the change: It would make *The Green Light!* the first serious musical since *Show Boat* to feature an interracial romance. It seemed absurd that Broadway hadn't investigated this delicate issue in greater depth. If he could pull it off, it would set his show apart, perhaps even earn it that most coveted of all accolades: "Groundbreaking!"

Still, Henry knew there would be risks. If the idea was poorly executed, the criticism would be intense. He might be chided for taking artistic liberties with an acknowledged classic. Some critics might even get after him for being racist. Anything was possible. But one afternoon in mid-August these concerns were rendered moot when Henry sat down at the piano and found himself improvising what started as a traditional twelve-bar blues but soon turned into a rousing gospel number. It was only then that he saw the musical implications. With a black Gatsby, he could give the score a jazzier feel—follow in the footsteps of one of his greatest heroes, George Gershwin, and turn the show into a modern-day *Porgy and Bess*. In fact, Henry grew so excited that he called Tamar and played her the song (later entitled "Praise the Valley of Ashes!") over the phone. With her seal of approval—an eloquent "That frigging rocks!"—he was off. For the next few weeks, Henry devoted himself even more assiduously to his work, reworking the script to take into account the new racial angle. Just like that, a first draft was complete. That was when Tamar, in late August, deemed the show ready to face the public.

"You won't really know what you have until you get it up on its feet, right?" she said. They were having dinner at his place, spaghetti prepared with the assistance of the trusty stove, Sebastian. "Do a reading like Glenn."

Henry took a healthy sip of wine. Any mention of *Hoo, Hoo! Haw, Haw!* still made his skin crawl. To his surprise, Glenn had been approached by a serious off-Broadway producer who was currently trying to raise funds for another workshop and possible production. Of course, Henry was jealous. On the other hand, he figured that if a piece of pretentious crap about three talking chimps could attract professional interest, then *The Green Light!* could be on Broadway in a week. Still, he wasn't sure. Though he had already spent a solid six months on the project, he had sometimes wondered if he'd ever have the guts to show it around at all. He knew that to write a musical based on one of the seminal works of American literature was a risky endeavor, perhaps even a bit presumptuous. If he pulled it off—if he managed to successfully reinvent the story of *The Great Gatsby* for the stage—it would be a stunning triumph. On the other hand, if it was bad, it could make *Hoo, Hoo! Haw, Haw!* seem like *Hamlet.*

"I don't know," Henry said.

"Henry. You've got to get it out one day, right?" She took his hands. "What's the problem?"

Henry sighed. "No problem." He smiled. "I'm just scared it'll suck."

Tamar took her own sip of wine. For a moment her slightly cross expression reminded Henry of the look on his mother's face after he had forgotten to take out the trash.

"First of all," Tamar said, "it won't suck." Then she kissed him. "Second of all, even if it does, I'll still love you."

"You will?"

Tamar considered the question. "Well, maybe."

Preparations got under way the day after Labor Day. First, Henry booked a small theater on 107th Street off Broadway for October 16, a Friday. Then Tamar got into the act. Drawing upon her marketing expertise, she wrote letters, made calls, and generally did whatever she could to convince theater pros from around town to come see it. Even more important, she bolstered Henry's spirits through a series of final rewrites. In fact, she seemed so devoted, so engaged in his life, that Henry soon began to consider broaching a subject that he'd kept in the back of his mind for the past five months. Henry had wanted to ask Tamar to marry him that very first night by the fireplace back in April. Though he had quickly relegated those thoughts to semipermanent cold storage, as work progressed on his show and he and Tamar came to seem more and more like a team, Henry thought it time to bring them out to thaw. Doug had once told him that he had proposed to Ellen when "it felt right." If what Henry was feeling toward Tamar didn't qualify as "right," then he didn't know what ever would. True, they hadn't known each other very long. True, he wanted to be sure not to scare away his future wife with a premature proposal. But with every fiber in his being crying out, "Marry her, goddammit! Marry her!" and with the shining example of those eight weddings, how could he hold back? After a few days' serious thought, including two hour-long consultations in 34 North (the vote: Glenn and Chimp Two, who contributed her opinion via speakerphone, propose; Ellen, wait a month or two; Doug, wait at least another six months), Henry realized he had no choice. The simple facts were these: He loved her. He wanted to be with her forever. Therefore, the only logical thing to do was to ask Tamar Brookman to be his lawfully wedded wife. It wasn't a question of if, but of when.

The decision made, Henry immediately began to allot major minutes to imagining exactly how he would do it when the time came. A romantic at heart, Henry wanted the moment to be special, a dream proposal for his dream girl. Though his first two choices were financially prohibitive (a weekend in Paris or renting a tropical island for a month), he soon came up with a list of workable alternatives:

1) A bubble bath, complete with candlelight, incense, mood music, and, the pièce de résistance, the engagement ring placed over the mast of a toy boat.

2) A singing proposal at a karaoke bar, featuring rewritten lyrics to "A Whiter Shade of Pale" or "Like a Rolling Stone."

3) The old standby, champagne and caviar atop the Empire State Building.

Each choice had its pluses. The Empire State Building would give the event historical resonance, while the karaoke would lend a humorous (and hopefully not too embarrassing) touch. Aside from being the cheapest option, the bath would offer complete privacy along with the added benefit of complete nudity.

The choice of locale was only part of the problem, though. Henry wanted to mark the occasion with words that would properly convey the full depth of his feeling. In that spirit, he began work on "Ode to the Woman I Adore," a six-page poem he hoped to imbue with heretofore unrecorded depths of feeling—a poem engineered to obliterate any doubts on the part of his intended with a single stanza. Unfortunately, Henry had set himself a goal that Shakespeare himself wouldn't have been able to match. When it became evident that he would be unable to capture the full intensity of his emotions in verse, he scrapped it and tried his luck with a slow ballad, "She's the Girl I Call Tamar."

> *(Rough draft—first verse)*
> *She's the girl I call Tamar*
> *She's daring. She's winning.*
> *She's brighter than a star.*
> *And I'm just beginning.*

Unfortunately, the second, third, and fourth drafts were no better. With his muse on extended vacation, Henry made a decision: When the moment was right, he would simply speak from the heart and hope for the best.

As for a proposal site, Henry soon got a daring idea. A week before his reading, he and Tamar were going to Adam and Melissa's for dinner to help celebrate the birth of their new son, Adam Junior. At two weeks old he exuded the same inner confidence as his dad. Henry was already intimidated. After calling his sister to RSVP, Henry remembered a similar dinner nine or so years earlier: the dinner where Adam, seemingly out of the blue, had dropped to one knee and asked Melissa to be his wife—in front of not only her parents but her entire family! Henry remembered being awed by Adam's guts. True, it had been somewhat corny, but classy as hell—a romantic gesture that had left Melissa, not to mention his mother, in tears. Even Henry had felt his eyes grow moist.

The more he thought about it, the more Henry knew that he had to do the same thing. Lay aside his insecurities and pull an Adam. There was no need to poll the court of 34 North on this one. No, Henry had the confidence to act unilaterally. And why shouldn't he? After all, he felt as good about himself as he had in years—possibly ever. Not only was he dating a terrific woman, but he was working on a show destined to do humanity the ultimate favor by closing down *Mamma Mia!* for good. Unspeakable riches were certain to follow. Better still, his parents weren't invited. Henry knew he could never pull off such a stunt in front of his mom, and it would be too distracting to watch his father making out with Amanda—or Maureen or whoever—while he was trying to pop the question. No, Adam, Melissa, and Jill were the perfect audience to watch him safeguard a family tradition. In their presence, he would drop to one knee, reach deep within, and create his own Hallmark moment, a memory he and Tamar would cherish for years to come.

So the decision was made. Still, Henry knew there was a final step to take. He was lacking the essential piece of hardware needed to complete the enterprise: the engagement ring. Though Adam had given Melissa a veritable rock (three carats), Henry's budget was a bit more modest. Even one carat in the simplest setting cost much more than he could have imagined. Though he considered trading down to sapphire, he reminded himself that he was only planning on getting married once, and for the moment to work the way he envisioned it (i.e., Melissaesque weeping), Henry required a diamond. As Glenn told him, "They look like cheap glass to me, but women love 'em." After some shopping around, Henry settled on a jeweler recommended by a friend of his father's. One carat, emerald setting. Cost, $4,500. By the time all was said and done, Henry was cleaned out, but that was alright. Wouldn't he make back the cost of the ring in years of everlasting love?

The first week of October, Henry was consumed by his reading. Rehearsals by day, rewrites by night. Just like that, the night of the big dinner was upon him. Though the sky was overcast and rain predicted, the temperature was a perfect sixty degrees with a classic autumnal chill in the air. Wearing a brown blazer, a denim shirt, and khakis (he hadn't wanted to give anything away by getting too dressy), Henry took a subway uptown and, ring in pocket, made his way to the Lexington Avenue Barnes & Noble to wait for his date. That morning he had called Tamar to subtly encourage her to be on time, passing off his own anxiety onto his sister, saying with a sigh, "You know how she gets." Despite Tamar's assurances that she would be prompt, Henry had a funny feeling that she was going to be held up. Usually, he took her tardiness in stride, but tonight was to be different. Didn't she know that this was going to be the happiest night of her life? That within hours she would be weeping tears of unadulterated joy?

Apparently not. By five after six Henry was already on edge. As five minutes grew to ten, he grew more annoyed. At fifteen, he was deep into a furious daydream that featured Tamar in bed with Eddie, Rick, and various imaginary members of the ex-boyfriend brigade. At twenty, she was begging Henry for his forgiveness, dropping down on a knee and proposing to him! At twenty-five, she was disloyal once more, this time in bed with Robert at his Fairfield mansion. Robert was just reaching for a bottle of champagne when Tamar finally emerged from the subway.

"God, I'm sorry!" she called, running up. "But you'll never guess who called as I was leaving work. Robert!"

"Robert?"

"Yeah. He said he was in the neighborhood. So we grabbed a quick drink."

Henry was stunned. Had he somehow acquired magical powers? Or had something unprecedented in the long history of his fantasy life finally occurred? Had one of them actually hit near the mark?

"You're kidding," he said.

"No," Tamar said. "Again, sorry to be so late."

She gave him a kiss. Henry forced a smile, still not quite able to comprehend what had happened. Tamar had actually seen Robert. The millionaire investor. The sailor. The asshole. Evil incarnate. Indeed, if ever there was just cause for taking his jealous side out for a spin, this was it. Unfortunately, Henry's own plans stood in his way. How could he throw a fit and then hope to propose an hour later? He had no choice but to stick to the high road.

"So," he choked. "How is he?"

"Fine, I guess," Tamar said. "Same dull life. Making money, sailing his boat. It's so narrow, you know?"

Henry smiled. Clearly, Tamar was rewarding him for his measured response, doing what she could to let him know that he had nothing to worry about. Though he didn't fully believe her, he appreciated the effort.

"Yeah," he said wryly. "Money is such a drag."

Tamar smiled. "I hate it, too."

"Liar," Henry said.

Tamar kissed him again.

"Relax," she said. "Robert means nothing to me, OK?"

Henry hesitated.

"Henry? I mean it."

Henry forced himself to relax. After all, it was just a drink.

"I know you do," he said finally.

Apparently, Tamar wasn't so sure. In an effort to put Henry's mind completely at ease, she dedicated the short walk to Melissa's apartment to putting an even more negative spin on the man who now qualified as ex-boyfriend number three. It was an impressive performance. Indeed, in five short minutes, she dismissed Robert's sailboat obsession ("a macho fetish"), his unhappy marriage ("repressed Catholic wife"), and even his children ("spoiled idiots"). Though Henry realized that he was an easy mark, by the time they reached 93rd and Fifth, he had caved completely. Clearly, Tamar was telling him how much she loved him. What else could possibly matter?

Still, as he stepped into Melissa's cavernous lobby, Henry began to feel his nerves. Given the circumstances, he knew that there was more than love at stake. The more germane question was whether Tamar was ready to make a lifelong commitment. Of course, Henry had assumed the answer was yes. Was pretty certain of it, in fact. (Hadn't he just dropped his life savings on the goddamned ring?) Despite the expenditure, though, Henry knew he couldn't be absolutely sure. On the elevator, he glanced at his almost-fiancée and, for the first time since he had decided to ask her to be his wife, imagined the unthinkable: what it would be like if she said no. In front of his family, no less! Henry shuddered. He had no desire to be the first grown man Jill had ever seen cry.

"What're you thinking?" Tamar asked.

"Thinking?" Henry squeaked. After a second of stammering, he rallied. "Oh, just how pretty you look."

Indeed, Henry was constantly amazed at how Tamar was able to make traditional corporate attire, in this case a conservative blue business suit, appear sexy. She squeezed his hand. Seconds later they were at Melissa's door.

Over the past four years or so, when Henry visited his sister, there had been one thing he could always count on come rain or shine—that Jill would be there to greet him. Tonight was no different. Better still, she was wearing her favorite Knicks jersey with a big 3, the number worn by Stephon Marbury, their star point guard, on the back. Definitely a good omen. With Stephon on his side, what could go wrong?

"Guess what?" she said.

"What?"

By way of answering, Jill opened her mouth and proceeded to

wiggle an extremely loose left incisor back and forth with her tongue.

"Wow," Tamar said. "Looks ready to drop."

"Yeah," Jill said.

Henry held up his palm. Jill slapped it five.

"Is it your first?" Tamar asked.

But Jill already had other things on her mind.

"Want to play video basketball?" she asked Henry.

"Later, honey," Melissa said, walking up. "The adults need to socialize a bit first."

Though still carrying a little excess weight from the pregnancy, Melissa was already slimming down.

"It's fine by me," Tamar said. She turned to Henry. "Go play. I'll be alright."

Jill grabbed Henry's hand and began pulling him down the hall.

"I have a new version. NBA All-Stars."

"Are you sure it's OK?" Henry asked Tamar.

"Of course. Go!"

That was all Henry needed to hear. After a quick peek at the newborn, he left his bride-to-be in the care of his sister and followed Jill to her room. In truth, he couldn't believe his good luck. The perfect preproposal distraction had fallen directly in his lap.

"You can sit here next to me," Jill said, pulling up an extra chair to her desk.

Henry did as he was told. For the next few minutes he forced himself to concentrate on the somewhat intricate rules to Jill's new "NBA All-Star Hoops." Then they got down to business. Though Henry prided himself on being an above-average video player (he had won the Pac-Man award in his freshman hall), tonight was different. Within minutes, he was down by ten. Moments later, fifteen. Though there had been times in the past when he had let Jill win, this was different. He was doing his best, but his mind had wandered back to a troubling issue: What would he do if Tamar said no? Cry, moan, beg? Become an unwilling case study for his mother's next book, *The Tragedy of the Hopeless*? In any case, the big moment was nearly at hand. Sooner than expected, his sister's voice came echoing from down the hall.

"Dinner!"

It was a word to strike fear in Henry's heart.

"We'll finish later," Jill said.

"Can't we play a bit more?" Henry asked. The first warning signs of panic—shortness of breath, trickles of sweat, general edginess—were upon him. "I'm down by eighteen."

"Afterwards," the girl replied. "Come on."

Before he had time for even a quick "you de man" to the mirror, Jill took his hand and led him from the room. No more thinking about what to say or when to say it. It was time for action—to get down on one knee and propose to the woman he loved. There was no turning back.

Or was there? When he set foot in the living room, an upsetting sight met Henry's eyes. Though he had expected to find Tamar where he left her—in the kitchen chatting with Melissa—to his surprise she was talking to Adam by the grand piano. Of course, that sight in and of itself wasn't cause for undue alarm. Rather, it was Tamar's posture that caught Henry's attention. Leaning forward, she had a hand on Adam's shoulder, her face no more than three inches from his. Further, she was giggling. As Henry helped his sister carry the food to the table, her laughter carried all the way from the living room.

"Hey," Henry whispered to Tamar as they took their seats moments later. "What was so funny?"

"Nothing," she said, and flashed Adam what Henry interpreted as an admiring glance. "Your brother-in-law's a riot."

Now Henry allowed his imagination to get the better of him. Yes, he had shown admirable restraint in face of the reappearance of Robert (especially in light of his mature handling of the weeklong visit of boyfriend number two back in August). But flirting with his brother-in-law? That was where he drew the line.

What made it worse was that Henry could see the attraction. After all, Adam really was good-looking. He was smart. Women really did love him. Throw in his money, and the combination was devastating. Even worse, he proceeded to dominate the mealtime conversation, describing his work at the soup kitchen, making it difficult for Henry to get a word in edgewise, let alone find the right time to pop the question. And Tamar hung on Adam's every word. Or so it seemed. Time and again Henry told himself to relax—that he was just being insecure. By the time the main course was served, Henry was absolutely convinced that his future wife had a massive crush on his brother-in-law. So convinced, in fact, that he sulked the entire meal and answered any conversational gambits thrown his way with a grunt. He soon pictured Tamar sitting in Adam's lap, feeding him grapes.

Needless to say, the proposal was shelved. The moment he and Tamar stepped on the elevator to go home, Henry exacerbated the situation by confronting her. Unfortunately, two hours of seething had made it impossible for him to broach the subject with any sort of delicacy. Instead of simply stating his concerns in a straightforward, mature manner or defusing them with humor, he accused her point-blank. Incredulous, Tamar listened in silence until, in the lobby, she said, "Screw you," marched outside into a light rain, flagged a cab, and left.

"Cab for you, sir?" the doorman asked.

"No," Henry said. "I'll hoof it."

No sooner were the words out of his mouth than a flash of lightning lit up the street. Seconds later, a thunderclap boomed down Fifth Avenue. The rain got heavier and Henry was suddenly staring out into a downpour. Just as he was deciding whether to walk or wait, the sound of high-tops slapping against the lobby floor echoed the sound of the rain hitting the pavement.

"Henry!"

It was Jill, umbrella in tow.

"For you," she said.

Good old Jill. As Henry took the umbrella, he noticed that it was her own—a Bugs Bunny.

"No way, Jill," Henry said. "I couldn't."

Jill simply nodded toward the weather. "We've got others." Then, more hopefully, "Or you could come back up and play more basketball. Maybe it won't be raining then?"

Henry got down on a knee. "I'd like to," he said, "but I'm a little bit upset right now."

"Oh," Jill said. "About what?"

Henry looked down at the floor. He knew that to break down in front of a seven-year-old would be inappropriate, not to mention pathetic.

"Nothing," he said, managing to pull himself together. "I'm fine."

"Sure you don't want to play the second half of the game?" Jill asked.

Henry would have loved to (especially considering that he was so far behind), but he simply wasn't in the mood.

"Not now," Henry said. He forced a smile. "But that doesn't mean I won't whip your sorry little butt next time."

"Oh yeah?"

Henry patted her cheek. "Keep me posted on that tooth, OK?"

Jill wiggled it once more with her tongue. "Sure thing."

With that, she kissed him. Then Henry watched her skip, run, and shuffle all the way down the long lobby, where she turned, waved, and hopped (literally) onto the elevator.

"Cute kid," the doorman said.

"Sure is," Henry said.

He glanced outside. It was still pouring. He walked under the awning and opened Bugs Bunny. With a nod to the doorman, he stepped out onto the sidewalk and set out for the subway at a rapid clip. Despite the use of Jill's umbrella, his pants and shoes were soaked within a block. When a gust of wind blew it inside out, Henry decided he had had enough. The rain was warm. He closed Bugs Bunny, held his face to the sky, and continued at a leisurely stroll. As he walked, his mind began to roam to a strange place. Even for him.

Sometimes Henry felt Jill was the sole female on the planet he could be with with no heartache. As hokey as it seemed, she was the one person who appreciated him for what he was. "Christ," he said to himself, "sometimes I wish I could marry someone like her." He smiled. It was certainly an odd idea. An illegal idea, too, but given his woeful track record with the opposite sex, perhaps the Commonwealth of New York could bend the law a bit? He could just see the ceremony. No pomp and circumstance. Not for a kid like Jill. She'd forgo the traditional wedding gown for a Knicks jersey—and insist that Henry wear sweats. Instead of a rabbi, Barney would officiate. Her stuffed polar bear would be best man. And the reception? SpaghettiOs, no utensils. Then ice cream all around. Seconds, too. No dancing. Instead, the guests would be offered a choice: freeze tag, hopscotch, or finger painting.

Laughing, Henry crossed Madison Avenue, heading east. The gutters were beginning to flood, the rain unrelenting, but Henry was so wet he didn't even feel it anymore.

"Finger painting," he said to himself.

The whole thing was absurd, but the more he thought about it, the more he saw that the idea had a certain twisted logic. Who needed sex, anyway? As far as Henry could see, it was the one element that always screwed everything up. After all, how often had horniness actually gotten him to the promised land of satisfaction? Not very. More often than not, his sexual urges led him directly to that special room in hell where clingy, jealous losers went to die. And if he foreswore all pleasures of the flesh, wouldn't Jill, the one person he could always count on, be the perfect match? Unconditional love—wasn't that what it was all about? Married to Jill, there would be no "jealous side." No ex-boyfriends popping in and out of town. No idiotic hats or haircuts. No fits. The quintessential cool big brother, Henry would go out of his way to make their life fun—an endless string of ball games, trips to the zoo, and video basketball.

Another bolt of lightning lit up the street. As the thunder

resounded up Park Avenue seconds later, Henry realized that there was more he could do with Jill than merely enjoy her company as she was now. As Jill came of age, he could become her tutor and mold her into the perfect woman. Indeed, if he was a diligent teacher, by the time she was out of high school the most important knowledge known to man would be at her fingertips. As an addendum to her own graduation ceremony, he would even administer his own "Exam for Life"—a test Jill would pass with flying colors. Section one would be short answer.

1) Discuss the stylistic differences between the piano playing of Art Tatum, Oscar Peterson, and Bill Evans.
2) Explain why the works of Andrew Lloyd Webber are inferior to those of Rodgers and Hammerstein and Stephen Sondheim.
3) Write out from memory the first chapter of New York Knicks great Walt Frazier's 1970 autobiography, *Clyde*.

Henry laughed. *Clyde*. She'd ace that. But the perfection that would be Jill would go further than a mere cultivating of good taste and memorization of raw data. No, Henry's work wouldn't stop there. Rather, he would take care to instill in her the right kind of values, turning her into perhaps the first lady in the history of the human race who appreciated the right men for the right reasons. Section two of the exam, the essays, would concentrate on this all-important area.

Essay—respond to two out of three. Fifteen pages each.
1) Describe why it is important to love a man based on the depth of his creative soul as opposed to the size of his bank account.
2) "Nice guys finish last." To the extent this adage still pervades modern society, explain what we can do as a country to change it.

3) Discuss the history of the female's attraction to the archetypal "arrogant asshole." Explain why this is evil. Explain further why sincerity and modesty are traits that a woman should prefer in a life partner.

Henry was splashing along 89th Street by now. Though he nearly collided with a man running for cover holding a newspaper over his head, he didn't even notice. For Jill's education would not be complete yet. Not by a long shot. The next part of his training regimen would focus on her own personal relationships, making sure that her conduct in matters of the heart would be beyond reproach. This section would be an oral exam, using incidents from Henry's own life.

QUESTION: Would you ever dis-engage yourself the day before college graduation?
ANSWER: Of course not!

QUESTION: Would you ever, under any circumstances, dump a kindhearted artist and move to Seattle out of the blue?
ANSWER: Never!

QUESTION: Would you ever put down his new girlfriend at his tenth reunion?
ANSWER: An impossibility!

QUESTION: Would you ever, under any circumstances, cultivate an entire fleet of ex-boyfriends?
ANSWER: Out of the question!

A cab roared by, sending forth a giant sheet of water. Intrepid Henry barely flinched, grinning wildly, for a final thought was welling up inside him. A thought that took the form of one last question—perhaps the most important of them all.

Extra Credit:

Situation: A woman has been dating a mild-mannered musician for six months. They are in love. They go to a dinner party at his sister's apartment. At said event, the woman flirts shamelessly with the brother-in-law.

Question: What should the woman's punishment be? Outline and defend several possibilities. High levels of severity encouraged.

For Jill? Another slam dunk. Perhaps she'd find life on a chain gang commensurate with the crime. Then again, she might opt for something more creative, such as requiring the woman to write "Flirting is the pathway to hell" in hieroglyphics for all eternity.

Jill would graduate with highest honors. Summa cum laude! Once she had left for college, perhaps Henry would take a cue from his mother and distill the lessons he had taught his niece into book form, *How to Be Henry,* a self-help manual engineered to teach women how to tell the mensches from the schmucks. Following a year or two on the best-seller lists (both hardcover and paperback), Henry would find himself the titular head of a new movement, "Nice Guyism." Appearances on Oprah, Letterman, and the *Tonight Show* would follow. Then the money. World tours. Mobbed airports. Not to mention women chasing him down the street.

HENRYMANIA SWEEPS COUNTRY, the headlines would shout. EVERYONE WANTS TO BE A HENRY!

It wouldn't take long for the term to catch on.

Afternoon talk TV: "This man claims to be a Henry. She says he isn't."

A woman being set up by a friend: "Is he Henrified?"

After good sex: "Oh, baby . . . Henrilicious!"

Woman to macho man: "Work on your inner Henry. Then call me!"

Henry pictured it all. In fact, he became so consumed in imagining a universe in which he was the ideal (for he was now being interviewed on Japanese TV—"Sensei Mann? To what do you attribute your power over women?") that he failed to notice how quickly he was approaching the corner of Lexington Avenue. Further, he didn't see that the gutter was filled with a good foot of water. Just as he was envisioning being shown the Japanese countryside by a model from Sapporo, Henry stepped off the curb. Up to his ankle, he slipped, spun his arms in a manner not unlike a windmill, then went down, landing smack on his rear end—and this just as a policeman in a blue slicker was walking up the block.

Needless to say, Henry was instantly catapulted back from the Far East to the East Side. He could only imagine how he looked, sitting in a gutter, sopping wet, holding an unopened Bugs Bunny umbrella. He felt a bit like Gene Kelly at the end of his famous dance routine in *Singin' in the Rain*, stopped short by an angry cop. Luckily, Henry's was of a more friendly variety. Seeing that Henry was alright, he simply moved on with a bemused glance. Still, Henry wasn't taking any chances. Though he knew he hadn't done anything illegal, he suddenly felt that the policeman's presence was somehow symbolic—that after all these years he was finally to be arrested for the ramblings of his depraved imagination. What if the cop was out on a pedophile sweep? Or an incest raid? In fact, Henry jumped to his feet and jogged, then ran, the final three blocks to the subway, like a criminal on the lam. What had he been doing anyway? Fantasizing about his own niece? Was this what his life had come to? Henry turned on the afterburners, sprinting, as if trying to outrun his own sick mind. Moments later, he rushed into the subway station winded but safe. Then he collapsed on a bench on the downtown platform to wait for the train.

It was there that Henry reached into his wet jacket pocket, looking for what he hoped would be something dry to wipe his face. Instead, he came across something hard and square, covered with felt: the box that held the ring that by all accounts should have been on Tamar's finger by now. Henry snapped shut his eyes. When he opened them again, he stared blankly across the tracks. Slowly, a couple came into focus, about his age, sitting side by side, holding hands. The woman looked something like Tamar. Not nearly as pretty, of course (who was?), but with curly black hair and a similar if somewhat wider build. Henry imagined jumping onto the tracks, leaping the third rail, pulling himself up onto the uptown platform, and slipping the ring on the woman's finger.

"Marry me," he would say.

"Of course I will," she would reply. "I love you."

Henry closed his eyes once again, this time feeling like a perfect fool, for he suddenly realized that had he asked, the chances were good that yes would have been Tamar's answer, too. Indeed, he could have been back at Melissa's drinking champagne. Instead he was proposing to a stranger on the uptown track. What had brought him to such a sorry state? How could he have ever doubted the woman who had stood by him for months? Was it all due to a harmless drink with an ex-boyfriend and a few laughs with a good-looking brother-in-law? Though it pained him to admit it, Henry realized the answer was yes. Fueled by preproposal jitters and a healthy dose of insecurity, he had blown Tamar's behavior with Adam entirely out of proportion. Simply put, his jealous side had reared its ugly head and bit him squarely in the ass.

The headlight of his train appeared down the tunnel, but Henry already knew what he needed to do. In seconds, he was through the turnstile and out onto the still-rainy street. There he cut in front of a couple and grabbed a cab. It was rude, yes, but Henry didn't care. He needed to get across town to Tamar's apartment—fast. To throw himself on the mercy of the only court that mattered. To tell her how lucky he was to be with her. How much he loved her. How he would go into therapy—alone, as a couple, with a group, even with his own mom if necessary—anything to work this out. Anything to have her back.

When the taxi stopped at the corner of 83rd and Columbus,

Henry threw the cabbie some money, grabbed Jill's umbrella, and ran headlong for Tamar's buzzer, already planning his next move. His reading was in six short days. The minute it was over, he and Tamar would drive to Vermont. That night, they would sleep in a romantic inn, the kind with an antique night table and fireplace in the room. The next day, they would climb Mount Mansfield, Vermont's tallest peak. There, overlooking a wash of gorgeous foliage, he would go for the big Hollywood ending—take out the ring, turn to his love, look in her eyes, and . . .

"Hello?"

Henry rushed to the intercom. "It's me," he called.

A pause. "Oh."

"Can I come up? Please, Tamar. I want to apologize."

No answer. Another pause, Henry drew in a sharp breath. When he heard the buzz, he pushed through the door and rushed up the steps. A floor down from her landing, he heard a creak. He stopped short. Tamar stood in her doorway, eyes red.

"I love you," Henry said. "Please . . . let me explain?"

Tamar wiped her eyes, then looked him up and down, considering.

"You're soaked," she said finally.

With that, she walked back into her apartment—but left the door half an inch ajar. The opening was small, but it was there.

Henry took the remaining steps three at a time.

The next Friday afternoon at approximately three o'clock, Henry was standing in front of the Downhome Theater on West 107th off Broadway, waiting for his bride-to-be. Behind him, a largish, square poster, elegantly designed, was hanging on a wrought-iron door.

Friday and Saturday Nights
in October and November

The Downhome Theater Presents
THE DANZINGER TAPES
A play by Rebecca Chase

More significant, however, was the light blue flier that was taped directly to its left.

Today Only!
A reading of a new musical
THE GREEN LIGHT!
Book, music, and lyrics by Henry Mann
Based on F. Scott Fitzgerald's *The Great Gatsby*

Henry paced a small swatch of sidewalk in front of the theater, stopping occasionally to sigh, mutter, and otherwise talk to himself. Though a passerby might well have been excused for thinking him mentally ill, Henry was simply a man with a lot on his mind. Not that things were all bad. Hardly. His rain-soaked apology had gone even better than expected. Not only had he been forgiven, but Tamar had even admitted her culpability, confessing that she might have mentioned Robert and flirted with Adam in part because she was scared of how strong her feelings were for Henry—issues she claimed to be working on with her therapist. In the end, Henry felt that they had emerged from the evening even closer, each better understanding the other's desire to be in a serious relationship as well as the fears they were trying to overcome. So much so that Henry had left Tamar's apartment the following morning determined to go ahead with Plan B, the Vermont proposal. Later that afternoon, he had arranged for a rent-a-car, then reserved a room at the Breyer House, an inn near Mount Mansfield, described (on its own Web page) as "the quaintest in all New England." Arrangements made, Henry had devoted the remainder of the afternoon to postseason baseball. All in all, it seemed that things were better than ever. In one short week it would all be over—he'd be engaged and Broadway bound. Not too shabby.

So why the pacing? The muttering? Why the look of abject distraction? The truth is that good news can bring stress as easily as bad. While juggling the final week of rehearsals and rewrites, Henry soon discovered that it was beyond his capacity not to worry about how everything would all turn out. It boiled down to two simple questions. Would Tamar really say yes? Would the show be a hit? Yes, Henry knew that the odds were in his favor—heavily, even—but given the enormity of what was at stake, as the week stretched toward Friday he grew increasingly nervous. Now that the big moment was actually upon him, his emotional state was registering dangerously high on the anxiety meter, flip-flopping between "scared shitless" and "pre-basket-case."

To make matters worse, Tamar was running late—again. True, Henry had already cleaned the theater, pushed aside the set of *The Danzinger Tapes*, even warmed up the cast, but with the reading scheduled to start in half an hour there were still things to be done. Even though Tamar wasn't actually needed to do them, Henry knew he'd feel better having her close at hand. Although the bulk of Henry's energies over the past two months had been focused on this very event, it had always seemed slightly unreal, like something that would happen in the far future. That future had arrived with astonishing speed, placing Henry at the edge of a sharp precipice, a short half hour from taking the creative leap of a lifetime. There was only one drug on the market that could soothe his nerves before he jumped: Tamar.

Instead, he was forced to settle for his father. Mr. Mann ambled down 107th, dressed casually in a blue blazer, jeans, and cowboy boots—a sixty-year-old Marlboro Man.

"So?" he called as he approached. "How's the Broadway star?"

"Hanging in, I guess. A little tense."

Mr. Mann nodded. "Well, you've got a lot at stake, right?"

Henry smiled. If his father only knew. Strangely superstitious, he had kept these particular engagement plans to himself, secret even from the inner sanctum of 34 North.

"I mean, look at that flier," his dad continued. "Book, music, and lyrics by Henry Mann." He placed a hand on Henry's shoulder. "Your ass is most definitely on the line, my friend."

Henry forced a smile. He always appreciated his father's ability to say just the right thing at just the right moment. No fool, Mr. Mann could see that his comment had not been well received.

"Oh, relax," he said. "You know I think it's going to be great. And you know what? If it bombs, life goes on."

"True," Henry said ruefully. "I'll just have to move out of the country. Maybe be a Sherpa in Nepal."

"And freeze your butt off leading expeditions up Everest?" Mr. Mann smiled. "Drop me a postcard from the peak, okay?"

While Henry was picturing himself succumbing to altitude sickness at Base Camp Three, a cab suddenly lurched to a halt in front of the theater.

"I see the *Times* is sending a critic," Mr. Mann said.

Though Henry knew that the odds of a genuine reviewer from any paper at all, let alone the *Times*, emerging from that cab were nil, his nerves were so shot that his heart took a literal leap (or so it felt) and then proceeded to pound at an alarming rate until the taxi door swung open, revealing not a man but a beautiful woman, reaching into her purse to pay the driver. Seconds later (Henry didn't know why he bothered to feel surprised anymore), that woman whisked up to Henry's father and kissed him squarely on the mouth.

"Hi, sweetie," she said.

Clearly, this was no reviewer. Further, it seemed apparent that Amanda had been replaced. Not to mention stewardess Maureen. Mr. Mann turned to his son.

"Henry, meet Greta."

She was an elegant, shapely woman, about thirty, in a tightly fitting business suit. Nearly too disgusted to check her out, Henry looked anyway. Yes, his father had done it again—bagged another great-looking lady, well his junior. In the past, this might have rankled Henry enormously, but since, he'd met Tamar, his feelings toward his dad had changed considerably. Envy had shifted to pity. What had once seemed studly now seemed infantile. What was his father trying to prove, anyway? Why the hell couldn't he just pick someone within ten years of his own age and settle down?

But now was not the time for moral superiority. Rather, decorum dictated he take a moment to get acquainted with girlfriend number fifty-one (or was it fifty-two?).

"It is so nice to meet you, Henry," Greta said. "Your father has told me all about you. Such talent!"

Henry detected a slight German accent.

"Thanks," he replied.

"I love musicals," she continued. "I just took my nephew to *Mamma Mia!* We loved it."

At present, Henry was too preoccupied with his own hopefully brilliant contribution to the musical stage to take the time to lecture Greta about the evils of a culture that embraced dreck. His father, however, who had heard Henry's diatribe many times, took it upon himself to move things along just in case Henry was unable to restrain himself.

"Why don't we grab a seat, honey," he said.

As a response, Greta turned and kissed him again. Henry looked away.

"Are you coming, Henry?"

"That's alright. I'm waiting for Tamar."

"Very good," Greta said, moving toward the door. "Come on, Greg."

As Mr. Mann stepped toward the theater, Henry couldn't resist a tug at his sleeve.

"What ever happened to Amanda?" he whispered. "Or that stewardess, Maureen. They were beautiful."

Mr. Mann smiled wistfully. "Yeah, they were. But Maureen was just a fling. And Amanda? Unfortunately, she . . . well, let's just say she had a little stamina problem."

With a wink, Mr. Mann followed Greta inside. As Henry watched him go, pity quickly switched back to envy—then to awe. Somehow his father, a handsome but otherwise unremarkable gentleman, had been blessed with the sex drive of a teenager. Henry only hoped that there was something to heredity. If so, he and Tamar would be in business well into their nineties. That is, if he didn't kill her first. This was one day that she had absolutely promised to be on time.

"Come on," he said to himself. "Where the hell are you?"

By this point, Henry's anxiety level had outgrown mere pacing. Though he knew full well that it would do absolutely nothing to accelerate Tamar's arrival, he soon found himself walking half a block to Broadway and looking angrily toward the subway. A steady stream of people moved toward him, but no Tamar. Henry sighed and glanced uptown. Again, nothing. After a somewhat rabid flurry of cursing, Henry found himself reaching into his pocket for the cell phone he paid for each month but always forgot to bring with him, then staring at a pay phone across the street. It was extremely tempting. Should he? On the one hand, he didn't want to be a nag. On the other, wasn't a certain amount of nagging allowed in exceptional circumstances? And didn't excessive tardiness on the occasion of a soon-to-be-fiancé's first New York reading qualify? What if she had gotten sick? Or had hurt herself? Certainly she'd understand—maybe even be touched by his concern. Henry reached into his pocket. Armed with a quarter, he waited for the light to change, then jogged across the street.

Bill, a coworker, answered.

"Hello, Tamar Brookman's line."

"Hi, Bill," Henry said. "Is she there, please?"

"Sorry, Henry. She's out for the afternoon."

"Yeah, I know. I'm waiting for her. Do you remember when she left?"

"About an hour ago. Say, are you guys going on a trip or some-thing?"

"Yeah. to Vermont."

"I thought so." Bill sounded distracted. "She had a bag."

Now Henry was surprised. Tamar had left her things at his place. In fact, Henry already had them loaded in the trunk of the rental car.

"A bag?"

"Yeah. A suitcase."

Henry paused. Tamar was supposed to bring extra copies of the music to the theater, but even though the show was running a bit long, a suitcase hardly seemed necessary.

"Anything wrong?" Bill asked.

"No, no," Henry said.

"Can I take a message?"

Henry paused.

"No," he said. "No message."

It is sometimes astonishing how effectively the human mind can convince itself that nothing is wrong while knowing, at the same time, that something most certainly is. By the time Henry hung up the phone, his mind was already spinning with scenarios, each specifically designed to assure himself that everything was fine. After all, with the noted exception of his Adam-induced spazattack, he and Tamar had been getting along terrifically. True, she had been a bit distant that week—a fact she attributed to personality conflicts at the office—but wasn't that just part of the normal give-and-take of any relationship? Hadn't she told him hundreds of times that she was madly in love with him? Further, there were a million reasons why she might have brought a suit-case to work that day. Perhaps she really was using it to lug the ex-tra music to the theater. Or maybe she was borrowing it from a friend for an upcoming business trip; Henry knew she was going to Seattle the following week. Or maybe she was lugging her entire wardrobe to Vermont.

Of all the hundreds of possible reasons for the presence of that piece of luggage in Tamar's office on that particular afternoon, the one that Henry wouldn't allow himself to consider was perhaps the most obvious: that she was skipping town. Given the preciousness of what was on the line, the mighty forces of denial had mobilized quickly. They had dug a line of foxholes in Henry's cranium and settled in for a siege. It was a direct result of their valiant efforts that by the time Henry recrossed Broadway he was absolutely certain that Tamar would be along soon—either with or without a suitcase. The thing to do was to get busy. There was still plenty to be done before curtain.

As he hurried up 107th Street, though, Henry saw that his return to the world of *The Green Light!* would be delayed a bit longer. Waiting in front of the theater to say hi were Doug and his ever sprightly wife.

"Hey, you!" Ellen said as Henry approached. "Excited?"

Henry stopped by her side. Though he usually tried to be upbeat around the queen of pep, this was a case when he simply couldn't manage it.

"Sure I am," he said. "When I don't feel like throwing myself in front of a cab."

Ellen let loose a loud cackle. "Oh, you'll be great!" she said, then turned to Doug. "Won't he be great?"

Doug agreed. "He'll be great."

"See?" Ellen said. "Doug's never wrong. Right, Doug?" She tugged at the front of his shirt. "Right? Right?"

Henry still had trouble believing Doug put up with such behavior. In her more hyper moods, Ellen turned enthusiasm into a strange and frightening sickness.

"Right," Doug said, gently taking her hand away from his shirt and holding it. He turned to Henry. "By the way, the gang at work says break a leg."

Ellen couldn't help herself. She smiled broadly and leaned up to Henry's ear.

"Christine, too," she whispered.

"What?"

"Well, not really," Ellen said. "But I'm sure she'd want you to do well."

Henry wasn't so sure. After the awkward denouement of their short-lived involvement, they had barely spoken a word that didn't relate to the job. Though Christine had not been openly hostile, Henry didn't think that "Should I spell-check it, too?" constituted a major thawing in relations.

"I still can't believe I was such a jerk. I should've said something."

"You still can," Doug said. "There's no statute of limitations on apologies."

Henry nodded. He sometimes found Doug's uncanny ability to pull a mature comment out of thin air irritating. The last thing Henry wanted to do now was tender an apology for something that happened over five months ago.

"Anyway," Ellen said, kissing Henry's cheek, "good luck, OK?"

"Yeah," Doug said. "Do it for old 34 North."

Henry laughed. "Yeah. You know, I'd feel more confident if that's where we were having the reading. With the portrait of old man Albright looking down at us."

"You should've invited him," Ellen said.

"He's dead," Henry said.

"I mean the one who's still alive, then—Dean."

"And the barking hyena," Doug said.

"Yeah, right," Henry said. "I'm tense enough without a woman who's killed half the wild animals in Africa in the audience." He paused. "Then again, if it bombs, a bullet to the brain might be just the thing."

"Oh, you silly!" Ellen said, hitting him playfully in the chest. "It's not going to bomb! It's going to be fantastic!"

"Really?" Henry asked. "You think so?"

Henry knew, of course, that looking for reassurance from a

woman of Ellen's relentlessly upbeat disposition was on par with asking the pope if he still believed in God, but with Tamar missing in action, he needed to grab his moral support wherever he could get it. As expected, Ellen responded right on cue.

"Why do you even have to ask!" she cried. "My God, Henry. You're so talented!"

Henry smiled. No doubt about it. Perkiness had its advantages. Maybe Doug was on to something.

"Thanks," Henry said. "I'm just a little on edge."

"Don't sweat it, Gershwin," Doug said. "Let's get you inside."

When Henry had left the lobby fifteen minutes earlier, it had been virtually empty. Now it was about half filled, mostly with friends. Family, too. The very second Henry stepped through the door, he was greeted by an all too familiar voice.

"Henny, honey!"

Henry had hoped that his serious relationship with Tamar would compel his mother to downshift to a simple "Henry." No dice. He was now resigned to being "Henny, honey" for the rest of his living days—to his own kids, perhaps even professionally ("And the Tony goes to . . . Henny, honey!").

"It's a nice little theater," his mother went on, kissing his cheek. "A bit drafty." She smiled. "But maybe they can close down this *Dancing Grape* show and open yours? You should talk to the owner about it."

"OK," Henry said weakly. "I will."

"Don't forget, now."

"Oh, stop pushing him, Marian. He's a good boy."

Henry shuddered. Could it be? The squat woman who had so nearly blocked his path to Amanda at his sister's housewarming took root before him.

"You remember Joan Fitz, don't you?" his mother said. "My friend from the Pinafore Players?"

"Yes, of course."

She was still short, wide, and frighteningly makeup dependent.

"We're so excited, Henry!" Mrs. Fitz cried. "A musical based on *The Grapes* of *Wrath*. How clever."

Henry didn't even bother correcting her.

"I was just talking to your mother," Mrs. Fitz continued. "I think you should write an original musical for the troupe. You know, something historical. We have lots of colorful characters."

Holding back a smile, Henry imagined the first-act finale, "A Barrel Full of Losers."

"I'll think about it," Henry said.

"Good!" Joan Fitz replied.

Then she looked concerned and took a step closer to Henry.

"You know I believe in your talent, Henry, dear," she said. "Always have. But correct me if I'm wrong. Didn't they do *The Grapes of Wrath* on Broadway a few years ago?"

Henry was about to explain that Steinbeck's book and Fitzgerald's, though both written in the twentieth century, were not, in fact, the same. He was saved by a strong hand on his shoulder. Without looking, Henry knew precisely who it was: Adam. The aura of success was so powerful that he could sense it blindfolded at a hundred paces.

"Hey there," the brother-in-law said. "All set?"

"Absolutely," Henry said.

Once he had straightened things out with Tamar, Henry had forgiven Adam for being so charming. In fact, as promised back at the housewarming in the spring, at the last second Adam had pitched in to help pull the reading together. Only six hundred bucks, small potatoes for him, but still extremely generous. It seemed silly that at dinner a short week earlier Henry had hated his disgustingly good-looking guts.

"Thanks again for the help."

"Don't even mention it," Adam said.

It was then that Henry felt the familiar arms wrap around his leg. He leaned down and kissed Jill on the cheek.

"Hey, sweetie."

He hadn't seen her since their brief marriage a week earlier—the time when, for a fleeting moment, Henrymania swept the world.

"Hi," she said. "How's your show?"

"Why don't you tell me when it's over."

"OK," she said. Then she smiled, exhibiting an exciting development in regard to the state of her dentition: a missing right incisor.

"Hey," Henry said. "You lost the tooth!"

"Did the Tooth Fairy give you anything?" asked Adam.

"Sure did," Jill said. "Five whole dollars!"

Henry could barely contain his astonishment. When he was a little boy he got a quarter at the most. Once, when the loss of a particular tooth had caused an unusually large amount of bleeding, his dad had thrown in an extra nickel. How would he ever be able to afford kids when the going rate was five bucks a tooth?

"Inflation," Adam said sheepishly. "By the way," he went on, "Melissa and Adam Junior send their best."

"I got you something," Jill cut in.

Henry got down on a knee. "What's that?"

She handed over a card, homemade in crayon. On it was a picture of an otter. Underneath were the words *Benjamin Potter says, "Break a Leg!"*

"That's so sweet," he said.

"She spent all afternoon on it," Adam said.

Jill smiled, once again proudly displaying her missing tooth.

"Well," Adam went on, "we'd better grab a seat."

"Yeah, OK. I'll catch you after. Thanks again for the card," Henry said, and hugged Jill tight. Reluctantly, he let her go, then watched Adam lead her into the theater.

The minute Jill disappeared from view, Henry surveyed the crowd. The small lobby was suddenly full—terrifyingly so. Again, life as a Nepalese Sherpa didn't seem so bad, but with showtime fast approaching, Henry didn't have time for an anxiety attack. There was too much to do. Aside from more meeting and greeting, he had to check in on the cast, talk to the lighting man, even make sure there were enough refreshments on hand for intermission. On his way back into the theater proper, Henry realized that he had forgotten about the most important task of all: chatting up the big shots. So, with ten minutes until curtain, Henry delegated the smaller jobs and got to work introducing himself to the pros, doing his best to come across as the very picture of the confident up-and-coming composer, the sort of fellow that any producer would want on his team. Though three of the four reps who showed up were typical theater types (loose translation: gay men), the fourth, from the Musical USA Workshop, was a pleasant surprise: a drop-dead gorgeous twenty-something in leather pants.

"Hi," she said. "Dyllan Richards."

To his credit, Henry managed to get through the entire introduction and at least two minutes of chitchat without groveling excessively, panting, or, most significantly, launching into one of his habitual fantasies. No, he didn't have time to whisk this stranger off to a village in Nova Scotia and hump her brains out on a fishing scow. He had a reading to produce. Not only that, he was about to be engaged—engaged to a woman he loved more than he ever thought possible. As he took a rare free moment to contemplate his good fortune (again refusing to acknowledge the possible significance of that suitcase), Glenn suddenly appeared at his side.

"Hey, buddy," he said.

"Hey there," Henry said.

Glenn smiled mischievously and moved slightly to his left. "I think you remember this young lady."

Suddenly, Henry found himself face to face with Diana. He was stunned.

"Henry!" she said, flashing a big smile.

He hadn't heard her voice since the answering machine on the infamous afternoon of *The Doctor's Wife*.

"Diana!" he replied.

"Henry!"

"Diana!"

They paused. Suddenly, Henry threw caution to the wind and gave her a big hug. So what if he held it a bit too long? Glenn wouldn't think a thing of it. As far as he knew, Henry and Diana hadn't seen or spoken to each other in months. In such instances a long hug with the wife of a best friend seemed entirely justified. As he pulled away, Henry did take the liberty of a long look at Diana's body. The time out west had been good to her. The Colorado sun had given her a deep tan. Hours spent mountain-biking away her depression had made her body harder and leaner. When Henry glanced back toward the stage, he couldn't help but notice that a small dining room table, a prop for *The Danzinger Tapes*, stood off left.

"Good news," Glenn whispered to Henry, pulling him aside. "She's finally forgiven me."

"That's great," Henry said. "But what about Chimp Number . . . I mean, Rachel?"

"Purely a stopgap measure. When Diana told me she was willing to go to couples therapy, I ended it."

"Couples therapy?"

"Yeah. Great news, huh?"

Henry wasn't so sure, for he had been struck by a horrible thought. What if Diana told all? Even worse, what if she twisted the story? Made it seem like the trips to Colorado were Henry's idea? Would Glenn ever forgive him?

"There's something else, too," Glenn said.

"What?" Henry said nervously.

Glenn paused, then grinned.

"What?" Henry repeated.

"I'm quitting Albright."

For a moment Henry thought he hadn't heard correctly.

"What's that?"

"I'm quitting," Glenn repeated. "Out of that fucking place. Good-bye. Sayonara."

This time Henry knew his ears weren't lying.

"Please tell me you're kidding."

"Well," Glenn admitted, "sort of. Only for a couple of months." He paused for dramatic effect and leaned in close. "The producer found some cash for my play."

This time Henry couldn't withhold his astonishment. "You mean *Hoo, Hoo! Haw, Haw?*"

"He wants to bring it to a theater off-Broadway. Or off-off-Broadway. Or at least try. And Diana said she'd help support us for a while. Isn't that great?"

Henry felt as though he had been kicked in the gut. It was too incredible to be believed. Yes, he knew that the rest of the audience, inexplicably, had liked *Hoo, Hoo! Haw, Haw!* more than he had—much more, even. Still, he hadn't imagined that a producer would have raised the necessary funds. It was simply too outlandish for public taste.

"Anyway, I've got to get back. Hey! Good luck."

"Yeah," Henry said. "Thanks . . . and congratulations."

He watched Glenn take his seat next to Diana, watched Diana wrap her hand around his. Though he had always known it was inevitable that, one day, one of the gang would move on, it was hard to imagine Conference Room 34 North without Glenn to throw pencils at the ceiling.

"Hey, Henry."

He turned. The actor playing Gatsby, a large African American man with dreadlocks, wearing a bright pink suit, stood before him.

"Are we going to start or what?" he asked.

Henry looked at his watch. It was 3:35. Time to roll.

"Yeah," he said. "Right now."

Henry walked into the theater itself and looked over the audience. Nearly all the seats were filled. Doug and Ellen were up front. A few rows back his dad was chatting idly with Greta; his mother sat with Joan Fitz and Rye, who had arrived moments earlier, halfway up the left; Jill, in Adam's lap, gave him a thumbs-up sign and blew a kiss. Even the gorgeous woman in leather pants smiled at him (hmmm, from a certain angle she looked a bit like Jennifer Aniston, too). Everything was perfect. They were ready.

Except for one thing.

Tamar still wasn't there.

As a cab carried him downtown later that night, Henry would still not allow himself to believe that he had been deserted. Though taking heavy casualties, the stalwart forces of denial were still entrenched in their cranial foxholes, refusing to permit Henry to acknowledge the complete disaster his day had become. For not only had his bride left him flat, but the reading on which he had staked such high hopes had been a bust.

If the only thing wrong with the show had been its length, Henry would have felt grateful. Cutting was easy. But Henry knew the problem was much more serious. Within ten short minutes the audience was already suffering. What had started as a few isolated coughs had escalated quickly to crinkled programs, butt shuffling, and, most painful, occasional dozing (Jill was out cold in her dad's lap by the third song). Not that it had been all bad—even in his bulldozed state Henry realized that the gospel number had received a nice ovation. Likewise a first-act song for Gatsby, written in a last-minute rush, "My Honey Got Money." There were other good moments scattered throughout. Still, though the independent parts often worked, they somehow didn't blend together into a fluid, entertaining whole.

By intermission, Greta had left, along with three out of the four pros Tamar had worked so hard to get to attend. Though everyone else had gutted out Act Two, the room had taken on a somewhat funereal gloom. The 7/8 dance break got a nice ovation, but the twelve-tone instrumental completely died. Even the second-act showstopper "My Pink Suit" missed the mark. Yes, it had gotten a few stray chuckles, but they had rung false, as though the audience were trying desperately to like something, *anything*. On top of everything, in a futile effort to inject some life into the proceedings, Henry had pounded the piano keys so hard he split a fingernail.

Worst of all, Henry's masterwork had ended with a sad whimper. No standing ovation. No triumphant curtain calls. How could there have been when the owners of the theater had made Henry stop a full fifteen minutes before the end of the show?

"Sorry," the theater manager had whispered. "But it's seven. We've got to clean up for *Danzinger Tapes.*"

Henry had felt so defeated by that point that he hadn't even objected. As a result, Gatsby's funeral march, Nick's final aria, "Take Me to the Orgiastic Future!" and the choral "Boats Against the Current" had gone unheard.

Sucking his throbbing finger, Henry looked blankly out the cab window and remembered the aftermath. His friends and family, like mourners forced to look into an open casket, had traipsed up to pay their final respects. His father had been first.

"Not bad, Henry," he said. "Greta liked it, too, but she had to meet someone for dinner."

"Don't worry about it, Dad."

"I'll call you."

"Good."

Ellen had been next in line.

"Some really great stuff!" she cooed, chipper as ever, But Henry knew her well enough to be able to tell the difference between genuine enthusiasm and a hollow fake. This had been the latter.

"Yeah, some really good things there," Doug said, taking his hand. "We'll talk at work."

They were granted a reprieve when his mother threw her arms around him—but then she said what Henry himself had been planning to say to Glenn when he thought that *Hoo, Hoo! Haw, Haw!* was a bust. "Well, *I* liked it!"

"Oh, I agree," Joan Fitz said. "This was much more exciting than the novel. Much more!"

As he accepted the compliment, Henry couldn't help but wonder if Mrs. Fitz had been confused by the marked dearth of Okies in the cast.

Then Rye cut in. "Interesting angle on the 1920s, Henry," he said, rubbing his beard. "Especially your decision to make Gatsby an African American. The Jazz Age, as you know, was a period of great freedom and a certain carelessness, if you will, among the . . ."

Henry nodded for two solid minutes until Mrs. Mann took his hand.

"Now, now, Rye. Lectures later."

Then she rubbed Henry's shoulder and met his gaze with a compassion only a mother could show. If anyone in the theater had felt Henry's pain, it was she.

"I was impressed. Keep on plugging."

With his parents out of the way, the rest of the crowd had come one after another, dutifully doing their best to be encouraging.

Glenn: "Keep working at this, buddy. You're onto something."

Diana: "Good job." Then, whispered, "And you look great."

Dyllan Richards (handing him her card): "Needs work. But you definitely have talent. Give me a call and we'll have coffee and talk it over."

Adam: "I admire you, Henry. All that work! I don't know how you do it. And for no pay!"

Finally, Jill: "Sorry I fell asleep. But I'm still gonna whip your butt in video basketball."

Here, Henry had smiled sadly and gathered his niece in his arms for the second time that day. Yes, he was doing it again, but like the afternoon of the housewarming, this was one of those times when he would take his love wherever he could get it.

"Thanks," he said.

She kissed him on the cheek, then looked around the room.

"Hey," she said, turning back to Henry, eyes wide. "Did you find Tamar?"

He found the note on his bed when he got home, the word "Henry" scrawled in Tamar's loopy hand on a plain white envelope. It was a sight that made the remaining forces of denial desert in droves, for though he couldn't have known the exact words she would have used, Henry had a good idea of what it would say. Notes in plain white envelopes left on pillows didn't generally convey good news. Even so, there was a small, pathetic hope. Maybe there had been some family tragedy. Maybe she had hurt herself and was resting comfortably in a— He wouldn't even allow himself to continue the thought. Tamar was gone. Forever. All that was left to be done was to read why.

> *Dear Henry,*
> *Here I go again . . .*
> *I'll spare you a long note. Suffice it to say, I feel like the worst human being on the planet. Even more so, because I couldn't bear to tell you this in person, in part because I didn't want to ruin your reading. It went great, right?*
> *I'll get to the point. After Robert saw me he made a decision. This past weekend he asked his wife for a divorce, then came to my office on Monday and proposed. I know it's awful timing, but the truth, Henry, is that I never stopped loving him. The more I think about it, the more I realize that I was on the rebound, maybe idealizing your artsy life a little bit. But deep down, I realize that it's just not me.*
> *I know you'll never be able to forgive me for this. But I hope one day you'll be able to understand, maybe even look back and laugh. I'm sure I'll be seeing you, too—on next year's Tony Awards.*

Good luck with everything, Henry. You're a wonderful person who deserves better than I've given you. You'll find it soon.

With great affection,
Tamar

P.S. Hey, at least it wasn't by e-mail this time.
P.P.S. I'm so sorry!

Henry lay back on his bed, stunned. This wasn't the way romantic movie montages were supposed to end. With all due respect to Glenn and Doug, Henry had come to consider Tamar his best friend. Now all that hope, all that love, had been distilled down and explained away in a lousy Dear John letter.

Had he idealized Tamar as Gatsby had Daisy? Loved her out of proportion? Perhaps, but that knowledge offered little comfort at the moment. The fact was that the blissful future for which he had laid such solid foundations over the past six months was gone. Like Daisy, Tamar had picked another man. True, Henry knew he would meet another woman someday, but one thing was certain: She wouldn't be Tamar. In his current state of mind, that was enough to make life seem unbearable. With that thought, Henry closed his eyes, half hoping he could perform a medical miracle and will himself instantly dead. But he would have to live with his pain—which is when Henry did something he hadn't done since he was a teenager: buried his head in his pillow and cried.

9

daisy

time: The not so distant future. Place: Henry's apartment.

Watching TV one rainy Sunday, Henry hears a frantic set of knocks on his front door.

"Let me in!" a voice cries. "Let me in!"

Henry flips off the remote and walks slowly, a bit nervously, toward the door.

"Who is it?" he calls.

"It's me, Henry! Me! Please! I have to talk to you!"

He stops short. Could it be?

"Tamar?"

"Yes! I must see you! I must!"

Trembling, Henry reaches for the doorknob.

Moments later, she's pacing the living room, crying hysterically. Robert has left her—for a bullfighter!

"His name is José!" Tamar wails. "They met on our honeymoon in Acapulco!" She turns to Henry, drops to her knees. "Oh, my God! I made such a mistake!" Her arms wrap around his legs.

"He's gay, Henry! Gay! Please take me back! Please!! Please!!!"

Depending on his mood, there are two endings.

1) Henry gathers her into his arms for a romantic reunion of epic proportions.
2) He kicks her down his front hallway and out the door.

All in all, it was an extremely agreeable fantasy, one that Henry returned to again and again during the first few days following Tamar's sudden elopement. In fact, if Henry had been able to remain focused on this one scenario, he might have been able to muddle through the post-Tamar morass a bit more easily. Unfortunately, his mind was usually occupied by other, more upsetting thoughts. Repentant Tamar, the penitent woman begging for forgiveness, was routinely pushed aside by unfaithful Tamar, the should-have-been wife, screwing Robert, her should-have-been ex-boyfriend, on a Mexican beach. More excruciating still were the torturous images of the idealized future that never would be: barbecuing burgers with Tamar at their country house on a Sunday afternoon, watching their six-year-old twins in the school play, driving Lionel (the boy, for Hampton) to his first Little League practice, helping Emily (for Dickinson) write the high school valedictorian speech—the full mosaic of a life unled.

Of course, the members of Henry's inner circle were on duty twenty-four hours a day, visiting often, keeping frequent vigil by phone, essentially doing whatever they could to ensure that Henry didn't kill himself before he felt well enough to reenter the human race. Glenn called every morning to say, "Forget her. She's a bitch." Diana called each evening to add, "Forget her. You're a stud." To stave off possible starvation, his mother and Melissa brought grocery bags full of food (uneaten; Henry's diet consisted of bowls of Special K). Even Jill got involved in what his parents jokingly referred to as the "Save Uncle Henry" campaign, sending over another crayon rendering of Benjamin Potter the lovable otter, this time chatting with her favorite members of the New York Knicks. Finally there was Ellen, who personally delivered one of her own pinhole compositions, a brooding picture of a deserted alley, entitled "Awareness in Love."

Henry had more than just love problems. There was also the small matter of his floundering career. Here, he received support as well. His father and Rye regaled him with stories of famous businessmen and historical figures who had failed, only to rise to greater heights ("Franklin Roosevelt had polio, damnit! Polio!"). Adam called Henry from a plane to Hong Kong to insist that he still believed in his talent. On Day Three A.T. ("After Tamar"), Doug and Glenn seconded that opinion.

"Come on, Henry," Doug said. "It's just one lousy reading. You can't expect to be on Broadway in two weeks."

The trouble was that Henry had expected success, even felt strangely entitled to it.

"I guess," he said. Henry assumed his usual position, slouched and unshaven on his sofa, his attire a T-shirt and boxers. Glenn had pulled the desk chair to the middle of the room while Doug sat on the fireplace hearth. Both were fully clothed.

"There was lots of good work up there," Glenn said. "You know, I've been working on *Hoo, Hoo! Haw, Haw!* for two years." He held up his fingers for emphasis. "That's two."

Of course Henry knew. He had had to suffer through two years—that's two—of hearing about it.

"To tell you the truth, it's mostly Tamar's fault," Glenn went on. "She pushed you in strange directions. I mean, come on—a twelve-tone dance break?"

Henry cringed. "You have a point," he said. "But Jesus! Halfway through it hit me. A musical of the *The Great Gatsby?* Way too fucking ambitious!"

"That's where you're wrong," Doug said. "You could pull it off. Like Glenn said, you just need to give yourself some time."

Henry shook his head. "I wrote a song called 'My Pink Suit,' for chrissakes!"

"I sort of liked that one, actually," Glenn said.

"Catchy," Doug added. "Some good rhymes."

Henry wouldn't hear of it.

"Pure shit," he said.

"Henry," Glenn said, "you've got to stop beating yourself up already. I promise you that there was nobody in that theater who didn't think you had talent."

"I couldn't agree more," Doug said. "That's what's really important. Who cares if *The Green Light!* isn't ready for Broadway yet? You can rewrite it. Or else shelve it for a while and move on to something else."

Here, Henry showed that he was not incapable of unseemly displays of self-pity, not to mention melodrama.

"Maybe I could've," he said. "Anything seemed possible with Tamar."

Given his state of mind, Glenn and Doug let the tone of the statement pass. By now, they knew all about Henry's meticulous plans to propose atop Mount Mansfield.

"I know it's hard," Doug said. "But you'll meet someone else. Women love you."

Henry was in no mood to be patronized.

"Me?" he said. "Name one."

"Christine did."

"Christine?" Henry made a sound approximating a game show buzzer. "Doesn't count."

"Why's that?" Glenn asked.

Henry sat up—perhaps the first time he had moved since his friends' arrival half an hour earlier. "Disqualified on account of desperation."

"What?" Doug said. "Christine's not desperate."

"Not desperate?" Henry shook his head. In his current state of mind, he was incapable of mincing words, not to mention believing that any woman of value had actually ever liked him. As a result, he felt it his duty to be cruel. "Guys, in case you haven't noticed, she's got a crooked nose, not to mention a unibrow the size of the Great fucking Wall of China!"

With that, Henry sank back on the couch, wearing the defiant glare of a man who knows he's spoken a harsh but necessary truth.

"You're kidding, right?" Doug said.

"Kidding?" Henry couldn't believe his friend could be quite so dense. "It's hanging over her nose like some weird alien growth."

"Never noticed it," Doug said.

"Yeah," Henry muttered. "I suppose you wouldn't."

After all, Doug was too busy being a grown-up to get hung up by anything as trivial as a physical imperfection. Glenn, however, was another story. No aspect of a woman's appearance escaped his roving eye. Certainly he would take Henry's side. But before Henry had a chance to ask, Glenn shook his head.

"Sorry," he said. "Me neither."

Now Henry knew he was in trouble.

"How about the crooked nose, then?" he asked. "Don't tell me you haven't noticed that?"

"Well, sure," Doug said, "But it's sort of cute, if you ask me."

"And don't get me started on that xeroxed ass!" Glenn said, wagging his head in appreciation. "Whew, doggies!"

Exasperated, Henry roused himself from the couch (one of the few times he had walked in three days, Special K foraging trips and bathroom breaks not included), flopped onto the piano bench, and played a few random chords. He couldn't fathom how his two best friends, otherwise sensitive, observant men, had missed an imperfection so distinctive. Yet he knew he wasn't crazy. Those brows were as uni as the day was long.

"Listen, Henry," Glenn said, twirling the chair around to face the piano. "Christine isn't the point, unibrow or no unibrow."

"What is the point, then?" Henry said.

"This Tamar girl. She's not worth it. Isn't that right, Doug?"

"That's right."

"In my opinion, you were infatuated more than you were in love anyway."

"What?" Henry said. "I looked it up in the dictionary!"

"Screw the dictionary," Glenn said. "Screw definitions. Infatuated. Love. Who cares? You know what you've got to do? You've got to say 'fuck her.'"

Henry could have guessed that Glenn's solution would somehow include the word "fuck."

"Fuck her? As in sex?"

"No," Glenn said. "Fuck her! As in forget about her. Doug?"

Doug nodded.

"She's not good enough for you, alright?" Glenn said. He rolled the chair to Henry's side. "She was deceitful from the beginning. What was that lesbian stuff anyway? And those ex-boyfriends visiting her? And Jesus Christ! What kind of person dumps someone with a letter? And on the biggest day of his career! And forgive me for saying it again, Henry, but she pushed you into doing that reading before the show was ready! I mean, come on!"

It was an unexpected rapid-fire combination—one that had Henry back on the ropes, struggling to remain upright. Though his mind raced with things to say in rebuttal—that Tamar had believed in his talent, that she had broken her back to get the reading together, even that she had composed "Monkeys Love Show Tunes," a song that had lifted his spirits when he had trouble finishing the Act One finale—when Henry opened his mouth to defend her, no words came out. The bottom line was that Glenn was right. Despite all her wit, charm, and warmth, Tamar was untrustworthy. As Sheila had put it, a bit of a flake. A woman who, by her own admission, had idealized Henry's starving-artist lifestyle and then, when the chips were down, opted for Fairfield over the Village.

Henry suddenly found himself looping back to Christine. For the first time in months, he thought back on their wonderful date, her easygoing ways, her long, athletic body. Had he really turned down a woman with a unibrow of such microscopic proportions that two of his best friends hadn't even noticed it? A woman whose slightly crooked nose had been deemed attractive? A world-class butt xeroxer?

He had.

"Maybe when I'm up for dating again I can give her a call?"

Glenn rolled the chair back to the middle of the room. "Give who a call? Tamar?"

"No, Christine."

Henry saw Glenn and Doug exchange a glance. Clearly, they were in possession of classified information.

"Hate to tell you this, buddy," Glenn said, "but Christine's dating some teacher she met at school. His name is Paul, I think."

Henry instantly pictured a vagrant pushing him in front of a speeding truck. He now stood utterly alone with no options. With that realization his throat began to constrict; his eyes grew moist. While Henry was aware that, among sensitive men, tears were socially acceptable—even a sign of maturity—he was still an unfortunate prisoner of a certain brand of old-school American machismo that held that crying was for sissies. As a result, Henry quickly looked for a way to compose himself before humiliating himself in front of his two best friends.

In the past, he had found solace in the piano. Even though he was midconversation, he spun around to face the ivories. Unfortunately, this time his piano failed him. When Henry's fingers unconsciously made their way to "She's the Girl I Call Tamar," it was simply more than he could bear. The second he realized what he was playing, the tears came fast and furious. Embarrassed, he began to bang on the keys with both fists, an action he repeated with increasing intensity for a full minute before Glenn and Doug were able to get him safely settled back on the couch.

· · ·

Two weeks passed. Some relevant statistics:

> Hours Henry spent watching TV: 196 (14 a day)
> Number of pairs of underwear worn: 2
> Showers taken: 2
> Number of bowls of Special K consumed: 32
> (approximately 2.3 bowls a day)
> Amount of food brought by mother and sister actually
> consumed: none
> Number of trips outside apartment: 0
> Number of tantrums, involving fists and piano: 2 a day
> Number of fantasies about Tamar: too many to be tabulated

Indeed, it was a difficult half month. Not only did Henry miss Tamar, but his distress over the fate of his show continued unabated. For the first time in many years he suffered from insomnia. By night he would toss and turn in his bed. By day he would channel-surf, dozing fitfully on his couch. Awake, his mind was locked on Tamar. When he managed to sleep, he was invariably plagued by nightmares.

Such was Henry's state of mind on Monday afternoon, Day Seventeen A.T. Sleeping fitfully on his sofa (still in boxers, unshaven), he was awakened by the ringing of his bell. When it became clear that the ringing would not stop, Henry managed to rouse himself and stumble toward his door. To his surprise, he found the best-selling author of *The Inner You* standing in the vestibule, bearing trash bags, Spic and Span, a package of sponges, a mop, a container of matzoh ball soup, rice, and leftover brisket. Though carrying the accoutrements of a maid, Mrs. Mann was elegantly attired in a light blue pantsuit, Gucci shoes, and an Hèrmes scarf.

"I'm sorry to barge in like this, Henny, honey," she said, "but I came over to discuss something with you. Do you mind if we talk?"

In truth, the answer was yes—Henry was too distraught to converse with much of anyone, let alone his mother—but clearly her question was rhetorical. Just like that, she swept by him, placed the food on the kitchen counter, then took a seat on the piano stool. Still sleepy, Henry resumed his position on the couch.

"Again, I apologize for the intrusion," she began, "but this is something I've been thinking about, well, for some time, and I've just got to get it off my chest."

Henry could only imagine what it was. A career in accounting, perhaps?

"I have a confession to make, Henry," she continued.

"Yes?"

She got up and began to pace.

"Something a mother doesn't like to admit."

"Uh-huh?"

She stopped and shook her head fretfully.

"But, well, on the way to your musical I was nervous."

"Yeah?" Henry said tentatively.

"Frankly," his mother went on, "I was worried your show would be bad. Not because I don't believe in your talent," she added quickly. "I've always believed in you, Henry, as you know."

Henry let that one pass.

"But since college you've seemed so, well, so aimless. One day a novel, the next a symphony, the next a poem about, I don't know, a . . . a woodchuck!"

Henry had to draw the line somewhere.

"That would be an otter," he said.

"Woodchucks, otters, gophers," his mother said. "Whatever! Except for that one kids' musical about Paul Bunyan, you never really stuck to anything long enough to finish it."

Henry had a sinking feeling that this conversation was leading straight to a corner office with a jacket and tie.

"But then, Henry!" she said, taking an eager step toward him. "Then you proved me wrong!"

Henry blinked. Had his distress over Tamar affected his hearing?

"I did?" he asked.

"Yes, you did!" Her eyes were alive, excited. "At your reading. Sure, some of your songs were, well, not very appealing, but others were terrific. Now I know what you're really capable of. I see how hard you worked this summer. You can go places, Henry. You can't quit now!"

It was all Henry could do not to laugh. Leave it to his mother to take his worst disaster ever and twist it into a reason to keep on going. It sounded like a chapter from one of her books.

"What about law?" he asked.

"Law?" his mother said. She paused, seemingly confused. "Now whatever gave you the idea I wanted you to be a lawyer?"

Henry shook himself. Yes, his mother was pushy—but he'd never known her to be senile. Then he noticed that she was smiling. Could it be that she was also developing a sense of humor?

"I'm sorry if I haven't been more supportive." She sat down next to him. "You know, I just want you to be happy."

Henry nodded, thinking back to when Sheila had said the same words on the Hamden College green. Was he so miserable that everyone felt a pressing need to wish him well? In regard to his mother, Henry had never doubted that she wanted him to be happy. He had just taken issue with her tactics. Despite his best efforts to appear blasé, he was touched.

"Thanks, Mom," he said.

Henry liked her this way. On the defensive. Apologetic. Gentler. Certainly it was too good to last. He was right. Just then, his mother sighed deeply and took a long look around the room.

"Now look at this place," she said. "It's a mess."

Henry couldn't deny it. Cleaning had not been a priority over the past two weeks.

"And Henny, honey," she continued, turning to him, "you look awful."

Though Henry couldn't vouch for his looks (he had generally avoided the mirror), he certainly knew that he felt awful.

"I brought this for you," his mother said.

She reached for her pocketbook. Suddenly, Henry was holding a copy of *The Inner You*.

"Now don't give me that look," his mother said. "This book of mine has helped literally thousands of people get through tough times. While I straighten up a bit, you read. Come, now! Enough wallowing around in the muck. It's time to motivate!"

Henry knew better than to protest. Once his mother's mind had been made up, she was as unmovable as reinforced steel. So as she headed for the kitchen, Henry lay back on the couch and flipped open the book to its table of contents. Perhaps due to the little chat with his mom (his longest in over a week), he felt suddenly exhausted. So exhausted that he thought he might even be able to sleep deeply enough to avoid another nightmare. It was ironic, though. All week long when he had wanted to sleep, he couldn't. Now that he felt as though he could, it wasn't polite. What would his mother say if he dozed off reading her life's work? With nothing else to be done, he lay back on the sofa, chose a page at random, and began to get reacquainted with his mother's unique prose style.

Men—you need to get in touch with your inner woman! Your missing X chromosome is calling you! Though you may think you're a macho tough guy, deep down you're merely a little boy looking for a shoulder to cry on. Sensitivity is not a word co-opted by women! No! And again no! There's nothing unmanly about caring. And this doesn't mean you have to knit or play canasta or host Tupperware parties. No, today's man's man can play touch football in the afternoon, then come home and shed a tear with his son over the death of his goldfish. For a man today is really a woman in disguise.

Men, try this exercise. Imagine you're a woman going out on a date. What would you look for in a man? Now try to be that man.

That was as far as Henry got. Though his mother's book had been written to uplift, it had the opposite effect on Henry. Not only was it a self-help book that had helped thousands, but it also appeared to be a wonderful cure for insomnia. As his mother continued working in the kitchen, Henry let the book drop to his chest and closed his eyes. But instead of falling into the deep sleep he craved, Henry merely dozed. Suddenly, he found himself in the middle of another upsetting dream, perhaps the worst of them all.

Scene One: The Downhome Theater, the reading of The Green Light!

The first act is under way. But it's a disaster. The cast doesn't know any of the lyrics. The singers are flat. The actress playing Daisy is missing, and two members of the chorus are playing hopscotch in the corner.

Henry sits at the piano horrified as he watches his show unravel before his eyes. What's going on in the audience is even worse. Yes, all his friends and family are there, but no one is paying attention! His mother, father, Adam, and Melissa are arguing about where to spend next Thanksgiving. Jill is playing video basketball. Amanda, his Iowa-born wife and fellow musician, sits up front, milking a goat. In the back row, Tori West straddles the Handsome Intern against her seat. Two rows up, Sheila sits in between husband Frank and Bill Gates, counting wads of thousand-dollar bills. Farther down, Jennifer Aniston and the entire cast of *Friends* laugh at a joke. Only Christine watches—but her cute face is dominated by a two-foot-tall talking eyebrow. "Pluck me!" it cries. "Won't somebody please show some pity and pluck me?!"

Anxious, Henry looks back to the stage, where the entire cast is engaged in a robust game of Twister.

Scene Two: Gatsby's Entrance.

Then—hope! Enter the leading man! He's the quintessence of elegance. His skin is dark, his hair styled in a beautiful weave. His features are chiseled, high forehead, pronounced cheekbones, strong jaw. His beret is tilted at a jaunty angle. His suit, pink (what else?). He takes instant command, belts out "My Honey Got Money." The crowd is riveted. Suddenly, the show is a hit!

Now something surprising happens: Gatsby begins to ignore the other actors onstage. Instead, Henry sees him look his way, which makes Henry nervous. Why isn't Gatsby playing to the audience? Things get even worse: Suddenly, Gatsby saunters his way. Uncomfortable, Henry concentrates on his piano, but he can't deny the heat of the man's gaze. "Kiss her!" someone shouts. *Kiss who?* Henry thinks.

Then he finds out. Just like that, Gatsby is by his side.

"Hello, Daisy," Gatsby says, tipping his beret.

Henry blinks.

Hello . . . *Daisy?*

Henry looks down to see that his normal clothes have been replaced by a yellow ball gown. Indeed, he's Daisy Buchanan, the rich, beautiful apple of Gatsby's eye, the woman Gatsby has spent his entire adult life idealizing.

Henry gasps.

It's true. He's a woman!

Scene Three: The Dance.

Horrified, Henry stands up and shrieks. The audience cheers wildly, and Gatsby, ever poised, takes him by the hand.

"Would you care to dance?"

Henry doesn't know what to say. Suddenly, the crowd is on its feet. "Dance!" they cry. "Dance, you fool!" Should he? Dance with a man? He looks to the audience. They're going nuts. The show is a hit! So Henry allows himself to be led to the floor, where Gatsby takes him in his arms and engages him in a vibrant waltz.

"You dance beautifully," he whispers.

Henry is touched. The show is a success. Gatsby is charming. Scintillating. Much to his surprise, Henry finds that the embarrassment has disappeared. He is enjoying himself. Having the time of his life, in fact. It feels wonderful to be dancing with this handsome gentleman in pink. He feels secure. Attractive. Wanted. He flashes Gatsby a smile.

"As do you, Jay," he replies.

Henry notices his mother dabbing away tears. In fact, everyone is weeping, touched by the tender beauty of the elegant couple. As the song "My Pink Suit" builds to a crescendo, Gatsby holds Henry closer. He looks into Henry's eyes, forms his lips into a moist pucker. Henry puckers back. Gatsby moves his head closer. Henry closes his eyes . . . with this kiss his life will be complete . . .

Gatsby pushes him to the floor!

Scene Four: Crisis of Epic Proportions.

Just then Tamar glides onto the stage—on one of Robert's sailboats! Henry sees Gatsby run into her arms. As the music swells, the new couple locks in a passionate embrace. The crowd cheers. Henry pounds the floor. "No!" he cries. "No!!"

"Henry! *Henry!*"

Henry woke with an audible gasp, heart pounding. What a horrible dream! It was bad enough to live through his reading the first time. Now he had to go through it again—this time as the jilted ingenue? Had his life really come to this?

Before he could suss it out any further, his mother was sitting next to him on the sofa. Surprisingly, she didn't seem upset that he had dozed off while pursuing her magnum opus. Instead, it seemed that there was another item on her agenda.

"Are you awake, dear?" she began. "Good. Because . . . Well, I was thinking . . . Now, Henry, sitting here feeling sorry for yourself isn't doing any good, is it?"

"Uh . . . I guess not," Henry said cautiously.

Somehow Henry had a strong feeling that another apology wasn't on the horizon. Still, nothing could have prepared him for what came next.

"No," his mother went on. "It's not doing you any good at all." Now she smiled sweetly. "So, well, thinking of your best interests, of course, dear, while you were dozing I took the liberty of calling

Joan Fitz and signing you up to audition for the Pinafore Players."

Henry was stunned. It was a statement so completely out of left field as to seem surreal. After the unique level of coolness he had reached (if temporarily) with Tamar, was he really being asked to go back to the land of the living geeks?

"You what?" he managed finally.

"Come, now," she said, taking his hand. "You'll never get over that . . . that little sharpie if you sit around your apartment all day. You've got to interact with people. That's the cure. Heavens! Don't you see? Doing a show with cute women is the perfect way to get yourself out of your own head!"

Henry pulled his hand away. Over the past two weeks, he had made a solemn vow. Given that the world was populated by vicious, deceitful women, the likes of whom disappeared to foreign lands with married men, he would never date again. Ever. Although Henry realized that his mother had a point—that a little socializing might speed along his recovery—he figured he'd wait another ten years or so before starting the process. On his own terms.

"What's really so awful, anyway?" his mother continued. She was walking toward the piano now. "You like girls. You like singing. You like theater. Now you can have all three at once." She turned around. "It's not death by lethal injection, you know. People do enjoy it. A lot. And in case you need more incentive, Sally Harris broke her engagement!"

Although dating was the last thing Henry wanted to do, the inner depths of his psyche—the part that knew that despite his best efforts to the contrary, one day, probably sooner rather than later, he would want to become involved with another woman—prompted him to raise his left eyebrow. Such a detail could never escape a mother's notice.

"Aha!" she cried, wagging a finger in his face. "I knew you liked her! It's settled, then!"

Settled? Henry was about to object—vehemently, even—but as he was leaning forward to put his feelings into words, he stopped. Then he sighed. On the heels of that wrenching dream, he simply didn't have the energy to fight. Further, he saw her point. Starving himself, thinking about nothing but Tamar, and having nightmares was hard work. Maybe getting up and out would shake things up a bit.

But could he really join the Pinafore Players? It was a stretch. A *big* stretch. On the other hand, what was so bad about a bunch of people doing community theater, anyway? Maybe he had let the fact that his mother was a member cloud his feelings about the organization as a whole. After all, there were bound to be some normal people in it. Women, too—and not only Sally Harris. There had been other cute women sailors in *The Pirates of Penzance*.

"So," Mrs. Mann asked hopefully, "what do you say?"

Henry was still leaning toward no, but then he looked at his mother. It seemed to mean so much to her. Hadn't she said that all she wanted was for him to be happy? So was it such a crime to return the favor—just this once? To audition, anyway? There was nothing to say that he had to do it if accepted.

"Oh, what the hell," he said. "You win." Yes, he would enter the land of the living geeks—for at least an evening.

Mrs. Mann took a sudden step back, eyes narrowed. Having neglected to take into account the psychologically depleted state of her opponent, she hadn't expected such an easy victory.

"Really?" she said suspiciously.

Henry shrugged. "Why not?"

"But you hate Gilbert and Sullivan."

Henry couldn't believe it. He had finally agreed to try something his mother had been after him about for years, and here she was throwing his very own arguments back in his face!

"Fine by me," he said. "I won't, then."

Mrs. Mann was smart enough to know when she had made a tactical error.

"No, no, no!" she shouted, waving her arms. "It's such great fun! Of course you'll do it. It's settled, then. Oh, Henny, honey! You're going to absolutely love it!"

As she threw her arms around him, "Henny, honey" was suddenly certain that he had made the worst decision of his life.

"OK, then," she continued, as Henry pushed her away. "Shave and get dressed. Hurry now! We've got to get going."

Henry was perfectly happy in his T-shirt and boxers.

"Going?" he said. "Where?"

"Why, to the audition."

"Audition?" Henry said. It was an event he had assumed would take place in the far future. In the back of his mind he was already thinking of ways to weasel out of it. "Now? *Tonight?*"

"Of course!"

"But I thought you were going to make me dinner?"

"Make it yourself later on!"

"I don't have anything to sing!"

"I have music in my bag. Now move!"

Henry moved.

It was only when he and his mother were safely out of the building that Henry remembered that a copy of *The Doctor's Wife* had been in the VCR for the duration of her visit. Once the panic had passed, Henry grew thankful that he hadn't accidentally turned it on. Had that unfortunate event occurred, he realized, his alternatives would have been two: the oven or the window.

Despite a successful audition (in which he shunned his mother's choice of music and impressed the Pinafore Players committee with a rousing a cappella rendition of the Beatles' "Glass Onion"), Henry returned directly to his apartment, changed straight back into boxers and a T-shirt, and plopped himself down in front of the TV. Not that he had given up on his plan to get back in the swing of life. It would just have to wait a bit, for on the way home from the audition Henry realized that there was a final obstacle a few short days down the road that he had to get through before he could begin the slow creep back into the living world in earnest: his birthday.

Thirty-three years old. Not too young, not too old. A good age—but an age by which Henry had hoped to have accomplished so much more. After all, if he were Gershwin he'd only have five years to live. If he were Keats he would have been dead for eight. And then there was that Jesus guy. Not that Henry aspired to found an influential world religion, but ten or so unfinished projects, a kids' musical, and a twice-broken heart was not exactly a record to go out and celebrate. Still, family and friends tried to convince him otherwise. Ellen even offered to throw a party, but Henry refused, preferring to weather the storm in the solitude of his own home with the company of his TV and a bowl of Wheaties (he had finally switched). Though his mother and father each insisted upon dropping by to deliver gifts on the morning of the big day, Henry effectively staved off all other human interaction. Then late that afternoon, while Henry was watching Oprah lead a panel discussion on hair loss (one thing he could be thankful he didn't have—at least not yet), Glenn called.

"What are you up to tonight?"

"Haven't we been through this?" Henry said. "Nothing."

"Good. You're coming out with me."

"Guess again."

"Sorry," Glenn said. "This is a command performance. Write this down." He gave the address of the Sleepy Wheel, a club on 6th Street between Avenues B and C. "Be there. Eight o'clock."

"Glenn, I—"

"Henry, you're coming."

"At least tell me what it's all about?"

"It's your birthday, dork."

"I know, but—"

"You'll see."

The line went dead. Henry looked at the receiver. Just like that, it suddenly hit him. Diana! It had to be. The subject of dining room tables had come up in couples therapy. Names had been named. "Shit," Henry muttered, and slumped down on his couch. "Just what I need." Would Glenn really ream him out on his birthday? Henry wasn't sure. Just in case, he reviewed his defense.

1) That Diana found him attractive wasn't his fault.
2) He had turned her down.
3) Repeatedly.
4) He felt too embarrassed to admit it to Glenn.

In short, he was an innocent bystander, caught in the crossfire of a seemingly doomed marriage. There was nothing he could have done.

I'm OK, he thought nervously. *There's nothing he can say.*

That night Henry forced himself into a full set of clothes for only the second time in a month. Grabbing his jean jacket, he jogged down five flights, off to celebrate his thirty-three years on earth by being chewed out by his best friend. On the street, Henry discovered that he had a more immediate problem with which to contend—the temperature. In the week since his Players audition, fall had begun to turn to winter. With a muttered "damn," Henry craned his neck toward his window. Sure, it would be easy enough to jog back upstairs for a heavier coat, but three weeks of inactivity coupled with a poor diet and insomnia made what amounted to a five-flight schlep seem like a trek up Kilimanjaro. Besides, why trade in his jean jacket when the perfect way to increase his suffering quotient had been placed squarely in his lap? If he was lucky, maybe he'd get frostbite.

By the time he walked half a block, Henry knew that the cold was to be the least of his problems. Standing on the corner of Sixth Avenue, waiting for the light, he realized that every conceivable route east took him past a restaurant, coffee bar, or store where he and Tamar had been together in happier times. Indeed, the neighborhood was a virtual treasure trove of old haunts, memories waiting to explode in his face. Of course, there was an obvious solution: a cab. Why walk when he could be transported painlessly to his destination? There was a taxi idling right next to him, also waiting to cross Sixth Avenue, but just as Henry was raising his arm to flag it down, he saw a cab ride for what it was: a coward's way out. So what if a walk across town was painful? Shouldn't he be able to face his past like a man? Further, a brief if brutal tour down memory lane would fit in perfectly with his current misery regimen. The light changed. Though the cabbie glanced his way, Henry waved him on. Yes, he'd take a dash of good old-fashioned lovelorn angst to go with his frostbite. Steeling himself for the sweet pinprick of anguish, Henry turned up the collar of his jean jacket and got walking.

Despite his brave and somewhat masochistic willingness to face the most painful aspects of his immediate past, Henry was blindsided by the speed of the first assault. Half a block from his apartment stood a homeless man to whom Tamar had often given spare change. This short conversation took place:

HOMELESS MAN: Hey, where's your pretty girlfriend?
HENRY: She dumped me.
HOMELESS MAN: Loser.

Stunned, Henry watched his accuser wander into the night before finally managing an anemic "*My* pretty girlfriend? Where's *your* pretty girlfriend, jerk?"—a response he realized was as pathetic as it was uninspired. Though Henry had just vowed to walk all the way east, he was smart enough to know when to cut his losses. When he spotted another cab, he didn't hesitate. Seconds later, he was in the backseat, eyes closed, trying to block out the memory of the bluntly delivered "loser"—a characterization that suddenly seemed to be a brilliant and succinctly delivered summation of his life to date.

With the dreaded word continuing to echo through his mind, Henry opened his eyes and stared at his reflection in the window. His face had thinned out over the last month, the by-product of his all-cereal-all-the-time diet. His hair was on the long side, but still not long enough to obscure the final remnants of the famed blond streak. Henry cringed. Yes, he had seen it every time in the mirror for the past months. Despite his better judgment, he had even managed to convince himself that Sheila had been wrong—that despite all evidence to the contrary, the streak was indeed cool—but the sharp words of the homeless man, coupled with the chill November air, conspired to force Henry to see things as they were. Tamar had done more than dump him flat. She had made him look like a fool. Henry Mann? *Hip?* It was the mother of all oxymorons.

Henry sank low in the seat. A few short moments earlier he had looked forward to working himself into a state of near-poetic misery—a romantic suffering known only by the likes of Byron and Shelley—but he was now experiencing the downside of the life of Heathcliff. As the cab turned onto St. Marks Place, another glance at the streak made him so angry that it was all he could do to stop himself from punching at it in the window. Disgusted, Henry shifted focus and decided to use the window the way it was actually intended, as something to look out of. At that moment—as he gazed beyond his reflection to the world outside—something caught his eye. Henry sat up with a start. He pressed his face to the glass to get a closer look. Henry wasn't religious, but he knew a sign from God when he saw it.

"Driver!" he called. "Drop me here!"

Seconds later, Henry was pushing through the doors of the Astor Place barbershop, site of the infamous haircut. Yes, Tamar had played him for a fool, but that didn't mean he had to spend one second longer in the role. Though it was closing time, Henry parked his butt in the chair nearest the door. "Cut me!" he cried, gesturing wildly toward the front of his head. "Somebody cut my streak!" The nearest barber, a thin young man, backed away. As a second reached for her cell phone, poised to dial 911, the shop owner quickly saw Henry for what he was: a harmless hysteric in desperate need of a haircut. "Relax," the owner said. "My streak!"

Henry repeated, holding out a clump of hair. "Please!" Quick as a flash, a pair of scissors was in the owner's hand. With two expert snips, the hip Henry was laid to rest for good. Though no fee was requested, Henry dug into his wallet, threw a ten in the air, and burst back through the doors.

Back outside, something astonishing happened: A month of crushing sorrow and abject mortification washed clean away. Suddenly giddy, Henry glanced at his streak-free reflection in the barbershop window and found himself laughing. With a triumphant "Yes!" he began to run. Tamar . . . *who?* Wasn't she some girl he used to date? With another burst of laughter, Henry turned up the speed. After a month of misery, he couldn't believe how easy it had been to lay Tamar's memory to rest—as simple as a ten-second haircut! He couldn't wait to break the happy news to Glenn. In fact, he'd run all the way to the bar! "Check out my trim!" he'd cry. "Tamar is history! Drinks all around!"

It was a fine plan, but a plan that Henry never had the chance to execute. Indeed, the month spent sprawled inert on his couch had taken its toll. After moving six blocks east at a near sprint, he collapsed on a green bench in Tompkins Square Park, sucking wind. Sadly, that is where Henry's brief recovery fell to pieces. For seconds after sitting, Henry had a funny feeling that he had been on the same bench once before. At first he tried to ignore it, concentrating on catching his breath, but the feeling grew in intensity until, a moment later, Henry sprang back to his feet as though jettisoned by a slingshot. With an anguished gasp, he circled the bench, eyes wide. Could it be? While celebrating his freedom from Tamar, had his unconscious led him to the exact spot where they had once spent a late spring afternoon reciting Monty Python routines? Henry glanced around the small park to get his bearings, desperately hoping that he was wrong. Instead, his worst fears were confirmed—which is when the pain returned, hitting him like a tidal wave. Henry slumped against a lamppost. Indeed, the trip to the barber had been nothing more than an all too temporary placebo. Though he did his best to contain his emotions, Henry's eyes were soon misting heavily in sad contemplation of Tamar's dead-on recitation of the line "That's an ex-parrot!"

It took Henry a full ten minutes to tear himself away from the lamppost and then another five to make his way the final few blocks to the bar. By the time Henry reached the Sleepy Wheel, the emotional ups and downs of his journey had put him in a worse state of mind than when he had started. On top of that, the club seemed a total dive. The windows were black. There was rust on the doors' hinges. Though Henry considered cutting his losses and heading home, he knew he didn't have the energy to walk back through that minefield of memories. Who knew what other landmarks of lost love he had avoided while in the cab or when he had been running? There was nothing to be done but to walk down the stairs and cough up the five-dollar cover. Moments later, beer in hand, Henry pushed his way toward the back of the bar, looking for Glenn.

"Yo, Henry!"

Glenn was seated at a corner table. As Henry cut across the floor, searing heartache was partially displaced by raw fear, for he was suddenly certain that his initial feeling had been on the money—that Glenn had invited him here to enact some sort of drastic revenge. Perhaps he was planning to slip truth serum in his beer and force Henry to confess every lurid fantasy he had ever had about his wife? Then take him to an S&M parlor where he would be coerced into lying down on a giant set of electrified cutlery?

"Hey, man."

"Hey."

Henry hesitated and looked around the room. It was dimly lit, filled with around twenty other people, nursing drinks. A very Village scene. At least one article of black clothing appeared to be the ticket of admission. Given that Henry was in jeans and a maroon shirt, he half expected a bouncer to throw him out.

"So what's going on?"

"You'll see," Glenn said. "Have a seat."

Henry did as he was told.

"By the way,'" Glenn went on, "you didn't speak to Diana today, did you?"

Henry's heart took a seismic leap. He was right. Glenn knew!

"Uh, no. Why?"

"Nothing. She was going to meet us, that's all. And our machine is broken."

"Oh." Henry took a long swallow of beer. "So?" he asked. "How's that going? I mean, with Diana?"

Glenn shrugged. "We're working on it. Hey, I see you got rid of your streak."

"Yeah," Henry said. "On the way over."

What followed was the first awkward pause Henry had felt with Glenn in years—if ever. Normally, Henry would have used Glenn's mention of the streak as his cue to tell the tale of his harrowing trip east. Instead, he was overcome by a powerful urge to confess. Obviously, Glenn knew something. Why else would he be acting so strangely? Wasn't it better to come clean rather than stand accused? To get it over with once and for all?

"Listen, Glenn."

"Yeah?"

The two friends locked eyes. Though innocent, Henry suddenly felt like the world's most infamous adulterer, Lancelot to Glenn's Arthur. It was now or never.

"I just think we—"

Before he could go on, the lights dimmed further.

"Ah," Glenn said. "Here we go. Look."

Exasperated, Henry forced himself to bite his tongue. Though he hadn't noticed it, fifteen feet away, a microphone, acoustic guitar, and stool sat on a small stage. In his current state of mind he half expected Diana herself to be the main attraction, perhaps in a piece of performance art entitled "My Husband's Best Friend Is Satan."

Instead, something even stranger occurred. An attractive woman in a white T-shirt, black vest, and tight jeans stepped out of the wings. Henry squinted. Then he looked at Glenn. Then back at the stage. Which is when he fully comprehended who the attractive woman was: Christine! Her hair was up in a bun—a look Henry didn't usually like, but in this instance it highlighted her cheekbones, bringing her features into sharp relief. And the unibrow? Undetectable at twenty feet. No doubt about it—she looked good. As Christine pulled up a stool and adjusted the microphone, Henry upgraded that assessment to very good, then all the way up the ladder to excellent.

Henry looked to Glenn. "You son of a bitch."

Glenn winked. "Happy birthday, fuckhead."

Surprised and extremely relieved (no need for confessions now!), Henry returned his attention to the stage.

"Hi." Christine flashed a self-deprecating smile. "I'd like to sing you a few songs."

She strummed a chord and saw to last-minute tuning. If she had seen him, she certainly wasn't letting on. Truth be told, she seemed too preoccupied to care. After adjusting the microphone a few times, she was finally ready.

"This is by Joni Mitchell," she said. With that, she played the first few chords to ' "People's Parties." Then she lifted her head shyly, took stock of the audience, and finally began to sing.

To Henry's surprise, she had a strong, clear voice. Though she cracked on one of the first high notes, halfway through she seemed to gain confidence and perform with more feeling. When the song was finished, the crowd clapped politely. Christine took a sip of beer. With the first tune under her belt she seemed to relax a bit.

"OK," she said. "I'm going to do a few originals."

Henry was worried. How could her own songs hope to compete with Joni Mitchell? As he was soon to discover, they couldn't, but they weren't terrible, either. A bit folksy for Henry's taste, but sweet. Perhaps the best was "He Took Me Out," a ballad about a first date. Though the song made passing reference to a slow dance, Henry was relieved to find that the description was more romantic than graphic (i.e., no penises mentioned, erect, limp, animal, or otherwise). All told, Christine did six originals, then finished with "Hey, You've Got to Hide Your Love Away" by the Beatles. She got a rousing ovation.

"Not bad, huh?" Glenn called over the applause.

"Yeah," Henry replied. "But why'd you bring me here? She has a boyfriend, right?"

"Actually," Glenn said, "I hear he's on the way out."

Henry was surprised at the news. Also at his level of interest.

"Really?" he said. "Who told you that?"

"Oh, I have my sources."

"Come on. Don't be a—"

"OK, OK," Glenn said. "Relax. It was Ellen."

Henry looked back to Christine and smiled. Ellen—a good source, as reliable as she was perky.

"So," Glenn went on, "wanna greet the star?"

Moments later, Henry was standing near the back of a small crowd of well-wishers, waiting to say hello, but when Glenn struck up a conversation with a short woman with bright red hair who introduced herself as Alice, Christine's roommate, he began to wish he had slipped quietly out the back. A horrible thought had occurred to him. What if she knew who he was? The jerk who dumped her friend after a single date?

"I'm surrounded," he whispered to Glenn.

"By who?" Glenn said.

"Her friends. Maybe even her boyfriend. Or ex-boyfriend."

Henry glanced over his shoulder, scanning the crowd for good-looking guys. Or better yet, ugly ones.

"Will you relax already?"

Henry tried, but when he recognized a fourth-grade teacher from Christine's school, a middle-aged man with a handlebar mustache, he grew more and more self-conscious. Would he remember him from his poetry reading? And how would Christine feel about his coming to see her? Especially without an invitation? Her feelings might range anywhere from touched to furious. Never one to thrive on uncertainty, Henry feared the worst, but he had no time to run now. Soon Glenn was congratulating her. Just like that, it was Henry's turn.

"Hi," he said.

"Oh, Henry?" Christine said, surprised. Her tone was straight from the "I'm still pissed but too mature to be rude" playbook, not as bad as furious but a long way from touched. "You were here?"

Henry swallowed hard. "Yeah. You were great," he stammered. "I had no idea you sang so well. Or that you wrote songs really. I mean, you didn't really talk about it much, you know . . ."

"On our date?"

"Yeah."

"Well, I guess it didn't come up."

There was an awkward pause. As Henry was scrambling to think of what to say next, he was saved by the redheaded roomie.

"Great job," Alice cried, and held her arms wide.

Seemingly thankful for the interruption, Christine threw herself into Alice's arms. Henry stood still, feeling useless. Present but ignored. When the roommates finally pulled apart, Christine remembered her manners.

"Oh, Alice . . . This is Henry."

"Oh, hi," Alice said, and turned right back to Christine.

For a moment, Henry was slightly miffed. Why such short shrift? But as he was treated to a view of the back of Alice's head, he began to view her nonchalance in a different light: *His name had meant nothing to her!* Maybe—just maybe—Christine had never even mentioned him! Could it be that he was blowing the whole thing way out of proportion? For a change?

Just as Henry was allowing himself to enjoy the sweet release of relief, though, the pendulum swung again. In a horrible instant, he saw Alice turn back toward him, eyes wide. There was a deathly pause. Then she held a closed fist to her mouth, as though to stifle a laugh.

"Oh, you're *Henry*," she said.

Henry suddenly felt weak, as though the bones had been painlessly yanked out of his legs.

"Yeah," he said, looking for a chair. "That's me."

"You're famous," Christine said, flashing a look at Alice. "I told her about your musical."

"Right, right," Alice said quickly. "Your musical. What was it about?"

Henry didn't buy that for a second.

"*The Great Gatsby*," Christine said.

"Cool," Alice said.

"Thanks," Henry managed.

"Anyway," Christine said, "I should join some friends. Thanks for coming."

"Sure thing."

As Henry collapsed into a chair, Christine hurried toward the back of the bar to the fourth-grade teacher and a slightly goofy-looking guy in khakis Henry immediately assumed was Paul, the boyfriend. A few seconds later, he saw Alice join them, looking his way, giggling now. Henry realized that things were even worse than he thought. His first assumption was that Aliee's "Oh, you're *Henry*" referred only to his insensitive postdate behavior, but in the face of that giggle he suddenly knew it was much, much worse. *She knew about the slow-dance woody!* Mortified, Henry glanced around the room. He was suddenly convinced that everyone knew. The fourth-grade teacher! Goofy-looking khaki man! Even the bartender!

"So?" Glenn said. "Another drink?"

"No way," Henry stammered.

"What's wrong? Why are you sitting down?"

"I'm not," Henry said, standing again. "I'm outta here."

How could he stay? He was a walking humiliation. Bill Clinton post Monica. Pee Wee Herman post movie theater. As crushed as Catherine the Great post horse!

"Outta here?" Glenn said. "Come on. Let's celebrate. It's your birthday."

Henry was already moving toward the door.

"Now!" he said.

It wasn't until half an hour later, seated in a coffee shop on Astor Place over coffee and cake, that Henry was finally able to get out the whole story. As he had expected, Glenn was more amused than sympathetic.

"Let me get this straight," he said. "You really think she told all her friends about a hard-on? That you got like six months ago?"

Viewed with a little perspective, Henry had to admit, it seemed a bit implausible. Especially when he took one important fact into consideration: that he hadn't even been sure if Christine had felt it.

"Listen," Glenn continued. "I'd take one hundred to one odds that Christine was basically telling the truth. She told Alice about your music, that's all. Maybe mentioned your date at the time." He smiled. "I'm sure she's too grown-up to be as obsessed about your dick as you are." He motioned toward Henry's dessert. "Now eat your birthday cake. You're obviously weak with hunger."

Henry looked at the half-eaten piece of German chocolate cake and sank back in his seat, thoroughly defeated. Some birthday. He had braved near-Arctic temperatures, subjected himself to the nostalgia tour from hell, then imagined a public humiliation to put Hester Prynne's to shame. True, Glenn hadn't yelled at him, but was that really such a great trade-off?

And then, when Henry thought he couldn't possibly sink any lower, he sank even lower. Suddenly, Glenn's attention was diverted by something out the window.

"What is it?" Henry asked.

"Nothing," Glenn said. He looked back at Henry. "Forget it."

The answer came a bit too quickly to be credible. In fact, there was something about Glenn's tone that gave Henry a bad feeling—a feeling that there was something outside that window he wouldn't like but should probably see for his own good. Unfortunately, he was exactly right. When Henry turned, he caught a full frontal of Christine walking by arm in arm with a man. And not the middle-aged fourth-grade teacher. Or goofy-looking khaki man. No, this guy was decidedly devoid of goofy characteristics. He was muscular, in fact, with features that could easily be described as chiseled. Worst of all, he was blond. Henry hadn't remembered seeing him at the Sleepy Wheel but immediately thought of Hans. Why were his women always stolen away by hunky jocks?

"Sorry, man," Glenn said. "I heard they were on the outs."

Henry turned back around and forced a smile. "Apparently not."

He took an unenthusiastic bite of cake and washed it down with a lukewarm swallow of coffee. While he was dabbing his mouth with his napkin, Henry came to what seemed to him an important decision—one that laid the whole Christine/slow-dance issue to rest forever.

"Oh, fuck it," he said.

Glenn looked up from his own cup of warm coffee.

"Fuck what?"

Henry nodded toward the window.

"Christine."

"What about her?"

Henry picked at his cake with his fork.

"She's not my type anyway."

"Oh, really?" Glenn said.

"Really," Henry answered.

It was a lie, of course, but a lie that Henry allowed himself to believe—as a sort of a gift.

After all, it was his birthday.

10

mrs. henry mann?

henry's first shift back at Albright after an eight-week leave of absence was marked by a special event: Glenn's going-away party. Though under normal circumstances Henry would have looked forward to such a gathering immensely, he now viewed it with great trepidation. Despite a successful audition for the Players and the outing to the Sleepy Wheel, Henry knew that socializing was still a definite risk—that he still suffered from a marked tendency to whine and otherwise drone on about his current favorite subject: his broken heart. He was also well aware of the fact that he was too self-absorbed to do anything about it.

To Henry's surprise, though, the festivities were easier to bear than he had anticipated. Thanks to the decorating expertise of Doug and Ellen, 34 North had never looked better. Not only had they hung streamers and ribbons across the ceiling, but Wynn Hamilton Albright now wore a fake beard and mustache and, given the coming holiday season, a Santa hat. There was even a special athletic event: Glenn's final pencil toss exhibition. To his surprise (though the two quick beers may have helped), Henry cheered loudly and chatted easily with friends.

Unfortunately, the fun soon came to an end. Inevitably, the phone rang. Ellen answered. It was their supervisor, Steve. The room held its collective breath, everyone praying not to be the next victim. Then Henry saw Ellen turn his way. "Damn," he muttered.

"Sorry," she said, almost apologetically. "But it's for you."

It seemed only fitting that Henry's first assignment after a two-month hiatus would be with the great and hideous Patricia. Though his last encounter with the hyena had gone unexpectedly well, resulting in a free Chinese dinner, this time the beast's behavior was more in line with her reputation. Not only didn't the hyena recognize Henry as the proofreader who bore a taller, hairy, better-looking resemblance to her husband, but the first sentence out of her mouth included the most loathsome word in the night staffer's vocabulary: deadline. In short, Henry was presented with a foot-high stack of documents to be word-processed, proofread, xe-roxed, and sent out before Federal Express closed up shop for the night—the part-timer's equivalent of being parachuted into the middle of the Tet Offensive. Failure would not be tolerated and death was likely. As he wrote down the instructions Henry couldn't help but notice that there was a new addition to Gergen's wall of taxidermy: the head of an antelope. Henry found it alarmingly easy to picture his corpse impaled on the antlers.

Once Henry started working, something surprising happened: The pressure of the deadline turned out to be just what he needed. For the first time in weeks he was simply too busy (not to mention frightened) to think about Tamar. For two hours he ran around like a wild beast, taking orders, proofing, xeroxing, typing labels with remarkable skill and dexterity. (Though he hated to admit it, Henry was actually proud of the fact that, when the chips were down, he was a damned good legal assistant.) Despite Henry's best efforts, he was only one person. When he realized there was no way he would be able to finish the task alone, he did what any good soldier is trained to do in times of crisis: call in reinforcements. To his enormous surprise, the new recruit was none other than an old comrade in arms: Christine. Wearing a snug mock turtleneck and jeans, she looked trim, ready for battle. Her hair was down this time and hung loosely to the middle of her back, but the assessment he had made a week earlier still held. She looked good.

"Hey there," she said as she approached.

Henry was more than a bit surprised at just how hard his heart had started to beat. Glenn's assurances aside, he couldn't help thinking about Alice's giggle fit.

"How you doing?" he managed.

"Pretty good."

"I really did enjoy your show the other night. Sorry I was too tongue-tied to really say it."

"No, you said it. Thanks."

As she looked over the stacks of documents, Henry racked his brain for what to say next. While he was debating between two scintillating alternatives, "How's school going?" and "Do you have any more gigs lined up?" Christine plopped herself down at the terminal, clicked on the word processor, and said, "Let's get started."

With those words, Henry was off the hook, an unspoken pact signed. Both parties would pretend that they were nothing more than passing acquaintances, work partners called in to do a job. Ironically, Henry and Christine turned out to be as compatible with paperwork as they had been grinding hips to "Desperado." With Christine manning the computer and Henry continuing to proofread and xerox, they got the distribution out with seven minutes to spare. But once the job was over, there was very little to say. After they spent a few moments congratulating each other on making a deadline a lesser pair of legal assistants would have missed, Christine got out fast.

"Well," she said. "Nice working with you."

If one of Henry's concerns had been that Christine was too mid-western to understand the subtleties of irony, he needn't have worried.

"Yeah," Henry said. "It was good to see you."

Henry had to admit that it was. Of course, there was the unibrow (yes, in the bright office light it was still noticeable, *barely*, even if Glenn and Doug said it wasn't), but as Christine walked toward the elevators, he treated himself to a view of the famous xeroxed butt. Then he thought of what Doug had said outside the theater—that there was no statute of limitations on apologies.

"Hey, wait."

Christine stopped and turned. "Yeah?"

She had made it fifteen feet down the hallway.

Henry swallowed hard. "I know I should have said this ages ago. But I'm really sorry for how I acted."

Before Christine could answer, a cleaning lady walked by dragging an enormous vacuum. Though Henry suspected that the woman was of East European descent and didn't speak a word of English, Christine waited for her to round the corner before responding.

"OK," she said.

"And I'm sorry I never said it earlier."

Christine looked to the floor, then back to Henry. "Yeah," she said. "So am I."

With another awkward pause, Henry found himself praying for the cleaning lady's return. Christine picked up the slack.

"And by the way," she said. "I heard about your breakup. That's rough."

Henry was impressed. He didn't know whether he would have been so gracious if their roles had been reversed. Perhaps she felt a little guilty about her roomie's behavior the night of his birthday? Whatever the reason, Henry realized that there was nothing stopping him from returning the favor. Two could play that game.

"Yeah," he said. "Well, it wasn't meant to be, I guess. That's great about you and your boyfriend, though. What's his name?"

"Paul."

"Yeah, like I said," Henry went on, pleased with himself. "That's great. I'm sure he's a terrific guy."

"Yeah, well," Christine replied. "Actually . . . we broke up."

The tone she employed was matter-of-fact, as though she were telling Henry that he had forgotten to put a return address on the Federal Express label. Glenn had been right. Clearly, Paul hadn't meant that much to her. Perhaps he not only looked like Hans but suffered from a similar gray-matter deficiency? Henry imagined taking a nose dive for Christine's ankles and begging for a second chance, possibly even dragging her by the hair to the closest judge. Unfortunately, decorum dictated a more restrained approach.

"I'm sorry to hear that," he lied.

"That's alright," Christine said. "My decision." She glanced toward the elevators. "Anyway, I better get back."

Henry was relieved. With Christine's status suddenly on the table, lying there like a live grenade, there was somehow even less to say than before.

"Yeah, right. See you around."

"OK. Bye."

"Right. Bye."

As she walked away, Henry once again imagined that ankle dive, this time ravishing her by the recycling bin. But as she rounded the corner out of his line of vision, he took a moment to remind himself of an important fact: He still wasn't over Tamar. His renewed interest in Christine—if it was to last at all—would have to wait. He still needed time to heal, to indulge in life's simpler pleasures.

Back at 34 North he got an immediate opportunity. To Henry's delight, he arrived just in time to cheer Glenn on as he successfully lodged twenty-two pencils in a row in the ceiling—a firm record.

. . .

Like most sons, Henry hated it when his mother was right. Though never once in his recollection had she said "I told you so," Mrs. Mann had a way, unique to mothers, of conveying that exact sentiment with a look or inflection. In this case, Henry knew that he deserved it, for though it was antithetical to everything he deemed socially acceptable, it didn't take him long to realize that the Pinafore Players was exactly what he needed, the perfect pastime to save him from himself, sitting at home, stewing in his own juices. Yes, it was terminally unhip—the antithesis of everything he had tried to be with Tamar. Even so, the group had its advantages. After all, singing and acting were both activities he enjoyed, as was meeting new people, women in particular. Even though his mother had been notably wrong as to the status of Sally Harris (still happily engaged), he took the news in stride. It only took a conversation or two for Henry to see that they weren't suited. Yes, she was pretty, but her long blonde hair and air of entitlement reminded him of Sheila. He'd gone down that path before.

Still, signs of recovery were on the horizon. By early January Henry had noticed an energetic soprano with a penchant for bright red lipstick in the chorus, name unknown. Twice, during rehearsals, Henry caught himself imagining kissing her; once, imagining removing her shirt and laying her down on the grand piano. There was also the older woman (late forties, Henry guessed) with whom he had been partnered in the chorus. One night over Christmas break, Henry found himself constructing an elaborate fantasy that included staying in her lavish Park Avenue boudoir for an entire weekend while her husband and teenaged kids were out of town on a ski trip. He even envisioned a threesome involving the eighteen-year-old Spanish nanny.

Toward the end of January his father phoned him with some interesting news. Apparently, Amanda, the woman with whom Henry had fathered six (or was it seven?) children, had thought he was cute.

"Why not give her a call?" Mr. Mann said (this after observing that her rear end had been "a dream"). "You two had lots in common."

For a moment, Henry's world was turned completely upside down. Amanda, his corn-fed, goat-milked, Jennifer Aniston look-alike bride thought he was . . . *cute!?* Of course he'd call—in an Iowa farmgirl second. But just as the words "sounds great" were forming in his mouth, Henry reminded himself of something: Did he really want to get involved with a woman who had slept with his very own father? Not only that, but a woman who had stamina problems? When his father casually mentioned that Amanda suffered from a long-term medical condition that interfered with her ability to produce saliva, the decision was made. Still, when Henry hung up the phone, he indulged in a repeat fantasy. Once again, he and Amanda were in their Iowa barn, naked on a bale of hay, entwined in each other's arms. Into the VCR went the copy of *The Doctor's Wife*. Though Henry wasn't quite ready to jump back in the race, he was priming the engines.

That was still Henry's approximate state of mind a little over two months later in early April when *H.M.S. Pinafore* began its two-week run. Despite an opening-night mishap in which the mainsail of the ship came loose, flapped across the stage like a ghost, and wrapped itself around the leading lady during her big aria, the show was a great success. Nearly all the people he invited actually came to see it: Rye, Adam, Melissa, Jill, and his father and Greta (miraculously, they were still dating). By closing night, Glenn and Diana were the only ones left.

After the final curtain calls, Henry followed his shipmates up a back stairway to the lobby to meet his friends. With the cast members still in costume, the large room took on the feel of a pier crowded with sailors home for shore leave. In fact, the area was so jammed that it took Henry a few moments to locate Glenn and Diana standing across the way by the exit doors. Before he could reach them, however, he accidentally bumped into Joan Fitz, who had miraculously landed the role of Little Buttercup (though in

Henry's view there was nothing particularly little or buttery about her), and his mother, who, upon admiring the beautiful Victorian dresses worn by the female cast, had decided at the last second to join the chorus. After a delay in which Henry met his mother's publisher and masseuse along with Joan Fitz's entire extended family, he was finally able to spring himself and cut through the crowd to where Glenn and Diana were waiting.

Diana threw her arms wide. "You were great!" she cried.

With that, she hugged him tight. And the kiss? Perhaps a bit too close to his lips. In the past, this might have made Henry uncomfortable (especially with Glenn watching), but now he knew that, at heart, the gesture was friendly, not romantic. A few weeks earlier, he and Diana had finally met for coffee to talk things out. Despite their mutual attraction, Diana had taken the brunt of the blame. ("What can I say, Henry," she had repeated, as if concluding an essay on the subject of her sexual predilections. "I'm just one horny bitch.") Though their relationship had never been consummated—or perhaps precisely because it hadn't—Henry knew that he'd always carry a little bit of her with him. Indeed, he'd never sit down to a formal meal again without thinking about what might have been.

Eventually the reigning queen of table sex released him. Though it still pained Henry to notice, she looked great, wearing a tight blouse and short cotton skirt—this even though it was winter. If he ever had a wife who looked half that good at thirty-seven, he'd die a happy man. What was Glenn thinking when he cheated, anyway?

"So what'd you really think?" Henry asked.

"What did I think?" Glenn said. "Fuckin's A is what I thought!"

The rave review was followed by a high five. When Diana leaned close again, Henry feared another hug. Instead, she simply whispered, "You look hot as hell in white."

Embarrassed, Henry glanced down at his sailor suit. It had certainly never occurred to him that such a costume could improve his appearance. The first time he had put it on, he had felt like a jackass. By closing night he had merely felt foolish. Despite Diana's views on the matter, he looked forward to putting it out to pasture.

"Lemme get a little less nautical," Henry said. "Then let's get out of here."

After each performance it was the Players' custom to take over the large backroom of a nearby pub, the Tavern. Soon Glenn, Diana, and Henry were seated at a small table, surrounded by a sea of celebrating thespians. Many were already drunk; those who weren't were doing their best to catch up, Henry included. It was in this state of preinebriation that Mrs. Mann appeared at the table bearing three pieces of chocolate-raspberry upside-down cake.

"A closing-night treat," she said. "It was shaped like a ship. Have some. Go! Eat!"

Though Henry didn't usually mix beer with dessert, he decided to make an exception.

"Thanks, Mom."

"Mind if I join you for a moment?" Mrs. Mann said.

"Sure," Glenn said. "Pull up a chair."

Unfortunately, there was no nearby chair to be pulled. Mrs. Mann placed half a butt cheek on Henry's (nearly pushing him to the floor), then with little provocation began to discuss her new book, *The Outer Look Inward*, describing it as so ahead of its time that it was "self-help for the fourth millennium." It was a long ten minutes before she left to join Joan Fitz, her family, and like creatures at a nearby table. When Henry was finally left alone again with Glenn and Diana, the conversation turned to *Hoo, Hoo! Haw, Haw!* Apparently, the show was encountering casting troubles. As Glenn put it, "It's tough to find an actor with enough range to tackle the role of Chimp Three." This discussion was eventually interrupted by a gang of cast members who tried to push Henry into joining them in a reprise of the choral number "Gaily Tripping, Lightly Skipping."

"Go for it," Glenn said. "Serenade us."

Henry demurred. He viewed his tenure with the Pinafore Players as short-lived, a quick stopover to help him get over a traumatic period in his life. It was one thing to sing such a song onstage, but in a bar? That was tantamount to acquiring full-fledged citizenship in the Land of Dork. Every man had his limits.

"Sorry," Henry told the gang. "I'll take a rain check."

Undeterred, the cast members burst into an enthusiastic if somewhat shrill rendition of the song. After listening politely for half a minute or so, Diana decided it was time to get down to business.

"So, Henry," she said, glancing around the crowded bar. "Tell us everything."

"Everything?" Henry asked.

Glenn stirred his gin and tonic.

"Translation," he said. "Which ones do you like?"

"As in women?"

"No, idiot. As in sea horses."

"In that case, I like lots of them."

"Come on."

Henry shrugged. "I'm still not ready."

For a second the trio's attention was drawn by a new group of Players belting out a spirited rendition of "Sometimes When We Touch" at a nearby upright (Henry was always amused and sometimes appalled at just how much heartfelt singing occurred within the organization). A slightly chubby guy named Tim was at the keys.

"Not ready?" Diana frowned. "Come off it. Lots of these women would love a guy like you."

"I don't know about that."

"Sure they would," Glenn said. He surveyed the room. "Let me check out the talent."

Given that Glenn's standards in looks were a notch or two below his, Henry knew what the verdict would be well before it was delivered. In any case, he didn't need to be told that there were many attractive women in the Players. Glenn being Glenn, his friend took it upon himself to inform him of that fact anyway.

"This place," he declared, "is a fucking gold mine. Jesus, Henry, it would be morally unconscionable to walk away from this bar tonight without at least one phone number."

"My point exactly," Diana said.

Henry was sticking to his guns. "Too bad I'm not interested in anyone."

"Bullshit."

"I'm not."

"Who is she?"

"Yeah," Diana said. "Who?"

"Come on, guys. No one."

If Henry had been honest, he would have confessed that he had been spending an inordinate amount of time over the final week of rehearsals with his attention focused squarely on the soprano with red lipstick, now positively identified as Anne DuGot, a junior editor at a woman's magazine. Henry couldn't resist watching her rise from a table of giggling twenty-somethings and meander across the room to the piano. Glenn and Diana caught on immediately.

"Aha!" Diana said.

"Gotcha!" Glenn added.

"Christ," Henry said. "You guys are disgusting."

"Stop stalling," Diana said. "What's her name?"

Henry knew he was sunk, but in an effort to irritate his friends as much as possible, he took a large bite of cake and chewed very slowly. When he was through, he patted his mouth with a napkin, then reached for his beer. Diana grabbed his arm.

"Her name!"

Henry calmly removed her arm and drank anyway. By the time he put his glass back on the table, he was ready to talk.

"OK, OK. She's Anne. She grew up in Montreal. That's just about all I know about her."

"So here's your chance to find out more," Diana said. "Come on. It's closing night. Show off a little."

"Yeah," Glenn said, "Kick that fucker off the piano and play yourself. You'll blow her away."

Henry smiled ruefully. "Yeah," he said. "Maybe I'll play a few bars of 'My Pink Suit.'"

"Why not?" Diana said.

"Please! I was kidding."

"Hey, it was catchy," Glenn said, then began to lightly sing in a slightly Joe Crockerish tenor, "My Pink Suit. There's no substitute . . ."

Diana moved her head close to his and joined in.

"It's sure a beaut . . ."

Then with Glenn, "My Pink Suit!"

They kissed. Henry was happy (not to mention more than a little bit relieved) to see them getting along so well.

"She'd love it!" Diana said. "It's a great song."

"It's crap," Henry said dismissively. Still, he found himself looking at the piano. Should he play? One thing was certain, if he didn't he wouldn't see her again—probably ever. Tonight was the night to make his move.

"Henry," Glenn said more seriously, "it's time. Get back in the game."

"You think?"

The two friends locked eyes, and with the mock seriousness of a father informing his son that, yes, a shave might finally be in order, Glenn nodded.

"You're ready," he said.

Well aware that Glenn and Diana would badger him into action sooner or later, Henry bowed to the inevitable.

"What the hell," he said.

"Good boy," Diana said.

"And while you're up there, play 'Stairway to Heaven.'"

"Fuck you."

On the other hand, with the revelers now singing "Daydream Believer," "Stairway to Heaven" suddenly didn't seem so bad. Henry chugged the rest of his beer and stood up. Though he was a bit nervous, he was fully confident that his stint at the keys would be a success. After all, playing piano was a skill he could always rely on. Regardless of whether he ended up with Anne's number or not, it was only a sing-along. How could anything possibly go wrong?

He soon found out.

Phase One: Mrs. Mann sees Henry walk to the piano, stands, and shouts, "Oh, Henry! Are you going to play? Oh, everyone! Everyone! If you've never heard him, you're in for a treat! He's brilliant! Brilliant!" At the piano, she practically pushes Tim off the bench, crying, "Play, darling! Play!"

Phase Two: Henry plays up a storm. Nobody in the troupe has heard him before (except, of course, his mother and Joan Fitz, whom, with a few sharp looks, Henry encourages to stay in her seat). Anne briefly leaves to get another drink, but she soon returns and eventually sits next to Henry on the piano bench. Even better, she laughs at his jokes. They're hitting it off.

Phase Three: Henry, Anne, and the group of singers sing the sappiest rendition of "Looks Like We Made It" on record. At the end, the sheer hokiness of the number strikes everyone as funny, especially Henry and Anne. Soon they are laughing so hard it hurts. That's when Henry feels something funny in the back of his throat. Still laughing, he coughs. Anne slaps his back. Seconds later, a substance resembling liquefied chocolate-raspberry upside-down cake begins to stream violently out of his nose onto her dress.

Phase Four: The room hushes while Tim, the chubby pianist, attempts to administer the Heimlich. Finally able to convince his savior that he's all right, Henry apologizes madly as Anne leaves, weeping, her dress covered with the liquefied cake that emerged from Henry's nostrils.

Phase Five: After receiving a pep talk in the bathroom from Glenn, Henry marches back out, apologizes again to those who witnessed the unsightly eruption, then continues to play. Anne does not return. Henry does not get her number.

Later that night, Henry and Glenn stood in front of the tavern, waiting for Diana to finish in the ladies' room before catching cabs to their respective homes. It was an opportunity Henry took to smoke his first cigarette in years. Not having the guts to commit suicide, he figured that he would see what he could do about contracting a severe case of lung cancer.

"Never was a lady wooed in such fashion," Glenn said.

Henry forced a smile. "Yeah, I'm right back in the game, alright." He inhaled deeply and tried to hold the smoke in his lungs. "One hell of a way to get the ball rolling."

He coughed violently.

"Relax," Glenn said. He lit his own cigarette. "She overreacted. Everyone else thought the whole thing was funny."

"You think?"

"Well," Glenn said, "it's not every day a person gets to see upside-down cake gush out of someone's face."

"Gee, thanks."

"Anytime."

Just then a group of Players barreled out of the bar and stumbled up the sidewalk. Though mortified down to his bones, Henry had to admit that some small part of him was strangely glad the whole thing had happened. Yes, he had a ways to go before he would be completely healed, but that apoplectic laughter followed by the Old Faithful from his nasal cavity had been somehow cathartic, as if a major chunk of misery had been expunged, kidney-stone-like, in one fell swoop. Henry took another puff of his cigarette, this time being careful to inhale less deeply. He looked inside to where Diana was lingering in the ladies' room, then back to Glenn.

Suddenly, it seemed like a good time to finish what he had started in the Sleepy Wheel—to put his old life behind him so he could start anew.

"Seems like you and Diana are getting along," he said.

Glenn nodded. "A few kinks, but basically, yeah. It's nice."

"You know, Glenn—" Henry started.

His friend cut him off. "Don't bother, Henry. I know."

"You what?"

"You and Diana, right?"

Henry was stunned. "Yeah," he said. "But I never—"

"Relax," Glenn said. He smiled. "I know that, too."

"Couples therapy?"

A cab turned up 57th Street. Glenn took a long drag from his cigarette, then grinned. "It may have come up a few times."

"I swear . . . the night of my birthday I thought you were going to kill me."

Glenn shot him a glance. "I was."

"Really?"

"Yeah. My initial plan was to confront you about it in front of Diana, but when she didn't show, I took it as an omen. I guess I realized that it wasn't really your fault, you know? Shit, I probably drove Diana to it. If I hadn't cheated . . . Anyway, we talked some more with our therapist. Yeah, I was pissed you didn't tell me about it, but I can see your side now. It must have been awkward as hell. Plus, you aren't the kind of person who would screw over a friend."

Henry knew he had earned that trust by the slimmest of margins. After all, the Sunday morning after his first date with Tamar he had picked up the phone and dialed Diana's number, fully intending to arrange a visit. Now Henry looked to his friend. Given that confession seemed to be in the air, perhaps it was a good time to admit to something else. First, he chucked his cigarette in the gutter. Lung cancer would have to wait.

"You know what?"

"What?"

He waited as a garbage truck pulled up to the curb.

"I think about Christine sometimes."

"Well, well," Glenn said, obviously pleased. "I thought she looked like a Muppet?"

He held his right index finger to his forehead to signify the unibrow.

"OK," Henry said. "So I'm shallow. I admit it."

Glenn waved a hand. "Hey, no more shallow than I am. If I didn't think Diana was attractive, no way would I marry her. The thing of it is, that Christine is no slouch."

"I know," Henry said. "She looked great down at that bar."

She did, too—in her own way, just as good as Anne DuGot. And she and Henry were clearly a better match. Anne was too uptight, too prim. So what if Henry had spewed liquefied chocolate cake all over her clothes? Was that any reason to get in such a snit? If Christine had been in Anne's place, Henry felt sure that she would have kept on laughing, cleaned herself off, and gone on singing. Who cared about the unibrow anyway? She was sexy.

"So you don't think she's too . . . I don't know, midwestern for me, huh? I mean, she was a cheerleader in high school."

"And you were a geek," Glenn said. "In fact, despite that streak of dye you subjected us to, you still are. I doubt she holds that against you."

Henry nodded, then took a moment to watch two garbage men toss a pile of trash bags into the back of their truck.

"Do you think she'd give me a second chance?"

Glenn took a final drag from his cigarette and stamped it out on the pavement. "Dude, you know nothing about women. She liked you once. If you play it right, you're in."

"I hope," Henry said. "I just don't want to lead her on. I want to be sure I'm over Tamar."

"Well, make up your mind fast. Because pretty soon she's going to meet someone else and you, my friend, will be left with a big bag of nothing."

The friends were silent for a moment. Then Henry saw Glenn give him a knowing look—a look that made him nervous.

"Hey."

"Yeah?"

Glenn smiled. "This isn't about that boner, is it?"

Caught off guard, Henry couldn't stop the answer from reading all over his face.

"Christ, I knew it," Glenn said.

The truth was that Henry had considered inviting Christine to see him in the show, but putting together his invitation list, he had imagined a worst-case scenario: Upon opening the mail, Christine would turn to Alice. "Hey! Guess who invited me to see him in *H.M.S. Pinafore?* Captain Wood!" "Oh, really?" Alice would reply. "Did he address the invitation with his . . . you know?" Hilarity would ensue. Needless to say, that envelope was never sent.

"Jesus, Henry," Glenn went on. "Even if she noticed, I'm sure she took it as a compliment, alright?"

"You think?" Henry asked.

"How else could she take it? Hold on—lemme ask Diana."

Henry glanced over his shoulder and gasped. She had come out of the restaurant.

"Ask me what?" she said.

"Nothing," Henry said quickly. "Boy talk."

"Yeah," Glenn said. "We were just talking about Henry and Christine."

"Glenn!" Henry said.

"Relax," Glenn said. "I was just going to ask my wife if she thinks you two would be a good match."

Diana took Glenn's hand. "Considering I haven't met her yet, sounds great."

Glenn looked pointedly at Henry. "See? It's in the stars. So call her, OK?"

How could Henry argue with that?

"OK, OK," he said. "I will. Promise."

Moments later, Henry saw his friends to a cab. Though it was at least three in the morning, he turned downtown and began to walk. He needed to think something through. Now that he had made the decision to get back in the game, he faced a new challenge: to safeguard against rejection. After all, despite his apology to Christine at Albright, Henry knew the odds were against him. Bottom line, he had rejected her. Callously even.

As he walked, Henry became convinced that the only surefire way to ensure an affirmative response was to come up with a date idea so wonderful that Christine would say yes whether she liked him or not. The old standbys—coffee, dinner, movie, museum—wouldn't do. Sure, the Natural History Museum had a wonderful dinosaur exhibit, but somehow Henry couldn't picture himself getting back into Christine's good graces by asking her to spend an afternoon looking at fossils. The Met? Impressionism was fine, but there was always the risk of taking a wrong turn and ending up in a room of Egyptian artifacts. In Henry's opinion, tombs were not turn-ons. No, he needed a real winner. Something along the lines of "Hey, how'd you like to meet Bobby DeNiro in person?" or "Perhaps I didn't mention it the first time we went out, but Paul McCartney's a friend." Since Henry had no celebrity friends to lure Christine into another meeting, he realized that he had to get creative, to suggest something well off the beaten track. Not as far out as his freshman roommate, an animal husbandry major, who once took a woman to a chicken hatchery. Or an acquaintance at Albright who had reportedly once asked a woman if she cared to join him for a short trip to the third moon of Jupiter. No, Henry wanted to come off as charming, not insane. Clearly, the answer lay somewhere between coffee and chickens. Something that took place on the planet Earth would be nice, too.

Unfortunately, by the time Henry got home he was at a loss. Though he knew he was simply procrastinating—that a real man would pick up the phone the very next morning and by the sheer force of his sterling personality charm Christine into seeing him again—Henry felt that he would need time to come up with the right idea. After all, didn't major league baseball players need spring training before stepping back into the batter's box after a long off-season? That being the case, why shouldn't he take some time to gear up for his own opening day? So Henry flipped open his calendar, picked up a red Magic Marker, and wrote the words CALL HER in the box for April 18, the following Saturday.

One week, he thought. Time to gear up. To dust off his best casual phone manner. Also to get creative. The dream date. As Marlon Brando might say, a date she couldn't possibly refuse.

There was one phone call that Henry felt brave enough to make right away, however. During the run of *H.M.S. Pinafore*, he had begun to think seriously about his writing. Though he toyed with the idea of concentrating on one of his novels or on his kids' poems, perhaps even his symphonic tone poem, Henry realized that he wasn't quite ready to walk away from *The Green Light!* At least not until he'd had a professional opinion.

On Monday morning Henry fished through his wallet and found the business card of Dyllan Richards, the one theater pro who had actually sat through his entire reading. The one with the leather pants. After a few emphatic "You de man's," he left a message. To his surprise, she called back within an hour and, following a few minutes of chitchat, made good on her offer to meet.

So it was that Henry found himself walking into Freddie's, a midtown coffee bar, that Thursday afternoon. Though he was anxious, his nerves were tempered by the realization that Dyllan would never have been willing to get together simply to tell him she thought his show stank. After purchasing a four-dollar cup of

latte, Henry made his way to the back to wait. To his surprise, Dyllan was already there, reading a script.

"Henry?" she asked.

"Hi," he said. "Thanks for agreeing to meet."

"Happy to do it."

When she stood up to shake hands, Henry noticed that she was
much taller than he remembered. Close to six feet. Then he focused
on the large brown eyes, the auburn hair, and the seemingly perfect
body. He swallowed hard. This woman was even more beautiful
than he had remembered. Even without the leather pants. With a
slight feeling of loss, Henry realized how much he must have been in
love with Tamar not to have spent his entire reading pretending Dyllan was turning pages for him—naked.

"So," she said, as they took their seats, "I didn't think I was going to hear from you."

"I'm sorry," Henry said. "I've been in and out of town."

"Oh, really? Where?"

Henry hadn't expected to have to back up the lie with details.
Suddenly, he didn't have the energy to make something up.

"The truth is that I've been going though sort of a tough period."

"Oh, I'm sorry."

"But I'm finally coming up for air," Henry added quickly.

"Glad to hear it."

A moment or two of small talk followed, focusing mainly on the
Disneyfication of Times Square. Soon enough, Dyllan glanced at
her watch and brought the meeting to order.

"So why don't you tell me what you've been thinking?"

Luckily, Henry realized that she meant about the show, as opposed to her.

"Well," he said, stirring his coffee, "I guess I'm at a sort of cross-
roads. I'm not sure if I should keep working on *The Green Light!* or
set it aside and move on to something else."

"Well, you could set it aside if you want," Dyllan said. "But I
think a musical version of *Gatsby* could work."

It wasn't what he had expected to hear. By this point, Henry had almost forgotten what had attracted him to the material in the first place.

"You do?" he asked.

"Sure," Dyllan said. "It's a great American story. It has all the elements. I just think you took some things too far. Like . . . was there a piece in the middle that sounded like . . . Wait. Hold on a minute." She reached into her bag and flipped open a frayed notebook. "Oh, yeah . . . here's what I wrote. Too much Schoenberg."

Henry closed his eyes. His twelve-tone instrumental.

"Hmmm, hmmm," he said.

Dyllan referred back to the notebook. "Also, it seemed that the styles kept changing. One minute jazz, then gospel, then modern, then Irving Berlin. I kept feeling thrown."

Henry had realized that the pacing seemed off, but he'd never considered that it was because he had tried to do too much.

"Well, I could rework that, I think."

"You should." Dyllan laughed. "I mean, no offense, 'My Honey Got Money' was great, but there was also some really dull stuff."

Henry sank back in his seat. This was the woman who had actually liked it enough to stay? Maybe she had arranged this meeting to tell him that, in the interests of the American theater, he should quit the business. As it turned out, she wasn't finished, either.

"I don't know, Henry. I guess I think that the angle you took on the material was . . . well, a little pretentious at times. Don't you think?"

Hadn't he just gotten through saying that he was going through a tough time?

"Could be."

"Heavy-handed, you know?"

Henry fought the urge to stand and shout, "She made me do it! Tamar! The bitch who ruined my life!"

Instead, he took the criticism like a man.

"You could have a point," he managed (through noticeably gritted teeth).

Dyllan closed the notebook. Apparently, she was done.

"But it's not all bad," she said.

"Oh?" Henry said. "You liked the costumes?"

Dyllan smiled. "Don't take what I say too much to heart. Yeah, some of the material didn't work, but a lot did. Think of this as your first draft—a starting point. You've just got to cut, rethink, and get back to work."

More work? Henry had expected to be on Broadway two months ago already. His Tony was due in June. Still, he had done enough writing to know that Dyllan was right. The first draft was just the beginning.

"Don't be bummed. I think you can keep the tone light and still make the deeper points stick."

It actually made sense.

"No promises, of course," she went on. "But if you do a rewrite—or do something new, for that matter—I'd be willing to see what you come up with."

It was a baby step, but a step in the right direction.

"Of course, I don't have to tell you that musical theater is a mess right now. I mean, nothing is getting produced. At least, nothing good, anyway." She grinned. "Unless you consider *Mamma Mia!* good."

Henry smiled. At long last he had found the perfect audience for his anti–*Mamma Mia!* diatribe. As it turned out, Dyllan was with him every step of the way. She agreed that the theater was in horrible shape. That most of the musicals on Broadway stank. That ticket prices were an outrage. That tourists had rotten taste. Further, they agreed that if they only had some money they could change the situation single-handedly. All in all, it was an extremely satisfying discussion. So satisfying that Henry was soon considering the inevitable. Dyllan hadn't mentioned a boyfriend or husband. An investigation of both hands revealed no rings. Yes, he was scheduled to call Christine in two short days, but who knew where that would lead? He was still a free agent. The larger question was whether Dyllan was out of his league. When he walked in he would have said yes. Now he wasn't so sure. In fact, she seemed to be warming to the conversation, leaning forward, gesturing broadly with her hands. She laughed out loud when he called Andrew Lloyd Webber "Barry Manilow with bad teeth." She even asked if Henry's novel *Greener Pastures* would make a good musical. Perhaps he should try to get her number? They could go to a show. A musical even. Maybe she would enjoy his typical tacky date at the Lookout? Henry let the evening take shape in his mind. After the Lookout, his place? Now, that was a plan. All he had to do was sit tight and wait for the right opening.

Then something strange happened. To Henry's surprise, he found himself souring on the idea. While on his initial date with Christine, he had felt the sheer force of her personality alter his perception of her looks. Now the same thing occurred but with different results. The more he and Dyllan talked, the less her looks interested him. Well, of course, they still interested him—after all, he was still breathing—but Henry began to see through her stunning beauty to the woman inside. Yes, they had things in common. She hated Andrew Lloyd Webber. She loved Cole Porter. But that was the end of the line. Like most theater types, she was self-absorbed. Her jaunty self-confidence bordered on arrogance. Henry realized that he didn't appreciate the abrupt manner in which she had delivered her critique, either. Nude page-turning? Sure. A quickie at the Shearing Plaza? You betcha! But his girlfriend? No, sir.

Not that Dyllan was champing at the bit for him, either. As soon as the conversation began to lag, she glanced at her watch.

"I've got to get back," she said. "You have my work number. Give me a call when you've rewritten the show."

Henry smiled.

"You got it," he said. "And thanks."

"Sure thing."

With that, she shook his hand and headed for the door. At the last second, she turned around.

"Henry?"

Henry looked over his shoulder. Framed in the doorway, with the sun shining through her hair, she looked stunning. He felt his heart begin to beat faster. Maybe he had thought too soon. If she asked him to call her, would he be able to say no?

"Yeah?" he asked.

"I must have a lousy memory, but I clean forget. In the book, is Gatsby black?"

Henry released his breath. Who was he kidding? Dyllan probably had a boyfriend with shoulders as wide as a professional wrestler's.

"No," he said, somewhat disappointed. "No, he's not."

Dyllan nodded. "That was an interesting choice, but you might think about changing it back."

"Yeah," he said. "I was planning on it."

"Do that."

She was out the door. She rounded the corner, waved through the window, then walked down Broadway. Henry watched her go. Despite his assessment of her personality, he allowed himself to appreciate the wonder that was her legs as she headed into the heart of Times Square. But the moment she passed the Shearing Plaza, Henry looked up what he thought was fifty floors to the Lookout and let his mind drift back to Christine. Though he still hadn't come up with the right idea for a new date, he remembered their first one vividly—the wonderful conversation, the sensual slow dance (obviously), the tour of the hotel . . . the honeymoon suites, the piano bar, the gift shop. He even remembered how he and Christine had bought matching Knicks mugs. Though Henry had meant to give his to Jill, it still sat on his bedroom dresser. Perhaps he would bring it over that night . . . Or just give it to her the next time they played basketball . . .

Basketball?

Basketball!

Henry nearly choked on the last swallow of his four-dollar latte, risking a near repeat of the chocolate-raspberry upside-down-cake incident. Just like that, he had it. The dream date! Something even better than meeting Paul McCartney (well, almost). Ironically, a date that he and Christine had set up a full year earlier.

No way was he going to wait until Saturday to remind her.

The next week, on Sunday afternoon, Henry and Jill were on the West Side, walking in Riverside Park, dressed for some serious hoops. Jill dribbled a basketball as she went.

"So who is this girl?" Jill asked.

"Her name's Christine," Henry said.

Jill smiled up at her uncle.

"Are you going to marry her?"

"Marry her?" Henry laughed. "Sorry. That's taking things a bit too fast, don't you think?"

Jill shrugged.

"Maybe," she said, and dribbled ahead and took a shot at an imaginary basket.

Henry sighed. Was his sickness so severe that it was noticeable to an eight-year-old? Apparently, even though, recognizing his illness—his addiction, really—for what it was, Henry had taken some precautions. Two days after Christine had agreed to meet, he wrote the words IT'S JUST A DATE on a piece of paper and taped them to his bathroom mirror. The following morning, he added NOT A WEDDING!

Truth be told, though, as Henry walked up Riverside Park toward the courts, part of him still didn't see what was so horribly wrong with thinking ahead a bit. What was so terrible with a little projection, anyway? After all, everyone knew what was really at stake. The unwritten rules of male-female interaction were clear: The ultimate goal of any social meeting was to evaluate said person for suitability as a lifelong partner. To Henry, ignoring that simple fact was tantamount to saying the world was flat—an absurdity. Given that set of assumptions, wasn't it logical, normal even, to consider the ultimate goal? Even before the first baby step had been taken?

Then he thought back to a certain night a year earlier—the night he had stood on the platform of the uptown express train certain that he was going to marry one Tamar Brookman of Queens, New York. Henry remembered how, late that same night, he had imagined their wedding from the ceremony itself all the way down to his bride's underwear. He had been so hopeful then, so sure that it would work out. Now, as Henry took a moment to ruminate on the exciting highs and ultimately depressing lows of his association with Tamar, he reminded himself anew of a simple truth: that the inevitable flip side of constantly inflated expectations was disappointment. Yes, it was alright for a triathlete to visualize the finish line before sprinting for the ocean, but that was sports. Love was a different matter. If Henry had learned anything, it was that experiencing the seminal events of his relationships in the privacy of his mind before they actually happened was hazardous to his emotional health.

"It's just a date," he told himself now, walking up the tree-lined path toward the courts. "Just a simple date. One date. A date. Only basketball, is what it is. Just a date. Only hoops. Just a date. Only hoops. Just a date!"

"Henry! Catch!"

Henry held up his hands just in time.

"Who were you talking to?" his niece called.

"Talking? No one."

"Really? It looked like you were."

"Come on. Let's run!"

Jill didn't need any encouragement. They jogged up the park tossing the ball back and forth. As they ran, Henry repeated his mantra over and over. Soon enough the courts came into view. Christine had already arrived. She was dribbling her own basketball (behind her back, no less—she was good!), wearing cutoffs, an Ohio State T-shirt, and high-tops. She looked every bit as beautiful as she had the night at the Sleepy Wheel. Henry couldn't believe he had ever been so critical. As Glenn had said, no slouch.

As he watched her jump in the air and take a shot, he saw their entire life spin out before him. Their apartment on West End Avenue (bought with the proceeds of his two-million-dollar book deal). Their country home in Vermont. The kids. Then the Pulitzer (for drama). The PEN/Faulkner (for fiction). The Tonys and—

Henry stopped himself. What was he doing? Clearly, his quest to bring a sense of proportion to his life was going to take some time. He had mastered the art of leaping into the future. Now he had to force himself to go backward and learn how to walk, to take things one step at a time. As he headed onto the court, he renewed his vow. "Just a date," he told himself. "Just a game of hoops." Yes, he'd stick to his new mantra or die trying.

Jill was dribbling the length of the court now, driving to the hoop. Henry jogged to Christine's side.

"Hey there."

"Hiya."

They looked down the court. Jill missed, grabbed the rebound, and put it back.

"Nice second effort!" Christine yelled.

Jill grabbed the rebound again and dribbled back to Henry, who made the introductions.

"Try that layup with a left hand now," Christine told Jill.

"OK!"

Jill was off. They watched her go, then Henry turned to Christine.

"Hey, I'm glad you gave me another chance."

Christine shrugged. "Well, you sounded so pathetic on the phone."

Henry smiled grimly. He deserved that. Even though he had apologized twice already—his first night back at Albright, then again when he had called about the date—he suddenly felt the need to assuage his guilt one more time.

"Listen," he began. "I really am sorry for—"

Christine chucked him her ball—hard.

"Will you shut up already? You're forgiven, alright?"

Henry blinked. "Really?"

"Oh, why not? I mean, let's get real, Henry. It was just one date. It's not like we were engaged or anything."

Henry broke into a broad smile, then laughed.

"What's so funny?" Christine asked.

"Oh, nothing."

"What?"

Henry threw the ball back to Christine.

"Listen, do you wanna play or what?"

"Hey, that's what I've been waiting for."

Henry caught Christine's pass and dribbled down the court toward Jill. Christine sprinted behind, stole the ball, and sank a medium-range jump shot.

"Nice," Jill cried.

Christine got her own rebound and tossed it back to Henry. He held the ball at the top of the key, considering what to do.

"Dunk it!" Jill cried.

"No way," Henry said. "I can't jump that high."

Indeed, his days of going for a slam dunk the first time off the block were over. Rather, Henry took a few easy dribbles and lofted an easy eight-footer toward the rim. A high-percentage shot . . .

"Nothing but net!" Jill called.

Christine smiled.

"Nice," she said, gathering in the rebound.

Yes, Henry thought. He was back in the game. Just then, Christine lofted a pass his way.

"Catch!" she called.

Now if he could only keep his eye on the ball.